A WORLD OF POSSIBILITIES

"Are you new here?" Dr. West asked.

"Yes," said Ellen, forcing herself to speak.

"Is it your first time away from home?"

"Yes." Ellen looked at him, feeling shy. He looked like ivory, but without any rough edges to sand and polish.

"Are you homesick?"

"No," said Ellen, perplexed. What had made him say that?

"I confess I still get homesick sometimes," he said, and his eyes were kind. Dr. West sipped his juice, and then, looking up, his eyes curious, he asked, "Are you like most women?"

"I don't know most women," Ellen answered, feeling confused as she looked at the other girls in the room with their tiny babies. "There weren't many people in Unaganik and we lived a ways from the village."

Dr. West smiled. It was the most perfect smile Ellen had seen in her sixteen years. "I do know something," she said, feeling she could trust him. "I know I don't want to get married and have children and stay here forever."

He smiled again, and at that moment Ellen believed that anything was possible. . . .

LONG SHADOWS

Susan Saxton D'Aoust

BANTAM BOOKS
NEW YORK · TORONTO · LONDON · SYDNEY · AUCKLAND

This edition contains the complete text
of the original hardcover edition.
NOT ONE WORD HAS BEEN OMITTED.

LONG SHADOWS
A Bantam Book / published by arrangement with E. P. Dutton

PRINTING HISTORY
E. P. Dutton edition published September 1988
Bantam edition / September 1989

*Hut Sut Song by L. Killion, T. McMichael, and J. Owens.
Copyright © 1939 by Brenner Music Inc.
Copyright renewed and assigned to Chappell & Co, Inc.
International Copyright secured. All rights reserved. Used by
permission.*

ISBN 0-553-28272-7

Published simultaneously in the United States and Canada

*Bantam Books are published by Bantam Books, a division of
Bantam Doubleday Dell Publishing Group, Inc. Its trademark,
consisting of the words "Bantam Books" and the portrayal of a
rooster, is Registered in U.S. Patent and Trademark Office and in
other countries. Marca Registrada. Bantam Books, 666 Fifth
Avenue, New York, New York 10103.*

PRINTED IN THE UNITED STATES OF AMERICA

O   0 9 8 7 6 5 4 3 2 1

To my daughter,
Renée

ACKNOWLEDGMENTS

In seven years of researching this novel, I met many Alaskans who opened their homes and hearts to me. Their kindness and generosity facilitated travel to places where I would not otherwise have gone, and I am deeply grateful.

For their willingness to share the hard-won experiences of their lives, I particularly want to thank the following Alaskans:

Henry Swanson, Unalaska's lively storyteller, who recounted ninety-two years of adventures and gave permission for them to be used in the novel; Dr. Francis J. Phillips, M.D., FACS, FRCP(A), who heard the call of the Yukon when he was an army doctor in the Aleutians during World War II, and later became a leading Alaskan specialist in the treatment of tuberculosis; both Bob Berkholder, a retired pilot biologist, U.S. Fish and Wildlife Service, and Eric Manzer, a halibut fisherman, proofed the manuscript in various stages and guided me through fog and williwaws. Elmer and Geneva Smith, who welcomed me to Aleknagik with open arms and always answered my interminable questions; Lydia Gardiner, of Aleknagik, who shared her *maqi*; David Carlson, who kept a careful diary, and his wife, Mary Emily, a nurse; Bill Bright, the benevolent fish buyer at False Pass; the late and famous bear guide, Mike Uttick; Governor Jay Hammond and his wife, Belle, for teaching me the fine art of set netting; Dr. Betty Elsner, M.D., who survived several hair-raising flights during medical rounds of the villages; Abi Dickson, Unalaska's balcony cheerer; Leonard Weimar, of Seward, for his humorous stories of life as a village health aide; Pat Williams and Ann Hatch of Seward; and George Max and Bob Van Cleve of Sitka, who helped me understand life under the tall trees. From Anchorage: Carl V. Novak, for flying stories and an introduction to the Pilgrim; Carolyn Smith Owens, Nancy

Kroon, and Steven McGlashen; Captain Wolstenholme, for Aleutian songs and adventures. A special thanks to the Shaman, who drummed me to the center of the earth.

In the Lower 48, many veterans of Alaska also assisted my research. My grateful thanks to: Mr. and Mrs. William C. Bland; Dwight Dougherty; Ralph Lund; Fanny Nerup; Mr. and Mrs. Stanley Peratrovich; and Grace McRae, who introduced me to Alaska, thus beginning my love affair with the people and country.

I read dozens of books but particularly want to record my debt to the following: Brian Garfield, *The Thousand Mile War;* Irma Drooz, *Doctor of Medicine;* Morris Gibson, *One Man's Medicine;* Max Miller, *The Great Trek; Uutuqtwa,* a publication of Bristol Bay High School.

Not only Alaskans assisted with this novel. I am indebted to: my beloved mother, Dr. Dorothy E. Saxton, M.D.; Dr. Gordon Baker, M.D.; and Meredith McFarland for their medical expertise; Jean Bryant for her faith in the process; Lynda Hyde and Jane Morse Thompson, fellow poets and gardeners; Bob Bower, for visuals and tours; Michael Robinson for his actor's instinct; and to Table One for providing comic relief. My family deserves praise: my husband, Brian, for expanding my vision; my son Ian, for his relentless honesty; my son Tony, for his champagne; and my daughter Renée, for being a sounding board and midnight muse. I am also indebted to my agent, Chris Tomasino, and my editor, Jeanne Martinet, for their enthusiasm and perceptive editorial suggestions.

For their wonderful exhibits and information, I want to thank: Sheldon Jackson Museum of Sitka; Anchorage Museum of History and Art; Seward Public Library; Resurrection Bay Historical Society Museum of Seward; Alaska and Polar Regions Archives of the Elmer E. Rasmuson Library, University of Alaska, Fairbanks; The University of Alaska Museum; Instructional Media Services, University of Alaska; Seattle Public Library; Museum of History and Industry, "Life on the Homefront" exhibit, Seattle.

The characters in *Long Shadows* are fictitious; where they came from remains one of the mysteries of the imagination and blessings of the universe. Any resemblance to people living or dead is purely coincidental. Unaganik and Harold's Point are fictitious places based in Bristol Bay, as are other place names not found on the U.S. Department of the Interior's geological survey map of Alaska. The Yup'ik spelling, where possible, conforms to the *Yup'ik Eskimo Grammar* published by the Alaska Native Language Center, University of Alaska, 1977. Any errors are strictly my own.

LONG SHADOWS

A WEATHERBEATEN CABIN PERCHES on the edge of a steep bluff in the southwest region of the Territory of Alaska. It faces eastward across a vast body of water called Bristol Bay. On the eastern edge of the bay, beyond the view of the cabin, snowcapped volcanic mountains grace the Alaska Peninsula and continue through the Aleutian chain to the Bering Sea.

Far to the northwest, separated from the bay by an expanse of tundra, a single mountain sculpts the surface. Velvet green moss, purple lupines, berry bushes, and scrub spruce cross the tundra and disappear into space.

A shiny new stovepipe reaches skyward like rigging holding the small cabin to the earth. Nearby is a sweathouse, called the *maqi,* a smokehouse, a cache, and a variety of homemade birdhouses. Farther away stands a privy, with a crescent moon on the door. There are accumulations of driftwood and willow, snowshoes piled in a dogsled, wooden salt kegs, and torn gill nets. A large gardening box leans against the south side of the cabin. Tethered on hummocks on the opposite side of a bubbling creek are five sled dogs, one of which is arthritic and old.

It is June 1937.

PART
ONE

1

E LLEN LAY ON THE cot, wide awake. Her thoughts were like salmon caught in a gill net, silver and flashing through the twilight.

On the same cot, head at the opposite end, Bonnie slept like a rag doll. Ellen moved her feet away from her younger sister's and snuggled deeper under the worn patchwork quilt. She touched the piece of blanket Mother stole when she ran away from the orphanage, the knotted wool from pants Mr. Stokes wore up the gold trail, and finally a strip of tartan from Daddy's old necktie. Ellen rubbed the soft tartan between her thumb and forefinger and rolled onto her side. The cot squeaked.

"That you?" hissed Stewart from the far side of the main room.

Ellen tightened her eyes, knowing what her thirteen-year-old brother was going to say next.

"We gotta go." Stewart tugged at her quilt. "We gotta get ta the end o' the nets afore low water." He said that as if, because she was only twelve, Ellen didn't know.

She swung to a sitting position. The quilt slipped down and the cold bore into her until she longed to curl against Bonnie. She looked at the pale sky dusting the east window and wondered if she had slept at all.

"I'm away." Grabbing four rounds of hardtack, Stewart clomped to the door.

Ellen finger-combed her black hair, separated it into three strands. With a red satin ribbon lying along the center strand, she plaited it, Eskimo-style, into a single thick braid.

She pulled on her clothes, tied a wool *blatook* over her head, and swung Mother's old oilskin from the hook by the door. Five-year-old Charlie moaned. The big bed creaked in the alcove beside the kitchen.

In the windbreak, a lean-to protecting the back door from the wind off the tundra, Ellen slipped into her knee-high beach boots and tucked the shoulder ropes into the sides. She felt foggy with lack of sleep, and when she heard a deep voice say, "Are ye off?" she jumped.

"Can ye manage, me wee blue goose? Ye sure?" Her father, Angus MacTavish, stood at the door looking pale and ghostlike in his flannel nightshirt.

"Yes," she nodded. Didn't she have to pick the fish so Daddy and Stewart wouldn't fight?

Daddy peered at her through the gloom of the windbreak. The Lord knew he got little sleep between working at the Unaganik jail and cleaning the nets at each tide, but still he wished his wee lassie didn't have to help.

"I can do it!" Ellen spoke loudly.

"Let me tie up yer straps," said Daddy, coming closer.

"No," said Ellen, "I can do it myself." She hated tying her long boot ropes over her shoulders. It made her feel like a fish being squeezed into a can.

When Ellen left, Angus MacTavish lifted his nightshirt and relieved himself beside the empty potato box outside the windbreak door. When he stood straight, Angus stood six feet. If the country had bowed him in the past thirty-nine years, well, so had it bowed—indeed killed—many a taller and stronger man. Angus had broad shoulders that could carry a two-hundred-pound Dall sheep, and a broad square face with red veins lacing his large nose. His white eyebrows tufted above deepset blue eyes, giving him a puckish look that fooled only the most naive *cheechakos,* although newcomers rarely came to this remote part of southwestern Alaska.

Once blond, Angus's hair at sixty-seven was pure white, although a few streaks the color of old gold appeared when he pushed his square hands up through his thick tumbling mane. There was no hair on his face. He had started shaving in his first year at Glasgow University and continued to shave every day of his life with a straight-edged razor he sharpened on a leather strop, and a reindeer tail brush he swathed with soap oozing from an enamel cup.

Angus dropped his nightshirt and returned to the house. Behind him, Wolff, the lead sled dog, strained against his chain, smelling something on the wind.

Baby Bruce lay in the center of the double bed, wrapped in a red fox fur. Angus bundled the baby and moved him to Stewart's cot. Charlie, in the next cot, smelled of ammonia. Angus stifled a sneeze and settled back into the double bed, pressing his cold feet against his wife's flannel pajamas. Her back warmed his chest. Slowly, insistently, Angus stretched the elastic of her pajama bottoms over her wide hips. Adjusting his position, holding the soft flesh of her waist with his scarred hands, he rubbed his growing penis against her until she angled forward and settled onto him. Angus slipped up and down, thrust higher and higher, and seconds before the final release, he jerked out and came into the flannel. Five children was enough. Take out your pipe before you spit, Dr. Visikov had warned, or you'll have a dozen.

Ellen hurried to the nets as fast as she dared, hugging the sides of the treacherous trail that dropped toward the beach. Just when the fierce beach wind threatened to toss her into the air, she touched something human. "Augh!" she cried, swaying. Strong hands gripped her wrists, holding her down.

"I came back for ye," Stewart said in a perplexed voice. "Dinna ye hear?"

Trembling, Ellen smelled the salt air against the smell of Wildroot which Stewart had ordered from the catalogue and had taken to slicking, in spite of Angus's scorn, into his hair. Stewart was as tall as Daddy, with blond hair and a strong nose. Proof, the doctor had said, explaining Mendel's laws to Ellen, that there must have been a Russian trader somewhere in Cheok's family background. The other children, in contrast to Stewart, had their mother's coloring, her dark narrow eyes and her round flat face. Only Stewart spoke with Angus's Scottish accent. To Ellen, watching their constant battles, it seemed the last bond between them.

Ellen caught her breath. "Why do you have those?" she

asked, pointing at the shoepacs knotted together and hanging around Stewart's neck.

"I'd best go ta the village when we finish," Stewart answered, "and I dinna want ta wear me waders."

"Are you going to Unaganik to get away from Daddy?" Ellen traced her finger over the welt Daddy had made when he smacked Stewart at the nets yesterday.

"Dinna worry, Ellen," Stewart said, taking her hand. "I willna be letting Daddy touch me agin."

Stewart continued down the trail and Ellen, hugging the steep shaggy sides of the bluff, followed. Out on the vast bay, beyond the talley scow, gaff-rigged double enders sailed for the fishing grounds. A flock of seagulls winged noisily over the lapping edge of the receding water. Sandpipers hopped on the wet mud. The water bubbled with caught salmon. Ellen and Stewart hauled the skiff over the pebbled beach and climbed in. The tide was ebbing and there was barely enough water to float the skiff.

When they reached the first iron post, Stewart shipped the oars and pulled up the loose folds of gill net which hung between deeply anchored posts. He laid the cork line over the gunwale of the skiff. The net was full of salmon.

Ellen grabbed a fish tail with her left hand. With her right, she curved an ivory pick between the gills and mesh. Lifting the linen threads away from the gills, she twisted her left wrist, yanking the tail. The salmon flicked out of the net. She dropped it into the skiff and reached for another. Curving her hook against the gills, she raced against Stewart, who worked twice as fast. Moving out with the tide, they pulled the skiff along a hundred and fifty feet of net, picking salmon as they went.

"No dead men yet!" Stewart teased as they started at the last stretch of hanging net.

"Shush," shuddered Ellen, seeing, in her mind, the bloated grotesque body that had washed up on the beach last winter.

A large King salmon, in a determined effort to escape, had thrashed itself into a mesh pocket. Ellen shook the net to loosen the tangles. If they're only paying us eight cents a fish, I want ye to keep the big ones, Daddy had said. When Ellen freed the King, she dropped it into a burlap sack to take home.

"The linen's torn," she said, inspecting the tangled mesh.

"Fix it later," said Stewart. "I want ta finish and get ta the village."

Looking at Stewart, Ellen noticed that he had ropes, as well as his fancy new suspenders, holding up his hip-high waders. When the suspenders had arrived on the first boat since break-up, Daddy had jeered, "Aye, and we've got a dandy." Thinking quickly, Stewart had replied, "They're ta hold up me boots." Ellen dipped her hands into the tops of her knee-high boots where she had tucked her shoulder ropes and stared at her brother, wondering why everything he did made Daddy so mad.

Stewart batted a small stray steelhead toward her. Ellen caught it and tucked it into the sack. A treat for Mother.

The tide continued to ebb. The sky changed to dusty blue. Ellen licked the salt from her lips and sucked in her cheeks to moisten her mouth. Her arms felt like lead weights. She dropped the net off the stern of the skiff as if she were dropping an anchor and chain. When the last salmon was picked from the far end of the second net, three hundred feet into Bristol Bay, she permitted herself a sigh. Finished. And now, she thought, cuddling the idea around her like a quilt, I can sleep until high water.

"I kin take the sack in, if yer that tired," Stewart said, watching her.

"I can do it," Ellen said, although her body shook with exhaustion.

"Ye sure?"

Ellen nodded and stared at the thick grey gumbo separating them from the washed pebbles at the base of the bluff.

"Leave the sack at the foot of the trail," Stewart said as he slipped the oars into the locks. "I'll carry it up when I get back."

Ellen shrugged. It seemed strange to talk this far from the beach, as if she had entered another universe, where language was superfluous.

"Promise?" said Stewart, and knowing he wouldn't

leave until she did, Ellen nodded. She felt like rubber. Parts of her stretched away, disconnecting from her aching body. The shore also seemed to move, to get farther away the longer she looked. Ellen hunched her shoulders, cradled her arms around herself and turned the other way, to look across the vast bowl of water. The fishboats had disappeared over the edge, as if they had left Alaska and gone to another part of the world. Someday I'll go too, she thought, and a deep part of her knew she needed to leave, knew she needed more than fish, salt water, and mud. Someday, she thought, if Daddy lets me, I'll go Outside to school.

"Tide's still going out." Stewart pointed to the water.

Gathering what remained of her strength, Ellen swung over the side. The water sloshed around her calves. The mud sucked at her feet.

"Tie yer straps," said Stewart. "Ye'll get a licking if ye lose yer boots."

Avoiding her brother's gaze, knowing that they both knew that as many times as Daddy had beaten Stewart he'd never ever laid a hand to Ellen, she said, "Are you still going to Unaganik?"

"Yes, but I'll be back ta pick the nets at high water." Bending, he lifted the burlap sack of fish and heaved it overboard. With a thud, it hit the iron post holding the end of the net. Then Stewart stood at the long oars and, facing the talley scow, rowed the skiff, heavy with the morning's catch, toward it.

The noise of the oarlocks jangled into the distance. The gulls left. For a long time Ellen stood alone in the thick silence of the mud flats. The wind had died. The silence was as thick as flour in a calico bag.

Picking up the two ropes tied to the front and back of her left boot, Ellen tugged on them and, despite her stiff fingers, tied them over her left shoulder. Bending, she reached for the ropes that were attached to her right boot. They were caught under her foot. Balancing on her left foot while she freed the ropes from her boot, she reached for the post to steady herself. She missed. For a brief fraction of an instant everything seemed as motionless as the sky on a windless day. Then she swayed forward. Her head cracked against the iron post.

A tern squawked. Her spirit climbed to meet it. Separated, Ellen looked down. An exhausted shell of a body lay alone on the mud. Behind her a light warmed her, beckoned her. She thought of Daddy, Mother, Stewart, of how they needed her. The next instant she knew nothing.

There was no sound except the foaming of the water as it drained into the bay, where it would change direction at the lowest of the low-tide marks and rise relentlessly back toward the bluffs.

2

BABY BRUCE, ON STEWART'S cot, gnawed his lips. He let out a series of short whimpers, which soon exploded in a wail that woke Cheok from a leaden slumber. Tugging on her pajama bottoms, she lurched out of bed, picked up the trembling bundle of fox fur, and, fumbling with the buttons on her pajama top, plopped into the overstuffed rocker in front of the wood stove.

The anxious baby rooted for her breast. With a loud slurp, he pulled the nipple into his mouth and began to suck contentedly. Cheok smiled. Rocking back and forth, she crooned a lullaby that she remembered from the long ago days before the orphanage.

Cheok was twenty-eight. The Eskimo village where she had been born no longer existed. When she was ten, government men from the Bureau of Indian Affairs had found her wrapped in fur, her feet digging into the sod floor of her dead parents' house. A *kass'aq*—white man—had carried her, kicking and screaming, to a boat moored in Bristol Bay. While the motor wracked her ears and billows of gaseous blue smoke seared her lungs, Cheok watched flames blaze across her village, burning the dead. The soil is too thin to bury so many, the white man explained, but Cheok knew only Yup'ik.

The government men took Cheok to Unaganik, where an orphanage had been hastily organized in buildings donated by the cannery. White people burned her clothes, shaved her head, called her Rose, and slapped her for speaking Yup'ik. Cheok ran away to find her brother, who had gone north to learn reindeer herding under a program started by Sheldon Jackson. A *kass'aq* returned her to the orphanage, where she was locked in the basement for three days.

When she was fourteen, Cheok ran away again. Mr. MacTavish married her, thus preventing the orphanage from forcing her back. Cheok took her Yup'ik name, although Mr. MacTavish still called her Rose when she did something wrong—something she didn't understand in this white man's life.

Baby Bruce, who was part of this life, pushed Cheok's hard brown nipple out of his mouth. Cheok transferred him to her other breast. Spittle gathered at the corners of his blistered lips and he pushed her away with a tiny pink tongue. Cheok burped him over her shoulder the way Dr. Visikov had taught her with the first baby, Stewart, *ciuqliq*, born nine months after her marriage to Mr. MacTavish.

Stewart rowed a load of salmon toward the talley scow. Soon, he thought as he strained his arms on the heavy oars, I'll have my freedom and won't have to take any more whippings from Daddy. Stewart stopped for a rest, breath gushing out of him like a whale about to break surface. Flying, yes, that's what he wanted to do, would do, when he'd saved enough from the odd jobs he picked up in Unaganik.

Stewart had fancied flying ever since an old JN₄D landed in Unaganik in 1927. The Jenny had been flown by a survivor of the Great War who later hit a cloud stuffed with rocks—which is what they said when a plane crashed into a mountain in the thick of fog. That didn't stop Stewart from longing for wings, from longing to soar over this interminable drudgery.

His thoughts were interrupted by the noise of the tug heading toward the talley scow. Stewart shouted frantically. Daddy would have his hide if the tug pulled the scow away without their catch.

A thin talley man wearing a blue peaked cap waved from the side of the tug. He held a cigarette between his thumb and first finger. As soon as Stewart maneuvered the skiff alongside, the talley man stuck the cigarette into his mouth and jumped into the scow. He grabbed a pue—a long-handled pick—and began tossing salmon one by one behind him into the scow. Ash dropped from his cigarette. He held it in one half of his pinched mouth as he breathed through the other half. His forearms rippled as he tossed salmon into the scow in one continuous motion—up with the pick, down into the gills, up. He and Stewart counted the salmon as one by one they landed in the scow. Three hundred and five, at eight cents a fish. Twenty-four dollars and forty cents, calculated Stewart. A fraction of the price of a new linen net.

"Got something for ya," the thin man said after Stewart had signed the chit recording the exact number of fish. He handed over a tattered book. "It belonged to the Bellanca pilot. He loaned it to me."

Stewart stuck his hands under his waders and wiped them on his wool pants. He took the book. There was no cover.

"The Bellanca went into the soup over by Dutch Harbor," said the talley man, taking a drag on a fresh cigarette. "The pilot won't be needing a book where he's at. You're welcome to keep it." On the first page, the title read bold and clear: *We* by Charles A. Lindbergh.

"I'll be thanking ye fer this!" Stewart was so excited that he could barely mouth the words.

"Read it myself," said the man.

"Lindbergh signed it!" Stewart studied the handwriting inside the title page. "Fancy having a book Lindbergh himself signed."

"It's come down from Nome," said the man. "Lindbergh must've given it to someone up there when he and the missus flew through in Thirty-one."

"I do thank ye," said Stewart, and tucked the book under his suspenders. Forgetting his plans to go to Unaganik, he rowed toward the beach. He was that anxious to be home and reading.

The tug pulled the scow off in a rush of water that ruptured the silence of the bay. Stewart, bending over the skiff's oars, facing the open bay, pulled as fast as his weary arms would allow. He angled to shore and then hauled the skiff over the mud and above the high water mark using a tump line of reindeer hide that Mother had beaded in the pattern of her family. When he reached the trail up the bluff, Stewart looked for the sack of fish that Ellen had promised to leave. It was not there.

Ellen dinna carry it in, he reasoned. She was that tired. He shaded his eyes and saw a hump far out where the tide had turned. Cursing the tug of mud on his boots, keeping his eyes lowered, he heaved himself forward to the water's edge.

A tern squawked. Stewart looked up. The bundle moved. "Ellen!" His voice cracked. The grey gumbo of mud pulled against him. His chest split from the strain of trying to move faster than the mud allowed. "Ellen!" She didn't move again.

Panic-stricken, he yelled "Ellen" over and over. Just before he reached her she stirred, curling her feet away from the tide that lapped at her ankles.

A bump the size of a Klondike nugget had burst on her forehead. Stewart dropped to his knees, cradling her head. She opened her eyes and stared at him. His back straining, although Ellen weighed considerably less than a load of salmon, Stewart picked her up and started homeward. Ellen struggled.

"I have ye," he said, soothing.

Ellen screamed.

"I have ye," he soothed, bending over her, cradling her in his arms, seeing the dark centers of her eyes widen until they seemed to obliterate the white. "Yer that safe."

Angus bolted out of bed. "Where's Ellen?"

Cheok dozed in the rocker with the bundle of fox fur in her arms and her pajama top unbuttoned. She shook her head.

"Ellen dinna coom in?"

Cheok again shook her head.

Angus slapped on his clothes and boots. He roared like the tundra wind down the bluff, unknowing what beset him but sure that something had happened to his wee blue goose. Sure enough. She screamed on the beach. He heard her voice whistling through the air and, knowing her to be in some terrible danger, grabbed the only weapon he had upon him. His belt. Of thick tough leather, it snapped out of his belt loops and sizzled through the air.

His darling screamed. Through blurred watering eyes, Angus saw the shape of a man. He snapped the belt across the man's back. Ellen screamed louder.

A second time Angus drew back his arm. The belt unwound. He snapped his wrist as if mushing a dog team.

The belt twanged through the air, cutting the flesh of the man's ear. Blood dripped onto Ellen's cheek.

"Don't," she screamed. "Daddy! Don't!"

Angus raised his arm again. He blinked the tears from his eyes and recognized Stewart. "Wha' hae ye done!" he bellowed like a bull moose in rut.

"Daddy! No!" cried Ellen and the words shook her body. "My boots. In the mud. Get them. Please. Please get them!"

Angus dropped the belt. He spread his hands over his face. Ellen wrenched sideways. Stewart tipped her over, laying her on the beach where she vomited until her eyes felt like they'd drop from her head.

Without a glance at Angus, Stewart turned away and slogged again through the mud until the water sloshed around his knees. The tide had come in that fast.

3

WOLFF BARKED. HE BEGAN with a low rumbling in the back of his throat and worked up to a full-pitched roar. The other dogs tugged on their chains and howled. Paying no heed to the dogs, a domesticated herd of reindeer chewed across the new green of the tundra. They passed within a mile of the MacTavishes'.

Inside the three-room house, Stewart awoke at the first bark. He dressed quickly in his warmest clothes, then slipped his fingers into the patch of his quilt where he had ripped the stitching to make a hidden pocket. He extracted his life savings, collected by hustling work at the saloon, jail, and cannery, counted some out and dropped the rest into a skin poke hanging from his belt loop. Burrowing along the edge of the loose quilt patch, he bunched up the cloth until he found a small hard object tucked in the deepest corner. It was a jade labret, a relic he had found in the tundra. His good luck piece. He licked the smooth hard stone and then polished it on his sleeve. Stewart pulled on his shoepacs and fur parka and tiptoed to Ellen's cot. She opened her eyes.

"Here," he whispered, tucking five silver coins into the warmth of her neck. "Fer yer new boots."

"It's not your fault," Ellen whispered, moving away from Bonnie.

"Maybe not," said Stewart, "but ye still need new boots."

Ellen clutched the corner of his wolverine-trimmed par-

17

ka. She kneaded the fur and said softly, "Why are you wearing this to the beach?"

Stewart's blue eyes didn't leave her face. He loosened her small fingers from the fur and took her hand in both of his. He caressed it a second, and when he dropped it back onto her quilt, she was holding the jade labret.

"Shh," he said, backing away from her, a warning finger on his lips.

Shutting the windbreak door behind him, Stewart beat a trail toward the pawing, grazing reindeer. Their grey winter coats were peeling off, leaving splashes of soft brown underneath. High, branched horns dominated both male and female deer and stood even with Stewart's shoulders. Their legs were slim and dark. The beard under their necks was almost white, and white brackets of fur enclosed their twitching noses. A copper bell chimed at intervals as the sled reindeer moved. Feeling the dull jangle of his nerves, Stewart looked back, fearful that Angus followed. The house slept.

When Stewart was close enough to smell their sweet musk, several of the larger male reindeer reared their heads. Their ears, protruding flat and dark against the pale sky, were nicked on one side. Stewart rubbed his own ear where Angus had cut it. He moved closer. The reindeer studied him with steady brown eyes, and then, unconcerned, dropped their heads to a clump of white reindeer moss and started nibbling.

A black dog, lean in comparison to the sled dogs Stewart had left behind, raced toward him. The dog stopped to sniff Stewart's ankles, as if to nip him into the herd. Following the dog, the Eskimo herder, wearing a four-cornered Laplander hat with red tassles, called, "*Camai!*"

"*Camai,*" answered Stewart and came closer.

The herder could have been twenty-five or sixty-five. He was round, like Cheok. When he walked, it looked as if he was planting one foot into the center of the earth and balancing it there until the next foot was ready to move. A smile ballooned across the herder's smooth copper face and lit up his black almond-shaped eyes. He showed a sparse mouthful of brown teeth ground close to the gums. "*Kituusit?*" he said in Yup'ik. Who are you?

"Kin I join ye?" Stewart asked, praying that the herder

would have him. He'd not spend another night under Angus's roof.

The herder, one of few surviving Yup'ik who had not had an orphanage education that taught him to speak English, answered, "*Canaluten-qaa taiguten*?" Did you come for any particular purpose?

Berating himself for not learning more of his mother's tongue, Stewart tapped himself and said, "Stewart." Then he pointed to the reindeer herd.

The man touched his broad chest. "Mutuk." He pointed to the dog. "Qimugta." Then he pointed southwest. "Mutuk, Qimugta, Togagung."

Stewart tapped himself and pointed. "Stewart, Togagung."

"Stewart, Togagung," repeated the herder, and grinning and nodding so hard the red tassels on his four-cornered hat jiggled, he indicated that Stewart could join the herd. Mutuk liked company and did not need the familiarity of language to know a man's soul.

Ellen knew Stewart had gone. She threw off her quilt, intending to go after him. The hard bruise on her forehead ached and her stomach churned from the aftermath of yesterday's concussion. Forgetting Stewart in her misery, she darted through the windbreak to throw up the bilious contents of her empty stomach into the potato box. Her mouth tasted sour. The cold sheared her bare skin. A reindeer bell rang across the tundra. Aching in every curve of her body, Ellen slipped back onto the cot, coiling her feet against Bonnie's and pulling the warm woolen quilt to her chin. The piece of jade lay on her pillow. The hard stone dimpled her cheek.

Two hours later, Angus dragged himself out of bed. He moved Baby Bruce away from Cheok, who opened one eye and watched him as he dressed.

"Ach, and the lad's already gone," Angus said, noticing Stewart's empty cot with not a small measure of pride. "He'll be after pickin' the nets alone if I donna hurry."

"He be a good boy," said Cheok quietly.

Angus looked at her. Had she heard what happened on the beach?

Cheok returned his gaze, her face as implacable and composed as ever.

Angus turned away and checked on Ellen, who breathed as if in a deep sleep.

"She coom through the night a-right," said Angus.

"My smart girl be fine." Cheok stretched her plump body to fill the bed.

Angus pulled on his waders and slicker in the windbreak and hurried outside. Antlers marked the horizon like bare branches against an empty sky. Reindeer, he thought briefly as he headed down the treacherous bluff. He near burst with pride as he imagined Stewart at the nets, working like a man.

At water's edge, Angus shaded his eyes. The net popped with salmon but no one worked beside it. Turning quickly, Angus saw the skiff high and dry on the stones. His heart raced. Had the lad fallen? Sure that he'd see the broken body of his eldest son crumpled on the stones, Angus searched along the base of the bluff. Clumps of tundra fallen from the disintegrating soil lay in his path. He overturned sod large enough to crush a boy's body. No Stewart.

Angus looked again to the beach and felt oppressed by the need to clean the nets before the tide turned. He didn't have time to find Stewart and pick salmon too. Sighing, Angus dragged the skiff to the water. As he yanked fish out of the mesh, his worry crested into a mighty anger.

"Gone ta Unaganik, spoiling fer fun," Angus raged as he cleaned the nets with reckless speed. "Spoilin' fer a beatin', that's wha'!"

The day was grey and windy. The sun was a pale disk behind the clouds. Angus's lips dried. He felt hoarse with rage. Further along the net, two big Kings had ripped halfway through the diamond mesh. Their whipping tails had snarled the threads. One still thrashed. Angus dug the sharp point of his hook into the top of the silver head. He jerked the hook back and forth until the convulsions stopped. Angus tied the broken mesh with clumsy cold hands, cursing the old rotten threads and the lack of money to buy a new net. With the bloody cannery paying pennies, he'd be sore put to make any gains this season.

Finally he reached the end post. The skiff was now full

of fish. Angus pulled out a dozen salmon for the dogs and dinner and rowed to the talley scow where the thin man counted up the catch.

"Seen me lad?" asked Angus after he signed the chit. He controlled the angry tremors in his voice with difficulty.

"Wasn't on the wharf when I left," replied the man.

"Donna mean he dinna go ta Unaganik," said Angus, mostly to himself. "He coulda' taken the trail o'er the tundra, or gone along the beach."

"He could be hanging around," said the man, "and I wouldn't of seen him." Angus tied his skiff behind the scow. He joined the thin man on the tug.

"Cigarette?" offered the man.

Angus shook his mane of white hair. Reaching into the breast pocket of his tartan shirt, he pulled out a pouch of pipe tobacco and his briar pipe. Angus knocked the pipe against his hand until it was clean, and tamped it down with a concentration that hushed the talley man. Soon the smoke from the briar pipe and the thin man's cigarette filled the wheelhouse like fog over Dead Man's Shoals, and, like dead men, they said nothing.

The thin man had troubles of his own. He kept silent in the presence of Angus and the other independent fishermen. Even though he came from Montana, he knew their complaints, but he had a job to do and didn't want to lose it and lose the chance to buy the family farm back from the bank. He'd take his money and get out in September. It wouldn't be soon enough.

"I'll be thankin' ye for the ride," said Angus, breaking the dull, thudding silence when they reached the dock in Unaganik. The village of Unaganik teetered on one side of the river, the cannery on the other. A wooden footbridge crossed the river like the arm of a scale, balancing the two sides.

The cannery consisted of three long broad warehouse buildings built of wood shipped up from Seattle twenty years after the purchase of Alaska from Russia in 1867. The buildings had weathered, had been patched, and now leaned under the wind. Behind them, a motley collection of canvas and skin tents housed folk who had drifted down from the

interior to find work during the big fish runs. A few crewed
on the double-ender boats owned by the cannery, but only
white men were hired as skippers, and only a handful of
natives were hired to work in the cannery itself.

The abandoned orphanage was also part of the cannery.
It now housed the Chinese packers. The Chinese, unlike
Cheok's experience in the same building, ate their own food
and spoke their own language. Although the stench and steam
was often unbearable, no one complained or tried to change
the system. For that, both cannery bosses were happy.

The talley man tipped his blue peaked cap. "Do you
want me to take the skiff back for you?" he asked. "I'll be
leaving before high water."

"I'll be thanking ye fer that, too," said Angus. "The
woman can start at the nets. Will ye blow the whistle on the
tug ta let her know?"

The thin man nodded and after Angus climbed onto the
dock, he headed the tug across the river to the cannery, to
offload the salmon.

The *Yethl,* an unfamiliar seiner, bumped against the
village dock. An Indian lad of Stewart's age gutted a salmon
on the aft deck. His dark skin, high cheekbones, and prominent nose reminded Angus of a Tlingit guide he and Joe
Stokes had once hired to take them prospecting north of
Juneau. A scar cut through the lad's right eyebrow, splitting
the dark hairs. It gave the right side of his face a look of
innocence and wonder that contrasted with the ancient knowing in his eyes.

Angus gave the stranger a brisk nod and hurried off the
dock and up the riverbank toward the village. The wind, by
now, had blown off the clouds and the June sun shone from a
sky that looked as if it had been scrubbed. A platoon of bugs,
including the white sox, which were no bigger than a pinpoint
and twice as sharp, swarmed into action. Angus ignored
them. An old Eskimo woman leaned against a doorway, as if
propping up the tar-papered shack around her. A boy the age
of Charlie rolled stones into a mud puddle and took no notice
of Angus. A mangy dog snarled. Angus booted him away.

Angus continued down the road, his mind on Stewart
rather than, as was usual, his growing problems with the
cannery. He detoured around a heap of tin cans, rusted claw

traps, a chewed bear rug, and empty oil drums. He carefully avoided the droppings of dogs. He nodded to Mrs. Vlabidy, a buxom white woman, who dumped a washtub of suds into the road, splashing her starched white apron. At the end of the road, he reached the Mud Dog Saloon. The saloon was empty except for a lone drunk whose lighted cigarette cast a red glow. It wasn't Stewart.

Across the road stood the jail, a one-story frame building on concrete blocks. The front steps had been forgotten in the shipment from Seattle a dozen years ago, but the only person discomfited by this three-foot rise was Mrs. Meriweather, the owner of the Mud Dog Saloon.

Angus climbed into the jailhouse. He rolled his waders over his knees.

"Have a big catch?" asked Robertson Sharpe, the head jailer.

"I'm late," said Angus, who was as honest as the Alaskan summer day was long. "Best dock me pay."

Robertson pushed himself up from the oak swivel chair behind the two planks that served as his desk. A half-empty coffee mug rattled on the planks. He leaned against the wall and studied Angus with his one good eye. His left eye had been chewed by a brownie. Some said in the Mud Dog that the enormous grizzly, after taking a great chunk out of Robertson's face and dismembering his left arm, had left, finding Robertson tasteless.

Miraculously alive, Robertson had dragged the remains of his body two miles to the MacTavishes'. Angus got him onto the dry sled and into Dr. Visikov's office within thirty minutes. Now major injuries were flown to Anchorage, but at the time Angus brought in Robertson, Dr. Visikov, fresh out of heroin, had to sew him back together without a painkiller. Robertson ended up with one good eye and a nose that sat straighter on his face than it had prior to the accident. His right arm was capable of locking and unlocking the jail and clipping a recalcitrant bugger if the need arose. It was no good for arm wrestling in the saloon, but he had trained himself to use a rifle. Even before meeting the bear, Robertson had spoken with a hiss that was hard to decipher. He hissed now to Angus, "I'll return before high water."

"Thank ye fer that," said Angus and he raised his

puckish white eyebrows in the direction of the corridor and asked, "Anybody in?"

There were two cells at the far end. One cell was large and called the Main. The other, called the Guestroom, held criminals with class.

"Friend of yours in the Guestroom," slurred Robertson, winking his good eye, "and Sour Pete and Toothless Ed in the Main."

4

As SOON AS ROBERTSON Sharpe left the jailhouse, Angus barreled down the hall, fingering the hook on his belt, expecting to catch Stewart in the Guestroom. He jabbed the key into the lock. It was open. He kicked the door.

A pole-shaped man swayed up from the mattress in the corner. "Angus MacTavish," boomed the voice, fulsome for someone so gaunt.

"If it inna Joe Stokes!" Angus felt bowled over by the voice and by his own surprise. He moved his hand from the belt he had intended to snap across the occupant's face, so sure was he that Robertson had meant Stewart when he said "friend of yours in the Guestroom."

Now old-timers, Joe Stokes and Angus MacTavish had met on the Chilkoot Pass Trail thirty-nine years ago, had joined forces in the search for gold, but had made more money running mail across the Arctic with dog teams.

Joe, at sixty-three, had twice as much hair on his face as he had on his head even in gold rush days. His bald pate was the color of rusted pipe. His eyes were green above a beard that was mottled white, red, and brown, as if simultaneously changing coats from winter to spring to summer. Joe's six foot three had bent like a willow wand to five foot eleven. When Angus grabbed Joe's elbow and said, "How are ye?" it was a shock to feel the strength in his friend's arm, so slight did he seem to the eye. There was a lot of time between the two men—time when they parted not knowing if they'd meet again, time when they came as if called, not knowing the other needed help.

25

Joe, years back, lived with a northern woman and had two children, Martha and Joe Junior, before the woman died of tuberculosis. Later, Junior, cleaning the .22, had killed the sister by accident, although who knew what had really happened in the lonely bush cabin along the cutbanks of the Yukon River?

Angus had been in a roadhouse near Nettles when he got a pressing itch to see Joe. He found him sitting beside Martha and quickly buried her below the frozen sod. He rescued Joe, most said, from certain death, yet all that was really known was that together the men came down to Bristol Bay. When Angus married Cheok, Joe went upriver to trap and fish. He still lived by his traps, his wits, and his ability to make do.

"Got a cuppa?" Joe asked, moving toward the door.

Angus smiled. "Unless yer here fer somethin' I should know about."

Joe was snapping on his suspenders and made no remark.

Angus leaned against the doorjamb and said in a loud voice, "Yer either turnin' daft or deaf or ye shot a mon."

Joe looked up sharply. "Someone dead?" he asked.

"Not that I know of," said Angus.

"Weren't me who shot him if he is," laughed Joe, and he banged his knee. "Merilee Meriweather was busy last night so I come here to sleep."

"She's working a wee bit fer the union," said Angus.

"Was a boss man," said Joe.

"That's wha' I mean," said Angus, and he pressed a square finger to his lips—no need to tell further. With the finger he felt the bristle of his beard and remembered he'd not shaved. I'll beat Stewart for that, he muttered to himself, stiffening his back and knowing that, if Stewart had helped with the nets, he would have had plenty of time to shave. I don't know the lad, thought Angus with a rage stirring inside such as he had not known since the days his own father switched him for lesser misdeeds. Shirking his duty!

From the Main came the drunken bellow of a man wearing the last of his booze. "Git me some *hootchinoo*." The floor boards vibrated.

"Shut yer trap, bucko mate!" Angus bellowed back. "There inna volcano juice in the jailhouse."

"Boil me some Hills Brothers," bellowed the voice, "or

me brains will burst and bloody these here blasted blue walls.''

Angus twanged the locked door with his key ring. "I'll bring ye some brew when I bring it.''

Angus dropped the keys onto the desk. In a back room, behind the front desk, he fired up a Coleman and set on a pot of water. When the water boiled, he threw on a handful of coffee and let it continue boiling until the contents of the pot looked like molasses. The thick roasted smell seemed to peel the paint from the walls.

Angus lit his pipe while his cup of coffee cooled. "Did ye ha'e a brae winter?''

"Got my quota of silver fox and beaver,'' said Joe after a loud slurp. "Took the pelts down to Harold's Point and hopped a ride up here on a seiner. Couple of fellows you might like to know. The name's Kleet.''

"From the *Yethl*?'' asked Angus.

Joe nodded. "They're wondering what we're doing about a union. The skipper's trying to start one in the Southeast. They've got them big traps there and don't buy from any independent fishermen.''

"Tell the old mon we dinna ha'e eno' men around here ta beat the cannery,'' stormed Angus, using the nautical term for skipper.

"Careful,'' cautioned Joe. "You'll burst a blood vessel.''

Angus sipped his coffee and heard the fast beating of his heart.

"They've got you all over a salt barrel,'' Joe said, rocking his cup side to side on the table. "You don't sell your fish, you don't get no money.''

Angus, quieter now, thought of the lad on the *Yethl*. He was as dark as Stewart was light, as hardworking as Stewart was a slackard, a dandy. I'd be proud of a son like that, Angus mused.

Joe slurped the last of his coffee and poured a second.

"So what are yer plans?'' asked Angus, changing the subject so quickly that his pipe quivered between his lips. "Ye canna sleep in the Guestroom all summer. Be a rare season we dinna ha'e a killing and need it.''

"I was thinking to roll my bed across the river,'' said Joe, meaning the ground behind the cannery.

"Indeed, ye might get caught in the middle," said Angus. "If there's trouble, the bosses'll think ye started it."

Joe spat coffee grounds through the large gap in his front teeth.

"Ye kin help me with the set nets."

"And what about Stewart?"

Angus banged down his mug and poured seconds of the sludge remaining in the coffeepot. Joe had never talked about his family problems and the Lord knew he'd had plenty. Angus would not either. They'd been friends for too long to spoil it by idle chatter.

"Yer that welcome at the house," Angus said, ignoring the question.

"Jee-zuz," said Joe, "I can't sleep with folks sucking up all the air."

"Ye kin have the *maqi*."

"What does Cheok have to say 'bout that?"

"Ye think it's up ta her, mon?"

"She likes her steam," Joe insisted. "I can sleep on the ground."

"And ha'e the mosquitoes feast on ye?"

Joe scratched his beard with both hands.

"Coom tonight, at least," said Angus. "Yer must coom ta say hello."

Joe drank with Merilee Meriweather in the Mud Dog Saloon until Angus finished his shift at the jail. As Joe and Angus headed down the road through Unaganik, they saw two men looking through the windows of the one-room schoolhouse. Angus recognized the younger man from the seiner.

"Ted Kleet, Captain of the *Yethl,* and Ted Junior," Joe said, introducing the two men. "And this here's Angus MacTavish."

"Yer tha' welcome ta coom ta supper," Angus said. "Be glad ta hear about yer union."

In silence, they hiked over the tundra, through the white birch with their new buds yellowing against the sky, past the low lying scrub spruce with its sharp blue needles, around the drift willows lining a large bog. The ground was soggy but all except Joe had worn fishing boots.

"May we see your fishing site?" Ted Senior asked when they reached the little house on the bluff.

"Doon there," said Angus, pointing to the trail. The Kleets headed down the bluff and Angus unhooked the leather thong holding the door closed to the *maqi*. It was a low-lying log building with a battered Yukon chimney and two rooms. Rough benches lay along two low walls of the outer, changing, room. A bottle of Lily of the Valley perfume stood on a small shelf next to a half-height door. That door led into the steam room proper, where there was a barrel stove, a pile of spruce, two five-gallon cans of spring water, a basket of a plant Cheok called her Eskimo medicine, and a large bird wing that she used to flick and pat her sweating skin.

"Drop yer bedroll," said Angus in the outer room, "and coom ta the house. If Cheok's cleaning the nets, we'll nae ha'e ta do it." Or Stewart, he added under his breath, wondering if the lad was back.

Naked, Ellen lay in her cot with Baby Bruce, showing him her favorite picture in *Our Wonder World, Volume III*. A lion stared up from the page like a bearded ancient crowned with wisdom. "Someday I'll take you to see one," Angus heard her croon to the baby and wondered why he had plucked that red leather book out of a snowbank and carried it for years only to have his wee blue goose read it and talk about leaving.

Angus picked up the wool quilt and tossed it over Ellen and Bruce. "Are ye better?" he asked.

"I'm hot." Ellen threw off the quilt and, leaving Baby Bruce in the cot, gave Joe a hug as she always did when he stopped by the cabin. His trapper's hands pressed against the smooth copper skin. He moved his hands down the fine balls of her spine. She felt like a bird, all hollow in the bones. He pressed his cheek to her feathery lips and dared not move his own. He found it near impossible to keep his green eyes from the tiny red-brown nubs of her breasts, from the smooth slit where her lithesome legs met.

Ellen danced away to put on her clothes, and Joe thought, Jee-zuz, I can't stay here and keep my sanity. If Angus knew my thoughts, he'd have the gun to me as . . . as . . . The memory clouded over him. The words he'd told no one opened like a well into the earth, as if he'd been hiking through the tundra and stepped into a bottomless hole.

Leaving the house, Joe crouched by the potato box and

looked at the thin peach-colored line cutting the sky. The shot his son had fired at Martha had been meant for him, and over the long twenty-three years since that day, Joe had wondered if his son had known that Martha had died instead. He suspected Joe Junior had escaped to the Lower 48 and some day, before he got old, Joe planned to search for him.

Joe never knew what Angus knew, if anything, about the shot Joe Junior had fired, and why. Now, despite the insistent memory of that experience, he found himself feeling for Ellen as he had felt for Martha, as he had felt years past on the unbroken prairie for a bit of a girl who had been the preacher's daughter and who knew all there was to know about sinning.

Cheok climbed up from the beach with the Kleets behind her. Fingering the jade labret that she had tied around her neck with her red satin hair ribbon, Ellen watched Ted Junior. He seemed as old as Stewart but easier, as if he was not encumbered by an excess of restlessness or emotion. When he walked along the edge of the bluff, studying the ground, she followed him, savoring the freshness of the wind sweeping the heaviness of Stewart's leaving from her thoughts.

Ted stopped. Ahead, tucked into a tussock of thick grass and spagnum moss, almost invisible, lay two spotted olive eggs.

"Tern," said Ted, stepping around the nest and heading inland from the bluff. Ellen stood beside him and they looked at the sky. Over the bay, a flock of seagulls screeched and fought. A tern flew in, circled, and, wary of their presence, darted back over the water.

"Where do you live?" Although he was a stranger Ellen felt comfortable with this person.

"In the tall trees," he said. "They're ten times bigger than any of the trees around here."

Ellen was about to ask what it was like, coming from so far away, when he said, "I like the tundra." He stretched out his arms, indicating the vast space around them. "You can see the bears before they reach you."

"The bears run if they hear you first," said Ellen.

"Are you afraid of them?" he asked.

"No." Ellen planted her hands on her hips. "I'm not

afraid of anything." But when he looked at her, with those quiet eyes that seemed to search her soul, she knew she was afraid. Afraid for Stewart, for where he might have gone.

"A dude came to take pictures of the bears one time," said Ted. "The old man warned him not to camp on the bear trail, but he didn't listen."

"Daddy told me about those kind of *cheechakos*," Ellen said, smiling. "They knew more than the Sourdoughs."

"This dude didn't get a chance to learn much," said Ted. "A grizzly ate everything but his right foot."

Ellen's laughter filled the air. "For goodness sakes," she said, catching herself. "I shouldn't be laughing at that."

"My mother says laughing's as good as sunshine."

"Daddy says laughter's the work of the devil."

"I don't see one around," Ted said, twirling around and around in a circle, his arms out, his hair flying like a raven around his head.

Ellen opened her arms and spun until she felt like she was flying like a tern above the tide flats, seeking a home.

All through dinner, while the men plotted ways to get all the canneries to pay a fair price for fish and to hire natives instead of bringing foreigners up from Outside, to permit gas boats on the bay and ban the big traps, Ellen watched Ted Kleet, Junior. He seemed so much like his father and yet independent at the same time. Stewart was so different from Daddy, like they were opposite sides of a silver dollar and only one side could win the bet. She'd not miss the battles and the feeling that she needed to keep them from killing each other. But she grieved for Stewart so much that to think his name brought tears. Ellen rubbed her eyes and, looking up, noticed that Ted Junior watched her as if he was reading her mind.

At the end of the meal, when she left to carry water to the dogs, Ted joined her. "Do you go to school?" he asked.

"No." Ellen shook her head.

"Is that because they won't allow natives?"

"No," said Ellen, astonished because she had not thought of herself as a native. "Unaganik only has eight grades and I've done them all." She poured water into Wolff's trough and returned to the creek to refill her bucket.

Ted took a second bucket from the bank and filled it

alongside Ellen. "Do you want to go to high school?" he asked.

"Yes." Ellen looked down at the cold rushing water and remembered another fear, the fear that Daddy would never let her leave home. She yanked the overflowing bucket from the creek, splashing water as she hauled it toward the panting dogs. The mosquitoes buzzed.

"When my mom and the old man moved my sisters and me from our village to town so I could go to high school," Ted told her, "the people in town said I had to go to boarding school with the other natives. Since the old man didn't want me to live away from our family and the old ways too soon, he and my mom got winter jobs at Sheldon Jackson's boarding school in Sitka. I go there and in summer we fish."

Ellen crouched beside Wolff, patting his head and talking into his ruff of hair. "You're lucky," she said, her voice breaking. She felt her eyes brimming with tears. It seemed as if she'd never get to school, as if she'd be stuck in Unaganik for the rest of her life. She buried her face in Wolff's fur, feeling hopeless. With Stewart gone, there was no one to see her side of things and to understand how much she longed for something more.

"Some people have to make their own luck," said Ted quietly. He crouched beside her until Ellen could smell the salt crystals on his gaunt, high-boned cheeks and the Lifebuoy soap in his glistening dark hair.

5

THE NEXT EVENING, BEFORE high water, Angus had not returned. "Can this girl go look for her daddy?" Ellen asked Cheok in the old language.

Cheok nodded from the rocker where she nursed Baby Bruce.

Ellen ran along the trail to Unaganik. Daddy was not at the jailhouse or Dr. Visikov's, and she entered the Mud Dog, hoping Daddy wasn't drunk. Sounds of music from the pump organ rolled down the stairs and Ellen climbed them slowly, hearing Daddy's booming voice in song.

Mrs. Meriweather's knees pumped the side bellows. Her feet, in high-heeled white shoes, rocked back and forth on the pedals. Her brightly painted nails flashed over the ivory keys. Angus stood beside her, his eyes on the grey roots of her bottle-russet hair. "Oh, ye take the high road and I'll take the low road," he sang, and Ellen smelled whiskey all the way across the room.

She dropped onto the maroon couch. When Angus ended on the last Lomond, Mrs. Meriweather broke into a dance rhythm. Angus turned and saw Ellen.

"Coom here, me wee blue goose," he boomed and, reaching for her hands, swung her so they faced the same direction. Holding her right hand up, her left hand down and in front of him, he called the steps of the schottische: "One, two, and three hop, and four, five, six, hop, one hop, two hop..." Around they went, circling the rug, the furniture. Mrs. Meriweather played. They were skimming past the open

33

door for the third time when Joe Stokes entered with the two
Kleets.

Angus swung Ellen to Ted Junior. "Here ye go. I'm
needing a libation."

Ellen, still dancing in rhythm, crossed her left hand to
Ted's left hand and clasped her right hand in his right,
holding it high.

"One, two, three hop," clapped Angus while Mrs.
Meriweather played. With the music tapping through their
feet, Ted, with few stumbles, got the rhythm. Ellen liked the
feel of his hands. He held her with a strength that made her
imagine she could fly like a tern whenever she wanted.

Ellen felt freed of worries. There were no salmon popping in the nets, no Stewart disappearing over the tundra, no
desperation to go to school. She started to laugh and Ted
Junior, distracted by the chime of her voice, stumbled and fell
sideways onto the couch. Ellen fell beside him, and the two
of them looked at each other, laughing until their stomachs
ached.

The music stopped. The men talked but Ellen rested in
the soft comfort of the couch, unaware that her hand still
remained enclosed in the young man's.

Despite his feelings for Ellen, or perhaps because of them,
Joe Stokes lived at the MacTavishes' all summer, staying out
of the *maqi* when Cheok took her steam. Ellen never went
near the low-lying building and Joe pushed down his thoughts
about her—except for once.

That was a day so hot, so muggy, that the heat seemed to
drop like sweat from the sun, which had hung high in the sky
for the duration of two tides. There was no wind. Ellen,
standing on the tide flats, peeled off layers of clothes, leaving
a piece strung over the net here, a piece over the net there.
Joe Stokes watched her and kept his longings under control.

Ellen was barefooted, as always. She had not bought
beach boots with Stewart's money. She had feared what
Daddy would say, that he would think she knew where
Stewart had gone, for surely Stewart was not dead.

The sound of Daddy's belt burned in Ellen's memory
although Daddy had never so much as put a hand across her
backside. Ellen could not put away the thought that if she had

tied her boots like she should have, she wouldn't have stepped out of them, wouldn't have lost her balance and hit her head, and when Stewart had carried her to the beach, she wouldn't have cried because her boots were stuck in the mud. For Daddy to beat Stewart because she was crying about boots was too strange to understand. If all that hadn't happened, and surely, except for her, it wouldn't have happened, Stewart would be picking fish with her instead of Mr. Stokes.

Stewart's leaving was entirely her fault, Ellen knew that, but it still didn't change the fact that she liked bare feet rather than being tied into her boots. The feeling of being completely bare in this heat she liked even more, especially being far enough away from the shore so the sand fleas didn't bother her. Ellen imagined that that brush of wind on her skin was what those fine ladies in New York City felt when they wore silk dresses. And the flecks of sunlight dancing on her skin, she imagined, looked like real diamonds.

Joe Stokes said nothing, but watched Ellen shuck her clothes piece by piece. Her thin, hard body shaded the sun. The rays glowed around her like rays around the ikons in the Russian Orthodox Church. The bay licked the shore with a lace-edged tongue and Joe ached to lick Ellen's juicy folds, which seemed so close. Ellen's deep dark eyes, round flat face, and tiny lips disappeared in the blackness of the shadow she was with the sun behind her. Joe forgot it was Ellen, and Angus's daughter. Angus was rowing the skiff to the talley scow and this was a girl-woman and they were alone.

When Ellen stretched her hands as if to embrace the sky, Joe moved toward her. He held her around the middle, tossed her up and let his hands clasp under her flat bare buttocks. His fingers longed to explore that secret place he had thought about so many lonely nights. His breath banged against his chest and he held it, afraid for the moment to change. Ellen clasped her arms around his neck, thrust one leg up over his shoulder. That special place widened.

And suddenly Ellen was around his neck, seated on his shoulders. Her hands tickled his bare head. She was pressing that place into the bony spines of his neck and saying, "Will you carry me to shore, Mr. Stokes?"

The water trickled in behind them. Joe hauled his mud-laden feet forward, one after the other, carrying a bundle more precious to him than all the fish in Bristol Bay or all the silver fox along the trap lines. By the time he set Ellen on the stones, his iron will locked down his emotions and his breath came free and easy. He turned toward the net with no other plan than to retrieve Ellen's clothes before the tide rose.

Later, much later that night, lying by the smudge and hearing the skeeters buzz beyond it, Joe felt such a weight it was as if he was once again hauling grub up the perpendicular trail to the Chilkoot Pass and was meeting Angus MacTavish and Merilee Meriweather en route, and they were all young in a prime they never imagined they'd lose.

No one spoke of Stewart. Joe wondered, but did not ask.

There were any number of places Stewart could have gone, Angus reasoned in the privacy of his own head. He wanted to believe that Stewart was safe and would return as a man of the country, not someone who acted like a fop.

Meanwhile the fish continued to spawn upstream. After the early run of Kings came the big run of the blood-red salmon they called Reds. Then the Humpies, with their strangely deformed backs, and finally the Chum, which were not good for much but the dogs. Even with Joe Stokes's help, Angus worked long hours without sleep, and often his eyes stung like spruce needles and his lips were raw and bleeding from the salt wind. He went from picking the nets to his shift at the jailhouse, and then back to the nets, grabbing forty winks when and if he could. There was no time to plan a strike against the cannery and men who looked to Angus for the initiative were mad.

"Hold off till next year," Angus said, rolling his "r" so long the men who had gathered at the jailhouse wondered if he'd ever stop. "Nae's the use tipping our honds before we're good an' ready."

By the end of summer, when it was dark enough to see the aurora borealis, the MacTavish household, with Joe Stokes's help, had caught and sold nine thousand salmon, had smoked, for winter, two thousand pounds, and had gathered and dried three barrels of the small, red low-bush cranberry.

One night when they were eating *akutaq*—or Eskimo ice cream, fat whipped with berries—Joe announced, "I'll be getting on with my traps."

But first Joe helped Angus undo the beach nets, to bluestone them, and haul them up the bluff to be stored for winter next to the smokehouse, where flat sides of salmon still hung by their tails. When that was done, Angus said, "Aye, old mon, it's time to settle up. Let me pay ye yer fair share."

Joe scratched his beard. To refuse would be to scorn Angus, to suggest that Angus needed the money more. Joe searched for an easy answer and, finding none, blurted quickly, "Keep it for Ellen. For her schooling."

"Nae," said Angus, "ye've earned it and ye deserve it. The Lord knows what may happen to ye this winter."

"I won't starve as long as there's moose in the woods and fish in the streams," said Joe. "The money's for Ellen."

"Nae." Angus's eyes sparked. Joe took the unfamiliar paper bills without another word. There was no arguing with a man who valued his reputation for honesty as much as other Scots valued theirs for parsimony.

"Ellen's nae going away ta school," repeated Angus in a tone that sounded familiar to Joe. "She's that young and her mother needs help with the bairns."

They entered the cabin. Joe picked up Ellen and held her tight against his beard, forcing the muscles in his arms to overrule his trembling hands. Then Angus and Joe Stokes headed off through the tundra to Unaganik, where they tied a few on at the Mud Dog Saloon.

What with fishing season over, men were wild. Angus and Joe walked a fine line between taking part and keeping their distance. With this crowd, and this mood, it didn't behoove a family man to get too close.

It wasn't near midnight when Sour Pete tossed a glass into the smoky air of the saloon and pumped it with bullets. One bullet hit the beveled edge of the mirror behind the bar. It spun out the open door and hit the temple of the thin man who had just collected his summer's pay for running the talley scow. The thin man slumped to the ground.

Angus ran for Dr. Visikov, who pressed his stethoscope to the thin man's chest while Joe escorted a drunk Sour Pete to the jail.

"Quite dead," said Dr. Visikov when he climbed up into the brightly lit jailhouse several minutes later.

"Never knowing what hit him," said Joe.

Dr. Visikov looked at Joe through his hooded, half-raised eyelids. The doctor was a grey man—grey about the drooping jowels, grey about the head and hands, with cavernous lines connecting his eyes with his receding jaw. His jaw hung like an afterthought, as if the Creator, seeing a space between the doctor's mouth and neck, slapped on a boneless flap of skin.

"I've got to find his kin and send off this poke of money he's got on him," said the doctor wearily, as if the act of doing such was more than his medical expertise could encompass.

"The Stinson's flying in tomorrow," said Joe.

"I'll meet it," Angus said, and stayed all night in Unaganik in order to send the money and news on the bush plane in the morning.

During that all-night wait, Angus MacTavish drank Joe Stokes under the table. Merilee Meriweather entertained one of the cannery bosses in her upstairs room, getting him to tell her next summer's plans in order that she could inform the growing organization called "the Union."

The thin man was the only shooting death of the season, although a father of five caught it on Dead Man's Shoals, sinking with a double ender, for which the cannery forced the dead man's family to pay.

"We'll hit them next season," men muttered around the Mud Dog and made plans to run their own bloody business themselves, by God, and return the profits to themselves, instead of to some goddamn plutocrats who didn't even live in the country.

6

I N JANUARY, ANGUS HUNG the 1938 calendar on the wall above the water bucket. It came from the cannery bosses, who spent winters in Hawaii. When Ellen stared at the picture of palm trees waving in a pink sunset, at blue water warming white sands, she longed to go there, longed to escape the frozen snow-covered tundra stretching beyond the cabin in a vast stillness.

Every morning Cheok lost her breakfast and what was left of her dinner in the slop bucket in the windbreak. It seemed to Ellen that mother did not want this new baby, but no one talked about that, as no one talked about Stewart. No one ever talked about anything except the weather, the difficulties with the cannery, whether the fish runs would be big this year, whether Mrs. Meriweather's order of alcohol would last the winter and who had spent the night in the jailhouse.

Ellen had moved into Stewart's cot. She wore the jade labret around her neck on the red satin hair ribbon and still thought that his leaving was her fault, that she must watch herself so that she caused no one else so much harm. Most days she huddled by the stove, sunk so deep in worry that her forehead creased and her shoulders folded forward. Those days even Baby Bruce, crawling over her legs, pulling her braid, or sucking her fingers, could not reach into the depths of her despair.

In three weeks Ellen would be thirteen and it felt as if her life had stopped. She wanted to make what Ted had called her "own luck," but how to get it overwhelmed her. Every day she seemed to repeat their conversation in her head and she was therefore not surprised when Daddy arrived home late one afternoon with Mr. Kleet Senior.

"Ted wanted me to tell you hello," Mr. Kleet said when he and Ellen found themselves alone in the windbreak.

Ellen, feeling shy, said nothing.

"My boy wanted to come with me," continued Mr. Kleet.

"Is he at school?" asked Ellen, finding her voice.

Mr. Kleet nodded. "He thought you might be too."

"I wish—" Ellen blurted but bit her tongue when Daddy burst into the windbreak with an armload of wood.

All night Mr. Kleet and Daddy ran over and over the same old problems: how to get all the canneries to allow gas boats on Bristol Bay, how to get them to stop using the massive fish traps in the Southeast and on the Pacific side of the Alaska Peninsula. Ellen fell asleep with their deep voices thundering through her head.

When Mr. Kleet left for Harold's Point on the Stinson he had flown in on, Ellen sunk deeper into despair. Only the picture on the calendar roused her. I'll go to school there, she told herself over and over as she stared at the palm trees. The idea charged her and gradually lightened the wearisome chores that ruled her days.

Meanwhile, the only place she would be going was Beaver Lake, for wood. Daddy always took the whole family there for what he called their winter holiday. Finally he was getting ready. He oiled his shotgun and Winchester rifle, made extra bullets, filled the grub box with dried fish, bacon, and rice. He sharpened his axe.

One cold dark morning, when the wind was still and there was no fresh snow, Daddy harnessed the five dogs, with Wolff in the lead. The dogs snarled at one another until Angus cracked the whip with a ping on the side of the house and the dogs stopped.

Ellen and Charlie pulled on their mukluks and their winter clothes and set off ahead of the dogs. The air was motionless. There was no sound except the crunch and creak of their snowshoes. Charlie hummed.

"Be quiet or we'll wake a bear," said Ellen.

"Silly, everyone knows bears sleep in the winter."

"Who told you that?"

"Teacher."

"How did she know?"

"She read it from a book."

"People who write books are fallible too," said Ellen.

"Fallible. What's that mean?"

"Look it up next time we're at Dr. Visikov's office," said Ellen.

"I can't remember that long."

"Practice. Remembering is something you have to practice."

"What about bears?" Charlie's winter parka was made of squares of red and black wool, padded with a Chinaman's coat that had washed up on the beach. He looked like a walking checkerboard.

"What about bears?" Charlie asked again.

"Have you seen their paw prints in the snow?"

"Yes."

"So what does that tell you about bears?"

Charlie tilted his chin in the air. "They walk around in the winter?"

Ellen clapped her mittened hands together, laughing. "Does that mean they sleep all winter?"

"Sure they sleep," said Charlie, warming to the subject, keeping his stride even with Ellen's. "But they wake up sometimes and they're awful hungry when they do."

"And that's when you have to be very careful of bears," said Ellen.

"I'll tell teacher when we go back to school," said Charlie.

"I think teacher's gone Outside," said Ellen. "I heard Robertson Sharpe and Dr. Visikov talking about her. She got knocked up and quit."

"Who knocked her up?" asked Charlie.

"How would I know?"

"I bet it was Joe Stokes."

Ellen stopped in her tracks. She raised her black eyebrows at Charlie. "Why would Mr. Stokes do that?"

"Why wouldn't he?" asked Charlie as he scuffed up a loose drift of snow with the pointed tip of his snowshoe.

"Talkety talkety talk," said Ellen. "Your mouth is too big."

"You're jealous," said Charlie.

Ellen raised a hand to punch her brother. She pretended to follow through. "Now I know you're stupid," she said.

"I saw him looking at you."

"Charles T. MacTavish, you are the world's worst liar, and you are only six. Mr. Stokes never looked at me, and besides, he's almost as old as Daddy."

"So what," said Charlie. "Daddy's a lot older than Mother."

"*Ahlinqnakfar!*" said Ellen. "For goodness sakes, when I fall in love it's not going to be with anyone from here."

"How are you going to find a man if he's not around here?" Charlie asked, stopping to pack a snowball.

"I'm going Outside." Ellen astonished herself with the conviction in her voice.

"Why do you want to leave Alaska?" pestered Charlie. "You want to live in Bristol Bay for the rest of your life?"

"Yes," said Charlie, and with enough strength to shake his entire bundled body, he heaved the snowball into the air.

"You think this is the whole world," said Ellen, ducking to one side as the snowball fell. "You're just six, but you talk like an old man."

"Maybe I am an old man," said Charlie. "Mother tells me old men come back again and maybe I was an old man before and came back."

"Don't listen to Mother's stories," said Ellen. "She doesn't know what she's talking about. You were born in that same bed that I was born in and Bonnie was born in and Bruce was born in, and Stewart..." Her voice caught. She cleared her throat. "And there you popped out and were a baby. You were not an old man, and I don't want to talk anymore."

Bells tinkled in the distance. Soon the sled approached. White powdery ribbons fanned up from the runners as they creaked over the snow. Bonnie and Baby Bruce were tucked out of sight under the furs. Cheok was two dark eyes in the midst of the wolverine fringe on her parka hood.

"Ye all right?" called Angus as Charles and Ellen jumped out of the way of the racing dogs.

"Yes," Ellen called. Looking up at his sister, Charlie

echoed her call. The sled disappeared in the distance, leaving behind five sets of dog prints, runner tracks, and Angus's mukluk tracks in the snow.

Ellen reached over to Charlie's cheek and pinched a white frozen circle until it returned to the copper color of his flesh. She pulled his scarf over his mouth and nose until only his eyes peered through. "Come," she said, following the tracks, "let's go."

At Beaver Lake, Angus slowed their pace through the grove of spruce. "We'll stop the night at Joe's trapper cabin," he said, "and I'll go back for Ellen and Charlie."

"Let them walk," said Cheok from the depth of her fur fringe.

"It's that cold," said Angus. "Might be they willna make it."

"When my people that age," muttered Cheok, "they run behind a pulka."

Angus slowed the dogs to a walk and looked behind. Ellen and Charlie were nowhere in sight and he debated between stopping the dogs altogether and waiting. The dogs' tongues dripped with saliva. Wolff lifted his rear hind leg but, although his bladder burned from the need, did not urinate. Old Wolff was nearly blind and his hearing was limited to a few commands. Without his indomitable will and unerring sense of direction, he would have been useless on the trail.

It's past time to shoot him, thought Angus, but that sentiment drove him to crack the whip, canceling the thought of doing away with his favorite lead dog. "Mush," he shouted and down snapped Wolff's leg. The dogs charged through the close-packed spruce bordering Beaver Lake. The sled bells rang.

The blue-tinged and sharp-needled trees were weighted with snow. Their tips touched the ground, and occasionally, as the sled sped past, large comforters of snow slithered off the branches and onto the winter tundra.

Angus gee-ed the dogs right, haw-ed them left, and the old thrill came back, the power of the beasts listening to his voice and obeying his commands. He hopped on one runner and clung to the post. Around one more grove of trees and they'd be at Joe's cabin. The frozen lake spread before them.

The beaver dam lay on the left. On the right . . . Angus braked the sled in alarm. Wolff skidded on his hind legs and dropped his behind to the snow. Angus's startled eyes met the black and still smoldering remains of a trapper's cabin.

Cheok's scream dug like a needle into her throat. For a second, she saw her burning village and smelled the char of human flesh.

"What's this?" Angus said in a loud, harsh voice, ignoring the evidence.

Bonnie peeked up from the bundle of furs. "A fire."

As if spurred by Bonnie's reply, Angus searched the site, reading the message of survival in marks in the snow. "Someone rolled here," he said, pointing at the ground.

Baby Bruce gasped for breath. Lost in memory, Cheok was smothering him. The baby squirmed and Cheok returned to the present. Wriggling her pregnant body free of the fur wraps, she, too, examined the marks in the snow.

"Mr. Stokes, he roll here," she said, indicating a large area that was also marked with charred pieces of cloth.

"Lord!" said Angus, picking up a piece that looked like a remnant of a winter parka. "Not Joe!"

"It be him," said Cheok, bending in spite of her heavy shape. She walked away from the place where they found the cloth, following indistinct footprints marking a trail around the lake. "Look, Mr. MacTavish," she said, pointing them out to Angus, who kept shaking his head in disbelief. "You go."

"Get in!" Angus's voice echoed across the lake.

"This mother waits for Ellen and Charles," said Cheok, planting her feet wide apart.

"Nae," said Angus. "If something's wrong, we'll need ye."

"Those little old people walk far enough," said Cheok, mouthing each word as if Angus was a child and she needed to make him understand.

"Fer Lord's sake, woman, get in the sled. Dinna ye just tell me ye ran fer miles when ye were that age?"

"This woman Yup'ik." Cheok glinted into Angus's eye and stood as tall as her five-foot-two could stand. "They little old half-breeds."

"Get in, Rose!" shouted Angus.

Without another word, Cheok climbed in amongst the furs on the sled and took Baby Bruce from Bonnie's arms.

Ellen and Charlie reached the woods. When they were several yards into the woods, Ellen stopped and pointed to large hoof prints in the snow adjacent to the sled tracks and seemingly more recent than the sled and dog prints.

"Moose," she told Charlie. "Keep your eyes open in case he charges."

"What would a moose want with me?" retorted Charlie, throwing out his small six-year-old chest. He chugged carelessly ahead.

Ellen looked around and, as she followed her younger brother, she continued to look from one side to the other. Suddenly she stopped and sniffed. Beyond the spicy odor of spruce there was something else. A smoldering odor. A smell of burned meat.

Ellen stopped, shivering. The odor of warmth, of heat, made her nervous and cold. She sniffed again. Was it possible something bad had happened to Daddy and the others? The sides of her jaw ached. She stuck out her chin and pushed forward, imagining the worst, and already planning how she would get Charlie bedded in the trapper's cabin in the horrible event that they were all alone.

Bear, lynx, moose, *irrcingquqa,* the dwarfs who took the shape of animals and the little people with the big heads that mother talked about, were out there in the dark, waiting for them. Ellen shoved those fears from her mind to make room for the uppermost fear, that something had happened to her family.

"Look!" Charlie called from the lake.

Ellen's stomach dropped at the sound in his voice. "What?" she called, hurrying as fast as she could on her snowshoes.

She saw the charred remains of the trapper cabin, saw, in a glance, the sled runners leading around the other side of the lake, saw, in a quick glance to the sky, that it was going to be dark before they made it to the next shelter. "Come," she said to Charlie, who was lying in the snow with his eyes closed, "now you're all wet and you'll get cold."

"Will not," said Charlie.

"Hurry. We've got to follow the runners while we can still see them."

"I can't move," said Charlie and pinched his eyes tightly together so they looked like narrow lines.

"You have to move," said Ellen. "It's going to be colder when it gets dark."

"Daddy'll be back."

"Maybe he will, maybe he won't, maybe something's happened and he can't." Ellen forced the words through her shivering lips. Why didn't he wait?

She reached down and pulled her brother's arms. The weight of him popping up all of a sudden unbalanced her and she plopped on her behind into the snow. Charlie giggled.

"Isn't funny," said Ellen. "We *have* to get going."

"I'm not," said Charlie.

"Oh yes, you are, and you're moving on your own two feet."

"What would you do if I stayed here?"

"I'd leave you alone to freeze to death." Ellen stepped forward, walking on her snowshoes between the dog prints and the marks of the sled runners. Oh, she was tired. She wouldn't mind lying in the snow with Charlie and closing her eyes. But there was no choice. If she did that, surely they'd both die. They had to keep moving and get to the next cabin. Move, Ellen chanted to herself, over and over, as she moved her snowshoes along the track of the sled listening with one ear for Charlie's shuffle behind her.

Joe Stokes was almost unrecognizable when Angus found him in the trapper's cabin on the other side of Beaver Lake. He had no hair, no beard, no eyelashes. His face was bloated beyond recognition. His eyes were slits. It was as if someone had taken a pump and blown air up inside his skin, coloring him pinkish red at the same time. He smelled like roasted meat. Burned meat. Joe mumbled and writhed on the wooden bed under a thick lynx fur that must have been in the cabin when he arrived.

Cheok stomped the snow from her boots at the door and entered. She stared at Joe for several seconds, then pulled the fur from his body. Living in the lynx were a colony of fleas who were biting what was left of Joe's blistered and naked skin. His clothes had burned off his back. His penis hung charred and swollen between his legs. Remnants of his leather boots still stuck to his bare skin.

"My Lord," said Angus, staring slackjawed at his oldest friend, "he must have been here for days for the fleas to hatch."

Cheok's eyes widened and widened. She dropped the flea-infested fur back onto Joe and, screaming, rushed outside.

Bonnie slunk closer. "What's wrong with him, Daddy?"

Only then did Angus notice that Joe's mouth was seared shut, and that Joe could scarcely get a breath.

Angus unsheathed his knife and, pressing his fingers to mark the outlines of Joe's blackened lips, plunged in the blade, cutting through the heat-sealed flesh. Joe sucked deeply, pulling air into his lungs, and expelling it with a rasping, sizzling sound that penetrated the chinks in the log walls and seemed to reverberate back and forth. Angus said quickly, "Lord, mon, we've got ta get ye out o' here." He picked Joe up from the bed, lynx fur, fleas, and all, and carried him out to the sled. The moon glared through the trees, marking eerie shadows across the snow.

Angus set Joe onto the bundle of furs, then lifted Joe again and asked Cheok to move the furs, so they could cover him. Cheok stared down at Baby Bruce and didn't move.

"Coom, woman, kinna ye move yer furs? I've got ta get Joe under cover and ta Dr. Visikov's."

Cheok said and did nothing.

Bonnie yanked the furs off and onto the snow. Angus laid Joe down and covered the furs over him, then lifted Bonnie onto the sled. Cheok started to moan.

"Stop, woman, fer Lord's sake. It's nae happening ta ye."

Cheok moaned and Joe, who was buried under the furs, lay silent.

"Stop, Rose. I said stop."

Bonnie nestled against her mother's arm. Baby Bruce sucked his tongue. Cheok bit her lower lip and let the tears fall.

Angus turned the sled around. "Mush," he called to the dogs. Old Wolff struggled and nearly collapsed from the strain.

Angus cracked his whip. The old dog, his tongue drooling against the ruff of his fur, strained forward. Angus rocked the runners from side to side. The sled flew.

Ellen and Charlie heard the bells in the distance. They waited, happy. Charlie hummed a little tune. The sled passed in a whirr.

"Wait," they screamed, and Ellen, lifting her snowshoes high, pounded after the sled screaming, "Wait! Wait! Daddy, wait!"

Cheok turned to Angus, who ran with one hand on the sled handle. "Stop," she said.

"What's the matter with ye, woman? We hae ta get Joe ta Unaganik."

"You want to leave your wee blue goose?" Cheok spoke low and the words came hard from the back of her mouth.

Angus pulled the sled brake. The dogs spun their heels. Angus listened hard and when he heard the faint sound of Ellen's voice calling "Wait! Wait!" he pressed his forehead to the sled handle and waited, breathing hard through his mouth, feeling the hard painful ache in his chest.

7

"**M**USH," SHOUTED ANGUS. THE cold air sizzled with the crack of his whip. The dogs stood still. Only Wolff, operating on years of habit, pressed feebly against the harness. Angus rocked the sled from side to side, breaking the runners from the ice. "Mush!" Wolff whooped to the other dogs harnessed in pairs behind him, but did not move. The sled bells jingled, an idiotic and hollow sound in the vacuum of the night.

Joe Stokes lay on the sled under a pile of furs. Cheok, who had been dozing over Baby Bruce, opened her eyes when the sled had stopped.

Angus lifted the furs from his old friend and saw the puffs of warm breath steaming from his swollen mouth.

"Be Mr. Stokes alive?" asked Cheok.

"Aye and that he is," he said. "Ye'll hafta walk, Cheok, and take the children with ye. The dogs kinna pull the weight nae more."

Ellen and Charlie, and Cheok carrying Bruce, rolled off the sled. The cold snow bit into their feet and faces. Ellen stamped her feet up and down for a few minutes, before clipping on her snowshoes.

"I can't walk," wailed Bonnie from the cozy confines of the sled.

Cheok, in a flash of movement that was almost invisible in the dark, cuffed Bonnie over the head. "*Mikelnguq,*" she growled. "Child!"

Bonnie cried and ducked under the covers, out of sight. Cheok, in a burst of energy although she, too, was cold and tired, flung the robes from the child. In her own fury at having to walk the dark distance, she jerked Bonnie's arm and Bruce, precariously perched on her hip, tumbled into the snow.

Ellen went to him. Bruce whimpered but was unhurt. He was a weak, slight child, still not walking at one year. But Ellen loved him, as did the whole family. And since he was to have been the last child, they babied him as long as possible. Soon enough, everyone thought, he will have his share of work. They carried him, and played with him, and in so doing got some relief from the unceasing chores of winter.

"Come my little gosling, night is nigh and we are walking home." Ellen imitated the singsong voice Mother used when she talked in Yup'ik to her friends in Unaganik. Although she knew many of Mother's words, Ellen rarely used them. She didn't use them now, crooning instead in her own translation of the old Eskimo lullaby, trying to warm the ice chipping at her lungs, solidifying in her bones.

Ellen looked at Charlie out of the corner of her eye. He was weaving back and forth and she surreptitiously moved sideways, to catch him in case he fell. No point embarrassing him by saying anything. If they had to walk, he had to walk too. No matter that he had already walked miles today. And Ellen could not carry him because she was already carrying Bruce, who weighed more by the hour.

Angus rested the dogs until they breathed easier and icicles no longer formed from their dripping saliva. He, too, felt the ice in his lungs. But he wound his scarf higher, and with his eyes burning out of his head, mushed the dogs and continued down the trail, soon passing his family.

"Stay together," he called back to them.

Cheok suddenly turned around, staring behind them. "*Yuilrig?*" she said, her voice fearful.

"Get on with ye, woman, there is nae ghosts!" The sled bells tinkled in unison to Angus's parting bellow. The sled whooshed out of sight, the bells dimming, then dissolving into the darkness. Now there was only the crunch of their snowshoes on the ground, and the heavy breathing of Cheok weighted by the unborn child in her belly.

"Help," whimpered Bonnie as she sunk to her knees.

Cheok lifted Bonnie off the ground with one hand.

"Carry!" Bonnie lifted her arms and wavered forward.

Cheok chugged on, ignoring Bonnie, who continued to whimper.

Ellen looked at Charlie, a little old man, his eyes half open, walking in a stupor and not complaining, even though he was four years younger than Bonnie. "Hush," she hissed to Bonnie, "you'll wake the haunts."

Bonnie's eyes darted wildly. She started to scream but Ellen quickly pressed her hand over Bonnie's mouth. "I didn't mean it," Ellen said. "I was only joking. There's no such thing as ghosts!"

Bonnie's shoulders heaved. She swallowed, and swallowed, and when Ellen removed her hand, gulped for air.

Slowly they moved into the dark, their snowshoes squeaking on the iced snow, their legs like axe handles striking steady blows against the ground. On they went, following their breath, thinking nothing, feeling only the will of their bodies to find warmth.

Not voicing even to herself the worrying thought that his lungs might freeze, Ellen tucked Baby Bruce against herself, cradling him in her arms. "*Nengllirpaa!* How cold it is," she was thinking when Charlie dropped into a heap on the ground.

"Mother!"

At the sound of Ellen's voice, Cheok turned. She lumbered back, slapped her hand against one side of Charlie's head, then the other. No response. Charlie might as well have been dead.

Cheok held him up with one hand. "Put him on my back."

Ellen laid Baby Bruce on the ground. She struggled with Charlie. With her strength nearly gone, she could not move him. "Help!" she hissed to Bonnie. Bonnie had her mitten off and her thumb in her mouth.

"Help me with Charlie," shouted Ellen, but Bonnie held her other, mittened hand, over her fingers and sucked loudly on her thumb.

Cheok and Ellen struggled together and finally hoisted Charlie onto Cheok's broad back. His arms dangled over her shoulders. Cheok gripped them as she bent forward and once again put one snowshoe in front of the other.

Ellen's arms felt light, easy, without the baby. He lay in the snow in his fox fur. The redness of the fur was blackened by the night and one could have stepped over him like a log except for the breath drifting in spurts from his tiny mouth. His breath was shallow, slow. Startled by the sight of it, Ellen bent down and rubbed his chest under the fur, warming his lungs. His breath didn't change.

They moved onward behind Mother until suddenly they bumped into her. Cheok was bent to one side, as if leaning against the darkness. *"Chewgamuck,"* she said. "Hurry up. The wind comes off the bay. It is nearby. *Ukaqsigtuq.*"

"I don't smell the wind," Ellen said, unwinding the scarf she had wrapped around her face and sniffing loudly.

"This mother does," said Cheok, and Ellen stopped arguing. No one ever questioned Mother's sense of smell.

They moved forward in a trance, shuffling one snowshoe after the other, too tired now to lift them. The cold deadened their spirits, and the sound of their movement seemed to come from somewhere else, not from the shuffle of their feet.

Yes. There was the salt wind off the bay. And the deeper cold because of it. Ellen tightened her grip on her precious bundle and breathed slowly so as not to pull the bitter air into her lungs.

When they reached the cabin, it was Bonnie who opened the door. Ellen's arms felt as if they had frozen in position around Baby Bruce. Cheok's arms were melded to Charlie's. She dropped him into his cot and pulled the heavy quilt over him. Bonnie rolled into her own cot and with her boots still on closed her eyes and was immediately asleep. Ellen, with a start, realized she had her snowshoes on. How had the others got theirs off? And where had the time gone since Daddy left? She had lost that time, lost her energy, too, but now revived with the heat that came from Cheok's quick lighting of the stove.

Ellen laid the baby in the crib Daddy had built for him. She moved the crib close to the fire and took off her snowshoes, her parka, her mittens. She flexed her fingers, and when the kettle steamed, took a cup of Hudson's Bay tea from Mother. Around her Bonnie and Charlie breathed with rasping labored noises. But Baby Bruce hardly breathed at all.

"He's sick, Aana," said Ellen, using a rare pet name for Cheok.

Cheok held her hand over his pale thin lips.

"Isn't he?" questioned Ellen.

Cheok leaned close to his face.

"Isn't he?" Ellen spoke louder. Bonnie grunted from her cot and, curling onto her side, grabbed the quilts and covered herself and her boots.

Cheok's hands formed a triangle on her face. She sniffed deeply several times and with her mouth open, blew her own warm air into the baby's face.

Bruce lay like a limp rag on the cot. His breath moved like a thin wisp of smoke.

"Put your hands on his chest," said Cheok. "Warm his air pockets." By which she meant lungs.

Ellen laid her hands lightly on Bruce's limp body. Cheok left the cabin, leaving behind a blast of cold air from the windbreak. She soon returned with a bundle of the dried spiked leaf plant she called Eskimo medicine.

Cheok crunched the leaves into the steaming kettle. A faint grassy odor filled the room. They moved the crib closer to the stove.

Cheok loosened Bruce's coverings, lifted up his wool undershirt and rubbed a round white stone over his heart. Bruce's chest was so blue, so thin, that Ellen thought she saw the red chambers of his heart pulsing against the stone.

Ellen and Cheok took turns hovering over the baby. When Cheok's eyes drooped, and her mouth gaped with snores, Ellen burst awake. When Ellen's head plummeted to her chest, Cheok's eyes opened as if she had heard a thud. It was as if they were right and left hands of the same body—one doing the work when the other could no longer operate the machinery.

Baby Bruce wilted before their frantic eyes. His breathing became shallower. His frozen lungs melted into pulp. He worked against them, drawing in, expelling, up and down in tiny, almost imperceptible movements. His chest continued to expand, contract. At one point, holding her ear down over his gaping little mouth, Ellen thought he had given up. She rubbed the stone in tiny fast circles over his heart. Another breath came, faint, but fair enough for hope.

Bonnie and Charlie slept. In the background, the bay waters drummed against the bluffs, charging in as if nothing were happening, as if the world was not about to stop. Ellen wanted that roaring noise to cease so she could hear Bruce better, but then, no, she wanted it to continue. As long as the water challenged the shore, she believed that Bruce would breathe.

Angus mushed the dogs over the familiar packed trail to Unaganik. The stars stung the sky like white hot embers. A single star shot across the sky ahead of him. It dropped into the void, leaving the merest thread of a tail.

Dr. Visikov stumbled out of bed to the pounding on his door. He lit the gas lantern. Jamming his stocking feet into his slippers and his arms into his dressing gown, he picked up the lantern and made his way to the front room. "E gawds, man," he said, seeing Angus's flushed face covered with tiny white frozen spots. "Come in before you're thoroughly frostbitten."

"I've Joe Stokes," said Angus. "Kin ye see ta him?"

"Bring him in," said the doctor.

While Angus hurried to the sled, Dr. Visikov shuffled to his sleeping quarters in the rear of the building. He slipped his round gold spectacles on his nose. With a trembling hand, he picked up a tortoise shell comb and drew it through his thin grey hair thinking, as he looked at his sunken eyes, how each man chose his own way to dull the inner pain and what he did to himself was nothing compared to what men did to themselves over and over in this godforsaken country. The doctor sighed and prepared to face another crisis in his long years of dealing with man's pitiful efforts to tame the wilderness. Taking the lantern, he returned to the front room.

Angus held Joe with the reverence of a newborn. Dr. Visikov opened the door to his examining room, a stark white room that took up the glow of the kerosene lamp and made it a partner with the shadows. The doctor put his bleached white office gown over his nightclothes and began to peel the lynx fur off the unrecognizable form that lay on his examining table.

"Shall I light another lantern?" asked Angus.

The doctor shook his head. He did not need to see more

to know what damage was done. It was easier to clean up if you didn't have to see the pustulating flesh.

Joe moaned. Fleas spilled into the air in a cloud as the doctor dumped the fur on the floor. "E gawds, Angus," he said, "couldn't you find something better than lynx? You know they hold the fleas like no other."

Angus didn't respond. If Joe hadn't found the lynx in the cabin he might have frozen to death, no matter that his flesh burned with heat.

Dr. Visikov pursed his lips and studied Joe from the tip of his hairless head to the pieces of leather stuck to his feet. He fixed his eyes on Angus for a second, back to Joe, and then went to Angus and shook his shoulder.

"Get over to the wireless," said Dr. Visikov, "and get a plane down here at first light. We'll have to send him up to Anchorage."

The eerie sound of Joe's anguish haunted the room.

"Will ye nae gi'e him a shot?" asked Angus as he jerked to his feet.

"Give me time," said the doctor. "But you be off. Wake up Shushanuk and get a wireless up to Anchorage for a plane."

Angus left. Dr. Visikov opened his supply cupboard. For the past eleven years, since the awful day he'd had to sew up Robertson Sharpe without a painkiller, he had been sure, despite his own need, to save enough heroin for emergencies. He uncorked the bottle, tapped a little powder into a spoon, and warmed it, with distilled water, over his gas burner.

Dr. Visikov drew a syringe with the maximum dose that would put Joe under but not kill him. He shot a drop through the end, tapped the side of the hypodermic. No bubbles. Finally the doctor plunged the needle into Joe's charred flesh and prayed that it would take.

"Joe," said the doctor in a quiet, controlled voice, "I've given you something to take off the pain, and tomorrow you'll fly up to Anchorage. You'll wake up in the hospital."

"Not going in one of them goddamn flying machines," said Joe through his oozing lips.

"Yes, you are," said Dr. Visikov, his voice allowing no dissension. "The doctors up there can take better care of you than I."

"Take my poke," Joe mumbled. The leather bag of money was gone.

"I'll take care of it," said the doctor. "You can give me some furs when you're back on the trail."

The slits that were Joe Stokes's eyes closed. Dr. Visikov poured boiled water into a sterile pan, added tannic acid powder, dipped strips of old sheets into the tea-colored solution and slowly, patiently, bound Joe's burnt body. By the time Angus had stomped the snow from his boots and opened the office door, Dr. Visikov was ready to cover Joe with full-sized, well-worn cotton bedsheets.

The kerosene flickered. The doctor rolled Joe to one side and said, "Lay the sheet down." Angus complied and, looking at the scorched body of his oldest and dearest friend, wondered if Joe would last the night.

Angus lay on the floor of the examining room and tried to sleep. In the dim light of late morning, he heard the faint whirr of an engine. By the time the Stinson wagged its wings overhead, Angus had his dogs back in their traces. The sled bells tinkled. Rather than the thrill of the days when he and Joe raced their dogs across the north, hooting at each other, at the freedom of speed and motion, hearing the bells now gave Angus a spasm of despair. He felt as if a blizzard had buried him and he couldn't see the breath in front of his face. It was too much. Forty years was too much. He could go home, now, and face them all. But there was no home back in Scotland. Home was here, with his wee bairns and the woman who had given them to him so late in life.

"Give me a hand," called the doctor.

Angus returned to the examining room. He held Joe's legs. The doctor held Joe's head. They laid him on the bed of furs in the sled and gee'ed the dogs to the outskirts of the village in time to see the snow spraying from the Stinson's skis as it ran to the end of the landing strip.

"Thank the Lord ye had eno' dope," Angus said when they bent Joe into the idling plane. "Or we wouldna be getting him inta this contraption."

Dr. Visikov handed the pilot a note for the doctor in Anchorage, and a roll of bills. "Send a wireless when you get there."

"Will do," said the pilot. He leaned into the plane, brought out a length of line, and tossed one end to Angus. With each of them holding an end on either side of the wing, they dragged the rope across to chip off the ice that had formed in the long flight through the mountains from Anchorage. They did the other wing, and then the pilot was in his seat and taxiing down the narrow strip. Airborne, the pilot wagged the wings and headed northeast.

"Those fly boys are changing everything," Angus muttered as they watched the silver dot disappear into the faded blue-grey sky.

"World's got to turn," said the doctor, "or we'll all fall off."

Angus jammed his pipe into his mouth and chewed on the end.

"There's talk of a hospital for Harold's Point," said the doctor, turning toward Angus. "Will that upset you too?"

"Ach!" Angus said, taking his pipe out of his mouth and punctuating the air with it. "Ye aren't of the country and ye dinna unnerstand."

Dr. Visikov wiped his glasses and admitted he did not.

"Will ye coom home with me?" asked Angus, changing the subject. "I want ye to take a look at Cheok. She's big with the wee bairn."

The doctor dropped his black bag into the sled. He wound his scarf around his face and tucked his spectacles into the pocket of his mink coat.

"Get in," said Angus, indicating the sled.

"I'll run with you," said the doctor, although he rarely ran, even in extreme emergencies. Today he wanted to run from the lingering sight of Joe's burned flesh and his frustration at being unable to give more care. But the doctor knew, more than he cared to admit, that whatever combination of will and spirit Joe possessed would pull him through, more than anything a physician could prescribe.

"Mush," called Angus and the dogs, despite their exhaustion, charged over the snow. Dr. Visikov, his pulse racing, kept pace for a few yards. Then Angus stopped the dogs and the doctor climbed on the sled. Old Wolff slumped to the snow. Angus cracked his whip. The ailing lead dog struggled forward.

"Home," called Angus.

As if they finally understood, the tired, hungry dogs yipped encouragement to one another and moved over the snow. Angus jumped onto the sled and rode with one foot on the spreader, one hand gripping the waist-high handle.

Wolff, out of sheer habit, found the familiar trail away from the village, through the grove of stunted trees and over the tundra. As they approached the little house on the top of the bluff he strangely put on speed.

"Whoa," called Angus, but the old dog, mindless with exhaustion, headed straight for the side of the cabin. At the last minute, Angus rammed on the brake. Old Wolff reared back on his hind legs and spun sideways. His harness tangled. The other dogs howled. Wolff's body convulsed into knots. His eyes rolled back, exposing the whites. With shaking hands, Angus struggled to undo the collar. It was no use. Wolff had made his last run.

Dr. Visikov stomped his feet in the windbreak, hung his coat on a nail. His glasses steamed up as soon as he entered the stuffy warm cabin with the faint aroma of Eskimo herb. He stopped to wipe them.

Cheok and Ellen crouched on the floor on either side of the crib, sound asleep. Their foreheads pressed into the frame. The kettle burned dry on the stove. Dr. Visikov took one look at the baby. He snapped open his black bag, removed the stethoscope, and touched it to Bruce's chest.

There was no sound.

8

AT HIGH NOON, WHEN the limited winter light was at its best, the villagers who had gathered en masse to mourn the death of Bruce MacTavish circled the Russian Orthodox Church three times, following the tiny closed coffin. Other preachers had more recently tried to get a following in Unaganik, but the Russian missionaries, there for over a hundred years, continued to touch the people's hearts and bury their dead.

The mourners wrapped their arms around themselves, more to guard against the ghosts that surely haunted the ancient graveyard than as scant protection against the wind. The graveyard, with its old wooden fence, leaning crosses, and mounds of drifted snow, faced east to west on the north side of the clapboard church, on the edge of Unaganik.

The current occupant of the Guestroom, a man who had axed his wife and seven of his eight children, had chopped a hole in the frozen ground under the supervision of Robertson Sharpe. A traditional three-bar Russian Orthodox cross, built by the priest, stood at the head of the open grave. Burned into the wood was: BRUCE MACTAVISH, DEC/36–JAN/38.

Incense from the silver censer smoked like a skeeter smudge and perfumed the snow. Cheok, feet planted wide apart, stared straight ahead. Angus bowed his head, getting no comfort from the priest droning on in Russian. Ellen, Bonnie, and Charlie huddled together, jaws tight, fingers clenched inside their beaver overmittens. Overhead, a raven squawked.

Around the gravesite stood the villagers: Merilee

Meriweather, whose russet hair was covered by a blue and
gold blatook; Shushanuk and his wife, Ooguk; the new
schoolteacher; the cannery caretaker, called the winterman,
and his wife; Toothless Ed, home from his trap line; Burley
Jones, who held Buddy, his four-year-old son, tightly in his
arms; and Johnny the Jap, who had slipped away from his
Chinaboss one winter and hadn't been Stateside since. There
were Stinky and Red Cap and Olaf, regulars at the Mud Dog.
There were Dr. Visikov, Robertson, and the priest, who wore
his gold headdress and ankle-length turquoise robes. On the
back of the robe, one arm of the gold fabric three-barred cross
flapped in the wind. The cross had needed sewing since the
last funeral service, two weeks past, when the wind blew so
fiercely across the tundra that the coffin slid six inches over
the snow.

"What's he saying?" hissed Charlie, as the priest lifted
the thick red leather Bible over the small pine box.

"I believe in one God, Father of all sovereigns, Maker
of heaven and earth, and of all things visible and invisible..." Ellen translated the Russian prayer, which the priest
had taught her.

The priest handed Dr. Visikov the Bible, and signed the
cross. Ellen and the others copied, except Cheok, who saw
nothing.

"He's still talking," said Charlie, louder this time, as if
no one else were hearing the deep droning voice.

"I look for the resurrection of the dead," said Ellen,
whispering, "and the life of the age to come."

"What's resurrection?"

"Look it up in Dr. Visikov's dictionary." Ellen's back
was sore from bending against the wind, from bending over
Bruce's crib. If Stewart had been there in his customary role
as acolyte, he would have carried the red leather Bible high in
the air, would have tended the tiers of burning candles in the
church, would have...

"What's he saying now?" Charlie's insistent voice continued. "What?"

"Let us pray, also, for the repose of the souls of the
servants of God who have fallen asleep, that he may be
pardoned all his sins, voluntary and unvoluntary..." Ellen

rubbed her back as she leaned over to whisper in Charlie's ear.

"Stupid," said Charlie. "Bruce ain't asleep. He's dead."

"*Isn't,*" corrected Ellen.

To the sound of Gregorian chants sung by Mrs. Vlabidy, they watched the tiny coffin slip into the shallow ground, the head to the west so that, if Bruce stood, he'd face east and the sunrise. They had kissed him in the open coffin in the church, had said "Godspeed," and now dirty snow covered the closed box. Merilee Meriweather tossed a red satin rose onto the top.

No one cried.

Merilee served tea in her rooms upstairs at the Mud Dog Saloon. Cheok talked in her own language with Shushanuk and Ooguk. She wore a brown wool skirt over her wool pants and a wool shirt of yellow and green that Angus had ordered for her from the catalogue and hidden until that morning.

Angus, with his hands gripped behind his back, talked to no one. Dr. Visikov spoke Russian with the priest, whose long, thin grey hair, freed from the gold crown, drifted around his neck, meshing with his long, thin grey beard. Mrs. Vlabidy and Mrs. Meriweather bustled in the kitchen and Robertson Sharpe stood by the long table, fingering the embroidered linen cloth with his one hand. Ellen inched toward Angus. Bonnie and Charlie, like two squirrel tails on her sleeves, swayed beside her as she made her way across the red carpet that covered the floor. Two maroon plush sofas faced each other across a mahogany table, low to the ground, which held burning red candles in a filigree silver candelabra. Red velvet drapes cut out the winter dark. More candles burned on the pump organ against the wall, opposite the tiled wood stove.

The last time she had been in that room, Ellen and Ted Kleet had danced the schottische. For an instant Ellen felt the reassuring pressure of his hand on her own, as if everything would turn out all right. She sat on the rug, hands clasped around her tightly bent knees, wondering if Bruce wasn't lucky after all, in a place where surely there were no fish to pick, nor fires to burn you, nor bears to maul you. Could she leave her body and fly there to find out?

"Help yourself to Peak Freans, children," said Mrs. Meriweather, referring to the square tin of English cookies.

"Tea?" She turned to Angus and proffered a thin china cup with gold trim.

The cup rattled against the saucer. Angus balanced the saucer on the palm of his square hand, grasped the delicate gold-painted handle against the root of his distended thumb. With four fingers straight up on the other side of the handle, he raised the cup. In the old days, Angus's prim mother curled her pinkie when she held a teacup. Angus remembered that when the cup was halfway to his mouth and looking around the room, remembered, also, that red was the sign of the devil's presence.

Angus studied his broad thumb—a few grey hairs on the knuckle, the nail ridged as a horse's tooth and just as yellow. He superimposed the thumb over the image of his mother, then tossed the contents of the cup into his mouth without touching his lips.

In deference to the occasion, Mrs. Meriweather had used the tea as a disguise for whiskey. The tincture burned his throat. He held the cup while Merilee, smiling at him in a conspiratorial way, poured straight whiskey from a sterling silver teapot with engraved curlicues on its sides.

"Come, Angus, sit beside me on the loveseat like old times," said Merilee after Angus had downed his second cup. They had been friends since Angus met Merilee in Skagway in 1898, en route to a dance hall in Dawson.

"You've had some hard sledding," Merilee said when they reached the loveseat in the far corner.

"Nae more than most." Angus perched stiffly on the edge of the divan, his eyes on the teacup, as if to balance it required his absolute attention.

"Do you have any regrets?"

Her perfume wafted over him. "Donna push me, Merilee," Angus replied in a gruff voice, turning to her. "I wanted ye once and ye said no. Donna taunt me agin."

"I said no, Angus, because marriage ruins a fine friendship— as I'd discovered five times before."

Angus hooted and then, remembering it was the funeral of his youngest child, stopped in mid breath.

"Doesn't mean you can't come by once in a while," said Merilee.

"I get all I need," said Angus shortly. "Yer busy eno'."

"Not in winter, and I do miss my wee Angie." Merilee traced her tongue seductively over her lips.

Angus looked away from Merilee to his young wife. Cheok's dark eyes looked sad in the dim candlelight. She seemed larger, more pregnant than before. Maybe the death of Bruce has sagged her belly some, Angus thought. Has loosened the muscles.

Merilee followed his gaze. "When her time's closer, you'll want to come 'round," she said.

"I may want ta," said Angus, "but I willna. I kinna talk to ye if ye keep propositioning me. Keep our friendship and take yer wares elsewhere."

"Where do you suggest I take them?" asked Merilee, her voice matter-of-fact. "Robertson Sharpe's half a man, the priest is a eunuch, Dr. Visikov's an—."

"Merilee, if ye say another word I'll toss this likker in yer face."

"I do believe you will," said Merilee and, gathering her red skirt, fairly floated to the organ where she trilled her red-painted fingers over the ivory keys. "Abide with me," she sang in a deep gusty voice.

Dr. Visikov joined in with a shaky tenor. Robertson Sharpe, Cheok, Shushanuk, and Ooguk hummed, and Angus belted out all three verses.

The priest took the opportunity to slip away. That morning, before the funeral service, he had discovered a mute Yup'ik lad hiding in the church and was concerned about leaving the lad alone for too long. He suspected that the lad might be a surviving son of the crazed man Robertson had in the Guestroom. Whoever he was, what the lad had seen had shocked him into silence.

Noting that the priest had gone, Merilee switched into the rollicking gold rush melodies. Angus, his voice liberated by neat scotch, sang, "There was a wee copper who lived in Fife, nickety nackety noo noo noo, and he has gotten a comely wife . . ." Merilee, beside him, echoed the noo noo's and roo roo's. After several songs, Merilee crashed out the final chords of "Johnny Schmoker" and, spinning around on the piano seat, exposing her shapely knees, she pointed at the floor.

"Mine three bairns," said Angus, and there was in the

room one of those poignant moments when everyone's thoughts were stilled as they looked at the remaining children of Angus and Cheok, still alive but very much asleep.

Angus, brusque, broke the silence. "We must be away. Wake them, Cheok."

Cheok, heavy with sudden associations, could not move.

"Leave them here," Merilee said. "They can have my bed."

"Where will ye sleep?"

"I'll have the couch."

"Ach no," said Angus.

"It won't be the first time," said Merilee with a knowing look.

"Leave them," said Dr. Visikov. "You only have the hand sled, and it's too cold for them to walk. Let them sleep."

Angus and Cheok walked home past ghosts dancing in the reflection of the moon. Cheok kept her eyes on Angus, avoiding the spirits that haunted the trail.

Warmth hung in the center of the cabin, but the corners were cold. Angus lifted the lid of the stove. The last red embers of the morning log flared. While Angus built up the fire, Cheok stared at the empty crib. Swallowing the lumps in the back of her throat, she pushed the crib through the door and into the windbreak.

The fire crackled and roared. Angus peeled out of his clothes, layer after layer, until knotted around his thick neck and lying against his whitened chest hairs was his only tie, the Glasgow school tie with gold Scottish lions stitched upon it, worn in honor of Baby Bruce.

Tears filled Cheok's eyes and tumbled silently down her cheeks. Angus held her and moved backward until he was sitting in the upholstered rocking chair with Cheok cuddled on his lap. Angus pressed his face into Cheok's hair and tried to think of words to comfort her. Her belly stirred and he laid his square work-worn hands over it, feeling the first movements of the unborn child.

Angus cradled this mother who had brought bairns to him so late in life, especially his favorite wee blue goose. Strict Calvinism was his background, and he had read the evil of sex in his mother's tight lips, in the cane his father had used when he found Angus asleep with his hands on the soothing comfort of his penis. But, thank the Lord, Merilee had taught him to forget all that and to enjoy the urges of his body and hers during cold dark nights on the trail to Dawson.

If she hadn't . . . Angus shook his mane of white hair and wondered at the path his life had taken, how rich he had come to be despite the limited gold he had found in the creeks.

Cheok wiped her eyes on the Scottish tie still hanging around Angus's neck. Bruce had been buried, and there was yet another baby in her belly, and work to do tomorrow. With a deep sigh, she rested against Angus. His curly chest hairs tickled her damp cheek and she was amazed, as always, that he had hair where no Eskimo man ever did.

Slowly Angus wound his fingers through Cheok's hair, marveling at how the light spun across it, across her dark skin. He undid the buttons on her new wool shirt and cupped his hands under her heavy breasts, feeling the moist line where they hung against her chest, feeling their weight.

Cheok rubbed his back, stroking his spine, his shoulder blades, his muscled biceps, feeling the magic of his skin beneath her hands. At the orphanage no one had hugged her. Desperate for the warmth of another's touch, she and her two young roommates had snuggled in bed together as had been their custom in their own village. Caught by a *kass'aq,* they had been isolated in separate rooms, the worst punishment of all.

Cheok stood and began undressing in front of the fire. Angus watched her and felt the urge deep within him to become something to this woman who had given him so much, who had lost a baby while he saved the life of a friend. Before she put on the familiar flannel pajamas, he reached for her. Her skin seemed to flow toward him in the dim fire-lit room, and he realized, with a start, that he was seeing her naked for the first time. There had been Cheok's awkwardness in the early months of their marriage, when she was just fourteen and afraid to show herself undressed to this strange white man who had become her husband. Then Stewart came, and Angus felt constrained with a son in the same room. Tonight, with Ellen, Bonnie, and Charlie safe at Merilee's, and Bruce not sharing their bed or needing a breast, Angus reached for Cheok in a way that he never had before.

He drew her to the big bed in the kitchen alcove and lay on his back. Cheok crouched beside him. She grasped his penis with both hands and studied it for the first time, playing with the tip, the root, spreading the flap of skin over the head. Marveling at the children that had come from this throbbing shaft, Cheok guided it to the valley between her breasts, holding her breasts around it.

Angus, surprised, stroked her hair and felt his heat as he grew larger. He moved over his wife's body, tracing with his tongue the broad expanse of her belly, her line of pubic hair. His excitement soared as his tongue explored the salt-flavored marsh between her legs.

Cheok arched her back, thrusting her pelvis off the bed, moaning without caution because there were no children to worry about wakening.

Angus massaged her with his tongue as if he were circling the universe. Entranced by the swelling of her skin, it seemed as if her body were engorged with pleasure, as if it would explode before him and disappear like stars before the morning sun.

9

MUTUK CLAPPED HIS HANDS and pointed to a three-month-old fawn suckling its mother at the edge of the herd. Qimugta, the dog, took off, a flash of black against the green moss. Seconds later, bleating, the fawn raced toward them, Qimugta nipping at its heels. Mutuk flung it down and cut a triangle in the right ear, a thumb span from the tip, while Stewart held the flailing hooves. Thus they branded, over several days, two hundred newborns that they slaughtered later, in August, selling the meat to a trader and the tails to an old crone who made them into shaving brushes. Stewart, stroking his chin, remembered how Angus used to lather soap over his face with a reindeer-tail brush, never missing a day, no matter what the circumstances. There were no hairs on Stewart's face, and he wondered if, when the time came, he, too, would shave with a straight-edged blade as his father always had.

When snow first covered the ground in the winter of 1937–1938, Stewart lay under a reindeer hide that had shed so much fur it had lost its warmth. He felt hands at his neck and doubled his fists for a punch that was suddenly blocked by a heavy weight of fur. Mutuk was tucking the edges of his own mountain sheep fleece around Stewart's shivering body.

Stewart curled into the warmth, tears filling his eyes. Ach! he thought, pained by the quickness in him to distrust Mutuk. It was Angus taught me that. Taught me to keep up my guard. Stewart trembled with the knowledge that he still feared this reindeer herder who had surely saved his life by coming past the MacTavish cabin at just the right moment. I'd kill myself rather than go back to Angus, Stewart thought as his muscles softened under the fleece. Kill me or kill him! There's not eno' room fer us both.

"Go for sheep," Mutuk said the next morning in Yup'ik. With his rifle slung over his shoulder and wearing his long Laplander parka in which he could sleep, he strode alone toward the white mountains rising in the distance.

Stewart held the dog with one hand and shaded his eyes against the glare of the snow with the other as he voiced an old Russian prayer for Mutuk's safe return. The herd pawed the snow. Feeling the isolation guard him like an unfriendly stranger, Stewart forced the loneliness from his mind. Thinking does nae' good, he told himself, but by the end of the uneasy day he had no energy, as if it had all been used in keeping the foreboding images from his brain.

At dark there was no sign of Mutuk, and Stewart, although he knew Mutuk thought nothing of walking fifty miles at a stretch, tried not to expect him. Streamers of green aurora flicked overhead. Stewart watched until his head had emptied and the Great Bear had turned in the sky.

In the slate dark of morning he pumped the primus for tea. There was a waiting in the air, a feeling of impending doom. Nothing rustled. Stewart felt the ears of the earth point upward, like a reindeer's when it senses danger. The herd circled nervously, breaking up only when the dog, on Stewart's orders, nipped their heels.

Bit by bit through the short day, the air seemed to suck up the sky until Stewart felt as if he, too, would disappear. He was certain he saw *irrcingquqa,* and walked around the tent in the same direction as the sun, to keep them away.

The air collapsed. Stewart could barely breathe. Then the night air rushed in, dark and ominous, blowing across the tundra like empty sleeves. "Mutuk!" Stewart screamed into the dark. The wind howled.

In a terrifying crash of thunder, the storm broke and with it Stewart's nerve. Holding the dog, he burrowed into the tent. Deep wracking sobs resonated through his body like old enemies. Drained by the sobs, by the overriding rage of the storm, he was emptied of his own rage at Angus, his own immobilizing fear. Calmed, he looked up and saw the tent billowing in and out with the wind. He clutched the sides, holding them down. The dog threw himself against the folds, trying to get out. Stewart untied the flap and Qimugta burst into the gale seconds before the howl of wolves rang through the haunted darkness of the night. The wolves' voices eerily caught the wind so that Stewart could not be certain if they were near or far, until the ground shuddered beside him.

The blanket of snow seemed not to dampen the thudding of the stampeding herd but magnify it, carrying the sound through the earth like colossal waves crossing a storm-tossed Bristol Bay. Qimugta yapped nearer, farther. The wolves howled. The dog answered.

Stewart peered through the flap, not breathing. The cold sliced across his bare face. The wind lifted the strands of hair covering his eyes. He saw nothing, smelling only the sourness of frenzied deer and hearing only the clicking of rampaging hooves.

The storm raged. The wolves howled. Stewart clung to the tent for hours, or days, until the storm passed. Stillness dropped around him. He unbuckled his fingers from the tent hide and sniffed. The scent of reindeer musk was gone. Stewart went outside into the dim light of mid morning.

The bloody remains of three yearlings lay in the middle of a vast trampled area. Snow edged the area where the circling hooves had cleared the tundra. Imprinted in the encircling snow were wolf tracks the size of Stewart's outstretched hand. Qimugta was nowhere to be seen.

Stewart set off across the snow, following the reindeer tracks. The cold bit through his tight shoepacs. The wilderness seemed to stretch to nothingness. He lengthened his stride until miles had passed between him and the tent. He breathed in unison with the easy movement of his body, feeling a happiness he had not known before. Was it gone, that old wariness of being beaten? Despite the cold, Stewart felt a warmth around him as if someone had tossed him a fur. Mutuk, he thought, passing a hand across his sweaty brow, pushing the long hair backward under the ruff of his parka hood, is Mutuk on his way home?

The sudden realization of what he'd thought stopped Stewart in his tracks. "Home" was a skin tent pitched on a snow-covered tundra, not the wooden cabin at the edge of the bluff above Bristol Bay. Smiling, he strode on until he found the herd, with Qimugta on watch, near a grove of scrub spruce. It was useless to try to move them back to the place of the wolves. Seeing that they were safe, Stewart turned and retraced his steps.

As he neared the tent, the rich aroma of mutton drifted through the cold air. Stewart, catching a whiff, felt his hunched shoulders drop with relief. Mutuk stood near the tent stirring the cooking pot with a long wooden ladle. Thick globules of fat burst around the rim and Mutuk's flat broad face grinned through the steam. A grey fleece lay on the snow beside him.

"Kaigtua. Elpesmi?" Mutuk asked. I'm hungry. How about you?

While they ate, Stewart told, in halting Yup'ik, the story of the night of the wolves. Mutuk asked many questions and Stewart repeated himself many times. Finally Mutuk laughed. "Such wolves. They as smart as a man and know you here alone without a gun."

Stewart looked at the herder and voiced the fear in his heart. "Are you mad I didn't save the three yearlings?"

"What could a boy have done alone without a gun?" Mutuk said, surprised.

It's true, thought Stewart, sighing to himself, but other things had been true and had made no difference to Angus's response.

That night, after they had repitched their tent next to the reindeer and Mutuk had cleaned and reloaded the rifle, Stewart sat on his new sheepskin, smelling the lanolin and rubbing his frost-bitten toes in the thick fleece. Mutuk picked up Stewart's shoepacs and banged the soles together. A thin clap resounded in the lamp-lit tent. Qimugta jerked his head, twitched his nose in the air.

"A boy needs mukluks," Mutuk said the next morning before pumping the primus for their tea. He spoke in Yup'ik and Stewart, relieved, wriggled his cold toes and nodded.

Motioning Stewart to hitch up the sled deer, Mutuk loaded on the tent and got underway. The flat winter land soon disappeared in rolling hills where the visibility was limited by the next rise of land. Just before dusk on the third day, both Mutuk and Stewart, parched from the cold and longing for a tea break, failed to stop the deer from detouring to a patch of fodder buried eighteen inches under the snow. Knowing the deer had been able to smell the moss, Stewart sniffed loudly. Mutuk, imitating Stewart, wrinkled his nose and sniffed. Stewart sniffed again, sticking his nose into the snow. Mutuk bent over, sniffing long and hard.

Stewart started to laugh and great bellows burst from Mutuk's mouth. What reason to frown? Life had always been hard. But these times were better than those of Mutuk's childhood, before Sheldon Jackson started the reindeer program to feed the starving villagers. Now there was always meat and shelter walking with him on the hoof. Life was good.

Soon the two of them were rolling in the snow, overcome with laughter. But Stewart sobered a little, thinking of Cheok, and wondering if she still laughed as she sometimes did in early morning, before dawn brought memories that overwhelmed her.

The next morning, in a fresh downfall of snow, Mutuk and Stewart edged the herd onto the previous day's track. Late in the afternoon they stopped at a thick willow grove blocking a lake of black ice. The telltale hump of a beaver den rose at the east end of the lake. Mutuk slashed a path through the willows wide enough for the reindeer to pass through. Cutting one uncommonly long tree, he stepped onto the ice, holding the tree across himself as a precaution in case the ice broke. Qimugta twitched ahead, his nose inches above the ice.

Stewart remained on shore, his body tense; Mutuk shuffled one foot ahead of the other, testing the surface. Beside Stewart, the reindeer nibbled on willow bark. Occasionally a soft nose nuzzled against his shoulders, spraying him with a sweet moist smell.

When Mutuk had crossed the lake, Qimugta returned. He yapped at the reindeer and forced them into the pass through the willows. The reindeer moved onto the ice. They were halfway across when one of the yearling bucks threw out his ears in alarm. The herd clenched together like the fingers of a fist.

"No!" Stewart windmilled his arms and tried to keep them moving.

Mutuk motioned Stewart away from the reindeer. Carrying the pole, Mutuk walked cautiously along the path where he had first crossed, humming to the reindeer in a soothing lullaby voice.

"Look," Mutuk called above the grunt of the herd and the yap of the dog. He pointed his pole to wolf prints frozen in the ice. "Foolish beasts," he said to the reindeer, "to be frightened at paw marks."

Abruptly the reindeer headed to the opposite shore and Stewart, amazed, watching them instead of his feet, plunged as suddenly through soft ice. Freezing water clutched at his legs.

"Awgh!" he called, throwing himself forward. One knee buckled and he caught his foot on the ice behind, stopping his plunge into the water. There was an ominous sound as the ice splintered again. Stewart thrust himself forward and stretched his free leg at the same time. Desperately he wriggled on the slick icy surface of the lake, trying to yank his submerged leg free. The leg remained in the hole, getting colder by the second.

Shuffling forward, the willow pole across him, Mutuk approached. When he was close enough, he held one end of the pole and slid the other end toward Stewart. Stewart clung to it; Mutuk pulled. The pole slid through Stewart's iced mittens. He bit them off and, reaching for the pole with his bare hands, heaved himself sideways. The ice cracked beneath him. Mutuk kept pulling until Stewart's leg inched out of the water. Mutuk pulled until Stewart reached solid ice. Unable to stand, Stewart wriggled forward until Mutuk felt it was safe enough to grab Stewart's hood and drag him like a sack over the drum ice edging the shore.

The reindeer grazed. Mutuk wrapped Stewart in both mountain sheepskins. He built a huge fire of willow. He boiled snow, made tea, and forced Stewart to drink cup after cup until Stewart was warmed from the inside out.

Mutuk talked about the reindeer. "Ayagnaurtukut," he said. "Go! When they circle! Cut man to shreds. A fallen fawn go like that." Mutuk held his palms upward. "It's almost like this. Nothing." He stared at Stewart and added, "Worse than breaking through the ice."

"Yes." Stewart felt the pain of hooves where his legs had felt the icy water.

"Keep out of their way," continued Mutuk, gesticulating with his hands.

Stewart feverishly nodded his head. He no longer worried that he could have saved the yearlings on the night of the wolves. The reindeer had their own good sense to form a circle, to fend off attack with their antlers circling the herd. But to circle because of wolf prints? Reindeer are stupid, Stewart thought, his head slumping to his chest.

Mutuk grabbed Stewart's head and shook it from side to side. Stewart's eyes flung open. He stiffened his shoulders.

"Keep out of deer's way," Mutuk said, removing his hands when he saw that Stewart was awake. "I not be able to save you from them."

And it seemed to Stewart that this man who knew nothing about his past life cared more for him than his blood family ever had. Except Ellen. Her long braid with the red satin ribbon seemed to dance through the flames. He missed her that much!

The next day Stewart walked vigorously, pumping the blood through his legs so that he did not even remember that they had nearly frozen. At dusk they reached a small village of log and mud huts.

In a hut with a sod roof and a dirt floor, an old woman sat on a short-legged stool next to her fire. Three tattoo lines ran down her chin, which slanted inward from the absence of teeth in her lower gums. She grinned at Mutuk and stared when he introduced Stewart.

"Mukluks?" asked Mutuk, pointing to Stewart's feet.

The old woman leaned forward and pulled off the shoepacs.

"I've got money." Stewart reached under layers of clothes for his poke.

"Money bad," said the old woman in Yup'ik, dribbling the word over her sunken lips with a trail of tobacco juice. "What this old woman do with money?" She wiped the back of her hand against her watery dark eyes.

At the same time, Mutuk pressed a hand on Stewart's arm. "We kill reindeer for her," he said. "Be best."

"Best," muttered the old woman.

"Forehead for sole of boots. See!" Mutuk spread his fingers over his own forehead, showing the fur going every which way, copying the way the fur grew there on reindeer. "Hold you on the ice," continued Mutuk. "Not slip."

Stewart's eyes stung with the smoke, dampening his vision as if to enhance the ability of his ears to pick up the guttural, lyrical Yup'ik sounds. Rather than feeling strange at being between the first walls since he had left the MacTavish house on the bluff at Bristol Bay, he felt—in some way he did not understand—as if he had been here before, as if he'd known this old woman in another time. He squatted by her low stool. Refusing the chewing tobacco she offered him, he rocked back and forth on his heels and felt the heat ease the aches his body had stored from the long trek.

After Mutuk and Stewart chose a deer and slaughtered him, they roasted strips of meat on a green twig and ate with the fat dribbling down their chins. The old woman chewed the eyeball.

The hide soaked in their urine until the hair peeled off in handfuls. When it was scraped, the old woman studied Stewart's feet and cut their pattern into the reindeer skin with her sharpened *ulu*. While she crimped the cut pieces with her teeth, Stewart asked for beading on the toe, remembering the beading Cheok had done on the tump line for the skiff.

"What pattern?" muttered the old woman as she crushed more tobacco leaves to stuff into her mouth.

Stewart drew his mother's pattern in the dirt floor, naming the color of the beads he wanted and in what order.

Mutuk, bending over the design, crossed both hands over his heart. His dark eyes narrowed. "Where goes the little old red?" he demanded.

Stewart poked the tip of his little finger into the holes for the red beads. The old woman was already threading her ancient supply of beads onto a thin bone needle, following the color pattern that Stewart had described.

"Where a boy get that pattern?" Mutuk's eyes glinted.

It was forbidden to use another's bead pattern, Stewart knew, but this was his mother's, and he said simply, "My mother, Cheok."

Mutuk bounced from one foot to the other. "This man know Cheok," he said, and his eyes were narrow slits from the hugeness of the grin across his face. "Know her brother. We learn herding together and this be his bead pattern."

The smoke from the fire filled his head and Stewart felt like he was not only caught in the fog, but was the fog itself. He knew his mother had a brother. She had waited for him to save her from the orphanage, but when the brother had not come, she married Mr. MacTavish instead.

Mutuk flung himself around the small room with excitement. He slapped Stewart's back. Stewart choked and Mutuk slapped some more, bringing Stewart's lungs to the point of collapse. The old woman hobbled to the water bucket and, dipping in with a blue enamel mug, scooped a drink for Stewart.

"Cheok," said Mutuk at last, pushing the word from his mouth as both hands pressed his heart. "She alive?"

Stewart nodded slowly. As far as he knew she was alive.

"Her brother thought she and everyone in village dead. We go there but he leave quick with his herd. Place full of haunts."

Thus Stewart, in the time that it took the old woman to sew the boots, learned what Mutuk could tell him about his mother's village and about her early life with the "Real People," which is what Yup'ik means. When the boots were fitted to Stewart's feet, Mutuk rounded up the wandering reindeer with Qimugta.

"*Natmurcit?*" asked Stewart, nervous about the purposefulness of Mutuk's movements. "Where are you going?"

"We go Bristol Bay," said Mutuk, his face a huge grin. "We see Cheok and speak of her brother."

There were days in which Stewart wondered what it would be like to see his family again, days in which he plotted to leave Mutuk and strike out on his own, days in which he knew he could never again be under the same roof with a man who had beat him, despite his longing to see Ellen.

The air warmed. The snow melted into rivulets that covered the ground. For Stewart and Mutuk, walking on the water-soaked ground was often impossible, but the reindeer, happy with new moss, frolicked with one another. Both male and female grew new antlers. Soft fuzz covered them, darker than the pussy willows that gradually opened along the melting creek beds.

One early spring day, restless from the warmer weather,

the reindeer spied caribou on the snowy ridge of the next hill. Ignoring Mutuk and the attempts of Qimugta to hold them back, the reindeer joined the caribou, mingling among them. Fearing he'd never get them separated, Mutuk approached the thousand-strong herd of caribou, humming in a singsong voice, trying to attract his own animals. All at once a single wolf darted over the hill and grabbed a yearling. Slowed by the weight, the wolf just missed being gored by a raging stag. The stag grunted a low warning.

Qimugta yapped a warning at the edges of Mutuk's heels as a family of wolves appeared over the ridge, enclosing the herd. The stag bellowed an alarm. The sun glinted off the barrel of Mutuk's rifle. A shot rang through the air. One wolf fell.

Horrified, Stewart watched as Mutuk jumped away, only to have his long Laplander parka snagged by the wide brack of a whirling reindeer. Mutuk jerked back. The parka ripped, throwing him off balance. Stewart raced forward, his heart pounding. Antlers met him. The herd spun like a wooden top, around and around, with Mutuk somewhere in their midst.

A yellow globe of sun perched above the southern horizon. The deer circled counter to its path, moving with the young attached to their mothers so that the larger beast looked as if it had eight legs. Qimugta whined, a low mournful sound. Stewart's spine prickled.

The thunderous circling continued. The wolves, heads down, noses forward, looked for a way to go in for a kill. Stewart raised his arm. He raged at the setting sun, at the circling reindeer, again and again, as the wolves, pausing on the hummock, saw defeat in the whirling mass of antlers and retreated.

Frothing at the mouth, breath steaming from their quivering nostrils, the reindeer stopped. They moved southward, out of the trampled circle. It had happened so fast it seemed not to have happened at all. Stewart waited for Mutuk to materialize. He walked forward, slowly, thinking to himself: *"Uitalria-wa tayima cali tamaani."* Maybe he is still there.

A fawn had fallen. Mangled flesh, shards of skin, splintered bones, bloodied the dirty snow. Bile rose in Stewart's mouth. He searched the ground, praying Mutuk had bedded himself into a depression, protected himself with his heavy skin coat.

Stewart bent over, spreading a tangled mass of gore. He uncovered the metal barrel of the gun—the rifle that Mutuk had been carrying. The bile rose again and Stewart vomited until his eyes pulsed from the force of his overturned stomach. The reindeer's pounding hooves had pummeled it all— the sled, the fleece bags, the cooking gear, just as Mutuk had warned. Stewart found the iron pot, buried under the trampled ground. So there were two things left, but nothing of his friend, only blood turned brown by the snow and splintered bones like toothpicks on the trampled ground.

The silence dug into Stewart's bones, gnawing the marrow until his skeleton wanted to collapse and splinter. Avoiding the feeling, too numb to pay attention to the threatening silence around and within him, he scuffed his way through the trampled ground. And there, lying in the snow at the edge of the trampled circle, he saw Mutuk's four-cornered hat.

Reaching down, stuporous, Stewart caught up the hat and twirled it around his clenched fist. The tassels danced in the pale sunlight. Stewart ran back to the spot where he had last seen Mutuk and flung the hat into the air. It balanced, briefly, on an updraft, like a lost bird taking new bearings. Then the hat sailed toward the trampled ground.

Stewart knew one thing. He must leave. This single thought pushed all else from his mind. He turned his back on Qimugta, whose nose twitched like the tassled hat it touched. In a dream Stewart turned north by northeast, into the distant hills, far from Unaganik. The sun set. The aurora borealis spun through the sky in shades of green and blue and yellow. God's lantern, Mrs. Meriweather used to say. Hung in the window of heaven to keep us from getting lonely in the dark night. But to Stewart it seemed like the sky reflected the bruises he felt in his whole being.

He walked until the past disappeared, until the arctic clock, the Great Bear, crept past the zenith. At last there was nothing except this cold, lonely moment. He built a spruce fire, blew it to a red blaze, and sat rocking on his heels, his arms pressed against his empty stomach.

10

E LLEN'S DEPRESSION AFTER BRUCE'S death mystified Angus. He far more missed old Wolff than wee Bruce, Bruce having been with them but a year and Wolff for thirteen. Bruce's death made one less baby in the small house, particularly with Cheok growing larger by the week with her latest pregnancy. Indeed, Angus convinced himself, life had to go on. No pioneer survived if a tragedy did him under as it was obviously doing to Ellen.

Ellen sat on the floor, knees bent, hands clasped tightly around them. Although she sat as close to the fire as she dared, since Bruce's death she had been unable to get warm. The cold she felt was different from the storms that blew tunnels of snow over the country. It was an inner cold, not bitter but deadening, as if it had come from and ended in nothing. She rocked. The floorboards creaked beneath her. The fire crackled and the wind knuckled the window. Ellen heard nothing, not even the deep-freezing of her own soul.

When the storms had abated, Dr. Visikov stopped by. Ellen saw the steam misting the doctor's gold-rimmed spectacles but made no acknowledgment.

"I dinna ken what ta do wi' her," Angus said in a voice that indicated he thought Ellen could not hear. "She's nae with us."

"I'll put her to work," said Dr. Visikov. "She needs to be busy. Get her mind off herself."

The next morning, when Bonnie and Charlie left for school, Angus told Ellen to walk with them. She did not hear. Her real self hung separate, looking with pity on the wooden

person, stacked like a stick in the woodpile, waiting to be
tossed on the fire by someone else's hand.

Feeling desperate about Ellen, Angus followed Dr. Visikov's
prescription for her himself and got to work training a new
sled dog to replace Wolff. The new dog was eight months old
and a born leader. Blond-haired, a mixture of Golden Labrador
and Husky, the dog's mongrel strains had been traced to a
famous mother dog brought to the Klondike by a hopeful
prospector. To avoid jealousy among the older sled dogs,
Angus refused to favor the new dog, whom he called U-Prince,
short for Unaganik Prince to distinguish it from the hundreds
of other northern Princes. Angus would not have looked with
disfavor, however, if Ellen had wanted to pet and coddle the
new dog. He'd be grateful for anything to take her mind off
Bruce's death, to get her moving again.

Ellen rocked until it seemed like the weeks on the
Hawaiian calendar swam together into one moment. No past.
No future. No going on to school. No going to the Lower 48.
No more imagining herself under a palm tree, bare-hearted to
the sun and wind. Not even *Our Wonder World* excited her.
When Angus set the book beside her, opened to her favorite
photo of the lion, Ellen stared at it, indifferent.

One morning after a fresh snowfall added another two
inches to the six feet already covering the tundra, Cheok took
her ivory story knife from the apple box shelf tacked onto the
wall behind her bed. She went outside. Ellen followed. No
one had said anything to her, but it was as if arms had
grabbed this stick that was herself and carried her to the open
air.

Cheok bent at a right angle over the snow. Her large
belly was caught by her tight fur parka.

Ellen crouched beside her mother and felt warmer for
being outside.

"Years before," said Cheok, drawing many moons and
suns in the snow with the point of her story knife, "before
this time"—she drew the three-room house with the shiny
new stovepipe—"this girl lived in a little old village." Cheok
drew a row of many smaller houses and a round meeting
house with smoke twisting up from the center of the roof.
"Her father hunted and her mother made clothes and food,"
she said, drawing stick figures as she talked. "One day this

girl took a wooden bowl of food to her father in his kayak and he was gone three days. When he return he had fur seal. That seal got plenty money at the trading post." Cheok drew a pyramid of coins. "Now there is no fur seal, no money," she said, scratching out the pictures, "and no father, no mother, no little old village." She drew the story knife back and forth, cutting the snow pictures into deep crevices.

"But this girl," Cheok continued, "she live here." Cheok drew trails of smoke from the stovepipe atop the house, and as she continued in a story-telling voice, she drew stick figures that Ellen recognized. "She live with her smart girl, her *akutaq* boy, her good girl, and Mr. MacTavish. They all live because she give them secret Yup'ik name of spirit who protect them."

"Did you give Bruce an Eskimo name too?" Ellen asked. It was the first time she had spoken for days. Her voice sounded hollow as a loon's.

"Mr. MacTavish say not give anymore Eskimo name. He say it silly but I know spirit of dead person take care of baby until baby's spirit strong enough to live alone. That spirit bring you in from the tide. But Bruce not have any wise old spirit from dead person to watch over him, and he die."

Tears filled Cheok's eyes. She tucked the story knife into her right boot and reached for Ellen. Ellen wept in the encircling warmth of her mother's arms. She emptied her tears for Bruce and found more for Stewart, then more for herself, for the void in her own life. Where was that warm light she'd met above the tide flats? Could she find it again?

The next morning, Ellen snowshoed into Unaganik with Charlie and Bonnie. They stopped to examine tracks. Five massive toes lay above a huge pad the size of a man's head. Curved claws dug deep into the snow.

"A brownie," said Charlie. "I'll have to tell teacher."

Ellen grinned. She left Bonnie and Charlie at school and walked through Unaganik until she reached Dr. Visikov's.

"Scrub your hands," the doctor said when she entered his examining room. Robertson Sharpe lay on the bench. Dr. Visikov, using a pair of tweezers, was picking shards of glass out of Robertson's bear-scarred face.

"Thank God it missed your eye," muttered the doctor.

"What happened?" asked Ellen.

Robertson looked at her with his one good eye. "That rotter who dug Bruce's grave is still in the jailhouse," he explained in his customary slurred voice. "Smashed his fist through the window in the Guestroom just as I was pissing underneath. The glass hit my face."

Ellen waited for her reaction to the mention of Bruce's name. There was no huge uproar. What had changed? She looked inside herself and saw that Bruce was still in her heart and, like Stewart, she could carry both of them there and move on with her life.

"You know what they say," said Dr. Visikov when he finished Robertson. "There's three sides to every story."

"Our side, their side, and Morningside," said Robertson, referring to the Stateside mental hospital.

"Put that crazy man in a straitjacket," said Dr. Visikov, "and send him to Morningside. You don't need any more trouble than you've got."

"I've been waiting for the magistrate," said Robertson.

"You might not be able to see him when he comes," said Dr. Visikov, stern. "When this eye's gone, you'll be blind."

Shaken, Robertson left and Dr. Visikov showed Ellen around the examining room and taught her how to sterilize the tweezers. He then gave her a grey book with a plain red cross on the front cover: *First Aid Textbook*. Ellen took it with a thrill she could not explain. It was a well-worn book with pages that felt like Mrs. Meriweather's satin sheets. She flipped the pages and they fell open to a drawing of a skeleton. "Thank you," she said, her voice hushed at the detail of the picture.

"When you've finished looking at that," said Dr. Visikov, "I'll introduce you to the microscope."

Ellen was engrossed in examining blood cells under the microscope when Dr. Visikov reminded her that it was time to meet Charlie and Bonnie. "Come back tomorrow," he said. "I'll have work for you to do."

"If Daddy says I can, I will," said Ellen and hurried to meet Bonnie and Charlie, who were just getting out of school.

Throughout the rest of winter, Ellen assisted Dr. Visikov.

She learned how to clean and dress boils after they had been lanced, how to treat a head full of lice with kerosene. She dispensed mineral oil to people with the chronic winter complaint, constipation, or castor oil if they were really impacted and Dr. Visikov's examination showed no other complications.

When Martha Jones carried her son Buddy in with a cut on his knees, Ellen soothed the Yup'ik woman. "Burley kill me if something happen to his boy," Martha wailed.

When Sour Pete Berglund struggled in from his trap line complaining of a pain in his side, his breath smelling of rotten apples, Dr. Visikov made a quick rectal exam and then showed Ellen how to drop ether. When the trapper was under, the doctor cut into the abdomen and exposed the small sac of bowel from which the grossly inflamed and ominously grey appendix was suspended.

"Early gangrene," said the doctor, removing it carefully. "Remember the smell of his breath. It's a dead giveaway."

Ellen watched him sew up Sour Pete with tiny catgut stitches and doubted if she could ever take a knife to a human body, no matter what the need.

"She's a natural," Dr. Visikov said to Angus late one night when Ellen was supposed to be asleep in her cot. She heard, and an idea came to her that seemed so utterly preposterous, so completely unattainable, she immediately dismissed it.

But the idea popped into her mind again at Easter time as she stood in church, waiting for the stragglers to gather. In that relaxed moment, listening to the melodic peal of the bells, seeing the tall white candles flicker and the gold-encrusted ikons, smelling the strong odor of incense, Ellen wondered if she'd still be here next year and the years after.

The mute boy, who the priest had discovered the morning of Bruce's funeral, assisted at service as Stewart had once done. Not knowing his real name, the priest called him Jonah. Ellen watched Jonah and thought of how Stewart had disappeared. She could never do that to Daddy. It would kill him. Soon the incense, the Gregorian chants, the prayers, seeped into her and calmed her by their sameness. Transported, Ellen slipped into a space where she heard nothing, not even the priest giving communion to the congregation.

Bonnie nudged her arm. "Ellen! It's over."

Jerking her head, feeling the ache in her legs from standing still so long, Ellen followed her younger sister, feeling like a sleepwalker. Outside the church, she saw Ted Kleet standing in the snow beside the path, talking to Daddy and Mother. She blinked her eyes several times. Was she dreaming?

"Will ye join us to bake kulich at Mrs. Meriweather's?" Daddy was saying as Ellen and Bonnie approached. Kulich was the traditional Easter bread.

"Thank you," said Ted, "but Gus will be expecting me back at the plane."

"What are you doing here?" Ellen asked, catching her breath.

"I was in Anchorage visiting my uncle. A pilot friend of his, Gus, had to fly some radio parts over for Shushanuk, and I came for the ride."

Ellen stared at him. "It seems a long way to come just for a ride."

"It's easy by air," Ted said. He grinned down at her. His right eyebrow, the one with the scar, remained still when the rest of his face softened.

"Gi'e me regards ta yer father," Angus said as he, Cheok, and Charlie headed down the road to the Mud Dog.

"Are you coming?" Bonnie asked, pulling on Ellen's parka sleeve.

"I'll be along later," Ellen told her younger sister. "I want to talk to Ted."

Bonnie ran off and Ellen stared up at Ted, surprised to see him again.

"I ran out to your place to see you and when you weren't there, I figured, since it was Easter, that you'd be in church," he said. "I don't have much time. Gus wanted to leave as soon as he dropped off the parts."

Looking at him, Ellen thought he looked taller and leaner than she remembered, although he had the same intensity to his eyes. His shoulders, stiff in a tight wolfskin parka, looked broader than before.

"The old man told me you were still in Unaganik," Ted said.

Longing for an education churned inside her. Ellen tried

to shrug it off, and when Ted continued to stare at her she stammered, "They need me here. Mother needs me. She's having another baby, and I'll have to help." Her voice trailed off under the intensity of his gaze. Unnerved, she started to walk to the end of the village. Ted walked in silence beside her until they approached the red Pilgrim tied to barrels at the far end of the snow-covered landing field.

"I still can't believe you'd come all this way," Ellen said as they reached the plane.

"Gus thinks that someday there'll be more planes in the territory than dogs," said Ted.

"Will you come again?" For the Saturday afternoon service, Ellen had unbraided her hair. It hung straight and heavy down her back. Ted was looking at it when he replied.

"I'm going Outside for four years. I'm going to a Bureau of Indian Affairs school in Arizona."

Ellen reached for the jade labret tucked under her old brown sweater. She held the stone to her lips.

"B.I.A. might help you go to Arizona," said Ted.

"I want to go to Hawaii," said Ellen, thinking of the cannery calendar.

"Why don't you ask the bosses? You might be able to live with one of them in Hawaii and go to school."

Ellen stared at Ted as if he was out of his mind.

"You can ask," he said.

"That's not our way," said Ellen, her voice soft. She slipped the labret back under her sweater, feeling its comforting pressure against her skin.

"Our ways are changing," said Ted. "We have to, too." He smiled. His right eyebrow, where the scar cut through, was raised.

"How do you know which way to change?" Ellen asked, perplexed by the emotion she felt at his words. Why was he talking to her like this? Didn't he know there were some things you just didn't do?

"I know that some day you're going to leave Unaganik," said Ted.

"How?" blurted Ellen. "How can you know that?"

Gus had climbed into the Pilgrim and was revving the engine. "I don't know how or when," said Ted, "but anyone can see you don't belong here."

*   *   *

One Friday when the tundra dripped with the last melting of snow, Ellen forgot her parka at Dr. Visikov's when she went down to the school to meet Bonnie and Charlie. They went home, but Ellen stayed to talk to the schoolteacher about a book she had borrowed, *Ivanhoe*. She was curious about Rebecca's power to heal.

"Staying in Unaganik tonight?" Robertson called from the door of the jailhouse when Ellen headed back down the road in the late afternoon.

"No." Ellen shook her head. "I'm just getting my parka. I forgot it."

"There's bears about," said Robertson. He waved at her with his one arm and cautioned, "Be sure you make lots of noise."

"Yes," said Ellen, feeling shivery. While she was pulling on her parka in the doctor's windbreak, she heard groans from the rear. She pushed open the door and hurried down the hall.

Dr. Visikov huddled in a huge bed with carved wooden pineapples on the four corners. He was inside a kapok sleeping bag. A feather comforter covered his head and shoulders. His face was flushed and his sunken eyes seemed the same color as the maroon orchids on the bedroom wallpaper.

"Are you sick?" asked Ellen in a worried voice. She came closer and at that moment a log spat in the stove. The doctor jerked his head and said in a voice that years before had given orders in a big city hospital, "Get more blankets."

Ellen darted down the hall to the examining room. Her temples pulsed in time to the frightened pump of her heart. She grabbed three blankets and returned to the doctor, who struggled to swing them over his shoulders. When Ellen reached toward him to help he shouted, "Don't touch me!"

Ellen clasped her hands together, as if they could comfort each other for their unexplained trespass.

"Put more wood on the fire," ordered Dr. Visikov, even though sweat rolled off his forehead into his bloodshot eyes.

The Howard stove flared with heat. Ellen opened the isinglass door and jammed in another log. The flames scorched her cheeks.

"It's cold in here," said Dr. Visikov and stared at Ellen

for so long she wished she could find his spectacles and put them back on his nose. They made him look alert, no matter if he had been up all night cleaning a burned body, as he had done that night with Mr. Stokes.

Ellen hesitated, but seeing the doctor still shaking despite the heat, she dashed down the narrow hall, across the street, and into the Mud Dog Saloon. Mrs. Meriweather leaned over the counter, staring at a rising yellow sun on the red label of a Midnight Sun Beer.

"Can you come?" Ellen called. "Quick?"

Mrs. Meriweather, wearing a black wool cape lined with red velvet, rushed with Ellen across the road. The doctor wailed in the back bedroom like a yearling fox caught in a six-pound steel trap.

"Saints be!" said Mrs. Meriweather, standing at the foot of the bed, her hands on her hips. "Are you out of a fix?"

"No," said Dr. Visikov. "No." And after a long pause in which the fire spat and Ellen felt as if she'd pass out from the heat, he said in a shaking voice, "No. I don't want anything. I'm going off the stuff."

"Happens every spring," said Mrs. Meriweather. She sounded annoyed. She turned to Ellen and, with a dramatic swish of her black cape, said, "Run along home. It's getting dark and there's talk of bears."

"What about Dr. Visikov?" Ellen's voice quavered.

Taking Ellen's elbow, Mrs. Meriweather steered her down the hall to the door. "Run along. I know what to do." She disappeared into the examining room and Ellen, peeking through the crack in the door, saw Mrs. Meriweather unlock the drug cupboard and take out a hypodermic syringe.

All at once things began to make sense. Old whisperings about Robertson not getting anything to take away the pain when the brownie chewed him swept back into Ellen's mind. Had the doctor used it? Feeling sick to her stomach, Ellen dashed outside, banging the windbreak door behind her.

Robertson Sharpe saw her racing toward the tundra trail. He took his new Winchester 45/90 from the hooks by the door, locked the jailhouse, and tried to catch up with Ellen. It might be for nothing that he followed her, but Stinky and Red Cap had been out that morning and had assured Robertson, before quenching their thirst at the Mud Dog, that brownies were on the prowl. He owed Angus favors enough and it was no chore to hustle home with Ellen, if she'd slow down.

Robertson released the safety catch on his heavy lever-action Winchester. The weight didn't bother him—not that he wasn't a good enough shot to kill a bear with a thirty-ought six—but having one arm prevented rapid reloading, and he felt safer with the heavier caliber. Robertson reckoned the brownies knew more about him after having had a taste, so he'd better be prepared.

Unaware of Robertson Sharpe, Ellen hurried along, head bent, arms swinging. Stars twinkled above the bay. Low in the west a strip of blue-grey light lined the sky. Ellen paused, briefly, to smell the birch buds, smelling ever so faintly of spring and sunshine. She continued on, filling her head with thoughts of summer and sun and ways to go Outside to school, cramming them in to shove out the sight of Dr. Visikov cowering in his bed, to shove away the painful knowledge of his imperfection.

The scrub spruce darkened the trail. The light changed. A winter ptarmigan, its feathers hinting at spring, burst through the underbrush ahead of Robertson. He called out, "Ellen! Ellen MacTavish!"

There was no answer.

Ellen rounded the corner of the woods. Straight ahead, clear as the dome on the Russian Orthodox Church, she saw the bear. In the second it took to stop on one foot, she saw his massive head, long nose, squinty eyes, ears flattened in alarm. Her knees sagged like the tops of hip boots as she saw, in one glance, his distinctive hump, his famous silver-tipped fur, his long sharp claws.

A low "woof" came toward her. The great beast lifted his head, and sniffed. Ellen's heart clogged her windpipe. She could not scream.

The great beast swung from side to side. Foam frothed at his mouth, his teeth clacked. The grizzly reared onto his hind legs, his forepaws raised, sharp claws extended. "Woof!"

Ellen spun into the trees.

Lunging forward, the grizzly charged. Its powerful legs covered the yards between them with lightning speed. Clods of earth flew in all directions. Smelling the foul breath like decayed fish, imagining she felt the bear's breath against her neck, Ellen leapt for a spruce, grabbing the spiked trunk as if it were satin.

Clutching the tree, the needles stinging her palms, Ellen climbed. The bear swiped his long claws toward Ellen's right foot. She jerked it out of the way.

The bear's teeth clacked. Lifting his right paw, he batted at the tree.

Her heart pounding, Ellen scrambled to the narrow tip of the spruce. The spruce swayed and Ellen, hanging on, screamed.

Robertson heard the sound on the wind. Cursing his bum leg, he raced as fast as he could down the trail. Rounding the corner of the woods, he saw the huge beast. The bear had reared on his hind legs, extending his claws toward Ellen. Holding the rifle to his good shoulder, curving his body to absorb the impact, Robertson lined up his sights at a spot on the bear's neck. He fired. The air exploded.

The brownie crashed against the tree. Screaming, Ellen lost her grip and tumbled onto a heaving mass of fur. Robertson, fearing he'd shot Ellen by mistake, dashed the rifle to the ground. He covered his face with his hand.

Sliding off the grizzly, Ellen rushed to Robertson and clutched his arm. The brand new Winchester smoked on the ground beside them.

11

THE WORST BLIZZARD IN fifteen years occurred three weeks after Robertson Sharpe shot the bear. The blizzard caught Angus in a whiteout on his way home from Nachook where he'd gone to talk to people about a strike and where, truth be told, he had hoped to find Stewart. That Stewart had cut him off, much as he had cut off his own father, never occurred to Angus. He missed the lad and, forgetting their battles, wanted to tell him he meant naught by the strapping. It was a foolish mistake made by a foolish man fearful over his favorite daughter. When he found Stewart, Angus planned to beg forgiveness, even though in his heart of hearts he knew that Stewart, in spite of his dandy ways and impulsive temperament, was of the country in which he had been born, a country giving no second chance for a mistake.

And now was no time for mistakes. At zero visibility Angus gave U-Prince the lead, and hung onto the sled. They reached the house on the bluff two hours later. Angus was overjoyed. Never in all his years of training and running dogs had he had such a dog as U-Prince. The thrill of that overcame his disappointment at not finding or hearing word of Stewart.

Although the inland villagers had agreed to boycott the cannery, since the bosses hired so few of them anyway Angus doubted that it would make much difference. Certainly the few local white men cut little ice. He, Burley Jones, Stinky, Red Cap, Olaf, and Toothless Ed gathered at the Mud Dog on lighter spring nights to talk about taking the fishing business into their own hands and keeping the profits in the country from which they came.

One night, tired of the talk, Angus returned home early. The unborn baby had been jostling Cheok's ribs, keeping her awake. When Angus fell into bed, the baby kicked. "Ach, and it wants out," he said.

Cheok wriggled to get more comfortable.

Angus stroked her. Her skin felt like rubber stretched smooth by this healthy living being underneath. He slid his fingers down, savoring the silkiness of that other part of her, the part where the baby would come in good time. Angus stroked her slowly, steadily. Her skin seemed to have a life of its own, to respond to some inner part of himself that reached for her. Forgetting Dr. Visikov's reminder to leave Cheok alone these final months, he slipped in, staying inside her, losing himself in the pleasures of her body. His tense limbs relaxed. He dropped into a dreamless snoring sleep.

Iingirtuq, thought Cheok to herself. He is snowblind. He doesn't see who this woman is. She rolled onto her back and tried to find patience in the thought that winter would pass as it always had, that this baby would come as the others had, as birds nested and fish swam up stream.

At last the ice started moving. A stake had been frozen into the ice last fall and the person who guessed the date and time when the stake dropped would win the Ice Pool. Daddy had put money into the pool and Ellen, excited, raced home from Dr. Visikov's to find him. She looked for Angus in the sweathouse, the smokehouse, and finally asked Cheok, "Where's Daddy?"

"At the Mud Dog," Cheok replied. She lay on the big bed as she did every afternoon. Her huge stomach was propped up with goose feather pillows.

"Getting drunk." Bonnie, home with a bad cold, spoke with a sniffle.

Ellen grabbed a drink of water from the snow melting on the stove. "Daddy has a chance to win the Ice Pool," she said when she finished swallowing.

"Wrong day," said Bonnie. "Daddy's day is tomorrow."

"I remember exactly," said Ellen. "He put May eighteenth at three-twenty P.M."

Bonnie pointed at the palm tree calendar. "Today's May seventeenth," she said.

"Is not," said Ellen. She stomped over to the wall. Seeing Daddy's crossed out numbers, she discovered, to her dismay, that she was wrong.

"Do you see?" Bonnie asked.

"Yes." Ellen nodded at her little sister and it was almost worth being wrong just to see a smile on Bonnie's puffy fevered face.

Floes drifted past the S.S. *Baranoff* that had been stranded for weeks in the middle of Bristol Bay, waiting for the thaw. The S.S. *Baranoff* contained grub, diesel oil, beer kegs, catalogue orders from Sears, and other essentials needed in the isolated villages along the shores of Bristol Bay.

In the case of Unaganik, the S.S. *Baranoff* also carried a wife for the priest. Russian Orthodox priests, if they have no desire to progress to the bishopric, are permitted to marry. The Unaganik priest, needing a mother for Jonah, the mute boy, had sent word to Seattle for assistance in his search. When a woman volunteered, he and Jonah had taken a plane to Anchorage and another to Seattle for the wedding. There the priest sent Jonah to a child psychiatrist who had left Hitler's Germany after two of his Jewish colleagues had mysteriously disappeared. After five sessions with the psychiatrist, Jonah told how he had flattened himself against the outer wall of his father's cabin beneath a bearskin tacked there to dry. He told how he hid until the screams stopped and his father dropped the axe and left. He never did tell his real name, so as Jonah he officially became the priest's son.

The new wife refused to get in a mechanical bird, and came north on the steamship instead. The trip took several months, including a layover in Seward, a month around the Chain, and now weeks in the middle of Bristol Bay, waiting for the thaw. The new wife waited each day on deck, wearing a high-fashion hat that flaunted her oval face. The hat had a brim decked with layers of ribbon on one side and a huge bow on the other. The new wife was past the age when most women marry and it was the death of her parents that had necessitated the event. However, the good woman was determined to make the best of it, and her trunk of new clothes was testimony to that fact.

At Unaganik, the residents watched the Ice Pool stake. Mrs. Meriweather wore her flowing cape with the hood over her head. She had run out of hair dye and her grey roots showed even to the unobservant.

Red Cap, Burley Jones and his young son, a sturdy, curious lad with a habit of holding his hand to his chin like his father did, Toothless Ed, the wireless operator Shushanuk and his wife, Ooguk, all stood by the planked footbridge that crossed the thawing river to the cannery, where the winterman and his wife likewise watched the progress. Ellen raced breathlessly into the village just as the schoolteacher excused his eight students to watch this major event of 1938.

Dr. Visikov left his office polishing his gold-rimmed glasses. He joined the priest and Jonah who stood side by side with expressions alternating from delight to dismay. They had, in the intervening time, got on quite well with each other and had mixed feelings about the arrival of the new wife.

"How are ye, me wee blue goose," Angus said, smiling down at Ellen when she joined him by the heaving river, groaning like mother earth in labor. More and more water seeped through the leaks in the ice and flowed over the surface. Beneath, the heavy bluish chunks seemed to struggle for air, as if they were drowned clouds seeking a home in the sky.

Ellen did not see Angus's smile. She stared past the river, toward the bay, where one enormous block of ice shot into the air and splintered like a sheet of glass. The bay ice shifted. The river ice chittered like a flock of birds all talking at once. Suddenly Merilee Meriweather sang out, "The bridge!"

It happened so fast people talked about it for years after: how the ice suddenly bunched up onto itself as if some giant ghost had banged his fist on the ground, jarring the melting blocks together; how the ice knocked out the pilings of the footbridge; how, when the pilings went down the bridge smashed the thin center ice which broke and rode, crashing and bellowing and foaming and churning out into Bristol Bay where the ice had already thawed.

Merilee held her second husband's railroad watch. Even

in the confusion she noted the exact time that the stake went down. She'd have been run out of Unaganik if she hadn't.

"I've won!" Toothless Ed shouted through his gums.

"That old heart of his can't stand so much excitement," Dr. Visikov muttered to Mrs. Meriweather. "Give him the prize quick."

"He's confused," Merilee said with a sorry shake of her head. "Are you ready for his reaction when I tell him he's made a mistake?"

The doctor sighed.

"Gimme my money," Ed said, holding out a gnarled hand to Merilee.

Mrs. Meriweather took him into the Mud Dog, poured him a Midnight Sun beer from the last case she had left. She waited until he downed it before showing him the time he had written. "Five A.M.," she said, pointing a red fingernail. "That's yours and Stinky has five P.M. He gets the money."

"I *meant* afternoon." Ed's toothless face took on a murderous look. Merilee took the bottle of Seagram's Crown from its purple bag and offered him a consolation. He gulped a whole glass and swooned backward into Angus's arms.

Charlie and Jonah ran to Stinky's cabin on the far side of the windsock on the outskirts of Unaganik. They found Stinky wrapped in a bearskin for his rheumatism.

"You won the Ice Pool," Charlie said, bursting back out of the cabin, standing in the fresher air of the windbreak door, feeling almost asphyxiated with the winter odor of the man. Jonah held his nose.

"How much?" asked Stinky.

"Come and find out. There's a celebration at the Mud Dog."

"I'll have to pay it all out to Dr. Visikov," said Stinky, but he gathered the bear robe around him and, despite his aches and pains, kept abreast of Charlie and Jonah all the way to the Mud Dog.

Three weeks after the S.S. *Baranoff* offloaded its cargo, and after the priest's wife was made welcome with a grand party at Mrs. Meriweather's, the two cannery bosses flew in on their private Norseman. When the locals heard the sharp growl of the powerful radial engine, they stiffened their backs and prepared to lie low. The two bosses arrived full of plans to hire more of the natives. The truth was, there'd been trouble with the Italians down south and they wanted to avoid bringing too many dagos north on the cannery barge.

When no one local came forth to request one of the Spritz-rigged cannery boats, the bosses queried the doctor. The tall boss with the pin-striped suit and the polka-dot bow tie spoke first.

"Where is everybody?" he asked in a gruff voice. "Are people too stupid to know the fish are almost here?"

"They're not stupid," said Dr. Visikov wearily. He knew too much about the man to be taken in. Twenty-five years ago this boss had married and his pretty wife wanted to spend the summer with him at the "canree," as she called it. Because she was pregnant, Dr. Visikov, a third-year medical student needing a summer job, was hired to come north to tend to her and any of the Chinaboys who sliced themselves in the gutting room or burned themselves on the boiling metal tins in the canning room.

Having a wife hadn't stopped the boss from seeking favors from other women. He picked up lice as a result and, coming to the doctor for a cure, had been shaved in his private parts and scrubbed with kerosene until he screamed for mercy. Out of a mistaken notion that they should not sleep together at all during her pregnancy, the boss had not infected his wife. This put Dr. Visikov in the enviable position of being the sole person to know of the incident. This knowledge came in handy years later when Dr. Visikov committed an indiscretion of his own and had his privileges revoked at the city hospital in Seattle. He knew he could practice medicine in Unaganik and earn sufficient fees from the cannery during the summer to support the habit that had caused his discharge.

The second boss, an oily man with shiny patent leather shoes and an irritating habit of flapping his jeweled hand back and forth in front of his face as if there were mosquitoes everywhere, even in Dr. Visikov's examining room, spoke first. "My God, Visikov, is this a strike?"

"Ask them," said the doctor in a weary voice.

"We can get all the fish we need from the Eyetalians," said Number Two Boss, forgetting that he had wanted to leave the dagos down south, to teach them a lesson or two.

"Will they shoot?" asked Boss One.

"We should arm ourselves," said Boss Two. "Fly guns in on the Norseman."

Dr. Visikov pressed his hands to his temples and wished the bosses would leave. Last night, or rather past midnight, Burley Jones had banged into his office with his four-year-old son. Unbeknownst to the sleeping Martha, Buddy had been convulsing for hours. Burley, thinking the boy safe, had been at the Mud Dog exhorting the men to stand up to the cannery.

Wild-eyed and raging, Burley had trouble telling the doctor what had happened to Buddy. Finally the doctor calmed Burley enough to learn that the boy had swallowed a mixture of strychnine salts put out for the rats. The doctor gave the boy an intramuscular injection of phenobarbital but was too late. The poison had done its job. Burley sobbed his way to the church where the priest's new wife spent the early hours of the morning trying to convince him in a gentle voice to give her the boy so she could prepare him for burial. Someone told Martha, and terrified of what Burley might do to her, she hightailed it into the bush.

Dr. Visikov shook himself. There were times like last night when he wanted to forget everything and everyone in this godforsaken place.

The bosses left and remembering that Angus MacTavish was a rational, educated man, they got the winterman to take them with the gasoline boat to his set-net sight.

Angus stood tall, facing them. "I ha'e other plans fer summer," he said pleasantly when they asked him to skipper one of their sailing boats.

"We'll pay half a cent more a fish," said Boss Number One.

"Wha' about kickers fer the boats?" said Angus.

"You know yourself that motors will rip up the fish," said Boss Number Two. His hands waved back and forth and Angus pretended not to notice the large diamond resting on a scroll of gold.

"Motors on the tug boats aren't damagin' the fish," said Angus with such a long roll on the *r* of motors that the rest of the sentence blurred.

"You need a new net," said Boss Number One. "Bring the men back to fish for us and we'll give you one."

"If ye gi'e me one, will ye gi'e the others new nets too?"

"Come on," said Boss Number Two. "We ain't made of money."

Angus watched as Boss Number Two rubbed mud from his patent leather shoes. Then Angus nodded politely and continued hanging his old linen net.

The next day, at low tide, Boss Number One marched down to the beach. "We're offering two cents more per fish, and if you'll relay the word to the others, you'll get a new net. *You* get the net, remember—no one else."

"Thank ye," said Angus. "But I can'na accept that."

"Can't accept two cents more per fish?" The Big Boss ignored the sand fleas leaping around on his sweating face. After that summer when lice scratched his private parts, no bug had bothered him.

Angus paused and the boss, seeing his hesitation, said, "Talk it over with the men. Two cents a fish firm. The offer holds until tomorrow."

That night Angus asked Cheok to do what she could at the net, he was going to call a meeting at the Mud Dog.

At the next tide, Cheok, overburdened with the unborn child, waddled down to the beach, her hand gripping young Charlie's shoulder for support. The exertion was too much. She couldn't struggle any farther and after a spasm of pain contracted her abdomen, she said, "*Mimigtuq.* It turns over." Cheok pointed to Ellen out on the mud. "Go," she ordered, her breath coming in sharp gasps. "This mother be there later."

"Where's Bonnie?" Ellen asked when Charlie joined her at the net.

"Bonnie says she's making dinner."

Ahlingnakfar! thought Ellen. Bonnie's useless.

Ellen and Charlie worked fast, picking the salmon one by one. It was the first day's catch and Ellen loved being way out in the bay, its vastness all around her. She loved the first smell of salmon, the salt water, the terns darting overhead. The clouds screened the glare from the sun. The air was swathed in filtered light that made her feel invisible, as if she was once again above the mud flats with the tern.

Looking beachward, Ellen saw Mother squatting over the

stones and wondered how, with that overgrown belly, she could squat like that. She squinted her eyes and saw Mother's belly move.

"Stay here," she said to Charlie, and slogged shoreward, to see what she could do for Mother.

Ellen's feet caught as the mud sucked her down. She yanked herself forward, grunting with each step.

While Ellen struggled, Cheok bent over the robust female that had dropped between her legs. Mr. MacTavish loved the girls best. He held his wee blue goose so tight it was a wonder she didn't smother to death. He didn't need another.

Spreading her hand across the baby's face, Cheok let her fingers rest in the crook of the neck. Quickly, sharply, as if it were a bird and not from her own body, Cheok snapped the head. There was no sound. No bruise. And then the placenta delivered and Cheok checked it, as she had seen Dr. Visikov check the other placentas. It seemed whole. No pieces left inside. She would soon heal, and soon Angus would want her again. But no more. She had had all the children she intended to have, and if Mr. MacTavish wanted to take his pleasure, he'd have to find another place for his pipe.

By the time Ellen finished the long journey to shore, Cheok was digging with her hands into the bluff. Ellen's eyes widened as the hole in the bluff widened, as Cheok threw the loose clay onto the beach stones, handful by handful, and as she then, without a word, tucked the baby into the hole and covered her with the clay.

Had Cheok buried the child alive? Was the child born dead? These were the questions that tormented Angus when he returned two days later with a hangover. Finally he dug up the baby and took her to the doctor.

"Was she smothered?" Angus asked, hovering over Dr. Visikov's elbow.

"No." Dr. Visikov wore a mask tinted with oil of peppermint to obscure the smell. Angus seemed oblivious to the sickening odor of decay.

"No," the doctor said again when Angus refused to move. What else was there to say? Another child born in this country and standing less than fifty percent chance of surviving. Ten percent if it was full native and exposed to tuberculosis.

"Check her over," insisted Angus at his elbow. "I want ta know. Tell me the truth."

If you wanted to know the truth, why didn't you check her over yourself? You'd know her neck was broken sure as I do. But the doctor caught himself before saying these words out loud. He was losing his grip, he knew, and every night he dreamed that the men were shooting one another and he had no medications to treat the wounded.

"She wasn't smothered," the doctor said. "Just one of those things." He pulled a clean white sheet from the shelf under the examining table and wrapped the child. "Just one of those things," he repeated, hoping the god his former wife had called a Loving God would forgive him this shading of the truth. "Perhaps the cord was wrapped around the neck."

"Ach," said Angus, slapping his thigh with such force that for days after he would have a bruise. "If I hanna been after that fool cannery business, I'd a got ye in time ta help Cheok."

"It's that way sometimes," said Dr. Visikov as he laid the tightly wrapped bundle in Angus's arms. "I doubt I could have done much."

Angus left, his head bent over the bundle, and the doctor prayed that he would leave the body alone, and not check it over himself.

Angus went straight to the graveyard where he dug a hole inside the fenced-in grave where Bruce was buried. Calling her Flora, which had been his mother's name, he laid the baby down and covered her with lupines before the final layer of dirt.

12

"**J**UST AS WEEL, I suppose," Angus said to the doctor.

"I suppose," said the doctor noncommittally, not knowing what in heaven's name Angus was referring to. For the past year Angus had been dithery, breaking off in midsentence or picking up conversations that weren't there. The doctor wondered if it had started with the dead baby Flora, just as Burley Jones's decline had started with his son's death from strychnine.

"Wha' with a madman like Hitler on the loose," continued Angus.

"Have you heard the latest broadcast from Anchorage?" asked the doctor, glad to get the conversation on a firmer footing.

Angus shook his mane of white hair.

"Let's go to Shushanuk's and listen to the wireless," said the doctor. He locked his medicine cabinet and went into the November night with Angus.

With the invasion of Poland, talk in Unaganik had switched from the battles with the cannery to the war in Europe. Despite the Neutrality Act signed in November, the consensus in the Mud Dog was that sooner or later Roosevelt would tackle Hitler head on. He was already sending materiel, wasn't he? Soon he'd be sending men.

If Stewart were home, Angus knew he'd want him to sign up. He discussed it with the doctor, the first time he'd mentioned Stewart since the lad had left.

"He was sixteen in April," Dr. Visikov pointed out. "They can't enlist until they're twenty-one."

"He needs ta learn discipline," Angus complained. His own father had raised him with strict rules and hadn't he turned out fine?

I didn't beat Stewart enough, Angus decided, embarrassed that he could have considered the notion of asking his son's forgiveness. Spare the rod, spoil the child. Stewart's spoiled, that's what. Spending good money on fancy suspenders! What the lad needed was more whipping, not less. War would make a man out of him, Angus thought as talk of Hitler continued over the long dark winter of 1939–1940.

Stewart did not hear of the war in Europe until spring 1940, by which time he was far from Unaganik. The night Mutuk died, a prospector by the name of Lonesome Olie had come upon Stewart as he sat staring into the spruce fire. They had traveled the creeks and rivers together and were removing gravel from a vein of platinum on the tip of the southwest peninsula when a trapper hailed them. Over a dinner of beaver tails, the peaches and cream of the bush, the trapper relayed what he knew of the war, and how rumor had it that the U.S. military was moving to Anchorage.

Seeing an opportunity to get flight training, Stewart immediately made plans to take a bush plane to Anchorage and enlist. He took leave of Lonesome Olie and two weeks later was in a red Pilgrim flown by a pilot with a face like glaciated rock. Stewart felt his world expand in a way he had longed for but never imagined. The propeller whirred in front of them and he was flying. Flying! The world seemed so vast that he felt his eyes stretch in a million directions. How insignificant one ordinary everyday life was. How glorious to fly above it.

Two hours into the air the pilot, Gus turned to Stewart. "Want to take over?"

Stewart whipped off his oversized beaver mittens and clutched the stick slanting upward between his legs. The sun cascaded off the turquoise fissures cutting through the glacier below. He squinted to shield his eyes from the glare.

"Rest your feet on the pedals," Gus said, "but don't press down. Just feel what I'm doing and concentrate on the stick."

Stewart stretched his mukluks forward. He held the stick

and felt the play of the airplane at his fingertips. The sky played with the snow on the adjacent mountains bordering the glaciers, and Stewart, challenged beyond anything he had ever anticipated, concentrated on keeping his eyes inside his head and the plane level.

Gus leaned to one side and pulled a green tin of Copenhagen snuff from his pocket. He pinched a wad between his thumb and forefinger and stuck it under his gums.

"Want some snoose?" he asked Stewart, handing him the tin.

Stewart shook his head.

"First time up?" Gus asked.

Stewart nodded.

"You picked the best kind of day," Gus said, and Stewart felt the adjustment of the plane as Gus pressed on the foot pedals. "I've flown over this glacier and had to count from one end to the other to find the entrance to this pass."

"Fogged in?" Stewart asked. His hands sweated as the mountain range crept closer.

"Thick as boarding house gravy," said Gus. "Now we're coming up to the pass and I ain't liking what I'm seeing. Let me take 'er awhile."

They approached a low-lying cloud wrapped like a scarf around a mountain. It filled the top of the pass. Below, in the sharp V of the valley, the air was clear.

"We'll ease in here like a whore eases into her corsets," said Gus and, taking the stick, nosed the plane down until they slid into the narrow corridor above the valley. The mountain peaks hid behind the clouds. The sun faded. Stewart exhaled heavily.

"Relax," Gus said in a voice that seemed alarming in its calmness. "It'll be another story to tell the boys when we get down."

Balls of snow raced down the mountain crevices, stirred by the sound of the engine. Gus squinted at the left wing, inched the plane to the right, and suddenly, behind them, a heavy overhang of snow avalanched down the mountain.

Stewart's hands dripped sweat. His squirrel parka felt oppressive. His checked shirt stuck to his back. Gus turned the plane sharply left, then to the right. Stewart's gush of breath misted the front window. "Can'na imagine flyin' this without bein' able ta see at all," he said, trying to sound casual.

"Sometimes the hand of God dips down and guides you along," said Gus with a shrug. "I always thank him, even tho' I don't understand it myself."

Stewart wiped his palms on his mittens.

"You done good before we hit that interesting part," Gus said as they finally flew out of the cloud and back into blue skies. "I can see you'll be one of those fly by the seat of your pants boys. Go ahead and take over."

Hiding his relief that they were safely out of the weather, Stewart smiled and gripped the stick.

"What brings you to Anchorage?" Gus clasped his hands behind his head.

"I'm joinin' the air force."

"Hot diggety," said Gus. "I'd do that myself if I were the right age."

He studied Stewart for what seemed like a long time. Stewart concentrated on keeping the plane horizontal.

"Tell 'em you're twenty-one," Gus said, returning his gaze to the window.

"I am," Stewart lied, thinking Angus would beat him for it if he could.

"I was twenty-one at your age too." Gus knotted his face into a wink.

A vast range of sharp-tipped mountains raked the eastern border. Below, an inlet named for Captain Cook mirrored the sky. Far ahead, to the north, another mountain range enclosed the horizon. Tucked between mountains and water, crosshatched on a flat delta of land, lay the city of Anchorage.

"When's the last time you saw four thousand people?" Gus laughed as he took over the stick.

Stewart shook his head, speechless that so many people could crowd together in one small place. He felt hemmed in, suddenly, more suffocated than when they had been cradled in the mountain pass.

"Over there's thirty thousand acres," Gus said, pointing across a creek to a higher plateau. "Congress sent the War Department twelve-point-eight million bucks to make that an airfield. Hitler's in Norway and heading over the Pole to us."

Gus circled a runway, lined up with the remaining strip

of snow, and came in with the nose angled to the ground. "Watch close now!" Gus jammed the wad of snuff to the left side of his mouth. "You are about to see one hot diggety crosswind landing."

The wing on Stewart's side slanted toward the ground. The other wing was high. The plane veered to the right, toward a low building, and in that same instant Gus muttered, "Damn gusts," and brought the plane up into the air again.

"Always bad in the spring," Gus said as they circled the field for the second time. "I never know when to take off the skis and put on wheels. That's why we've got to use this runway and aren't landing into the wind. But hold your hat, we'll get 'er down one way or t'other."

Stewart gripped his seat.

"Hang on!" said Gus. He throttled back. The plane circled the runway. He lined up the approach. "Bank toward the wind, but punch the opposite rudder so the old gal knows she's not to turn." The Pilgrim bounced on one ski. In that bounce Gus straightened it out, put down the left ski, and they slid to the end of the only snow-covered runway left on the field in the first week of April 1940. Anchorage had had a mild winter.

Gus stopped his spanking red Pilgrim next to an ancient green Stinson with packing tape around one wing.

"Here," Stewart said, tossing Gus his leather poke. "Tak' wha' the trip's worth."

Gus tossed the pouch between two massive hands. "Gold," he mused. "There's been prospectors down in the southwest since the Nome rush and ain't a one of them found more than a grubstake worth of fines."

"It inna gold," said Stewart.

Gus undid the leather thong and opened the pouch, pouring grey metal the size of his fingernail into his palm. "Hot diggety," he said. "Rocks."

"Platinum," said Stewart.

"I'll tell you what." Gus dropped the nuggets back into the bag and handed it to Stewart. "You tell me where you found those and the trip's free."

Stewart took out two nuggets and tied the top. He shook his head.

Gus gave Stewart a pocket of silver dollars. "Change,"

he said. "If you go dropping platinum around Anchorage you'll start another stampede."

Stewart unbuckled his seat belt.

"Give me a hand with this seal oil," Gus said, leaning over his seat and reaching for something in the storage compartment behind them. "I'll never get another passenger if the container breaks."

Stewart chuckled, remembering the jars of *uquq* Cheok kept by the stove. He tucked his mittens into the front pouch of his squirrel parka, picked up the end of a seal bladder. Its pungent contents gurgled.

"Call Tilly Kinegak and tell her I've brung a cure for her cold," Gus called to a woman sitting behind a desk in the low building. The woman held her fingers to her nose.

Gus swung the bladder of seal oil onto a cart and turned to Stewart. "I'll be flying to the Southwest next week. Be glad to pass word along to your people."

"Dinna ha'e any," Stewart said curtly. His jaw tightened.

"Hot diggety," said Gus. "That's one for the books. We got an immaculate birth right here in Alaska."

Stewart turned on his heel and headed across the building to the door on the opposite side.

"Recruiting office is in City Hall, on Fourth," Gus called after him.

Stewart waved his fur mittens and left. Brown snow melted beside the road. He cut through a cemetery, looking for the familiar three-armed Russian cross and finding stone blocks, a marble angel, and single crosses instead. He jumped the stone fence at the opposite corner and headed toward the building he'd seen from the air. A red, white, and blue pole circled around and around on another corner. Seeing a man cutting hair, Stewart entered.

"Just in from the bush?" asked the barber as he swung a white sheet around Stewart's shoulders.

Stewart yanked off his thick beaver hat. His long blond hair tumbled around his shoulders.

"Don't have any lice in there, do you?" The barber spread the strands of hair and studied Stewart's scalp.

"Not the last time I looked," said Stewart.

The bald-headed barber flicked an ivory comb over

Stewart's scalp before snapping his scissors. "Shave you next time," he said when he finished.

Stewart rubbed his smooth cheeks. He studied himself in the ivory circled mirror the barber held up in front of him. As he paid the barber with one of Gus's coins, he asked, "Kin ye point me ta Fourth?"

"You're smack dab in the middle of it, son," said the barber.

Whistling, Stewart strode down the street feeling tall and proud. "A dandy," Angus would have said, and Stewart snapped his fancy suspenders, scrubbed clean but faded with age. But Angus was out of his life and he could look as fine as he wanted. And why not? Stewart grinned at himself in the wide window of the Northern Commercial Company, jiggled the coins in his pants pocket, and considered buying himself some city clothes.

He was still whistling when he entered a red stone building. A man in uniform stood behind a high oak counter, tapping a nibbed pen up and down between his fingers. The high-ceilinged room felt stuffy. Stewart took off his parka and mittens and laid them on the counter.

"I'm here ta join the air force." Stewart suppressed his excitement.

"Name," said the man as he dipped his pen into a glass inkwell.

"Stewart."

"Spell it."

The man printed slowly as Stewart spelled.

"Last name." The pen went back into the inkwell.

"MacTavish. M-a-c-T-a-v-i-s-h."

"Not so fast," said the man in uniform and wiped the pen on a blotter.

Stewart repeated the spelling. Should have made up a name, he thought. Or used Mother's last name. Then he realized that Cheok had never mentioned her family name.

"Age," said the man.

"Twenty-one."

"Do you have a birth certificate?"

"Ach and I'm here. Inna that proof I've been born?"

The man turned to look at a hexagonal clock on the far wall. The hands pointed to five minutes to five.

Stewart lowered his eyes from the clock and saw a young woman studying him. Had she guessed his age? Their eyes met, briefly, and then she turned to a black machine on which she moved her fingers. The noise sounded like reindeer clacking across the tundra.

"What's that?" Stewart asked.

"Lucy." The uniformed man spoke with sarcasm. "A woman."

"I mean the wee machine."

"You don't know?" The uniformed man replied in the same tone.

"Lots I dinna ken," Stewart said, hearing the gruffness in his own voice. Out in the bush a man wasn't expected to know everything. Angus and Joe Stokes had no end of stories about *cheechakos* who knew all there was to know about the country without ever being in it. Joe would begin one story about the fatal adventures of an arrogant know-it-all and Angus, with a slap on his thigh, would follow with another.

Stewart smiled to himself, wondering how this desk soldier would fare with Spit 'n' Polish Patty, who, the story went, got frozen in with two newcomers who didn't expect winter so early and hadn't brought up a supply of grub. When Patty was found next spring, there wasn't a trace of her companions and everyone believed she'd eaten them in order to survive. Cleaned them up real good, everyone said, which was how Patty got her name.

The uniformed man dipped his pen into the inkwell and with a tight hand signed the letter the young woman placed in front of him. Stewart became aware of her smooth freckled face, the smooth breasts under a fuzzy white sweater.

"Quittin' time," the man said to Stewart. "Come back tomorrow."

Lucy handed Stewart his beaver overmittens and said, "These are lovely." Her voice was soft, not hoarse like the woman he'd met in Badnews Bluff while he waited for Gus and the Pilgrim. When Stewart took the mittens he touched, for a fraction of a second, Lucy's hand. His cheeks flared.

"I'll show you the way out," she said, slipping on a navy wool coat.

Under the arch at the front door, Stewart put on his squirrel parka.

"Is it true that there's a story to each of these?" Lucy asked as she stroked one of the tails that hung, with red yarn, from his shoulder.

"Aye," Stewart said with half of his mind, thinking with the other half that she was like an innocent fawn. He hardly dared move.

A damp wind rushed down the street but Stewart, for the first time in however long he could remember, took no notice of the weather. He walked beside the young woman, past the construction for the Federal Building. A man whistled provocatively. Stewart wanted to punch his nose.

"I eat at Providence Hospital," Lucy said at the end of the second block. "The food's good, if you like moose meat, beans, and cornmeal mush."

Was she asking him to join her? Never, even when the mud held his feet and Ellen lay at the edge of the tide, never had he felt so helpless. He slowed his stride and said, "Me father fed mush ta the dogs when the weather hit forty below. He swore it warmed 'em up."

"Where are you from?" Lucy asked.

"Bristol Bay." Stewart smiled at her. He could almost feel her breasts in his hand, and he wanted her as he knew Angus wanted Cheok so often in the big bed. He felt a surge between his legs and was glad of the long parka.

"I visit with lots of the patients at the hospital," Lucy said in a warm voice. "There's someone from Unaganik, on Bristol Bay."

Stewart stopped still. He stared at the smiling eyes of this pretty young woman, frightened of what she was going to say next.

"His name's Joe Stokes," she continued brightly. "He's been here a long time and I sure do know he'd be happy to see . . ."

But Stewart didn't stay. He turned and ran down the streets toward the inlet that edged the town. He had to be alone. The city noises, the strangeness of everything, being beside a young woman—it had happened so fast. The one thing he knew for a fact was he didn't want to see Joe Stokes. At least not tonight when he felt unlike the self he'd come to know.

13

O NE EVENING IN EARLY May 1941, Angus stared slack-jawed at the man who stood at the Mud Dog Saloon. The man had a high bald head on which the skin was stretched so smooth it looked like wax. The glossy surface of his head and face was broken by tucks and ridges that looked as if someone had pinched the surface at random. The mouth was a hole without lips. The eyes, hunting green like a Scottish tartan, were the eyes of a man who had burned in his own hell.

It was the eyes that struck Angus. "JOE!" Angus moved so fast he banged his hip against the corner of a saloon table. Jarred, he lunged forward. Joe caught him.

"Joe!" Tears filled the creek beds of Angus's face. "Kin it be ye?" He held his old friend at arm's length and studied him closely. "Ye made it."

"Thanks to you."

Angus thought back to that long night when he'd discovered Joe in the trapper's cabin, burned to a crisp. And he would run him to Unaganik with the dog team again, even though it meant losing Baby Bruce and the lead dog, Wolff, even if there was no guarantee that Joe Stokes would live. Angus was not a man to revel in his own praises, nor was he a man to deny that he'd saved Joe's life—the first part of it. Dr. Visikov, the hospital in Anchorage, and Joe's iron will had done the rest.

Joe tugged at Angus's mane of hair. "You're whiter," he said.

"And ye . . ." Angus looked past the mutilated face into

the heart of the man and said in his thick brogue, "why ye're just the same fer a' that."

Now Joe's eyes filled with tears. Whipping a red handkerchief out of the pocket of a brand new pair of cotton worsteds, he blew his nose loudly.

Robertson Sharpe, having heard of Joe's arrival from the pilot who brought in the mail sack, limped over the jailhouse stoop and across the road to the Mud Dog. He pummeled Joe on the back with his one good hand. Joe turned and the two scarred survivors held each other's eyes until Merilee took the Crown Royal from its purple bag and poured her best whiskey into three heavy shot glasses.

Angus looked at the railway watch belonging to Merilee's second husband. It hung in front of the shot-pecked mirror behind the bar and next to the hurricane lamp.

"I'm taking the night shift," Robertson insisted, seeing Angus's glance. "Ain't every day an old friend comes back from the grave."

Then Joe Stokes and Angus MacTavish, old friends for forty-three years, laughed together, a private joke about other graves dug but not filled.

"Come on, you old bald sourdough," Merilee said, "give me a kiss." The soft flesh around Joe's lips was gone but Merilee puckered her own dark red ones and smacked Joe across the flat opening of his mouth.

"Ah, Merilee," said Joe. "There isn't a woman in Anchorage to touch you."

Angus raised his glass but a toast escaped his tumbled thoughts.

"To miracles," said Merilee.

"I've got another miracle to tell you about," Joe said when they emptied their glasses. "But sit down, first."

Angus perched on a stool, feeling as if every nerve in his body had gone on alert. The large room was still. The pool table, which had come up on the last steamship before winter, stood empty.

Joe Stokes had thought about this moment long and hard during the third year he spent in Providence Hospital. He downed another slug of whiskey, felt it sharpen his tongue. If someone knew where his son had got to, he'd want them to tell him, no matter the pain. And knowing that, he had decided to tell Angus what Lucy had told him of Stewart.

"I got to know this young woman when I was in Anchorage." Joe began his tale in the way of the bush—where there's time for details, time to begin at the beginning, and not rush through because people have other places to go and more important things to do.

"Saints be," said Merilee. "You've gone and gotten hitched."

Angus pulled out his pipe and concentrated on tamping down the tobacco.

Joe told of the nuns in their black habits, the overworked nurses, and finally of Lucy who spent her evenings visiting patients from out of town, and her days working in the recruiting office.

"Is it true they've brought troops to Anchorage?" Merilee asked.

"The first troop train arrived in June of Forty," Joe said. "Now they're building an airbase near the city."

"Sounds like they're expecting Hitler," said Merilee.

"There's talk about the Japs," said Joe.

"Never heard anything so ridiculous," retorted Merilee. "Jonny wouldn't hurt the hair on a flea's head."

Joe twirled his glass. He wanted to be rid of the news. Whether their friendship survived the telling, he wanted it done.

Angus puffed on his pipe. Merilee picked at the red polish on the finger where she wore the thin gold band from her fifth husband.

"This young woman, Lucy, got to see everyone who wanted to sign up for the service and so, one day last April, April 1940"—Joe watched Angus's square fingers whiten on the glass—"a very handsome blond young man comes through the door."

"Who?" growled Angus so sharply that Joe, for a split second, doubted his decision. But no. There was no point holding back.

"Stewart. Stewart MacTavish."

Angus hurled the glass. It smashed against the wooden molding along the base of the opposite wall.

Joe continued in an even voice.

"Stewart didn't get into the air force," he said. "Lucy said Dr. Visikov had registered his birth so they knew his right age."

Angus covered his face with his hands. Merilee slipped a tin cup onto the counter and filled it with her cheapest whiskey.

"After he left Anchorage, Stewart wrote Lucy at the recruiting office."

"Wrote 'er?" Angus's voice was gruff. Why hadn't Stewart written him?

"Where from?" Merilee asked.

"Unalaska. Down the Chain, by Dutch Harbor."

Angus reached for the tin cup and downed the contents. He banged it on the counter where Merilee poured and continued to pour until Angus's head hit the bar. Drink was the surest way any of them knew to wash out the miseries.

Joe hauled Angus up the stairs to Merilee's double bed with the red velvet dust cover. The next morning, Angus woke with a head as big as a buoy. He felt smooth satin on his unshaven cheek, smelled perfume, and knew where he was. But his head! It had been years since it felt scoured raw. He rubbed his eyes and slid off Merilee's satin sheets. Ach! She'd got him under the covers again, and what would Cheok say? Did Cheok care if he had another woman?

Angus fumbled with his clothes. They had shrunk in the night. He couldn't get the buttons straight on his new tartan shirt, which had come in on the first shipment since breakup. He yanked at a button in disgust. It spun across Merilee's floor until it stopped at the carpet in the next room.

Angus slunk down the stairs and was almost out the door before Merilee called from the bar. "Come and get breakfast!"

The smell of bacon tormented his nostrils. He bolted outside, heaving into the empty gasoline can that Merilee, from past experience, had learned to keep there. The morning sun pierced his eyes. Angus struggled back into the Mud Dog, pressing the sides of his head with shaking hands.

"What happened, Merilee?" His heavy eyelashes furrowed over his bloodshot eyes.

"You got drunk."

"I know that, woman, but..." He eyed her suspiciously. Had she taken him last night?

"Nah, Angus, you old coot. Nothing happened in bed. You had your chance and failed."

"Failed?" Angus pressed hard against his temples. Things must be bad if he couldn't get it up. But thank the Lord he hadn't. He never wanted to cheat on the mother of his children, even though Cheok wanted no more children and had refused him favors in bed since Flora's death.

While Merilee ate, Angus pushed the food around the plate, concentrating on thoughts of his children. There was some connection that he couldn't make.

"Joe went out to your place to tell Cheok where you were," Merilee said as she poured coffee into S.S. *Baranoff* mugs.

"Joe Stokes!" Angus tumbled his fingers through his hair. "He's back."

"And he had news of Stewart," Merilee added.

Angus's head pounded, but the torture in his brain was nothing compared to the agony in his heart. Stewart alive and well and not coming home. Ach, he'd be a man for all that, and part of him was proud that the boy could go it alone. But his heart ached and a longing to see his first-born overcame him so much that he blurted, "What do I do, Merilee? Do I look fer me lad?"

"Only to make peace," said Merilee, who had sent her own son Outside to live with a family when he was five and hadn't seen him since.

"Ye think I donna want that?" Angus sunk his head into his hands.

Merilee sat across from him on the high bar stool, silent. A man must do what's in his own soul, she thought, if he knows what's in there to do. And Angus asking the question he did bothered her. Had he come to doubt himself so much, this man who'd never wanted for action?

"I'm goin' doon ta Unalaska!" Angus said as the impact of last night's news penetrated his whiskey-dulled brain. "*Sea Rider* is o'er at Taryaqvak. They sent a wireless to Shushanuk lookin' fer crew. Cap'n Nordsen would be glad o' me."

"Been a long time since you were on a halibut boat," said Merilee. "And you haven't gotten any younger."

"I'm jist as strong," Angus retorted, "and dinna ye remember? Cap'n Nordsen's older than I."

Merilee laughed. "Some of you never know when to quit."

"The *Sea Rider*'ll be putting inta Dutch Harbor," Angus continued, referring to the large protected harbor on Unalaska island. He banged his fist on the bar. "And I'll hop a ride ta Taryaqvak wi' the pilot who brought Joe in. If he's still here."

Merilee nodded. "What about Joe?"

"I'll ask him if he'll coom too."

Merilee locked the bar and followed Angus into the road. Holding his bruised head as carefully as if it were an Aleut basket full of King Crab, Angus headed across the tundra for the cabin on the bluff.

Ellen stared straight ahead when Angus announced his plans. She had always held the notion that she'd see Stewart again, and if Daddy wanted to look for him, that was Daddy's business. But there were so many buts. And how could they manage the nets?

"Can Joe Stokes help us?" asked Bonnie in a quiet voice.

"Ye kin manage on yer own," stormed Angus. "Yer sister started workin' the nets when she was yer age. Ye can gi'e 'er a hand."

Ellen looked at Mother, sitting motionless in the rocker. Cheok was thirty-two but she looked twenty years older and as hard as the iron frame that held the big bed. Since Flora's death there had been no sounds late at night from the big bed and Ellen worried that something terrible was wrong between Mother and Daddy. Was that another reason why Daddy wanted to leave?

"Is Mr. Stokes going too?" she asked, trying to rise above the emotions that seemed to creep below the foundations of the small house.

Angus smiled suddenly at this child of his heart. "I hope tha' he will," Angus said. "But donna ye worry yer pretty head. I'll be back in time ta put up the set nets, and I'll ha'e Stewart ta help us."

"What if you don't find Stewart in Unalaska?" Bonnie asked.

"Will you go further down the Chain?" asked Cheok. She looked at Angus with clouded eyes. That man hung onto Stewart like a starving dog to a bone. Didn't he see Charlie over there, a fine person, ten years old and longing like everything for his father's affection? Didn't he know Ellen would make like the man of the house while he was gone, even if it killed her?

That night, although Cheok still refused his lovemaking, Angus held his wife in his arms. He rocked side to side, swallowing the sobs that lumped at the back of his throat. He wanted Stewart home. He wanted to make amends, but in that dark place where he still held the hate for his own father, he knew it was too late.

Shushanuk always listened to the evening news from station KFQD in Anchorage. Afterward, the radio station relayed messages for people in the bush, but Shushanuk was still surprised to hear Cheok's name and the dispatch from Angus MacTavish and Joe Stokes.

"Leaving Unalaska to proceed down Chain aboard. Sea Rider. Will return in September, after halibut season."

At nine o'clock, Shushanuk set off for the MacTavish household. He was a short, stocky man whose dark eyes sparkled with intelligence. He had grown up, like Cheok, in the orphanage and had swiped spoons that he made into story knives for the girls to draw pictures in the dirt or snow. Shushanuk had advanced from spoons to crystals to the Marconi wireless and, had the opportunity presented itself, would have studied electrical engineering.

Song birds filled the trees with their music, the air was warm, the sky pale grey-blue. The bog at the edge of one patch of the trail had nearly dried up. Shushanuk breathed deeply, glad to be out of the wireless room with its prescient bad news from Europe.

Ellen was awake when he arrived. Cheok slumbered on the big bed in the alcove and Bonnie and Charlie lay like dough in their own canvas cots.

"Did they say anything about Stewart?" Ellen asked after Shushanuk relayed the message.

"No," he said, helping himself to a drink of water from the bucket.

Ellen tucked her ache for Stewart back out of sight. He was gone, Daddy was gone, and the nets needed to be mended and hung. When the salmon arrived in mid-June, Ellen insisted on using the full stock of gill net.

Cheok placed her hands on her broad hips. "We do one little old net."

"The cannery's paying extra this year, 'cause of the war," Ellen argued, as she had come to do since Angus left. "I'm putting up the second net. I don't care what you say. I'll pick it myself."

Cheok, looking at her sixteen-year-old daughter, saw a person with the same determination that had taken her out of the orphanage and into marriage with Mr. MacTavish. "This girl keeps that little old money from that net for her very own self," Cheok said in a quiet voice. "She use it herself."

The words did not sink in. Ellen stared dumbly at her mother.

"You pick that second net," Cheok repeated. "You keep that money."

At last Ellen understood. Mother knew! Mother knew she had to get away. Maybe Ted Kleet was right, Ellen thought several times throughout the summer. Maybe I will get away. I'll have money to fly to Anchorage. I could ask B.I.A. about going to Arizona. Is Ted Kleet still there?

Although on many days her body ached with exhaustion, Ellen stuck with the nets until the end of season, banking her share of the money in an empty Raleigh tin she kept under her cot.

In late August, when the bay churned into a mountain of foam and the waves crashed against the bluff, Ellen tried to conjure up a picture of Daddy in her head. A sense of panic overtook her. What if he drowned in the Bering Sea? What if he was drowning in this awful storm at this very moment? Ellen plunged her hands into a bowl of sourdough, kneading the bread with such force that the table underneath her arms thumped like a diesel against the wall.

14

THE STORM RAGED. THE Atlas engine beat in a steady rhythm. Angus gripped the spokes of the massive wooden wheel and steered the sixty-seven-foot *Sea Rider* to a pole where a red flag marked the beginning of a set of ten skates. Each skate was composed of a line with a hundred hooks baited for halibut, weighted to lie on the sea floor, joined to other, similar lines to make a set.

The wheelhouse lay aft of the working deck, which held two masts, reminders of the day when schooners traveled by sail. Captain Nordsen kept a gaff-rigged sail on the forward mast, using it to stabilize the boat when they raised gear or dressed halibut in heavy seas. Between the two masts was a lowered deck with a dressing—or fish cleaning—table covering the hatch into the hold, where the halibut were stored on ice.

"Jog on the gear," Captain Nordsen said as he flung his navy watch cap onto his bed behind the wheelhouse. "Twenty-five minutes at three hundred and thirty from the pole. Then turn."

The Captain turned to his grandnephew, Leonard, who stood next to Angus. "Mr. MacTavish will take the wheel trick and you keep watch. And mind, no fiddling in this sea."

The young man smiled. His violin lay in its case, tucked in a net hammock that hung from the galley ceiling and rocked free of the ship's roll.

"A black suitcase. Bad luck to take that on board," an old salt had warned when he'd seen Leonard taking it aboard the *Sea Rider* in Ballard in April.

"I can't take my violin without the case," Leonard had said with a furrow in his high pale forehead. "It'll get damaged."

"Don't give that squarehead an ear," Duke, a crew member had said. "It's superstitious fisherman talk."

The only superstition Captain Nordsen honored was not to leave dock on a Friday. A taciturn Norwegian who restricted conversation to business at hand, he now wiped his sweat-soaked forehead and said to Angus, "After two hours on the wheel, give it to Leonard."

Angus looked over his shoulder at the ship's clock and shrugged. Leonard would take over at eighteen hundred hours. Skipper's word was law.

"But keep an eye on him." The captain spoke from his room behind the pilot house. "I've seen the wind do a one-eighty in here and the kid's green."

Ach, yes, he's an in breaker all right, thought Angus, using the halibut fisherman's term for the most inexperienced man aboard. Too green to be fishing except for being the captain's relative. Sandy-haired like Captain Nordsen, with the same squareness of jaw, he was the opposite in build—slight with narrow shoulders and long lean arms that looked, with all their grand gestures, as if they should be steering an orchestra instead of a boat heading west along the Aleutian chain toward Siberia.

Constantly Angus compared Leonard to Stewart. Leonard was unlike any lad Angus had ever known, but when his eyes drooped from lack of sleep, Angus, seeing Leonard's blond hair, thought he saw his son. Stewart, for all his fine ways, had not been unlike Angus, who himself had been a sturdy headstrong lad wanting adventure, rebelling against the rigid rules of his father's household.

"Wake me when your trick at the wheel's over," said the captain, calling final instructions from his stateroom. "Sea might be calm enough to haul the gear." He was asleep before his feet left the floor.

Forty thousand pounds of iced halibut already lay in the hold. With war prices, the income from that was enough—even when shared among the crew of six—to keep a careful man for several years. Notwithstanding that, Angus would willingly trade the prospects of more money for the knowledge that he'd find Stewart somewhere along the Chain. But the captain had said Adak was as far west as he wanted to go, and if Stewart wasn't there . . .

Ach, he wished for the lad and was sure the harbor master in Unalaska, the one with the squeaky voice, wasn't saying all he knew. A scene of standing on the beach, ready to smash the information out of the man with his fists and Joe standing in the way, replayed over and over in Angus's mind. Who in the Lord's name had the right to withhold the whereabouts of his son?

How do men win the trust of their sons, he thought, remembering the two Ted Kleets and wishing he had the same bond. The Lord knew he loved Stewart.

A wave smashed against the salt-encrusted window. Angus gripped the wheel, his knuckles white. The window held. The spray cleared.

"Holy mackerel," said Leonard, waving his arm as if to wipe the window.

Angus put in the clutch, set the speed at dead idle, and wondered how long the old wooden boat would last. Even Captain Nordsen admitted he'd never seen conditions this rough at the end of August. It was as if that madman Hitler had set loose a torrential storm that spread from tiny Austria around the world.

A mountain of ashen water crested the rails, hitting the first mast in the center of the bow. Straining his eyes, Angus hunted for the flag through the towering waves of Seguam Pass.

"Back there," said Leonard, with a wide swing of his arm to starboard.

"Watch for a flat spot," said Angus, shaking his mane of hair out of his eyes. "We'll turn when we find one."

Angus strained to see through the waves washing the bow. While he waited for the sea to calm enough to turn around, he clamped his pipe between his teeth and reached into his inner pocket for his tobacco pouch.

"Watch out!" Leonard shouted.

A wave the size of the second mast shot up and out of the sea on the starboard side. Angus swung the wheel into it.

The wave broke against the roof of the pilot house. The diesel chugged ahead. The wave passed.

"Was that a williwaw?" asked Leonard, his teeth chattering.

"Ach, no," said Angus, speaking around his unlit pipe. "Williwaws are when the wind hammers down the mountain at a hundred miles an hour. I've heard it gusts here to one-twenty, but donna talk of it, lad, ye'll bring bad luck."

The sea flattened and Angus turned the wheel. They jogged back to the flag. The storm grew, and the ocean plunged into darkness. The engine chugged on. Angus clenched his empty pipe, wishing he was home by the fire, having a quiet smoke, or at least up in the relative quiet of the foc's'le where Duke, Joe, and the cook were chewing the fat.

If Stewart hadn't left . . . thought Angus, if Joe Stokes hadn't spoken . . .

Angus had given up going to sea when he married Cheok, and while he believed himself barely old enough to be Stewart's father, he felt, at seventy-one, too old to deal with the whims of Aleutian weather.

Angus recognized the sinking feeling that always came in his stomach when he realized he'd taken the wrong trail and had to fight his way through. He longed, suddenly, for the unending silence of the north, where there were simply himself and his dogs to rely on, not the manmade contraptions of engine and oil. Up north, if a man made a wrong turn he had at least a fifty percent chance of sweating it out, beating his way back. The sea, on the other hand, gave no quarter, and he didn't need that challenge anymore to feel he was alive.

If I get out of this alive, Angus muttered to himself, his eyes scanning the sea for that one wild wave they all feared.

At eighteen hundred hours Leonard took over. Angus watched him, prepared to take the wheel if the need arose. The barometer started dropping. There was a ripple of white caps on the pass, a bit of spray, and then the sea went flat. Angus woke the skipper.

"Do ye want ta haul the gear?" he asked. "The wind's doon."

Captain Nordsen's feet hit the floor. Instantly awake, he tilted his head. The steady rhythm of the Atlas pulsed through the hull. He looked out the window of the wheelhouse, then checked the barometer. It registered "Fair."

"See the glass," said Leonard, pointing to the barometer. "Weather's fine."

"Did it come up this fast?" The captain addressed Angus.

"Been droppin' steady," said Angus, avoiding Leonard's innocent face by concentrating on sticking his pipe into his inner pocket. "It's backed all the way around."

"Get the men and see if we can haul the gear before it blows us out of here," the captain ordered, taking the wheel from Leonard.

"Is this what they call the lull before the storm?" Leonard asked as he and Angus hurried across the foredeck to call the crew from the galley.

"Ach, it is," said Angus. "Mind ye keep alert, lad. It kin coom up that fast." Lights from both masts burned through the darkness. Overhead there was the inky blackness of a cloudy night.

They crossed the deck, avoiding the dressing table on which they cleaned the fish, and slid down the companionway into the galley. "Coom," said Angus as the cook handed him and Leonard mugs of boiling hot coffee. "Wanted on deck."

"What's happening up there?" Duke asked, pulling his oilskins from the hook by the door.

"We're goon ta get hammered." Angus had not the words from his mouth before the *Sea Rider* rolled. Leonard's coffee spilled. He yelped.

Duke hurried topside. Joe pulled on his wet-weather gear.

"Looks like we're in it," Joe said as he left.

Angus poured evaporated milk into his mug and gulped it down. Leonard waited and they headed up the companionway together.

The deck was awash. High-peaked waves crested the port rail. "Wait!" Angus shouted, but Leonard had already started toward the wheelhouse. Angus, knowing better, followed the lad. Leonard was so slight he didn't stand a chance in this roll.

Through the foam Angus could see Duke and Joe holding onto the rail around the wheelhouse. Their heads shook like windvanes. Joe seemed to be yelling, but no sound carried through the storm. Suddenly the *Sea Rider* pitched sideways and Angus pitched forward after Leonard.

" 'Wee, sleekit, cow'rin', tim'rous beastie, O what a panic's in thy breasty!'' A Robbie Burns poem came to him in the midst of another creaking, groaning, roll of the ship. For a brief second Angus wondered what had possessed him to leave the purple heather of Scotland. Then he reached for the dressing table, missed, and slid onto the deck.

A wave covered him. Angus hugged the deck. The wave washed down the icy surface. Angus slid with it. He smashed against the railing. The boat lay on its side and the wave carried Angus over the edge.

Dark green water bubbled in his eyes. A roaring sound burst through his eardrums. His boots filled. Kicking them off, his foot hit something hard. Angus lunged for it. His hands hit the mast lamp. He hung on.

Clinging to the lamp, thinking it and the mast had broken off the boat, Angus found himself rising out of the water. Wallowing from the weight of water on its deck, the *Sea Rider* struggled to right herself.

Pummeled by the waves, Angus clung to the light. The mast rose upward as slow as an anchor floating up from the ocean floor. Hanging tight, Angus felt himself rising out of the water.

"Help!" Angus boomed as the waves shifted off the deck and the mast headed into the air. "Help!" His voice lashed at the wind, at the waves. Joe Stokes and Duke had lurched to the stern and were searching the water. Angus screeched at them. The screams shook from his belly. He nearly lost his grip. Joe inched toward the bow, his scarred hands gripping the wooden rail.

"Here!" Angus screamed. "Up here."

Joe's head swiveled.

"Here! Up here!"

At last Joe looked up and was over to the mast, a rope coiled in his hand, before Angus could blink. The rope swung wide.

Joe reached him on the second try, but Angus, his head spinning, couldn't think what to do with the rope.

"Tuck it through your belt!" Joe shouted, showing with wild movements of his arms what he wanted Angus to do.

The movements reminded Angus of Leonard. He closed his eyes. Captain Nordsen's voice boomed over him. "Get down!"

Skipper's word was law. Angus, like a sled skimming over iced logs, plunged down, his arms circling the mast.

"The lad . . ." Angus choked as Joe helped him onto the deck.

"He's gone." The captain's voice sounded like it came from a megaphone.

"There'll be a calm patch. We kin turn back."

"Sea's bad. We've got to run with it."

Angus cleared his throat but had nothing to say.

At the next lull they dashed across the deck. Angus continued past the pilot house to the stern door. He slid down the ladder into the bunk room. The one-hundred-seventy-five-horse diesel Atlas engine kachugged in a steady rhythm on the other side of the thin wall. It sounded like the beating of his heart.

Feeling leaden at the loss of the lad, and confused by the relief that it wasn't himself, Angus thought, for a second, that he heard Handel's "Water Music" sweeping over the waves. Then he remembered the black suitcase in the galley. Should have tossed it over, Angus thought in a sudden rage at the sea. Might as well take all of the lad! What will he do down there without his violin? Then he fell into his bunk and prayed for sleep.

PART
TWO

15

"**I**'VE DECIDED TA SEND ye ta school," Angus told Ellen on his first evening home in the little house near Unaganik.

Joe Stokes sat at the table across from him. "If you get out of this alive," Joe had said to Angus during the longest night of their long lives, "you're going to send Ellen Outside. You're suffocating her, man."

"Wha' business is it o' yers?" Angus had said as the *Sea Rider* dove through a thirty-foot wave.

The wave plunged on and the *Sea Rider* bucked ahead. "I'm making it my business," Joe said, recalling his own daughter, how she had died in his arms and how he had kept her home too long and surely been punished enough.

"Ellen, I'll not send ye Outside," Angus continued on this September night in 1941. "Not when ye can get yer high school right close at Harold's Point." Angus brushed the back of his hand across his eyes and noticed that Joe watched him closely. He reached into his breast pocket for his pipe and, avoiding Joe, said, "I'd send ye ta the Lower 48, but I donna want ye so far . . ." Angus faltered. It wasn't just because of the war, the Lord knew, that he wanted her nearby.

Ellen stared at her father, dumbfounded. Charlie and Bonnie stared from Angus to Ellen, back and forth like wagging tails. Cheok stood by the stove, ladling cranberry cobbler into thick white bowls. She brought the steaming bowls to the table one by one. No one spoke. When everyone was served, Cheok sat down. Ellen picked up her spoon but did not eat.

"This boy doesn't want cobbler," said Charlie, pushing away his bowl of dessert. "He wants *akutaq*."

"My *akutaq* boy," said Cheok, and she rubbed the flat of her thumb against Charlie's cheek. "You pick those little old berries tomorrow and I'll whip them up with fat and sugar for your little old Eskimo ice cream."

"Picking cranberries is woman's work," Charlie said.

Suddenly Ellen came to. She frowned at Charlie. Hadn't he noticed that she had worked like a man all summer?

"Mr. Stokes will fly wi' ye in the Stinson ta Harold's Point and introduce ye ta the Berglunds." Angus spoke in a monotone. "Sour Pete's wife doona like ta be alone when he's workin' his line in the winter. Ye'll be able ta stay wi' her and keep 'er company."

"The Stinson sank on a glassy water landing at Lake Clark," Ellen said, staring at her father, her heart sinking. Would he still let her go?

"We'll send a message through Shushanuk for the Waco to come over from Taryaqvak," said Joe quickly, before Angus had a chance to change his mind.

"When?" Ellen asked, and Angus knew then that he'd lost her. She wanted to go. That comment more than anything else told him she was ready to leave.

The days passed in a rush. Ellen checked the numbers off on the calendar the bosses had sent from Hawaii. Shushanuk's wife made her a *qaspeq* of red and yellow calico, with a red ruffle around the calf-length hem. Dr. Visikov walked across the tundra to bring her a thin green vest pocket dictionary. Its pages were tinged with gold like the tops of the pages in her favorite *Our Wonder World*, which she was leaving at home.

Jonny the Jap, who had taken Angus's job at the jailhouse, gave Ellen a square-holed Chinese coin given him by one of the cannery workers when he decided to stay north at the end of fishing season. "It's good ruck," he told Ellen. She smiled and wondered what Ted Kleet would think of her luck now.

The priest's wife gave Ellen her eyelash curler and showed Ellen how to use it. Their Yup'ik son, Jonah, carved Ellen a killer whale from walrus ivory. The whale reminded her of the pod she had seen chasing belugas on the bay last summer. She smiled, and Jonah's face lit into a beautiful grin.

"I'll pay ye ta make me an ivory cribbage board," Angus said to the boy.

"Trade for something?" Jonah eyed the corner of the cabin.

"What?" Angus asked. "What ha'e I got, lad, that ye want?"

The lad pointed to the black case in the corner. Angus handed it to him. Jonah took out Leonard's violin and plucked the strings.

"It's yourn," Angus said, the dull notes a plague on his ears. "It's nae good ta me." He was glad to be rid of it and wished the captain hadn't thrust it on him to bring home to his bairns.

"For a cribbage board," said Jonah, laying the violin back in its case. Tucking it under his arm, he left the house at a run.

"What be that little old cribbage?" Cheok asked.

"I'll teach ye," said Angus, putting his hand on Cheok's shoulder, "I'll teach ye to play this winter."

Ellen observed Daddy in this uncharacteristic pose and laid her last fear to rest. They did not need her. And there was no baby needing her, either. Charlie was sufficient in school and Bonnie could set sourdough and make bread. Only Dr. Visikov needed her and he was glad she could go.

Ellen packed her new treasures and her few clothes in the faded carpet bag donated by Mrs. Meriweather. A four-seater Waco biplane roared across Bristol Bay and landed at the field at the edge of Unaganik. Joe Stokes climbed in the back with the gear. He locked his knees together to keep them from trembling. He had always feared flying and the torture of his flight to Anchorage, after Angus had rescued him from Beaver Lake, had done nothing to diminish his uneasiness. If it wasn't for Ellen, he would never have buckled himself into another plane.

Ellen sat up front. It was only then that the reality of what she was doing overtook her. For a split second, she wished she was not leaving. Or rather, she wished her family were coming too. Ted Kleet's family had moved when he had gone to school in Sitka. Had they moved to Arizona too? But that was him. Her life was different. Make your own luck, he had said, and here it was: exactly what she had longed for.

There was no door on her side and she asked the pilot to let her climb over him and get out. It startled Joe, who thought she had changed her mind. While the engine roared, Ellen ran to Mrs. Meriweather and touched her arm. She turned to Dr. Visikov. He held out his hand and when she took it in hers, he brushed his lips against her fingers. Ellen looked at him clearly for the first time since she had found him curled under the covers, freezing cold despite his overheated bedroom. He had shrunken since then and looked grey and wizened and older than Toothless Ed. His gold-rimmed glasses were misted and he did not bother to wipe them.

Tears clustered at the corners of her eyes and when Ellen turned away, she saw Jonah standing alone, opposite the crowd.

Ellen brushed her eyes, pretending to wave. Jonah clasped his hands in front of his heart as if he were praying for her to have courage. She moved toward the priest. He, too, clasped his hands together, fingers up, but his wife, stranger that she still was, kissed Ellen on both cheeks. Startled, Ellen wondered at this new custom. Did everyone kiss Outside?

In a whirl she nodded as she looked into the eyes of Robertson Sharpe, Bonnie, Charlie, and Cheok, whose eyes brimmed over. Then she crushed herself against Angus. He lifted her up, carried her to the plane and, leaning over the pilot, buckled her in. "Ye kin always coom home, me wee blue goose," he said in a thick voice. "Ye knows that."

Ellen straightened her back and looked ahead.

Harold's Point lay on one side of the wide Huvachuck River. It was flat country, with mountains far inland and the great bowl of Bristol Bay obscured by a long peninsula. Barrie's Cannery was here, a long building with a longer pier jutting into the river. The cannery's double-ender fishing boats, yellow to distinguish them from other cannery boats on the bay, were tied alongside the pier. Two hundred and fifty people lived in Harold's Point. There was one trading store, one co-op store, a small, privately owned library, a two-story jailhouse, a pool hall and tavern, a twenty-bed Alaska Native

Services hospital, and two churches—the Russian Orthodox and the Moravian. And, of course, there were the schools.

The high school was a brand new building with a coal stove, tall narrow windows crosshatched with wood, and ten wooden desks which were occupied by the older sons and daughters of both Eskimo and white members of the community. The younger children attended primary school in a building provided by the cannery, with their teacher being the wife of the cannery's winter caretaker, the winterman.

Miss Long, who had been teaching for more than forty years, presided over the high school. She assessed her students' strengths and weaknesses in the first few days, and planned an individual program for each of them. Determined to make up for lost time, Ellen plunged into her books and lessons, reminding Miss Long of a salmon fighting its way up stream. The more she gave Ellen, the more Ellen did. Resisting Miss Long's encouragement to mingle with her classmates at lunchtime, Ellen stuck to her lessons and as a result was called a bookworm behind her back.

Everything was new and strange to Ellen, but what felt strangest of all was to try to fall asleep to the rhythm of a clock instead of other people's breathing. Nights she lay between flannel sheets on the living room couch while a bell-shaped mantle clock ticked in two tones. Her wakefulness increased. After fighting to relax, to let go into the darker parts of an unconscious world, she'd light the kerosene lamp and open up her books. Often she overheard Sour Pete and Mrs. Berglund arguing in the attic bedroom on top of the house, and she'd cover her ears to avoid listening to the hurtful words they hurled at each other.

Two weeks after school started, the winterman at the cannery announced a dance in the mess hall. Miss Long asked Ellen to go with her. She was an older woman with hair as soft and grey as the buds on a willow, a face wrinkled like willow bark, and a voice that reminded Ellen of the brush of leaves in a gentle wind. She wore her hair in a bun secured by wire pins that looked in constant danger of falling.

"You are not going to the dance," Mrs. Berglund said when Ellen appeared after dinner wearing the calico *qaspeq* over her plain brown sweater and grey skirt. Mrs. Berglund was a big-boned woman with earlobes that dangled, pendulous and unadorned, beneath a braid of hair knotted above a face the color of the geranium that bloomed in the kitchen window.

"Miss Long asked me to go," said Ellen, keeping her eyes at a point in the center of Mrs. Berglund's large soiled apron. "She's stopping by for me. Why don't you and Sour Pete come too?"

"I don't dance," said Mrs. Berglund with a frown at Sour Pete.

"I don't either," said Ellen, "except the schottische which Daddy taught me once when Mrs. Meriweather played it on her organ."

"Did you know your daddy and Mrs. Meriweather used to be friends?" Mrs. Berglund's unhappy eyes took on the pleasure of a dark story.

"They're still friends," said Ellen and, taking the plates to the basin, washed away the scrapings of moose meat hash. She was finished by the time Miss Long called "Yoo hoo" from the windbreak.

"Who's that?" Mrs. Berglund said, her eyes wide. She shuffled to the gun rack in her purple backless slippers. Ellen stood in her way.

"It's my teacher," said Ellen. "She's come for me."

Miss Long poked her head through the inner door. Strands of hair had escaped the hairpins and she pulled off her wool gloves to tuck the pins back in. "Hello, Mr. and Mrs. Berglund," she said. "Are you ready, Ellen?"

In the windbreak, Ellen tugged on her sealskin parka and shoepacs while Miss Long talked to the Berglunds in the hot kitchen. Mrs. Berglund and Sour Pete grunted in response.

A diesel-operated generator ran the lights in the cannery and the hum could be heard throughout the village. People in their Sunday best called to each other across the flat land, recognizing voices through the darkness.

Ellen and Miss Long entered a large room. Dining tables had been stacked next to the kitchen except for one, which was set with a gingham cloth, mugs, and a cooking pot that held punch. Light bulbs dangled in a row from the ceiling. A black and white photograph of a string of Barrie boats being towed to the main dock hung on the wall near the door.

A bear of a man approached. He was so black Ellen had

to refocus her eyes to see him. "Dr. Constance," Miss Long said and introduced Ellen. The doctor smiled. Above his upper lip, two white dustings of moustache were almost overpowered by the ebony color of his face.

Do they call him *Tungulria,* the black one? thought Ellen, mindful of the Yup'ik custom of nicknames.

"Pleased to meet you," Dr. Constance was saying and Ellen blinked as the doctor turned to introduce a much younger man on his right. "Dr. Jason West. He's here from New York, assisting me as part of his public health training."

Nothing was out of kilter on this younger man's face. No scar where a fish hook might have torn the flesh or an axe scored the skin. Yet there was nothing to draw you to his face except his eyes. They were blue. Not sun bleached like Angus's, nor brooding like Stewart's, but blue as the Hawaiian calendar and clear as a summer sky when the wind had blown off the clouds.

Ellen stared into them and felt the stirrings of a world far from fish and mud, far from Sour Pete and sourer Mrs. Berglund. She forgot where she was, who she was, until suddenly the lively strains of music squeezed in on her. It was as if the world had begun all over again.

The winterman stood beside the gingham-covered table, tapping his foot and playing the accordion.

"A polka," said Dr. Constance, and bowed to Miss Long. She tucked a loose hair under a pin and put her hands on his shoulders. They joined the others bouncing around and around the warm room.

"Shall we?" asked Dr. West.

Mesmerized, unable to protest that she didn't know the polka, Ellen lifted her arms and put her hands on Dr. West's shoulders. He was as tall as Joe Stokes although not as gaunt, and under his stylish blue jacket, his shoulders were soft. He had a long neck with a prominent Adam's apple under which was knotted a silver and blue tie. A silver clasp with the initials J.W.M.D. held the tie to a starched white shirt. His wool trousers matched his blue jacket and were wide in the leg with folded cuffs. To Ellen he looked beyond imagination. She let herself relax into the arms that leaned over her and clasped themselves around her waist. The merry notes played around them. She felt herself lifted off the rough-hewn floor-boards into a glamorous and magical world.

"May I get you something?" Dr. West asked when the music stopped.

"Oh yes," said Ellen and moved to the side of the room, watching, spellbound, as this elegant stranger crossed the room to the refreshment table. It seemed unnatural that he was getting a drink for her when she was perfectly capable of walking across the room by herself. But she waited and smiled at him when he returned with two glasses of canned apple juice.

"Shall we?" he said, indicating the bench along the wall.

Suddenly tongue tied, Ellen sat down beside him and sipped her juice.

"Are you new here?" Dr. West asked.

"Yes," said Ellen, forcing herself to speak. "I came to go to school."

"Is it your first time away from home?"

"Yes." Ellen looked at him, feeling shy. He looked like ivory, but without any rough edges to sand and polish, like Jonah had done with her whale.

"Are you homesick?"

"No," said Ellen, perplexed. What had made him say that?

"I confess I still get homesick sometimes," he said, and his eyes were kind.

"Sick?" she blurted, surprised. "And you a doctor?"

Dr. West looked as if he were swallowing a piece of gristle. He sipped his juice and then, looking up, his eyes curious, he asked, "What will you do when you finish high school?"

Ellen sat crosslegged on the bench. "I don't know," she said, tucking the calico *qaspeq* over her knees.

"Are you like most women?"

"I don't know most women," Ellen answered, feeling confused as she looked at the other girls in the room with their tiny babies. "There weren't many people in Unaganik and we lived a ways from the village."

Dr. Jason West smiled. It was the most perfect smile Ellen had seen in her sixteen years. "I do know something," she said, feeling as if she could trust him, "I know I don't want to get married and have children and stay here forever."

He smiled again, and at that moment Ellen believed that anything was possible, even that secret plan she had tucked away so long ago.

The following week, Charlie Chaplin's *Gold Rush* was shown on the movie projector at the school. Ellen went with Mrs. Berglund while Sour Pete stayed home to grease and repair his traps.

"It wasn't like that," complained Mrs. Berglund, who had been seven when her fortune-seeking parents left her scrubbing floors in the Golden North Hotel in Skagway and headed to the gold fields without her.

But for Ellen, her first moving picture show was a thrill. Even more thrilling, however, was finding Dr. West in the hall after the film was over.

"May I walk you home?" he asked and Ellen nodded before Mrs. Berglund, huffing beside her, could say no.

The sky had darkened. Aurora flowed in white and green streaks and Dr. West stopped at the Berglunds' front door, gazing upward.

Ellen stood with the doctor and waited for Mrs. Berglund to go around the back to the windbreak. Instead, Mrs. Berglund shoved Ellen aside. Just as Mrs. Berglund had yearned for someone to protect her all those years and had hoped, in vain, that her parents would return to Skagway, now she would protect Ellen. She'd let no man get his filthy hands on anyone in her care.

"You leave this girl alone," Mrs. Berglund said, shaking a bloated finger under Dr. West's nose. "You hear?"

Miss Long watched the circles growing blacker under Ellen's eyes and noticed the liveliness in her fade week by week. In December, at the end of a dark school day, she invited Ellen to her apartment above the schoolroom. Miss Long served tea from a china pot with raised roses on the plump sides, poured it into two matching rose cups with petal saucers underneath. Afraid she might break her cup, Ellen's wrist jiggled when she lifted it up.

"Cookie?" asked Miss Long, offering Ellen cream-filled Peak Freans.

"No thank you," said Ellen, recognizing the cookies as the same kind Mrs. Meriweather had served at Bruce's funeral. It seemed strange to think of Bruce. What a long time ago that was. Ellen pushed the sense of him away and concentrated on the teacup and her teacher. The quietness of the room eased in on her. There was a peace here that was missing in Mrs. Berglund's house.

The teacher's shoulders loosened and Ellen watched as they gradually slanted downward, as if shrugging off the weight of teaching ten high school students in as many subjects. Then Ellen realized that she, too, had been holding her shoulders stiff. They felt as if they'd been in that position since she came to Harold's Point and as if, by holding them stiff, she could ward off the queer feelings generated by this new and different life.

Ellen's teacup rattled as she laid it back on the saucer. Feeling as if her nerves were stretched beyond capacity, that if she stayed any longer she would sling all her worries at Miss Long, Ellen stood up abruptly and said, "Thank you, but I have to go now."

Miss Long continued to sit in her chair and Ellen, standing by the couch, didn't know if it would be rude to move toward the door or not.

"Are you expected to do a lot of work for Mrs. Berglund now that Sour Pete has gone?" asked Miss Long in the unobtrusive voice Ellen loved.

"No." Ellen did not trust herself to say more. In fact she had less work to do at the Berglunds than if she had stayed at home. Home! The harder she fought to not think of home, the more it pained her when she heard the word.

"You're doing very well in your classwork," Miss Long continued, as if Ellen were still sitting.

"Thank you," said Ellen.

"I've asked Dr. Constance to teach you, if he has time. He can give you a better grounding in the sciences than I can with our limited facilities."

Why can't Dr. West teach me? thought Ellen, recalling that polished face she had not seen since Mrs. Berglund told him to stay away.

"I'm going Outside to visit my brother at Christmas and will bring back some advanced chemistry and biology texts for you," continued Miss Long.

"I might not come back after Christmas," Ellen said,

surprising herself as the words popped out. "I might not," she added, trying to firm the quaver in her voice.

"I'm sorry to hear that," said Miss Long. "If it's difficult living with Mrs. Berglund, I would be willing to help you find another place to stay."

"She's afraid to be alone after dark," said Ellen, "and I promised to stay with her as long as Sour Pete was gone on his trap line. That was why she let me come to live with her in Harold's Point and go to school."

"Sometimes we make promises without knowing all the circumstances..." said Miss Long, speaking so softly Ellen leaned forward to hear.

Ellen swallowed hard. Mrs. Berglund had grown odder as the winter darkened, although Ellen had hoped, without Sour Pete to fight with, Mrs. Berglund's mood would improve. She kept a loaded pistol by her bed and slept so lightly she had fired a shot through the roof when Ellen used the honey bucket after studying late one night. Mrs. Berglund had been convinced that a man was trying to break in and Ellen, astonished, had not found the words to persuade her otherwise.

"I'd hate to see you leave school," continued Miss Long as if she were talking to herself. "There's lots of ways to get your freedom, but to my mind, schooling is the best we've come up with so far."

Miss Long finally stood. As soon as she did, Ellen darted to the door and flung her sealskin parka off the hook. Her arms trembled. The parka twisted behind her back. Then Miss Long's hands were on her, guiding Ellen's thin arms into first one sleeve, then the other.

Ellen choked out a thank you, grabbed her schoolbooks, and fled downstairs. She burst into the black night before the dammed-up feelings exploded. Her cries tunneled through the dark and seemed to come from a place outside herself, a place as alien to her as she was to this alien and strange new world. A husky chained to a nearby cabin howled.

I'll hop a plane, Ellen thought. Mrs. Berglund will have to find someone else. A big lady like her afraid of the dark! It's too strange. I have money in the Raleigh tin. I don't need to wait for Daddy to come with the dogs. I'll leave as soon as Sour Pete returns from his trap line.

Wind howled over the snow. Ice chips flicked into Ellen's face, freezing her tears. She stifled a sob to listen to the wail of the wind. It sounded as if the wail came from the depths of her soul, as if the sound was her.

"Listening to the Alaskan love song?"

Ellen jumped.

A man in a store-bought green parka stood beside her. It was the winterman from the cannery who played the accordion.

"Didn't mean to scare you," he said.

"Hello," Ellen said, hoping he wouldn't notice her tear-blotched cheeks.

"Better get on home," he said. "Blizzard's brewing."

Home? Did he think she called the Berglunds' home? Ellen shook her head, suddenly knowing that Unaganik was not the place she wanted to be either. What had Miss Long said about freedom? Mother got free from the orphanage by marrying Daddy, Ellen mused. But she's tied in other ways. I don't want that!

Ellen listened to the wind sluicing over the snow-packed surface. She felt alone and lonely. Since Stewart had left, no one in her life understood her, certainly not Daddy, who never wanted her to leave. Feeling cut to pieces by her thoughts, by the knowledge that her life was as hopeless now as it had ever been, Ellen trudged blindly on. Outside the Berglunds' log house, she stomped her snowy feet on the back stoop, laid her books on a shelf in the windbreak, took off her parka, and opened the door to the kitchen.

Mrs. Berglund faced the door. She pointed a semi-automatic Colt .45 with one hand and an over-and-under Ranger with the other.

16

"IT'S ME. ELLEN. ELLEN MacTavish." The words rang through the kitchen. Ellen's feet froze to the rag footwipe just inside the door. She waited for recognition.

Mrs. Berglund's elephantine fingers shook on the triggers of both guns. Ellen sucked in her breath. The sound gurgled across the room. Terrified that it would prompt Mrs. Berglund to pull the trigger, Ellen froze.

The whites of Mrs. Berglund's eyes seemed separated from the dark black centers which revolved in independent directions. Her pupils looked through Ellen without form or focus. Faintly, from the living room, the clock ticked. Ellen heard words form in her mind but could not force them past the brick wall of her throat.

Mrs. Berglund's feet, in faded purple mules, were spread wide apart. The hand holding the Colt pointed straight at Ellen. The other hand holding the Ranger pointed at the geranium on the kitchen windowsill. Ellen followed the direction of the Ranger from the corner of her eye. The geranium looked limp.

Then Ellen thought of how Jonah had escaped his father's axe. His prayer for her, the smooth beauty of his ivory killer whale by her couch bed, filled her with courage. "Put those down, Mrs. Berglund," Ellen found herself saying with a deceptive calmness. "It's only me."

The Ranger went off. The blast shattered the window. Ellen ducked and snapped open the door behind her.

She crashed over her boots. Grabbing them and her parka, she tore into the blizzard in her stockinged feet. The blizzard pushed against her. Her braid banged against the back of her head like a whip, urging her on. There were no lights, no sense of haven in the dense turmoil of the storm. Panting, she stopped. She pulled on her boots, and, stamping up and down, trying to dull the needles of pain that shot up through her icy feet, she struggled into her parka.

The storm billowed around her, moaning and whining. A faint odor rode with a surge of wind. Steam...from the hospital furnace. Ellen followed the smell across the snowladen ground until she heard the hum of the generator. Soon a dim light shone through the blinding snow. Ellen felt her way to the door of the two-story hospital building, burst through the windbreak, and tumbled into the shock of light and warmth. She fell forward, faint.

Someone steadied her. She took a deep breath and looked up, expecting to see the black face of Dr. Constance. Instead she saw the young polished face of Dr. West.

"Hello," he said, and taking a linen handkerchief from his pocket wiped the sweat and snow gently from Ellen's forehead, from her broad cheeks, from her dimpled chin. Ellen put her right hand to her throat. She held the jade labret under her brown sweater.

"There's been a shooting," she said with a heave of her chest.

"Where?" said Dr. West. He stooped down and picked up his medical bag.

"At my house. I mean, where I live. It's Mrs. Berglund."

"I'll go," he said, hauling a black fur seal coat off a hook by the office door. "I remember where your home is."

"It's not my home." Ellen shook her head, feeling, all of a sudden, like a small child, like Daddy's wee blue goose.

"I understand," said Dr. West.

"No," said Ellen, "you don't understand at all. How could you? You aren't even from around here." Oh, where was Dr. Constance? He would know what to do without her saying anything.

"Dr. Constance is busy right now with a tuberculosis patient."

"I heard Mrs. Berglund tell you to stay away, that it wasn't right, and I don't want you to get shot," Ellen blurted loudly. "She's gone off her head. I hoped she wouldn't, but now she's—'' Seeing the guns in her mind, Ellen stopped talking, her mouth open, her eyes wide. It was too horrible for words.

Dr. West put his arm around her, steering her into the consulting room, slipped a chair under her and disappeared down the hall, returning with Dr. Constance almost before Ellen was aware that he had gone and come back.

"Trouble with Mrs. Berglund?" Dr. Constance asked, rushing into the consulting room ahead of Dr. West. "I've been worried about her."

"She tried to shoot me." Ellen felt detached now, calm, she had found her way through the blizzard and now these people could take care of everything.

"Let's go and get the marshal and get on over there," said Dr. Constance, "before it's too late."

"This blizzard's a bad one," said the marshal when he came stomping out of the jailhouse. "We'll have to take the dogs, to be sure we get back."

Ellen thought of Daddy coming down from Nachook last spring, swearing that there wasn't a dog to compare with U-Prince for getting through a whiteout. She wished so hard for Daddy she almost imagined he was Dr. West.

"Let's go," said Dr. Constance and, despite his sixty-five years, pushed himself as fast as the others through the storm.

Laboring to lift her boots through the heavy drifting snow, Ellen stayed by the lead dog, sensing the way back to the log house. She loosened her shoulders, feeling as if she were somehow detaching from her body, same as the time she had fallen on the mudflats and flitted through the air like a tern. She flattened the palm of her hand against her cheek, feeling the cold chill of her skin.

"Let me go first," said the marshal when they approached the house. He took off his fur mittens and drew his pistol out of the holster.

"No shooting, if we can avoid it," said Dr. Constance.

"She's a pretty big woman," said the marshal. "I'm not sure I can overpower her without firing this, at least as a warning."

"Wait!" Ellen suddenly felt alert, safe. It was her job to

take care of Mrs. Berglund and, pointing to the light stream-
ing past the jagged edges of the broken kitchen window, she
said, "I'll shout through the window and divert her attention.
While she's talking to me, you can go through the front door
and grab her from behind."

"What if she shoots at you?" Dr. West asked.

"There's a woodpile under the window," said Ellen.
"I'll crouch down on the other side of it. She won't see me in
the dark and if she does shoot, the bullet will stop in the
wood."

"Where's the door?" asked the marshal and Ellen led
him around the far side of the house to the little-used front
door.

As soon as the marshal had dug enough snow away from
the door to open it, he entered the darkened living room.
Ellen crawled on hands and knees to the woodpile. The
surface snow was soft and windblown but underneath was a
hard crust. She inched along, ignoring the cold that chilled
her knees.

"Mrs. Berglund," she called in what she hoped was a
comforting voice, "it's me, Ellen MacTavish. Are you all—"

A shot shattered her sentence. The glass remaining at the
edges of the window rained down. The geranium crashed onto
the woodpile. A second shot followed in quick succession.
Ellen covered her ears and cringed.

"Holy Hell!" The marshal's voice boomed through the
broken window. "Look what she done. Dr. Constance! Quick!"

Ellen jumped up and darted into the kitchen after them.
Mrs. Berglund lay in a hump on the floor, her legs crumpled
beneath her, slippers off. Her eyes had rolled up into their
sockets, showing only the whites. From a huge hole on the
left side of her head, blood and brains spurted in a creamy red
pulp. In her right hand lay the Colt .45.

Ellen choked. She clenched her teeth, trying to stop her
jaw from chattering. She stood stock still for several seconds,
then was drawn out of herself by the marshal, who jammed
his gun into his holster. The gun was unnecessary. Mrs.
Berglund had taken her own life.

Blood oozed over the floor. It soaked the rag footwipe
and gingham cushion, which had fallen off the rocker by the

wood stove. Ellen picked up Mrs. Berglund's purple mules before they got soaked, too, and set them on the rocker.

While Dr. Constance and the marshal busied themselves with Mrs. Berglund, Dr. West said, "May I help you get your things, Ellen? I think you should spend the night at the hospital."

"I agree," said Dr. Constance, looking up from the floor where he kneeled over the dead woman.

Ellen lit a candle and led the way into the living room. The couch was upside down, Mrs. Meriweather's carpetbag was turned inside out, clothes littered the floor. Ellen stared at the mess and went blank. It was too much to take in. She could only see the body in the kitchen.

"Maybe if I had come right home after school," Ellen said in a rush, "this wouldn't have happened."

"What could you have done?" asked Dr. West as they stood looking at the mess in the dim candlelight.

Ellen heaved her shoulders, feeling as if she was still carrying the load of Mrs. Berglund's madness. Obviously he was an Outsider and didn't understand.

"Ultimately each person is responsible for himself," he continued and as she looked at the jumbled room, she thought about what he was saying, and how Daddy would probably have agreed with him.

"We do what we can," Dr. West continued, "but sometimes everything everybody does is still not enough. You mustn't let this ruin your life."

Ellen looked up. There was a note in the young doctor's voice that made her wonder if he was speaking more for himself than for her. He bent over and picked up the ivory whale. "Is this yours?" he asked, handing it to her.

Ellen cradled the whale in her hand. Jonah had survived worse. She looked up at Dr. West, at his kind blue eyes. "Yes," she said. "This was given to me by a friend."

"Would your friend carve something for me?"

"Yes," said Ellen, tucking the carving into the pocket of her sealskin parka. She looked around the room for the rest of her things and found Dr. Visikov's dictionary among the mess Mrs. Berglund had made of the room. The Raleigh tin with her fish money was nowhere to be found.

When Ellen carried her bag back into the kitchen, Dr.

Constance was holding the Chinese coin. "This was in her apron pocket," he said.

"It's mine." Ellen took the coin and rubbed it between the palms of her hands while Mrs. Berglund was wrapped in a sheet and carried to the sled.

"I'll send my wife over tomorrow to clean up the mess," said the marshal as they prepared to leave.

"We better cover the window," said Dr. Constance, "or the house will be full of snow by morning." He smoothed his tiny white fringe of moustache and waited while Ellen and Dr. West nailed a table cloth over the broken window.

"When is sour Pete due back from his trap line?" asked Dr. Constance.

"He promised to be back by Christmas break," said Ellen, "so I could go to Unaganik."

"It's already December fifth," said the marshal.

"I guess we can wait till he returns to notify him," said Dr. Constance.

"Sour Pete wasn't much of a husband," said the marshal as he pulled on his fur overmittens. "But then again, I guess the missus wasn't much of a wife."

"Takes two to tango," said Dr. Constance, "but I've never been married, so how would I know?"

Ellen moved into an attic room under the roof of the two-story hospital. The night nurse prepared a hot water bottle for her. Ellen cradled it under the icy covers, trying to shove the day's trauma from her mind.

The next day she heard noises but did not stir until early in the afternoon when Miss Long tiptoed into the bedroom. "Ellen?" Miss Long said.

Ellen sat up in bed, the covers pulled around her naked body.

"I'm sorry about what happened," said Miss Long, tucking a wisp of hair into a hairpin.

Ellen did not want to talk about it. She did not want to think of that bloody mess of Mrs. Berglund anymore. It was like the moving pictures, only in color, and playing the same reel over and over.

"Can you get up now?" asked Miss Long. "And come for a walk with me?"

"I don't want to go out."

"The blizzard's gone and Grandmother Earth and Grandfather Sky are beautiful today."

Ellen dressed. She struggled into her parka and mukluks and went outside with Miss Long. The blizzard had pushed the old snow into swirls and drifts and brought new snow to cover the leavings of dogs and the maze of yellow stains. The sky was clear and pale and a sun dog, a prism of color, brayed at one side of the low winter sun. The snow sparkled and gave off no sound.

"Why did she do it?" Ellen asked as they walked together down to the frozen river on the other side of the Barrie Cannery. "Did I do something wrong?"

"Do you mean it's your fault?" The snow absorbed Miss Long's voice.

Ellen thought hard. So many things seemed to be her fault, like losing her boots and getting Stewart in trouble.

"Do you?" asked Miss Long.

"She was angry all the time. I couldn't please her."

They stood on the frozen edge of the river, where the bright yellow boats waited out the winter.

"It's impossible to please some people," said Miss Long. "The fault is in trying."

Miss Long stayed for dinner in the hospital dining room. She sat beside Ellen and they sat across from Dr. Constance and Dr. West. After dinner, Miss Long visited patients in the wards. Ellen stayed at the table, looking at her half-eaten plate of food.

"I'm sorry you had to see that last night," said Dr. West.

Ellen looked at the smooth whiteness of his face as if there were a message for her there, if she could read the print. Her thoughts tore against each other until she felt shredded into tiny pieces. Mrs. Berglund was dead, and she was supposed to have taken care of her.

"Did you sleep well?" asked Dr. West.

"I haven't slept well since I came to Harold's Point," she blurted. "It's been—" Ellen bit her tongue and fought for control. She clenched her hands. Her fingernails were chewed and a hangnail had been torn on her thumb.

"Did you know she was a fearful lady when you moved in?" he continued.

"I knew she didn't like me. That was obvious from the first."

"Maybe she was jealous of you."

"Me?" Ellen drew back. "Me?" she repeated.

Dr. West's eyes looked kind.

"Maybe she was jealous of your confidence."

"Me? Confident?" Ellen's astonishment showed in her voice.

"Must take a lot of self-assurance to do what you're doing."

What I'm doing, thought Ellen, remembering her conversation with Miss Long, is thinking of moving back to Unaganik.

Dr. Constance sent a message about Mrs. Berglund to Unaganik over the wireless. Shushanuk asked Jonah to run it out to the MacTavish homestead and Angus hitched up the dog sled and left an hour after Jonah arrived with the news. But by the time Angus reached Harold's Point, Mrs. Berglund's suicide was old news. The Japanese had bombed Pearl Harbor.

"I don't believe it," said Angus as they sat down at the table in the hospital dining room. "I don't believe it."

"Roosevelt has declared war," said Dr. Constance.

"Nineteen naval vessels sunk or damaged," said Dr. West, "and over two thousand people killed. At least by the latest news."

Angus shook his head in disbelief.

"Gargantuan damage," said Dr. Constance. "We might have hit some Japanese subs, but nothing compared to what they did to us."

"There were rumors of Japanese submarines down the Chain," said Angus slowly.

"Let's hope they aren't planning to bomb Alaska," said Dr. Constance.

"The Americans were building a naval base at Dutch Harbor last summer," Angus continued, his voice distant, as if he were thinking of other things.

Ellen reached for the jade labret hanging around her neck on a red satin ribbon. How had Stewart stayed away so long? Could she stay away, too?

"How planes fly in that Aleutian weather, I don't know,"

said Dr. Constance. "A pilot told me he used to put his hand out the window to feel the spray off the water in order to know if he was low enough to put down."

"No place for a novice," said Angus as he played with his fork. He ate in the Scottish way, with a fork in his left hand, his knife in his right, and Ellen had copied his style. In the past, when Angus had forgotten he was at table and had eaten off his knife, she had done likewise, only to be told, "Now me wee blue goose, eat like a lady."

Ellen smiled at Daddy. He had come to see if she was safe. It felt good to be next to him, feel his love. She rubbed like a puppy against his arm.

Angus turned to his daughter. "We'll be leavin' early tomorrow," he said. "We must away and tend ta yer mother and the other bairns. The Japs may hit Alaska next. Pack yer things tanight."

"Pack?" Dr. Constance's deep voice resonated through the dining room. "Now, Mr. MacTavish, she's safe with us. She'll live at the hospital, and I've got plenty of work for her. We can always use an extra pair of hands."

Ellen held her breath. If she returned to Unaganik now, she might never get the courage up to leave again. If she stayed, she'd live at the hospital! It would be wonderful! And the secret plan, plotted long ago at Dr. Visikov's, before Ted Kleet flew down for Eastertime, slipped back into her thoughts. To study to be a doctor. Suddenly it all seemed possible, as if, because of Mrs. Berglund's death, she had found the right path.

"I'll stay here, Daddy." She laid the fork on the rim of the plate and, adjusting her chair, faced Angus. "If the Japanese bomb Alaska they'll need me here in the hospital more than at Unaganik. I'm staying, Daddy. I have to."

Angus did not look at her. He scratched the plate with his knife, missing the slice of roast caribou that had been reheated from Sunday night's dinner.

17

"I'M GOING DOWN TO meet the plane from Anchorage," said Dr. West. He spoke to the group assembled in the hospital dining room for breakfast on Saturday morning, December 20, 1941. "Anyone want to come?"

"I do," Ellen piped up. "Miss Long's going Outside for Christmas. I want to see her off."

"I believe she's decided not to go," said Dr. Constance. Ellen looked surprised.

"Come along anyway," said Dr. West. "I'm expecting parcels from Mater and I'll need help bringing them back."

Ellen raced to the attic for her letters. One to Jonah with a request for a carving for Dr. West. One for the family at home.

No. She did not miss them. She squeezed her eyes. She was too busy with school and hospital work and preparations because of the war. She did not want to return home, but how hard it had been for Daddy to leave her! Feeling Daddy's pain like a cube of sugar in the center of her heart, Ellen held her letter to her chest and took a deep breath. Then she dashed downstairs where she met Dr. West in the windbreak. He helped her on with her parka.

"It's almost too small," she said, struggling into the sleeves.

"It's beautiful, though." He stood back to admire it.

"And yours too," said Ellen, reaching out to stroke the glossy fur.

Dr. West got the handsled from the hospital janitor while Ellen pulled on her mukluks. She met him outside.

"Mater will miss me this Christmas," said Dr. West, as he pulled the creaking handsled over the snow. "It's the first one I've been away."

"Who's Mater?" Ellen asked, and felt the pleasure of being alone with the young doctor for the first time since she had moved into the hospital.

"Mater is my mother," said Dr. West. "The finest woman you should ever hope to meet." Ellen concentrated on the feeling behind Dr. West's words, only partially hearing his recital of his mother's talents. Permanence, she thought. Not that awful wrenching and remoteness I always feel. He feels permanence with his mother. There's no separation, even though his mother lives far away in New York City.

They had reached the center of Harold's Point. The Berglund log house stood on the rise to their right. The awful image of Mrs. Berglund shifted into focus, like a bad nightmare daring to haunt a daytime world.

Ellen shuddered, remembering, too, how Sour Pete had reacted when he arrived in town and heard the news of his wife's death. He'd gone on a roaring drunk and after five days arrived at the hospital, smelling of his own urine, shouting obscenities at them for not saving his missus.

Ellen looked at Dr. West. The warmth and caring that had been there when Mrs. Berglund died was still present. But there was something more, something that made her want to touch him, to curl against him as she used to curl against Stewart when they slept together in the cot, before Stewart got too big.

They continued pulling the sled. The cannery stood by the wharf far to their left. The blue onion dome of the Russian Orthodox Church, the plain wooden cross on the Moravian Church, the corrugated metal of the Co-op Store, stood opposite each other on the wide, snowpacked road. A team of dogs rested in front of the general store.

Overhead the plane droned. The winterman hurried up from the cannery and the man with the dog team hurried out of the store.

"Did you know that Mrs. Berglund was ten years older than her husband?" asked Dr. West as the house receded into the background.

"My mother believes we're old people when we're born.

The old soul of us comes through into the new baby so it doesn't matter what age anyone is.''

''Is your father older than your mother?''

''By thirty-nine years,'' said Ellen, ''but they never talk about the distance between them.''

As soon as she said the word distance she realized she had meant to say difference. Yet there was both a distance and difference between Cheok and Angus. Cheok had never been more than fifty miles from home. Angus, it seemed, had been all over the world before he settled in the north. They were like earth and clouds, one rooted, the other always restless. And what did that make Ellen? Someone caught between them? Caught in the middle and feeling settled nowhere? Ellen wanted to touch this person next to her, feel his permanence so that she could also know her own.

She reached for him and in that moment the plane skidded to a stop on the frozen river. The propeller blasted snow into their faces. Dr. West fluffed his mittened hand across Ellen's cheeks, brushing the snow away.

''I'm not going Outside,'' Miss Long said to them as she arrived at the airplane empty handed. ''The war might prevent me from returning and then who would be the teacher?''

''That means room for me on the plane,'' said Lester Morton. His wife had recently died of tuberculosis. ''The Japs are coming and you'll all be eaten.''

A man in a military uniform climbed down from the six-seater Pacemaker.

''Lieutenant Hardwick, meet Dr. West,'' said the pilot.

''Can you put me up for a few nights?'' the lieutenant asked.

''We don't have any space at the hospital,'' said Dr. West. ''Our spare room is occupied.'' He smiled at Ellen.

''He can sleep in a bunk at the cannery,'' said the winterman.

''Thank you.'' The lieutenant followed the winterman across the snow.

''Will you take this to Unaganik?'' Ellen asked the pilot, handing him her letter. ''It's for Daddy.''

He took it and handed her an envelope in return. ''From your young man,'' he said.

Ellen shook her head. She was glad for a letter, her first

since she had arrived in Harold's Point, but she definitely did not have a young man. Ted Kleet was the only person remotely likely to write to her, and he didn't even know she had left Unaganik. Feeling strange about the letter, she walked to one side and quickly ripped open the envelope. It was a drawing from Jonah. Unsettled by what she saw, Ellen refolded the paper and stuffed it into her skirt pocket before returning to the plane.

The pilot was unloading Dr. West's packages and Ellen helped to stack them on the sled. They hauled it back to the hospital together, laughing at the steam puffing from their mouths.

"You were right about Miss Long," Ellen told Dr. Constance in the dining room, noticing how he smiled when she mentioned her teacher's name. "Lester Morton took her place on the plane."

Dr. Constance's enormous laugh filled the room. "Lester's fainthearted! Good thing his wife is gone. He'd have left her anyway, poor thing."

"A lieutenant came in on the plane," said Dr. West. "He's looking for recruits. I'm wondering if I should enlist."

Ellen's hands went cold.

"We'd miss you," said Dr. Constance just as a commotion stirred in the hall. The buxom cook entered the dining room with a tray covered with sourdough donuts. "Starring!" she announced.

Ellen greeted her friends from the Russian Orthodox Church. Nikolai Jones held the star. It was an eight-spoked wheel revolving around an ikon of the Virgin Mary and covered with tinsel and paper carnations.

Old Mr. Took stood beside Nikolai and handed an incense stick to Ellen. Dr. West flicked the lid off his Zippo lighter, rolled the blue flame up until it licked the end of the stick. The incense burned gold, then settled into a slow aromatic spiral of smoke. Ellen felt full of grace. The old Christmas traditions were so grand! Even here in the big village of Harold's Point. They were all connected: it was foolish to feel separate, remote, just because family and Stewart were so far away. The threads of smoke coiled up from the stick, and Ellen joined in the fun.

The star turned around and around on the bar attached to

the center. Little Elise Brandon started to cry and Ellen scooped her up and propped her on her hip. The child cuddled against her. With the star high above their heads, the group entered the dining room, singing Christmas songs in Russian and English. Dr. Constance joined in. His resonant voice dwarfed theirs and they sang louder, all the while eyeing the huge tray of donuts.

"One more song," said Dr. Constance. "Then you can eat."

"You choose," said Nikolai.

The doctor opened his large mouth and from deep in his chest came the opening lines of "Oh Mary, don't you weep don't you moan."

Everyone sang and clapped. Ellen stopped at "Pharoah's army got drowned," for fear she would cry, remembering Daddy telling how he almost drowned on the halibut boat and knowing she'd never have been able to go away to school if he had.

After stuffing themselves with donuts, the children sang and clapped through the hospital, then left to go starring elsewhere. Ellen went to the kitchen with the night nurse for hot chocolate. The doctors were there.

"Mr. Waylock has offered to shoot some ptarmigans for us for Christmas dinner," said Miss Herringbone, the night nurse.

"Please tell him yes," said Dr. Constance. "They'll be delicious with those sweet potatoes I've been saving."

"And Mater sent me grapes for Waldorf Salad," said Dr. West.

"What are grapes?" asked Ellen.

Dr. West's blue eyes widened in surprise. He grinned.

"Fresh raisins," explained Dr. Constance.

Nodding studiously, Ellen said: "If there's any little old berries left, I'll make *akutaq*."

"What's that?" asked Dr. West. Ellen looked at him, mimicking the same sense of surprise that he had shown to her.

Dr. Constance laughed and even Miss Herringbone, a sharp-nosed woman who had lost her sense of humor fifty years ago when her first patient died in childbirth, smiled.

"East meets west," said Dr. Constance, smoothing the

sparse white hairs of his moustache, not unaware of Dr. West's response to Ellen.

"Come, *child*," Dr. Constance said to Ellen, using the word purposely. "Come with me while I check on Mrs. Waylock before we turn in. She may have her baby in time for Christmas."

Ellen put her mug in the porcelain sink. She drew herself up. "I am not a child," she said in a voice comfortable in its firmness. "I am seventeen in January."

Dr. West sipped the dregs of his cocoa. There was the answer he had been looking for all day. She was too young. Certainly. Although truly, when one came right down to it, age meant nothing. The lateness of the hour, the excitement of the day, the parcels and letters from home, Ellen's tantalizing presence, filled him. He could not remember whether he had read somewhere that age didn't matter, or if it had been his own private thought.

When Ellen returned at eight from the nativity service Christmas morning, there were brightly wrapped parcels on the main table in the dining room. Heady from the three-hour service, her mind clotted with gold images and the strong perfume of incense, her legs weary, Ellen slumped on a chair. She had not thought of giving gifts, much less receiving them. Oh, there was much to learn in order to survive in this strange world outside of Unaganik.

Remembering that she had tucked Jonah's letter into her pocket, she pulled it out and was so absorbed in the drawing, she didn't hear Dr. West enter the hospital dining room.

"Merry Christmas," he said in a cheerful voice.

Ellen looked up, startled to see Dr. West in his fancy jacket and trousers.

"Ready for church?" he asked, pulling up a chair opposite her.

"I've gone and come back."

"This early?" Dr. West looked disappointed. "I was going to ask if I might accompany you."

"You'd have to have stood on the men's side of the room," explained Ellen. She looked at Dr. West, thinking how out of place he would have looked in his fashionable suit from New York rather than one from a Sears catalogue.

"Maybe it's as well I missed it," said Dr. West, settling more comfortably into the chair. "I feel as if I've been on my feet all month."

"I don't think you have to go to church to worship God," Ellen said.

Dr. West tapped the tips of his fingers together. "Mater would disagree," he said. "She raised me as a god-fearing Episcopalian."

"What's that?" Another piece to assemble in my new life, thought Ellen.

"Church of England," said Dr. West. "Sometimes known as Anglican."

"Oh," said Ellen, relieved. "My daddy told me about that church."

"Is that a letter from him?"

"My daddy doesn't write letters," said Ellen.

"Never?" Dr. West furrowed his high forehead in disbelief.

Ellen shook her head. "He used to deliver mail across the Arctic with a dog team and he swore he'd never put anyone to such trouble just to send a scrap of paper with a few words written on it." Ellen pressed her hand on the letter, flattening the folds. "This is from Jonah. The boy who carves ivory."

"Your boyfriend?" Dr. West's voice crackled like static on the wireless.

"What's a boyfriend?" Ellen asked.

"Someone you love?"

"He's from my village," said Ellen, perplexed by the odd tone in Dr. West's voice. "He lives with the priest and the priest's new wife."

"Will you write to me when I leave?" he asked.

"You can't be leaving," Ellen blurted.

"I plan to sign up with Lieutenant Hardwick. But I hope to be stationed in the Territory of Alaska." Dr. West looked at her with a strange expression. Ellen stared back, dismayed.

Distracted, Dr. West picked up Jonah's letter. On the top third of the paper, Jonah had sketched a picture of himself, standing on a bear rug, playing a violin. To his right was the blue dome of the Russian Orthodox Church, topped by the three-bar cross. To his left, fading into the distant corner, were seven young heads severed from seven round bodies. A man stood in front of them, leaning on an axe.

"Oh my God," Dr. West said, his voice choked. He raised his eyes to Ellen. "Forgive me for swearing"—he waved the paper—"but this is a very unusual Christmas card."

Ellen moved to his chair and, leaning over his shoulder, studied Jonah's sketch again. Dr. West, feeling her slight body against his, stiffened. He gripped the drawing and wondered if he dared ask the meaning of it, dared wonder about the depredations of human nature this gorgeous young woman had seen.

"Will you come back to Harold's Point?" Ellen picked up the stethoscope that lay on the table and rotated its wishbone-shaped earpieces.

In an even tone Dr. West said, "Do you want me to?"

Ellen did not reply. She had slipped the stethoscope around her neck and was listening intently to the beating of her heart.

That same Christmas morning, in Unaganik, the priest, having long given up the idea of an Orthodox Christmas on January 7th, donned his best blood-red robe trimmed with gold. He put a high gold crown on his head. After the long service, Jonah blew out the votive candles. With blackout, and the constant threat of a Japanese invasion, they wanted no light to guide the enemy.

Before leaving the sanctuary, Jonah handed the priest a painting of Jesus on a square slab of weathered wood. It looked like the ikons that adorned the church walls. The priest noted the likeness of Christ's face to his own and felt vaguely disturbed, vaguely pleased. He handed Jonah a present in return. It was a tuning fork, ordered from Seattle, to help Jonah restring and tune the violin Mr. MacTavish had traded for a carved cribbage board.

There were no presents in the MacTavish cabin on the bluff overlooking Bristol Bay. Bonnie helped Cheok boil fishhead soup, roast the "mousefood" nuts they had gathered from the nests under the tundra, and bake brown sugar pudding. Angus settled into a bottle from Merilee and spent the day sipping whiskey. His Raleigh pipe smoke filled the small house.

Charlie fed the dogs before racing into Unaganik to listen to the wireless. The Japanese had bombed and conquered places he had never heard of: Guam, Indochina, Thailand, Wake, Hong Kong. Two warships had been sunk west of Midway.

"It's here." Shushanuk pointed to a dot on the army orientation map.

Charlie studied the map while the voice from KFQD, Anchorage, continued. "Rationing for meat, oil, butter, sugar, and cheese will be in effect Stateside starting January 1942, but will not be in effect in Alaska."

"What's the word on the Japs?" asked Burley with a short bark. He stood in the background scowling as he had scowled since Buddy died.

Shushanuk held his fingers to his lips. The broadcast continued.

"We repeat," said the announcer, "that there is no substance to the rumor that Dutch Harbor and Kodiak are in flames, that Japan has bombed people in Fairbanks and has occupied Sitka and Anchorage. Major General Buckner of the Alaska Defense Command continues to order a constant alert at Fort Richardson and men have been called to arms. We are ready."

"They ain't telling the truth," said Burley.

"Shh," said the other men in the wireless room.

"Plans are in force to intern the resident Japanese," the voice went on. "They will be relocated . . ."

Charlie left the assembled men discussing their preparations for war and darted down the snow-filled road to consult the doctor's dictionary.

"Merry Slaviq," Dr. Visikov said, shaking hands when Charlie arrived.

"Merry Slaviq," Charlie repeated respectfully.

The doctor wiped his gold-rimmed spectacles on a linen handkerchief. "Any word from Ellen?"

"Not since the pilot brought the last letter."

Dr. Visikov replaced his glasses. He missed Ellen. He missed her quiet company, her ability to sense where she needed to put her hands when he was suturing a wound, her sensitivity with the patients. She would be a good doctor, and he had taken steps to be sure that lack of money did not prevent her from becoming one, if she had the inclination to do so. The notification that all was in order had come from his lawyer in Seattle on last week's plane. He was waiting until she returned to Unaganik to tell her himself.

Charlie and the doctor stood silent, connected by thoughts of Ellen. What was she doing during this season when they used to sing carols beside Mrs. Meriweather's pump organ, eat fruitcake laced with brandy, bless the Virgin Mother for bringing Jesus into the world?

Dr. Visikov sighed. "What's the news on the wireless?" he asked, not really wanting to know.

"They're ready in case the Japs bomb Alaska," Charlie answered.

Dr. Visikov looked down into the swarthy young face. In Charlie's dark eyes, so bright and curious, Dr. Visikov saw a will that he knew his own eyes lacked. He pulled off his glasses and polished them again.

"The Japanese have better maps of the Aleutians than we do," muttered the doctor, mostly to himself. "They mapped there in the thirties. Even pulled into Nazan Bay down at Atka and talked to a trader. He passed the word along to the authorities, and the coast and geodetic survey boys hopefully got to work."

"Daddy said the navy's building a base in Dutch Harbor," said Charlie.

"Hope the Japanese don't get that far," sighed Dr. Visikov, knowing that Dutch Harbor was a thousand miles closer to Tokyo than Pearl Harbor.

Charlie moved to the heavy dictionary on its carved oak stand. He leafed through the embossed pages to *I* and then to *R*.

"I'm going to see Jonny the Jap," he said all of a sudden. Leaving the dictionary, he moved toward the door. "He might be in trouble."

The doctor shuffled down the hall to his bed-sitting room in the back of the building. The fire burned in the potbelly stove. He had several hours before he and Mrs. Meriweather were expected at the priest's house for dinner. He dozed and his thoughts drifted to the days when he, too, had been bright and curious and in control of his life, to the days when he thought Alaska was miles of frozen waste and the good life was a thriving medical practice in the city of Seattle with a wife by his side.

In Unalaska, Stewart went to church on Christmas. Unaccustomed to long hours of standing, he fidgeted on the men's side. Gregorian chants drowned the sound of waves lapping on the beach, but above the blue-painted ceiling Stewart could hear the notorious Aleutian wind howling through the cupolas. He shifted position and his eyes met those of a young Aleut woman on the left side of the room. Her smile lit the dark spaces between them. Stewart forgot the cramps in his legs.

"Will you eat Christmas dinner with us?" she asked when church ended.

Stewart hesitated. Of course he could eat on the *Northwestern*, the old steamboat that housed the construction workers building the navy base. But he opted for this dark-skinned beauty and the possibility of some familiar food. "Thank you," he said, smiling.

Her name was Clara Sigs. Her sickly father led a procession of assorted peoples up the beach beside Haystack Hill. Carefree children, scantily clothed against the howling wind, ran here and there. One shot between Stewart's legs. He tossed him, laughing, into the air, and nearly missed catching him for the distraction of Clara's happy face.

Clara opened the door to a small house. Her father headed for the upholstered chair in the corner of the main room and pulled a fur robe, so worn its animal origin was obscure, over his frail shoulders. He coughed into a piece of torn sheeting. Blood seeped through the cloth.

Stewart looked away. He watched Clara working with the other women. On the creaking table they set mallard ducks, broiled with wild onions. Codfish cakes. Piroshki. Crab legs. Seal meat.

Blood dripped out of the seal flesh. Stewart, looking from it to the old man, felt sick. He pushed through the crowd of children into the open air. Rain slanted from an overcast sky. The snowcapped mountains across the bay had disappeared in fog.

Stewart felt earthbound, hampered by his age, by the bizarre fact that he could not fib here, even in Unalaska. Angus had tried to beat up the harbormaster, and had shouted Stewart's age as reason for them to tell him Stewart's whereabouts. When Stewart tried to enlist, he was hired, instead, as a nail banger on the base. "They might lower the enlistment age," the harbormaster said. "You can sign up then."

Still, the knowledge that Angus was looking for him had sunk in. Stewart felt his heart changing. He looked over his shoulder, half expecting to find the anger he had nourished so long. But it was gone. Why carry any more load than one has to, to survive? A foolish old man, that was his father. That Angus was old suddenly struck Stewart. Was Ellen caring for Angus as Clara Sigs cared for her tubercular old father in the upholstered chair? Perhaps he would go back to Unaganik if he could find transportation. Help out there until he could join the air force.

Stewart reentered the stuffy small house and smiled at Clara. She brushed a strand of coal-black hair from her cheek and smiled back.

18

STEWART LAY BESIDE CLARA, his mind as turbulent as the storm that pummeled the small house, his body as rigid as the chalkboard in the construction crew's conference room on the *Northwestern*. It was June and they had been lovers since the first of January. The loving was still new and he wanted her, but wanting was not enough, not tonight when he was so preoccupied with thoughts of war.

Slowly, lazily, Clara rubbed her hand down one side of Stewart's groin, up the other. When nothing happened, she rooted into the stem of his penis with her fingers. Stewart inhaled the fresh scrubbed fragrance of her body and tried to relax. For more than two weeks the area around Dutch Harbor had been on alert. It was only because of the storm that everyone in the town of Unalaska, and the adjacent Fort Mears, had gone to bed.

"What's the matter?" Clara propped up her head to look at him.

Stewart shook his head, amazed that she could not know what was wrong. She knew Japanese aircraft carriers had been spotted in the Aleutians.

"I wish you'd joined me in the *banya*," she said.

"How kin ye think o' steam when we're almost at war?" But despite the sharpness of his tone, past pleasures of mounting Clara on the bench in the *banya* surged through Stewart. He felt his rigid muscles soften into the thin mattress.

The wind howled. Waves whipped along the sheltered beach. There would be none of the famous Japanese Zeroes tonight, not when even the most foolhardy of local PBY

Catalina flying boat pilots refused to leave the ground. There was no reason not to enjoy her.

Stewart smoothed Clara's steam-dampened hair over her shoulders. She licked his neck, and with her finger played with the tip of his penis. The old father coughed in the adjacent room. Clara sat up.

"Are ye goin' ta him?" Stewart asked.

Clara shook her head no and straddled Stewart. He pulled her to him. His pulsing penis found its own special entrance and Stewart thrust hard and high, his pent-up emotions beating like stream-bound salmon through his blood.

"Easy," whispered Clara above him. She reached back and squeezed his testicles. Suddenly he had more time, more breath.

Stewart held himself as she had taught him those early days when he came too fast and she demanded her share of the pleasure. She rocked now, back and forth, rolling her inner lips across his weight. He burrowed his face in her breasts. Clara swirled like thick fog above him and she was Lucy, the girl in Anchorage, but then he was gone, spent, and still the wind howled. Clara moaned and rocked and finally she, too, got her pleasure. She sunk sideways, curling her back against his chest, and fell asleep. Stewart cradled his arm over her, cupping one of her breasts.

The old man wheezed in a half-sleep, but Stewart felt like mist floating above the williwaws that broke against the wild, rugged coastline of the Aleutian chain, felt caught between time and space, as if, without the storm clouds pressing down on the island, he would rise into the ether.

Stewart longed to stretch, but if he did, he was likely to push Clara on the floor. They had to sleep coiled together to get enough room for each of them on the single bed. He thought of Ellen and Bonnie sharing a cot. He thought of how Ellen had learned to stifle her restless limbs, and how she spent nights without sleep, unable to release her hold on the world for fear of disappearing from it.

Stewart could not tell how he knew these things about Ellen. The knowledge came from a place he did not analyze, but where he knew Ellen's mind, better—did he dare to believe?—than she did herself. He had rescued her, hadn't he? Surely it was no accident that he'd been given the book to divert him from going to Unaganik. Without that he would not have returned to the beach and saved Ellen's life. Without saving her life he could not have found the courage to leave Angus's beatings. Nor would he have found the platinum. Maybe there was something to God's plan. The platinum was safely stored on the *Northwestern* and soon he'd be able to take it home to Ellen, and she'd use it to get her education. Stewart went over the sequence of events as he had often during long nights in the past. Now it was different. Now he had reason to return, to make up to Ellen for his absence.

At dawn, the air raid siren wailed as usual. Clara slept, but Stewart lay wide-eyed and tense until the steady tone of the all clear sounded. Then he relaxed and prepared for whatever the day brought. Weak traces of dawn lightened Clara's broad face. Her long hair, still damp, circled her neck. Tempted to loosen it, he stopped his hand, not ready for the consequences of waking her.

Clara was shaped like a fish-packing box. She was square and much sturdier than Ellen, whose birdlike bones gave her a dainty look. But Ellen was deceptive. Under that daintiness was a will that wouldn't budge. In many ways Clara, despite her size, was soft as a woman should be soft. She'd become someone's wife and would be content to live her life within the treeless shoreline of Unalaska.

Stewart had these thoughts until, deep within the well of his ear, he heard the sounds the town had given up waiting for. Airplanes. He shot into his boots, parka, and out the door. Still distant, the planes droned forward, black notes on a drum of sky.

"Sound the alarm! Sound the alarm!" Stewart's voice boomed through the morning. The planes droned forward.

Looking toward the harbor, Stewart saw that the ships anchored there—a seaplane tender, two army transports, a coast guard cutter, a submarine, and a four-stack destroyer— were getting up steam in their boilers. They obviously knew about the planes and were not worried. The steamship *Northwestern,* where Stewart usually slept, was permanently beached on Amaknak Island. It had gone aground during a williwaw, and, secured by concrete ballast, there was no possibility of it getting out of the way in the event of an attack. Stewart worried about his poke of platinum on the ship and studied the approaching aircraft with apprehension.

The aircraft flew in a typical American formation. It's the fleet we've expected all along, he thought. American planes arriving to protect us. Stewart waved his arms in the air, excited, feeling himself up there navigating the wind. But when the planes sunk lower and started diving toward the army base, he saw solid red circles on the wings. Japs! A bomb dropped. One of the white frame barracks Stewart had helped to build went up in flames. Flak burst from the rooftop of Fort Mears.

A woman screamed. Her voice crossed the water and reached Stewart an instant before flak burst from one of the transport ships. Flames reached the grey sky. Black smoke spewed in a stench of burning wood. A flock of brant skimmed the water, looking for a place to hide. Stewart raced down the beach, the laces on his boots whipping around his ankles.

The high vibrating whine of the air raid siren sounded at last. The bells of the Russian Orthodox church rang, filling in the silence between the two-minute fluctuating alarm. Stewart, distracted, tripped and fell sideways. He looked straight up and into the goggle-covered eyes of a Japanese pilot who stared down at him through the curved glass cockpit of his Zero. The plane zoomed upward. Without waiting to see whether he circled for attack, Stewart scrambled from the ground and, reversing direction, headed full speed toward the foxholes hastily dug when Japanese warships were spotted in the Chain two weeks ago.

"Run!" Clara screeched from the door of the house. "Run."

Her father, alarmed by the fright in her voice, joined her at the door.

Stewart heard the plane, felt the stare of the pilot into his back, felt his own hands on the stick as if pulling himself up and away. Bullets from the wing guns whipped past his feet. He sprang into the air and dove headfirst into the deep foxhole. The dirt edging the hole collapsed, completely covering Stewart.

Clara ran to him. She clawed at the dirt like a blue fox,

spraying it behind her in grey gusts. Willy-nilly the Zeroes strafed, rose, and circled. The larger Kate bombers loosed heavier loads onto the islands and harbor. Dense black smoke grew like a rain cloud, but Clara did not notice. Stewart lay under the dirt.

Clara's old father hobbled to the trench, arriving at the same moment that Clara struck a boot. "Keep going, girl," he wheezed.

Clara did not need encouragement. Stewart, her Stewart, the father of the baby taking shape inside her, lay headfirst in this hole. Smoke dusted her hair, eyes, lungs. Her nose clogged with the smell of gunpowder. Her ears rang with the sound. She dug at the dirt, emptying the hole, ignoring everything but the spot where Stewart lay.

The old father kneeled beside her, his bony fingers raking away the dirt. He convulsed with coughing.

Intent on her digging, Clara ignored him until, too weak to spit, his bloody sputum dribbled on the dirt next to her. She looked up and looked straight into the gun barrel of an approaching Zero that she had not heard, so dulled were her ears by the bombing. Her old father, in a burst of remembered strength, threw himself on top of her. The plane passed over, shooting at two soldiers climbing a cliff to a concrete bunker.

Clara sucked on her cheeks for saliva and spat out grit. "How long can he live?" She choked out the words.

"He be fine," said the old father, who never, even in his own illness, admitted that he was sick. To admit sickness brought defeat. To admit Stewart would suffocate, ensured it would happen.

The pads of Clara's fingers bled. Stewart's leg was free. One leg. Then another. She worked with a fury, burrowing her hands through the dirt. "Get out," she screamed. "Get out!"

She hung over the hole, her hands grasping the skin on the sides of his waist. She dug her fingers into the band of muscle across his stomach and yanked. There was no response.

Stewart's knee-length parka had slipped up, exposing his blond hairy legs, his buttocks, and finally his testicles, which had turned blue.

"Keep on, girl," wheezed her old father.

Clara dropped into the hole, straddling Stewart. More

dirt caved in and she scooped out handfuls while the old father, wheezing, raked dirt from above the hole, widening it.

Then Clara crawled out. She yanked off Stewart's boots, tugged on his white ankles until the sockets in her shoulders snapped like bolts from a twisted cable. The old father put his bony arms around her waist, locked his fingers together and tugged with Clara. It was not her father's strength but his love that gave Clara the energy she needed. Stewart's limp body shifted. She let go of his legs. They dropped sideways.

Gunpowder filled her lungs like caustic soda. She thought she knew what it must mean to have tuberculosis: to suffocate.

"Again," urged her old father.

Clara prayed to Saint Nicholas, the miracle worker, whose ikoned face smiled from a wall on the Russian Orthodox church. She lifted up the parka and dirt cascaded into a vacuum that had been formed by the spread of Stewart's jacket.

Clara looked at her father and whispered, "He be in an airpocket."

"What I say," he wheezed back. "He be fine."

With the help of the good saint, Clara pulled again. Stewart shifted. Clara braced her feet, took a deep breath, and with one long pull hauled Stewart out of the hole. He tumbled onto the ground beside her, his eyes open but with only the whites visible.

The old father slapped Stewart's head back and forth. "Come here," the old father wheezed. "Come here."

Stewart felt the wind on his face, remembered his poke. He had to get the platinum for... "Ellen!" he called and opened his eyes. He stared at Clara for one brief second, bewildered that it was not his sister, then closed his eyes. The old father slapped his face, one side, the other, until Stewart rolled over and away. He rolled onto his knees and twitched like a sled dog at the end of a long run. Clara threw herself on top of him and hugged him until the twitching ceased.

"Hurry!" Clara grabbed his arm. "We get out of here."

"What?" Stewart was still bewildered. He teetered to his feet.

"We go to our fish camp." Clara's father stood between them, his bony hands on each of their arms.

"Can you walk it?" Clara asked him.

"I not stay here and be eaten by Japs," said the old father.

Back at the house, Clara filled a handmade basket with rice and another with tea.

"As long as tide goes out, we eat," said the old father, pushing her away from the kitchen.

Stewart pulled on his pants and started to roll up some bedding.

"We have plenty there," Clara said. "Let's go."

With the throb of guns behind them, they headed up the high dirt trail to the fish camp. The harbor disappeared into black smoke.

At the top of the second hill, Clara's father crumpled into a heap. Stewart, although feeling none too steady himself, picked up the sickly man and slung him over his back. The old man gnarled his fingers together under Stewart's chin and wrapped his legs around Stewart's waist. Stewart hoisted him higher over his shoulders and braced his legs with his arms.

Clara looked at him, her black eyes like the core of an Aleutian volcano. Stewart jutted his chin forward, motioning her ahead, forestalling any talk of whether he had strength left to carry her father. It had to be done.

Miles later, Stewart's back ached although Mr. Sigs weighed less than the hundred-pound sacks of coal he had hauled for Clara during the past winter.

The contrast between his own deep breaths and those shallow breaths of the tubercular man, the purity of the sea-tossed wind filling his own strong body, the debt he owned Clara for each clean breath, filled Stewart's soul. He felt something new, some fresh gulp of an emotion that had fermented since Mutuk died under the reindeer's hooves. It was an emotion not spoken in the MacTavish household and yet lavishly embroidered on the satin pillows sold at the canteen. *Love*. But for Stewart it was love at its undecorated best.

Overhead, clouds lowered and blackened. An eagle glided by on an updraft. The wind pushed sideways and Stewart struggled to keep his boots on the hill.

"Quick!" called Clara, swerving toward a huge round boulder. Stewart, with Mr. Sigs banging against his back, followed. Clara led them into a dank cave. The ground above them rumbled. Peering up, Stewart saw Japanese warplanes heading southwest into storm clouds, away from the island.

"Where be United States ducks?" asked Clara, using the native expression for airplanes. "I thought there be a secret base west of Unalaska."

Stewart shrugged. He felt as if he didn't know anything anymore, didn't know why planes hadn't come to their rescue or why Dutch Harbor had been bombed in the first place.

Sitting in this dank cave, resting his back, the old father coughing, Clara warm against his side, he tried not to compare this hole with the foxhole. Despite his will, he felt penned in. He wanted to dart out in the rain, get wet, anything but be enclosed in these dirt walls. Now that he had time to sit, to catch his breath, the experience of nearly smothering in the foxhole caught up with him. Yet this was no time to think about what might have happened. He was safe, thanks to Clara.

They huddled in the cave until the planes passed. Coming out, it seemed as if nothing had disturbed the world, as if nothing had changed in thousands of years. Vitas Bering and Georg Stellar had not arrived to label the wildlife. There were no *promyshlenniks,* fortune hunters from Russia with their own brand of massacre. A salmon steam gurgled over rocks, and Stewart breathed in the sweet smell of grass.

"Where's the wind?" he asked, feeling his hair flat on his head for the first time since he had been on the island of Unalaska.

"Don't speak of it," said the old father. "You'll bring a storm."

Stewart laughed out loud. A gull squawked in response.

A mile later they left the main trail and dipped over a moonlit hill toward the fish camp. Clara led the way down a ladder into their *barabara,* a dirt-sided dwelling cut into the hills. It was pungent with moisture, but as soon as his eyes adjusted to the dimness, Stewart found straw on a bunk and laid Mr. Sigs down. Clara covered her father with a fur robe. Then, as if sensing Stewart's tenseness at being underground again, she gathered up a large rug made of fur seal skins and taking his hand, pulled him outside to the hill. They climbed down the muskeg to the boulder-strewn beach. The tide was far out. The waves broke against sea stacks, the massive pinnacles of rocks standing offshore like sentries. Seaweed perfumed the air. Sea lions snorted into the water.

Clara wound her way down a narrow trail past the huge boulders. Stewart, following, drew deep breaths of salt air. He marveled at the feelings these sounds and smells brought racing back to him—of the hours picking fish with Ellen. He felt transported back to Unaganik, as if the ensuing years had vanished like stains on a bleached cloth.

Clara spread the fur on a level spot and they sat side by side, watching the waves roll under the gauze of moonlight that spilled through a fissure in the black clouded sky.

Taking a deep breath, Clara blurted, "Who's Ellen?"

"Ellen?" Stewart drew into himself. Had Clara read his thoughts?

"You called her name," persisted Clara.

"She's my sister," said Stewart slowly, remembering that he'd left his poke in his locker back on the *Northwestern*.

Clara, in her delight at his answer, forgot the night chill and pulled at Stewart's clothes.

"What's this?" Stewart drew her hands to him, kissed the raw pads on her fingers. He threw back his head, laughing and suddenly feeling free of everything, even the needs of this woman.

Clara smiled and pushed him back onto the fur. Its softness caressed his aching back while the salt air cooled the blond hairs just beginning to pad his muscled chest. He breathed deep and slow and felt no hurry. She could do what she wished. Clara caressed him until he no longer felt the damp chill off the water but only the warmth of her hands above the silky fur.

Stewart let himself feel Clara, as if he were feeling her for the first time. He felt the roundness of her belly without realizing that it had once been flat, so urgent, at other times, had been his need for intercourse.

Clara, sensing the difference in Stewart, responded as he traced his finger over the lines of her shoulders, her muscled upper arms, the broadness of her strong forearms that had saved his life. Her body softened. Feeling the delicious tingle of her skin, he closed his eyes. She cradled his head between her breasts. Stewart rolled Clara over, rolled on top of her, supporting his weight above her with his hands on the velvety fur. He thrust himself long and slow into her until her moans mingled with the wind and he felt as if they were intermingling with each other, with the universe, until none were indistinguishable. Then, except for the roar of water against the sea stacks, there was silence.

The tide turned while they lay rolled together in the rug. Stewart heard the approaching lap of water and woke. The sky was light beneath a continuously moving screen of grey clouds. Red-legged kittiwakes flew over the high water.

Stewart dressed quickly. He wrapped Clara in the rug and carried her up the hill and into the shelter where the old father's pulpy lungs bubbled for air.

Stewart rolled Clara into a second bunk and tucked the fur around her. He loved her, but he needed to get his poke of platinum and find a way to Unaganik.

Clara squeezed her fingers into fists until the raw pads of her fingertips screamed with pain. She wanted to blurt out about the baby growing inside her, their baby, but she did not.

Stewart grabbed the rungs of the ladder and left the *barabara*.

19

OBLIVIOUS TO THE RAIN stinging his face, Stewart scanned the sky. The distant drum of engines beat against his ear. The path that had seemed so silent and comforting yesterday had turned into a death trap today. There were no trees, not even scrub willows, and Stewart plunged across the mushy ground, searching for a cave.

Zeroes bellied in under the rain clouds. Before they could sight him, Stewart hunkered into a ball, pulled the fur parka over his blond hair, and prayed that the pilots, now overhead, would take him for a brownie on a hillside that had never seen bears.

The sound shredded the silence. When the planes disappeared toward Dutch Harbor, Stewart started to run in the same direction. The *ack-ack* reached him first. After pausing a minute to plan his next move, Stewart headed to the backside of the hill directly across the harbor from where the *Northwestern* was beached. He knew Vassily Trovich kept a kayak down there and, God willing, it would be an easy matter to paddle across to Amaknak and rescue his poke.

In addition to the Zeroes, heavy bombers circled overhead. Spikes of orange and red shot into the sky, collapsing downward into a blackened sea. The ships that had been in the harbor yesterday were gone and anti-aircraft guns from bunkers embedded in the hills surrounded the harbor aimed at the circling airplanes.

Stewart climbed the hill. As he reached the crest, he saw a thousand pounder spin from the bowels of an enemy bomber. Heaving himself the last fifty feet, praying for the safety of his poke, Stewart reached the lookout just as a second bomb landed on the rear deck of the *Northwestern*. He shuddered as screams broke between the chatter of guns and the crackle of fire. Horrified, Stewart saw the tiny shapes of burning men jump off the *Northwestern* and realized that his poke of platinum was gone in the blaze of the old steamship. Now he had no chance to help Ellen.

Gunfire roared between harbor and sky. A thousand pounder whistled so close by, its force seemed to shift the entire top of the cliff toward the harbor. Stewart dug his fists into the muskeg and hung on. Rocks sprayed down the cliff face and smashed a hundred feet below. The cliff resettled. Stewart tasted blood. He'd bitten through the soft fleshy inside of both cheeks.

Flames burst skyward, spreading the acrid stench of burning oil over the harbor. Must have got one of those new fuel tanks, thought Stewart and, gagging from the fumes, he ripped a band of cloth from his shirt and tied it over his mouth. His lungs felt pulverized. He forced himself to his feet, stumbling toward a bunker dug into the side of the cliff not a hundred yards to his left.

A bomber circled overhead and suddenly a flash burst in the bunker. An instant later it exploded with a thunderous boom. Stewart spun back, feeling utterly exposed on the barren ridge. Desperate, he turned right, without thought, toward the hopeful safety of another bunker. Eons later, he reached the second bunker, where a GI swiveled an antiaircraft gun at the sky while a soot-faced boy fed in the belt of bullets.

Stewart grabbed an unmanned rifle, but before he could find the trigger, the soot-faced boy pushed him away. "Over there," he screamed into Stewart's ear. Stewart jumped to the bullet belt to feed it into the anti-aircraft gun.

Gunfire ricocheted off the concrete walls. When the attackers dropped their last payload and disappeared over the island, Stewart barely heard the soot-faced boy say: "Butch is the name. Where'd you come from?"

Stewart took the proffered hand but before he could speak, the gunner banged his helmet and shouted: "Hey! Didn't we let go a salvo on those bastards! We taught them a thing or two with our Archies!"

Stewart ducked outside, crouched on his haunches, and waited for the clanging in his ears to cease. Smoke frothed from the *Northwestern*. He closed his eyes and saw a molten lump of precious platinum somewhere in the bowels of that ship.

"Lucky?"

"What the hell?" Stewart's eyes flared open. "Ye call that luck?" he almost said until he noticed that Butch was only offering him a lighted cigarette.

"Thanks." Stewart inhaled deeply. The bitten sides of his mouth smarted but the smoke soothed his lungs, replacing the acrid fumes that seemed to linger there.

Stewart handed back the cigarette, but Butch shook his head. He lit a second from a squashed pack in his breast pocket and then a third when the gunner joined them.

"Let's get down," said the gunner.

"Don't be in such a tall hurry," said Butch, settling into his smoke.

"Ye better wait till dark," said Stewart. "The planes might return."

"Don't wanna go down that trail in the dark," said the gunner. "Rather get killed by a bullet than step off that trail and smash onto the beach."

"I know the trail by heart," said Stewart. "I'll tak' ye down."

"You musta lived here awhiles," said the gunner.

Stewart nodded.

"Then maybe you can tell me something."

"Maybe."

"Who wants to die for Dutch Harbor?" sneered the gunner.

"You're not going to die today," Butch replied. "The Nips are gone."

Dark descended on the mountains and Stewart led the two soldiers down the trail, across the harbor with the skiff they had brought over, and finally into the mess hall at Fort Mears. He didn't even try to make his way to the *Northwestern*. He had already seen the bad news.

"Excuse me." Stewart hoisted his long legs over the bench. He left Butch at the table and headed to the end of the mess hall where he planned to try, once again, to join the air force.

A man known as Rosebud, because of the odor surrounding him, belched in a rum-soaked voice: "Here's a man for ye, Colonel Kelly."

The colonel, on assignment from the Alaska Defense Command, faced Stewart with his chin at a sharp upturned angle to account for Stewart's greater height, then lowered his gaze as if searching for hidden flaws. In a voice expecting an honest answer, Colonel Kelly asked: "Do you know Alaskan waters?"

"Lived here all his life," interrupted Rosebud. "And his father plays it straight. I know the kind of lad he'd turn out."

Damn you, cursed Stewart, surprising himself at the sudden flare of anger he thought gone. What do you know about Angus and me?

"Been on his own a long time," continued Rosebud. "Not afraid of a thing."

Only the *idigadich,* thought Stewart, thinking of Clara's stories of the "Outsiderman" who snatched up wandering children.

"You born here?" the colonel asked Stewart.

"You bet a sweet tittie," said Rosebud.

Stewart glowered at Rosebud. Unaganik was a good five hundred miles east by northeast.

"Part native," added Rosebud, as if it were a medal.

"I'm recruiting a special force of scouts," said Colonel Kelly.

Stewart studied the colonel. He stood not more than five foot five and looked as if he hadn't slept since the bombing of Pearl Harbor. "Kin I learn ta fly?" Stewart asked.

"Ain't old enough," interjected Rosebud, and at that moment Stewart hated him more than he had ever imagined himself hating anyone. Even Angus.

"Old enough for the Scouts." The colonel continued in a low voice that excluded their companion. "We've some tough missions ahead, but if you join us, I will personally see that you get a chance in the air when they're over."

Stewart stood stock still. The clatter of metal dishes, the chink of coins put down beside poker chips filled the mess hall. Special force? What was that compared to being a fly boy?

"Word of honor," said the colonel. "After we clear the enemy out of the Aleutians, I'll recommend you for flight training."

Stewart fought to keep his face still. Flight training. But he wanted it now, not after the war was over and the Japanese had gone home. "Have they landed?" he asked, sparring for time to sort his inner thoughts.

"That'll be your job to find out," said the colonel.

"Hardly vorth bothering about the islands farther out the Chain," said a Swedish Alaskan who had been lounging against the wall.

The colonel spun on his heel. "You know the country down there?"

"Not vat you'd call country," said the Swede. "Yust a bunch of rocks."

"Arne here can land a skiff where even a native wouldn't dare," interjected Rosebud. His breath fouled the air and Stewart stepped closer to Arne.

"Join me!" Colonel Kelly stared first at Arne and then back to Stewart. It was then that Stewart noticed the grey look in the colonel's eyes, the look of a man who had killed with bare hands and found it repugnant, but who, nevertheless, had the courage to teach others to do the same. "We're leaving on the *Dolphin* at fourteen hundred hours, providing the enemy isn't in our way."

Stewart studied Colonel Kelly and made no reply. The buzz of mess noise faded and he heard only the wind howling over the corrugated roof, tugging at the straps the construction workers put on the last time the wind yanked the roof off altogether.

"I'll expect you there." With that, the colonel turned on his heel and marched out of the hall.

It was too late to run back to the fish camp and to Clara. He wondered if he had ever intended to, after finding his poke. But then he realized that if he'd rescued the poke he'd have wanted to hitch a ride up to Unaganik, to take it to Ellen. Did Clara know he wasn't coming back? Would she wait for him? Did he want her to? Having no notion what he wanted to do next, knowing that if he couldn't join the air force anything else was a poor poker hand, Stewart tromped down the beach to Clara's abandoned house.

He woke in a sheet of sweat at first light. The Japanese gunner had been aiming for him and, when he looked at his eyes, they took on the shape and color of Colonel Kelly's. Stewart rolled out of bed, wide awake.

He climbed the hill above Clara's house. The air was calm. Tiny flowers bloomed white and yellow among new tufts of grass. Blackened shapes blotted the harbor. Stewart rested his eyes on the rugged volcanic peaks, visible in a rare display of beauty. He stretched backward onto a dry stony patch of ground and rested his head on his hands. For once, his impulse to act failed him, and he stared at the drifting clouds, wondering what he should do next.

Hours later, stiff and cold, he stood up. His muscles shook as if an electric current were passing through them. Stomping to bring his legs back to life, he noticed a grey seiner anchored offshore. Wondering if it might be a way to hitch a ride, he climbed down the hill. Borrowing Vassily Trovich's kayak, he paddled toward the seiner.

Although the boat was the *Yethl* and unknown to him, Stewart called to the Tlingit Indian coiling a hawser on deck. "Any chance ye might be goin' ta Bristol Bay?"

"We're supposed to evacuate the Aleuts to the southeast," said the young man. He was rock hard, but each movement blended with the sway of the boat like an eagle on an updraft.

"Aleuts? Why?"

"Government wants them off the islands. Don't ask me why."

Stewart shrugged, glad that Clara and her father were safely out of sight. Mr. Sigs would die for sure if he were moved from his favorite island.

Stewart shifted in the kayak. "Ha'e ye been ta Unaganik at all?" he asked, knowing that he wanted to make conversation just to postpone his decision about joining Colonel Kelly's mission.

"Not this year." The Tlingit's voice changed. He looked over the rail at Stewart. "But I'm going back there some day soon."

"Take a word fer me ta Ellen MacTavish." Stewart

looked up from the water at the bronzed face with its characteristic high cheekbones. The young man's expression anchored him, despite the bobbing of the kayak.

"I know Ellen MacTavish," said the Tlingit. His black eyes didn't blink.

"Ye do? Ye know me Ellen?" Stewart felt his pulse rise.

"Yes," said the Tlingit, seemingly without emotion.

"Do I know ye?" Stewart asked, wracking his brain to remember if he had met anyone from Southeast Alaska.

"Maybe." The young man motioned Stewart to the stern of the *Yethl* and dropped a line. Stewart tied the kayak to it and scrambled on board.

"Ted Kleet," said the young man.

About the same height, they both looked like young men muscled by hard work and heavy loads. Whereas Ted Kleet looked as if he knew his own mind, Stewart felt as if Ted could read the indecision clouding his thoughts. Stewart's blond hair dangled over his high forehead and drifted too long past his ears while Ted's hair was cropped to his skull and seemed blue-black under the dullness of the sky.

Ted Kleet stuck out his hand and grabbed Stewart's. "I'll hand wrestle you for her," he said. "If I win, you leave her alone."

"Alone?" Stewart's confusion deepened.

Ted Kleet mistook the meaning. "How well do you know her?" His voice sawed through Stewart, who recognized an assurance in it that he thought his own voice lacked.

"Who?" Stewart asked, feeling the grip on his hand tighten.

"Ellen MacTavish."

"I'm Stewart MacTavish. Ellen is me sister."

Ted almost shook Stewart's arm out of its socket. Then he let go and planted his hands on his hips, his eyes shining.

"When did you see her last?" said Stewart, aching for news and not fully realizing what was going on between him and Ted.

"Before the war." Ted Kleet stood with his legs apart, his hands still at his waist. He spoke as if he had known Stewart a lifetime and was only revealing the obvious. "Of course I'll marry Ellen when she's through school."

"Marry her?"

"Yes."

It was said so simply, so surely, Stewart could not doubt the outcome. He envied Ted Kleet, having his future so surely mapped. But marry Ellen? His little sister? "She's still a kid," he said. "And a stubborn one at that."

"I'm not marrying her now," said Ted Kleet. "I'm marrying her when she grows up."

How his words brought back memories. Hadn't Cheok been only a kid when she married Angus? Stewart ran his hands through his hair. It suddenly became clear how Cheok had been stunted by the death of her parents, by the orphanage, and how part of her had stayed at that young age. How had she ever managed to be Angus's wife?

Stewart tested the knot tying the kayak to the rail, seeing Clara instead of the rope. Had he used Clara the same way as Angus used Cheok? Was he, in fact, following his father's example in other ways. Such as the way in which he left home? Stewart knew Angus had never written home to Scotland, had let them all think he was dead. So many things seemed so obvious all of a sudden there on that swaying deck with this young man who was insisting that he would marry Ellen. More power to him. "May ye be happy," Stewart said, hoping his voice conveyed the words, although inside he felt suddenly and enormously sad.

Ted Kleet grabbed Stewart's hand and pummeled his back. "I'm forgetting my manners," he said. "Come into the galley."

"Tell me," said Ted when they were seated at the tiny table sipping black tea. "When did you leave Unaganik?"

"June Thirty-seven."

"Did you leave to go to school?"

"Nae." Stewart rotated the thick crockery mug in his hands. The steam lifted and whirled. "Other reasons. Nae. I dinna want ta go ta school, but did ye say Ellen was at school?" he added, perking up.

"She's gone down to Harold's Point," said Ted. "Or so I heard."

Stewart gulped a mouthful of tea, ballooned one cheek with the hot bitter liquid and bounced it into the other cheek. The sides of his mouth still stung. He gulped the tea, playing his tongue along the inner flesh of his cheeks, trying to smooth the broken skin. So Ellen had got the courage to leave home. She was going to school and he didn't need to worry about her. The *Yethl* rocked and Stewart looked out the salt-crusted porthole. A narrow sub slid through the water, maneuvering into the dock.

"I bet they don't have trouble with williwaws in that mousetrap," said Ted as they looked at the sub. It was called the *Dolphin*.

"I guess I'm goin' ta find out," said Stewart.

On deck, he shook Ted's hand. "All the best with Ellen. Tell her I . . ." But the words he really wanted to say didn't form so he nodded his head and climbed into the kayak without adding more.

"Good luck!" Ted called over the bow.

Stewart raised his paddle in salute.

"Spent most of my life trying to stay on top of the water," Arne said when Stewart joined him on the dock where the *Dolphin* was berthed. Arne carried a bulging Trapper Nelson pack that held treasures and curiosities from the sixty-five years of his life. A thick green rain slicker dangled over his arm.

Butch sauntered up to them. "You joinin' the cut-throats?"

Stewart nodded.

"They're up to some pretty tall shenanigans, I hear." Butch offered Stewart a Lucky and he took it, storing it in the inner pocket of his twill shirt.

Colonel Kelly marched down the dock. He preceded Arne and Stewart onto the bobbing surface of the sub. Stewart, taking one last look around, saw Ted Kleet standing on the bow of the *Yethl*. Their eyes met. I should have told him all kinds of things to tell Ellen, Stewart thought, but with Arne waiting behind him, he descended without delay.

The engines roared into action. Water rushed past the narrow sides of the submarine. It slipped out the narrow entrance to the inner harbor, past Mount Ballyhoo, and into the Bering Sea. Someone in the galley clanked a mug against the metal table. They heard him say, "To Victory!"

Stewart folded his arms across his stomach and hunkered down. His legs stiffened. It had been a long time since he had squatted like Mutuk, so long that he had to struggle to remember the smell of reindeer.

Colonel Kelly spread a map on the floor. It had been made during the Russian survey of 1812.

"That harbor on Akutan is the best you'll find," said Arne, pointing to the island east of Unaganik. "Wouldn't surprise me if the Japs had landed there. They were all over these waters in the Thirties, mapping the islands."

Colonel Kelly looked at Arne across the crowded bunkroom floor. "We're heading west to Adak," he said, and Stewart shivered, seeing the grey look in the colonel's eyes turn to steel.

20

ARNE ROWED THE RUBBER dinghy into the black night. They watched the *Dolphin* submerge behind them. Stewart, sitting in the stern, pulled his watchcap over his blackened hair and face. He wished for a Players, Navy cut, or even one of Butch's Luckies. Had he known three months ago, after that second and final attack on Dutch Harbor, what he knew about war tonight—Monday, September 7, 1942—he would have returned to Clara and never acquired a taste for tobacco.

That the future held the promise of flying seemed unworthy of attention. In five weeks of training under Colonel Kelly, Stewart had shed all but the ambition to survive. At last, at the end of the most grueling weeks of their lives, the colonel had proclaimed the "Scouts" his equal. For Stewart that unqualified acceptance was his graduation into manhood. It no longer mattered that he once wanted that acceptance from Angus. As he sat in the dinghy, shrouded by the long shadow of night, he suffered no pangs of unfinished business of the soul.

Arne rowed west into enemy territory. The black water slipped past. A splash suddenly soaked their bow. The Professor, a forty-year-old Nisei conscripted from a relocation camp by the colonel, jumped.

"A seal," Stewart whispered and grinned to reassure the Professor, who sat beside him. "If a seal can'na hear us, the Japs willna."

Quietly, their breath the only sound in the darkness, the four men slipped toward Kiska Harbor. The colonel had chosen carefully for this mission. Besides Stewart and the Professor, Arne the Swede had been picked because he could row without sound, a trick he had learned poaching fur seals in the Pribilofs.

The fourth member, the squat man who sat in the bow, was Sigori, an Aleut in his early twenties. Sigori swore that he knew every nook, cranny, and rock on Kiska from many seasons of trapping foxes. Furthermore, he knew each buried *barabara* where U.S. Navy weathermen, stranded on the island during the June 1942 Japanese invasion, might hide. But no one believed the navy men were still alive. They were not the purpose of this mission.

Soon they heard water hitting shore. Stark rock walls loomed above them. A sentry on top could not have seen them, so black was the night and so close the fog. Arne rowed adjacent to the shoreline, rounding a bluff known as North Head. Beneath them, anti-submarine nets crisscrossed the harbor entrance, a fact the *Dolphin* had discovered on other maneuvers.

The tenor of the waves changed, crashing louder as they rowed closer. Sigori jabbed his arm toward the cliff. Arne positioned the dinghy and they hung onto the gunwales as the dinghy swept through the crashing waves and through a cut in the outlying sea stacks. They entered an enclosed pool of calm water. Around them on all sides the cliff walls disappeared into the black sky.

"You'll be safe here," Sigori whispered.

Arne nodded. Colonel Kelly had ordered him to stay with the dinghy while Sigori, Stewart, and the Professor went ashore. Arne, who hadn't obeyed orders in sixty-five years, went along with the colonel, even though he had joined the Scouts only out of a sense of adventure.

Sigori leaped onto a scrap of beach, searched the base of the cliff for booby traps, then beckoned. The Professor alighted. Stewart felt his Bowie knife lashed to his left leg and then he, too, jumped to the ambivalent comfort of solid ground. Looking back at Arne, Stewart tapped his wristwatch, a present from the colonel. Arne patted his gold-scrolled pocket watch. If all went well, they'd meet here at four hundred hours. In five hours.

Sigori led up the cliff face. The Professor followed.

Stewart rubbed the cliff, found a handhold and heaved himself up. Above him, the Professor ascended into the darkness. The water crashing around the narrow cut through the sea stacks drowned out their sounds.

Sigori grunted. When he found another handhold, they continued up, their breath echoing between their chests and the cliff face. The wind rushed beneath them. An external force seemed to place Stewart's hands and feet in the right place. He felt protected, almost joyful despite the danger of infiltrating enemy-occupied territory and the more immediate danger of the hundred-foot cliff.

A tufted puffin flew from its nest. Deep below water foamed.

Stewart felt as if all his senses were on alert. He felt another awareness, too, and in the instant before it happened, he froze, wary, into the rock. Two soldiers, jabbering in Japanese, thudded overhead, their boots kicking against stones. When they left, the Professor whispered, ''They complain because the other two on patrol have trench foot and they must cover all the installations. It's luck for us.''

Sigori searched the clifftop for wires. Finding none, he, Stewart, and the Professor scrambled over. They raced toward the black ominous shape of an anti-aircraft gun, the only object on the horizon behind which they could hide. After a pause, and not hearing the sentries, they took off, three black humps against a dark and barren landscape. They headed inland, away from North Head, at a diagonal to the long harbor where they knew from aerial photographs that the Japanese were encamped. The camp was below a hill that leveled onto the only possible place for an airbase on mountainous Kiska.

No one wanted the dreaded Zeroes landbased in the Aleutians, especially with an Allied buildup planned for Adak, five hundred miles to the east. The Scouts' purpose was to destroy any equipment suitable for construction of such an airfield.

They ran crouched over the ground, until Stewart's boot struck metal. The sound echoed. The men dropped into the mud. Stewart, rummaging, found an axe and slipped it through his belt. Hand tools? He shook his head. The Nips won't get very far building a landing strip with axes.

"Spread out," whispered Sigori, handing the Professor the end of a heavy string. Taking the bulk of it with him, Sigori crawled into the night. Fifty yards away, he tugged the string. Stewart crawled until he reached the knot in the middle. They snaked over the muskeg, praying the string would locate any machinery they missed in the dark.

Mud oozed through their clothes, into their skin. The muskeg had been turned up, disturbed, but they found no tools larger than double-headed picks. Stewart pulled off his watchcap, patted his sweating face, being careful not to wipe the thick grease that blackened his skin. He checked his watch. Two hours gone.

Stewart yanked on the string. Sigori joined him. Together they reached the Professor at the same time a light slashed the darkness like a samurai sword. The Professor jumped. Stewart clasped his shoulder, trying to put his own sense of calm into the older man. It was a calm the colonel had cultivated in the Scouts, knowing their missions depended on it. The Professor, so called because he had once taught at college, had not had the same strenuous training.

The light moved along the bottom of the hill, parallel to their eyes. An Oriental voice spoke in English. "Dog? Whur dog?"

"He can't sleep without Explosion," grumbled an American voice.

The voices spilled up the hillside and onto the plateau where the Scouts lay motionless. Their breath knocked against the cavities of their chests. Stewart expected someone to notice. Then gradually the realization came that the people below were Americans, probably the captured navy weathermen.

Metal bars rattled. "He can't sleep without fucking the dog," said an angry voice in the same direction as the bars.

"Take it easy," soothed another voice in the distance. "He just wants to be sure Explosion is okay."

"How're we supposed to know where the dog is?" said a sleepy voice. "We're locked in this cage."

"Dog? Whur dog?" repeated the Oriental voice.

"Go to sleep," said the soothing voice.

Someone snored loudly, a mocking noise that grated the ears.

The Scouts waited, tense. They heard footsteps, watched

as a light shone on a door. The door opened and before he turned out the flashlight, they saw the Japanese soldier enter the base of the hill on which they lay.

Poor bastards, Stewart thought, they're living underground.

"Let's clear out," Sigori said.

"We can't leave them." The Professor sounded incredulous, but Stewart and Sigori knew it would be murder to release the navy men with no way to take them off Kiska.

"We'll coom agin." Stewart whispered in the Professor's ear, hoping his voice did not carry beyond the cup he made of his hands.

Suddenly an American voice, so loud it seemed to crash against their ears, said, "Jiggs, sing for us. I can't get back to sleep."

"You can't get back to sleep 'cause you ain't got room to lie down."

"Sing, Jiggs."

A clear tenor, as full and poignant as Russian bells drifting over the tundra, filled the black night. "Abide with me, fast falls the eventide."

Goose bumps traveled the length of Stewart's body. Ellen was on the rug beside him at Mrs. Meriweather's. Angus sang the old hymn.

"The darkness deepens, Lord with me abide."

Light cut the darkness and a voice shouted from the underground quarters. Gunshots flared against the black sky. There were more words, a door slammed, the light disappeared.

"What's he say?" Stewart whispered.

"He says he'll shoot the singer next time. Not right to sing when you're in a cage," said the Professor. "I'll warn them."

"No." Stewart grabbed the Professor, but his hand slipped. The frenzied bark of a dog pierced the stillness.

"Hush!" The Professor's voice brushed the night.

The bark changed to a low rumbling growl.

"What's the matter with Explosion?" said someone from the cage.

"Sing, Jiggs," said another. "It'll quiet him."

"No," called the Professor like a voice from the beyond, "don't sing."

"Abide with me," Jiggs began.

Stewart and Sigori flew, their muddy feet soft as goose down on the mushy ground. Light flared from the underground warren. A soldier rushed out, firing rapidly into the air. At the same moment, a single shot burst ahead. It had the dull thudding sound of a bullet impacting in a body. Sigori and Stewart paused, not knowing where to go next. Three more shots rang into the sky ahead of them. The universal alarm signal.

Arne? thought Stewart, just as Sigori slammed him into the ground. Running past them, the Japanese patrol they had heard earlier raced toward the encampment. Stewart and Sigori held their breath. The footsteps filled their ears then disappeared toward the confusion of light and gunfire at the encampment.

Sigori yanked Stewart's shoulder. They raced to the anti-aircraft gun. A body slumped against it.

"It's Arne," gasped Sigori, staring at the body.

"What's he doin' here?" Stewart grabbed Arne's arms, shook him. He pressed his two fingers to the large vein in his neck, found no pulse.

In the sudden quiet, a single shot rang out. "Hear that?" Sigori said.

The Professor, thought Stewart.

"Let's go," said Sigori.

They lunged over the cliff, jamming their boots into handholds, barely conscious that a mistake could drop them a hundred feet into oblivion. A sea breeze whipped past their soggy, mud-caked bodies. The cliff shrunk as the distance shortened. The water foamed closer.

Sigori stopped. Stewart, hearing the same noise, flattened against the cliff. Two shadowy shapes beached a lifeboat and, their backs to the cliff, jabbered away examining the Scouts' dinghy which was pulled out of the water.

Without pause, Stewart grabbed his Bowie knife, flung himself through the air and crashed onto the back of a soldier. He pushed the blade through the soft flesh of his diaphragm and up under the ribs.

Sigori dropped to the second soldier and knocked him out. He heaved the soldier's flashlight and rifle into the Japanese lifeboat and jumped in.

Stewart dug his knife deeper. His victim gagged.

"Get in," Sigori hissed. He held the oars.

Grabbing the stern, Stewart pushed the boat off the beach. He hauled himself on board at the same moment the dying soldier squeezed the trigger on his carbine. The shot smashed into Stewart's leg.

Sigori rowed past the sea stacks into the blackness. Drifting over them, Stewart was sure he heard, just before he passed out: "When other helpers fail, and comforts flee, Help of the helpless, oh, abide with me!"

Stewart tried to raise his head. He blinked and saw a dense, impenetrable grey. So this was it, this was what it was like when you crossed over. He tried to remember the green of Clara's hill, the gold of an early sky, the red of Ellen's ribbon. Here there was no color.

"Hi!"

Stewart blinked. A broad Aleut face smiled back.

"Hi."

It was sound. Stewart tried his voice. "Where am I?" The pain hammered through his leg. Then he knew he was alive although death could not be as bad as this.

"We are," said Sigori, "somewhere in the Rat Islands."

Stewart tried to move as if by moving he could escape the torment of his leg. Beneath him, beneath the wooden hull of the lifeboat, the ocean rolled. He raised his head and, looking at his leg as one would look warily at an *idigadich*, Stewart saw blood soaking the black wool trousers. His boot dangled from his ankle.

The *idigadich* clawed him, scraped his sides, scalped him. Stewart rocked in the lifeboat and tried to crawl away. Mercifully he passed out.

"Lie still," said Sigori when Stewart woke again, writhing in agony.

Stewart gripped his hands until his fingers turned blue from lack of circulation. "Where're we goin'?" he asked.

"To one of the Rat Islands."

"How long ha'e we been here?"

"Three days."

Sigori's face drifted away. Stewart blinked, forcing his eyes into focus. He remembered something else. "Where's the *Dolphin*?"

"We lost it."

"Why?"

"The compass be with Arne."

Through the thunder of pain Stewart remembered. Orders were to bear east on eighty-seven degrees and the *Dolphin* would pick them up, fog or not.

Stewart drifted. The wind blew and he awoke, feeling the change of water beneath the hull. "Where are we goin'?"

"The Rat Islands," Sigori patiently repeated. Stewart could ask a million times. He would answer a million times.

"Which one?"

"I don't know yet." The oars moved in a steady motion, forward through the air, back through the water.

"Need help? I kin help ye."

"Stay still," said Sigori. "I can do it."

The pain gripped Stewart, numbed him as if he floated directly on the freezing Aleutian waters. He sailed past and left the monster clawing, digging, demanding but getting no response.

"Wind's up." Stewart woke up much later, and tried to put his mind away from his leg. "Wind's up," he repeated, hearing the panic in his own voice.

"That be good."

"What about williwaws?"

"We'll get there before the williwaw."

"How do ye know?" Stewart heard his voice challenge this stranger who rowed so placidly, evenly, through the churning water. His voice sounded separate, not part of the real person inside.

"I feel the land. See? The air be different, warmer here." Sigori changed direction slightly. "Feel that?"

Stewart, too low in the lifeboat, felt only the growing choppiness of the waves. He shut his eyes. Had Arne stayed with the dinghy, had the Professor not warned the Americans, they would all be alive. And he wouldn't have this excruciating pain in his leg.

Then there was a definite change. The wind rumpled the sea. A big wave suddenly picked up the skiff, tossing it.

"Hang on!" Sigori stood up with his hands on the long oars. "We'll catch the next one." A roar of surf crashed around Stewart's ears. Dear God, he thought, sucking in his cheeks.

A wave lifted them. Sigori maneuvered the oars. The wave sent them airborne, smashed them down, soaked them.

"Next one," said Sigori. The lifeboat surfed the crest of the next wave. It rode high, higher. The wave dropped. Sigori jammed an oar into the beach, teetered against a boulder. The wave rode out. Sigori hung on. The lifeboat stayed. He jumped free and hauled the boat higher up the beach.

They were on solid ground.

"It stinks." Stewart looked at his smashed left leg as if it were a hunk of black crab meat. They had been on the island several weeks. The *Dolphin* had not appeared.

Sigori sniffed and nodded.

Despite the salt wind that blew steadily across this desolate rock, the stench predominated. The sides of Stewart's mouth tightened downward from the smell.

"Why donna ye clean it?" His voice sounded strange to his own ears.

"I have." Sigori squatted beside Stewart, his hands on his hips.

"Ach!" Stewart closed his eyes, remembering how the salt water had cut through his barriers to the pain, washing him closer to the surface of it until the pain had overwhelmed him and again he had passed out. He opened his eyes and looked at Sigori, avoiding the wound. "So why is it like this?"

"Bad problem." Sigori remained quiet, waiting for Stewart to see the solution he knew was inevitable.

"Ha'e no medicines in the Jap boat?"

"I have Aleut medicine." Sigori stood up, moved to the overturned boat and from underneath its protective cover removed a large green bundle. *"Cingatudax,"* he said, returning and setting the weeds down beside Stewart's bad leg. "This stop the bleeding. I know because I see it done."

"Bleeding? That's nae blood, 'tis gangrene. Gangrene!" The saying of it hurt his throat. Stewart closed his eyes, pressed his fingers to his neck, rubbing his Adam's apple. He wished the words away, willed the leg whole. Abruptly he opened his eyes, studying his right leg. It rested on the damp brown army blanket, strong, muscled, covered with blond hair. Perfectly normal. He inclined his head slightly, hoping by the time his gaze settled to the left leg that it would be better, be cured. That he would have made a horrible mistake, that his vision had been wrong, defective.

"You not live unless I take off." Sigori pulled a round grey stone from his pocket. Stewart watched the stone as Sigori rolled it and rolled around in his head what Sigori had just said.

"Use that," Stewart said suddenly, remembering Cheok rubbing a stone over his chest when he had a bad cold. "Make it better with the stone."

Sigori held the stone, and after a short pause said, "This not good for that. This is *qawag* stone."

"What's *qawag*?" Stewart relished the conversation. It gave more time for his leg to heal.

"Sea lion. He swallow beach stones so he can sit up in the water." Sigori patted the stone back and forth, hand to hand. "It good luck for us when we go back on the water."

"When we leave here, ye mean?"

'*Ang.*' Sigori, forgetting that Stewart did not speak Aleut, answered yes in his own language.

"Why? Why leave?"

"I take you to Adak."

"Adak? That's bullshit. 'Tis five hundred miles. We can'na make that. Donna be a smart ass." Stewart heard his voice run on, heard the nonsense babble out of him. He finally took a deep breath and said in what he hoped was a calmer voice, "We'll ne'er make it."

"My people travel long distances—"

"I know, I know," Stewart interrupted. "But that's in a *baidarka*."

"We not be here all winter."

Stewart knew it too, of course. Better they drown trying to save themselves than freeze in the howling winds of winter.

"If we be in the boat and your leg get more bad, nothing I can do," said Sigori. "I take it off before we go."

Stewart still did not hear him. "There's lots o' islands up the Chain," he said, reasonable, calm. "We'll stop along the way."

"Ang." Sigori clasped his hands together, pressing the stone between the toughened palms.

"So when do we leave?"

"Soon as your leg come off."

"No!" The sound exploded from Stewart and at the same moment his stomach lurched. Last night's meal of raw octopus heaved itself, partially digested, up and onto the bare rock. He leaned his head off the blanket and vomited until his eyes were bugging and bloodshot. Green bile finally heaved out of his stomach. It was as if he were vomiting the rot from his leg up through his groin, his stomach, and out his mouth.

"You think you lose your soul when you lose your leg?" said Sigori and, without waiting for an answer, continued. "That not be true. At mission school they told us people get cut open and not lose soul."

Stewart stared at him.

"See!" Sigori pointed to the leg. Stewart, exhausted from the vomiting, could not resist. He stared down at the leg he had tried to avoid. The sides of his mouth tightened again in disgust.

"See!" Sigori pointed to where the damage from the shot had moved up the leg, eaten off more flesh.

"Look," said Sigori and his forceful voice somehow calmed Stewart's stomach. "It climbs up your leg. It get past here"—he touched the joint between Stewart's leg and groin—"there be no help. Your meat be gone."

"No!" Were it not for the surf pounding the shore, Stewart's cry might have been heard by the Japanese on Kiska.

"You die if I don't take leg off," said Sigori, forging ahead, wanting to get the job done. "I seen it before."

"How will ye do it?" Stewart felt calm now, collected. The leg was smashed, useless. They could build him a stick, like Captain Hook in the school teacher's story of . . . His mind drifted. He could not remember.

"I get you drunk first," said Sigori.

"NO!" Stewart screamed above the pounding surf, above his own desperate knowledge that what Sigori said was true. But he'd do it without getting drunk. He'd seen what liquor did to the men at the Mud Dog, to Angus . . .

Stewart saw the axe, gleaming sharp in the dull light spraying through the fog. His axe. He had found it.

Sigori handed him an unfamiliar flask of clear alcohol he had found in the Jap boat. He tied a strip from his shirt well above Stewart's knee.

Stewart clung to reality, clung to his body, solid, whole, clung to running over the tundra after the reindeer, planting his foot on the shovel, digging into the gravel, finding platinum. The platinum that was to have sent Ellen to school. Sigori drifted close, then away, his black hair floating above his dark eyes. Stewart drank. He closed his eyes, thought of Angus, knew now why Angus drank, wondered why he didn't shut the world out more often. Stewart opened his eyes just as Sigori lifted the sharpened axe over his back.

"NO!" Stewart's voice joined the wind, blew over the island, tangled with the surf, lifted into the grey sky. His voice came back to him, hit the wind again. A flock of whale birds lifted as one black cloud at the sea's edge.

Sigori raised the axe over his head, aimed just above the knee joint.

"NO!" Stewart heard a raven, mocking him, spitting his own word back into the air.

Sigori swung the axe down. Screams rocked the island.

The sound of shattering bone covered the desolate rock. Stewart passed out. Sigori dropped the axe and, picking up the *cingatudax*, rubbed the featherlike leaves between his palms, making a poultice to heal the wound.

21

T HE HOSPITAL GENERATOR HUMMED in the distance, on its last shift before the janitor shut it down for the night. Miss Long sat in a rocking chair under the eaves in Ellen's attic bedroom. As she rocked, the shadow of the old school teacher took on the shape of a humpbacked whale. Ellen's smaller shadow had the sleekness of a porpoise. But she did not feel playful like a porpoise, she felt wind-whipped and tired.

"Are you packed?" asked Miss Long.

"Yes." Ellen shoved Mrs. Meriweather's carpetbag toward the door. Dr. West's letters were wrapped with red ribbon and tucked into the bottom. His location had been inked out by the censor, and Ellen, confused about how to get a letter to him, had not written back. The ivory whale he had ordered from Jonah was wrapped in cotton wool and rested beside her own carving, waiting for the day she saw Dr. West again.

Dr. Visikov's vest pocket dictionary lay inside the bag. She had given the Chinese coin from Jonny the Jap to little Elise Brandon when Elise's mother fell through the ice and drowned. She had given the eyelash curler from the priest's wife and the *qaspeq* to Abby, one of the patients.

It worried Ellen to think of thirteen-year-old Abby who, after two days of hard labor, had given birth to a baby girl. Because she had been pregnant and unmarried, Abby had expected to give birth to pups. Believing another superstition, she had chewed gum, hoping the pups would stick inside her and never come out.

190

"Don't forget your quilt," said Miss Long, noticing that it was still folded at the foot of Ellen's bed.

"I won't." Ellen thought of the time Daddy had brought it down on the sled, when he'd come to take her home after Mrs. Berglund died. How long ago that was. Daddy seemed like a person from her imagination and not the man who had ruled her life for so long. She sniffed the wondrous odor of woodruff in this room, the first of her very own, and wondered if she could ever go back to sharing a cot with Bonnie.

"Have you enough to wear?"

"Miss Herringbone gave me two of her uniforms." Ellen unconsciously patted her sides where the uniforms were too snug. The spinster nurse was as thin as *ooligan*, the needle fish Cheok caught in winter.

The gesture was not lost on Miss Long. Ellen needed clothes, but with a war on and her own spare cash going into war bonds, what could she do?

On the hospital scale Ellen stood five foot five and weighed a hundred and ten pounds. When she came to Harold's Point last year, her skin had been dark. Having spent a year at the hospital without a break in the sun at the fish nets, her skin had lightened. Her eyes narrowed in Eskimo fashion. She had a round exotic face, high broad cheekbones, and a firm chin with a dimple in the center.

Throwing alternating shades of light and dark, the bulb played across Ellen's waist-length hair. As Miss Long looked at Ellen, she saw no resemblance to the self-conscious child who had poured over her studies to the exclusion of everything else. Instead she saw a young woman, confident and intent upon taking her place in the world. It seemed an impossible change in just over a year. But Miss Long knew that one minute they were children, learning their colors, the next minute they were pregnant and having children of their own.

That reminded Miss Long of what she had come to talk about. She cleared her throat. "The men will be forward with you."

"Maybe." Ellen picked up the jade labret from its nest of cotton wool on the dresser and, taking a new red ribbon from the pocket of her pleated grey skirt, wrapped it around the center of the stone.

"What will you do when"—Miss Long coughed—"they, ah, make . . . make advances?"

"I'll smile."

"That will encourage them."

"Should I frown, like Miss Herringbone?" Ellen screwed up her face and sucked in her lips until they made a tight, fleshless knot.

"Polite women don't mock." Miss Long shook her head, exasperated. A hairpin flew out and fell to the floor.

"I'm sorry," said Ellen as she tied the labret around her neck.

"How can you be so casual?" said Miss Long, not the least fooled. "You know what happens. Look at little Abby, for example."

Abby's screams still rang in Ellen's ears, seemed etched into the cuts on her palm where Abby had dug in her nails. Ellen rolled backward on her bed, sweeping her hair up and away from her neck. She wished dear Miss Long didn't have to talk, that they could just share the quietness. She was tired of talking all day to Abby, explaining, comforting, trying to tell Abby to stand up for herself when the poor girl couldn't even fold the flour sack diapers into triangles. Abby seemed like a child playing with dolls, except it wasn't a leather doll dressed in furs, it was a real baby needing full-time care. Ellen sighed aloud.

"You do not need to go." Despite her resolution not to interfere with Dr. Constance's decision, Miss Long's precisely spoken words marched across the room like good samaritans bringing free advice.

Ellen rolled to a sitting position. Miss Long spoke again.

"You don't have to go. You can stay right here in Harold's Point."

"I want to go."

Miss Long pulled a hairpin from her hair and caught up the loose strands.

"There's a war on." Ellen spoke firmly, erasing, she hoped, once and for all any persuasive arguments Miss Long might have rehearsed.

"I can't help but worry. I'm sorry but I just don't think—"

"I'll be fine," interrupted Ellen, "I always am."

How does she forget so easily, thought Miss Long, not wanting to bring up the horrible scene with Mrs. Berglund. It had changed Ellen, that experience, and Miss Long had wished a hundred times since that she had asked Ellen to stay with her in the school that night. Since the suicide there had been an impenetrable core in Ellen that made her appear as hard and inflexible as iron. Her black eyes, which once reflected her state of mind, now appeared so opaque that Miss Long doubted they would ever sparkle again. But there was no use crying over spilt milk, no use rewiping a slate blackboard that, no matter what, would always show the faint outline of the chalk. What was done was done.

"What if the Japanese invade Alaska?" she asked, trying another tactic.

"Maybe they already have," said Ellen. "There's no knowing what's going on down the Chain."

"You're only hearing rumors," said Miss Long. "The government would tell us if the Japanese were that close."

"The government's not telling us anything."

"No doubt that's for our own safety."

" 'Loose lips sink ships.' " In a singsong voice Ellen quoted from the War Information poster the cook had tacked up in the hospital kitchen.

"Your tongue is going to get you, one of these days, Miss MacTavish, if you don't watch out."

Ellen grabbed her tongue with her fingers and tried to fold it in the middle. "Do you know what Dr. West told me?" she said, and without waiting for a reply added, "There are two kinds of people in the world. Those whose tongues crease naturally, and those whose don't."

"There are two kinds of people in the world," said Miss Long. "Men and women. And you are of the latter, gentler sex. Please remember that."

The gentler sex. Ellen's spine stiffened.

Miss Long sighed. "You're too young to be taking such a risk."

"I like risks." Ellen felt impatient. "I want to go." Closing her eyes, she plopped back down on the bed. She did not want to have to battle Miss Long as she used to battle Daddy.

The bulb swung. The rocker squeaked. Miss Long searched

her mind for the proper words to convince Ellen to stay. Soon they heard Dr. Constance's heavy footsteps on the first landing.

Ellen opened her eyes and stood by the rocking chair. "Will I see you tomorrow at the plane, Miss Long?"

"I couldn't bear to see you off." Miss Long reached for the handkerchief tucked inside the sleeve of her best white blouse and pretended that the drip from her nose was the beginnings of a sneeze.

Ellen looked at the carpetbag that held Dr. West's letters with their censored black lines. Although she had not answered them, he had continued to write from some unknown place. Would it be that way for her, too—that no one would know where she was, just as no one knew about Stewart? She rested her hand on Miss Long's shoulder. The rocking stopped.

Dr. Constance entered the small room with its slanting eaves. He was a large man and his tight curls brushed the ceiling.

"Come down to my quarters," he said to Ellen. "I have something for you."

Then Miss Long realized that she had forgotten to remind Ellen that young women must, at all times, protect their reputations and not go to men's rooms alone, even if it was a gentleman like Dr. Constance. Annoyed with herself for not giving Ellen the advice she would surely need, Miss Long followed Ellen and Dr. Constance down the stairs. Her sturdy, square-heeled shoes sounded regimental beside Ellen's fur slippers.

Dr. Constance rummaged through his pine bureau, and removed a twelve-inch gentleman's gold vest chain. He dropped it into Ellen's cupped palm.

Ellen dangled the heavy links between her fingers, away from the cuts Abby had made. Like tiny melodious cymbals, the gold links clinked against each other. Ellen undid the ribbon on her labret and handed the stone and chain to the doctor. The crystal lamp on the bureau caught the gold, spraying prisms of color over the gallery of framed photographs on the wall, faded sepia prints of men and women in overalls and straw hats.

"Oh my!" breathed Miss Long, breaking the spell.

Ellen found her tongue. "Oh thank you so much, Dr. Constance," she said softly. "Thank you so much."

"What a wonderful gift," said Miss Long, her eyes moist.

Dr. Constance nodded toward Miss Long with such tenderness that Ellen knew then what she had only guessed at before. Why is it so difficult for people who love each other to be together, she thought, wishing for Dr. West. He promised to come back after the war. What if he didn't? And where would she be by then? She worried this thought while Dr. Constance attached the chain to the jade labret.

As always on a dark winter Sunday night, Dr. Constance walked Miss Long to the door of her apartment above the schoolroom. When they reached the door Miss Long said, as always, "Would you like a nightcap?"

"If it's no trouble." Dr. Constance slipped off his shoes in the windbreak and while Miss Long fussed in the kitchen, he stretched on the couch. When Miss Long came in with a glass of Southern Comfort, her face flushed at the sight of his stockinged feet on the rounded arm of the couch. The big toe on the right foot stuck through the wool. What she had forgotten to tell Ellen was also true for herself. There was certainly danger in inviting a man to one's rooms, even though Miss Long thought herself beyond the age when it mattered.

Waking almost immediately, Dr. Constance swung his feet around. Miss Long poured his drink and, reaching for her sewing basket, said in a schoolmarm voice, "Hand me your sock, Doctor."

The usual protestations had not woken with him, Dr. Constance slipped off his sock and handed it to Miss Long. He picked up the Southern Comfort. "Here's to good health!"

"To health," said Miss Long. She slipped a wooden darning egg into the toe of the sock and, speaking evenly, carefully, hoping the doctor would not suspect that she was trying to interfere, said, "Are you sure this is the right move for Ellen?"

"Yes." Dr. Constance savored his drink, his one indulgence of the week.

"I don't see how you can spare her," said Miss Long,

weaving black wool thread across the toe as her maiden aunt
had taught her fifty years ago.

Dr. Constance rolled the sweet sting of Southern Comfort
along his tongue and then spoke in a voice of the Deep South
that he used only in Miss Long's company. "My dear, what is
it you really want to say?"

There was such compassion in his eyes that Miss Long
wished . . . but oh drat! What was the point of wishing?

"What is it, my dear?" continued Dr. Constance.

"Ellen's too young to be on her own." Miss Long forced
her voice to be stern rather than pleading.

"She'll be eighteen in January."

"Still young."

"How old were you when you came north to teach?"

She had been eighteen, sailing on the wooden steamer
Willapa to the northern village of Whaler's Point, where she
taught until she was asked to teach in the Unaganik Orphanage in 1918. Then she had been forty-one and, while she
missed her friends above the Arctic Circle, she no longer
relished the cold. When the orphanage closed, she had come
to Harold's Point.

"Things were different then." Miss Long looked at the
doctor.

"Ellen's stagnating here," he replied, his voice kind but
firm. "She needs to get out and try her wings and, when the
war's over, she'll have more opportunity to get to college.
She'll be unhappy all her life if she doesn't get to challenge
her mind."

"Morals are different these days." She lowered her eyes.

"Are human emotions ever any different?" Dr. Constance
smiled. "Ellen respects herself enough not to be, shall we
say, loose."

Miss Long handed him the sock, locking her sewing
basket and her lips. She had said what she needed to say.

Dr. Constance put on his sock, then pushed himself out
of the couch. "I've a heavy day in surgery tomorrow, my
dear, and need to turn in."

She carried the lantern to the door and, despite the rules
of blackout, let the yellow light spill down the stairs after
him. At the bottom he turned and she wished she had the

nerve to say, Spend the night with me, old man, and warm my lonely bones.

Joe Stokes flew back to Unaganik with the same pilot who brought Ellen's hastily scribbled letter. Joe had gone to Anchorage to train for the Signal Corps, but he was all thumbs on the telegraph keys. They dismissed him "with regret." Only his desire to get back to the bush as quickly as possible enabled him to test his luck at yet another plane ride.

He regaled them at the Mud Dog Saloon with tales of people sleeping in cars and chicken coops. "And twenty-six dollars a day wage for construction," he said. "And me not able to wing a saw."

"Ellen won't find a place to stay," Angus replied. "I better hitch up U-Prince and get down to Harold's Point and bring her home."

"If she's going with the army, they'll put her up," said Merilee. "And anyway, she didn't say she was going to Anchorage."

"I should go down there and change her mind," said Angus.

"You know you're not going to change her mind," said Joe Stokes and nodded to Merilee to pour Angus another draught.

Angus stared into his Glasgow mug, then lifting his tufted eyebrows, he banged the mug against the table and boomed, "Damn this bloody war."

"Let's go down to Shushanuk's and get the news," said Joe.

"Ach no," stormed Angus. "Charlie's doon there and he'll bring it home tonight. I'll hear it soon eno'."

"Are you off tonight?" asked Merilee.

Angus nodded. When Jonny the Jap had been rounded up for relocation, in spite of everyone's support of his innocence, Angus had returned to his former job at the jail. This week he'd worked double shift because Robertson felt poorly and old Visikov had ordered bedrest.

Although Merilee joked that Dr. Visikov ordered for others what he needed for himself, it was true that they all had felt their age since the war. Going without sleep was no longer as easy as it had once been and Angus wondered how he'd cope with a big fish run. Although Charlie helped at the nets, Angus didn't think he could handle them himself, not like Stewart had. Ach, he missed the lad more now that he was older, with no first-born to take the weight of the chores.

With Ellen it was different. She was never out of his thoughts and thus he did not feel she had really gone. He talked to her in his mind, told her things as if she could hear. Her absence only hit him when a letter arrived. He kept the rare notes folded in the pocket of his shirt until they had worn to tatters with the constant rereading.

Cheok found Ellen's latest letter on Monday when she and Bonnie scrubbed Angus's shirt. Cheok said nothing, but prayed that Ellen's restless spirit would find a home.

"Orders from the U.S. Army to pick up E. MacTavish," said the pilot as he jumped out of the Norseman just after daylight on December 21, 1942, a year and two weeks after the Japanese bombed Pearl Harbor.

The pilot, an older man with a lean frame that no amount of fleece-lined clothing could fatten, slipped his tinted goggles up over his fleece-lined leather helmet, glancing past Ellen even though she and Dr. Constance were alone.

"She's here," said Dr. Constance. "Take good care of her."

The pilot slipped his goggles back on and stared at Ellen.

"Is everything all right?" asked the doctor.

"Beats me." The pilot scratched under his leather helmet. "You sure the army knows about this?"

"Of course," said Dr. Constance. "I consulted with them myself."

"You sure you know what you're doing?" The pilot glared at Ellen.

"Yes." Unnerved by his glare, Ellen entered the rear of the single engine plane. Three men occupied three of the five passenger seats. Ellen settled into the tail seat, feeling cross. The tightness of her sealskin parka annoyed her. She yanked on the back of it, trying to get comfortable.

Dr. Constance stuffed the carpetbag into the storage compartment behind her. "Ellen," he said, handing her a piece of paper, "I've written something, in case there's any question."

This is to certify, Dr. Constance had written in his lacy script, the *T*'s crossed with a bold and determined hand, *that Ellen MacTavish has worked under me* . . . Ellen refolded the paper and looked into the dark eyes of the doctor. "They won't expect me to be a real nurse, will they?"

"They didn't specify nurses," said Dr. Constance. "They asked for able-bodied men with medical experience. They'll be pleased to put you to work."

"I hope so," said Ellen.

"Ready?" grunted the pilot from the front.

"Ready?" repeated Dr. Constance, looking at Ellen.

"Yes," she said and brushed a fleck of snow from his winter coat.

The radial engine up front roared. The pilot reset his flaps. One of the passengers, a rotund Yup'ik man, clasped his hands in prayer.

Ellen gripped the seat and forced herself to stay put. The roar filled her brain. The engine sounded as if it were sucking up spare parts and spitting them out on the snow. With a roar that scattered all emotion but stark panic, the plane skied down the frozen river and lifted off. Ellen looked down and saw the black face of Dr. Constance against the white snow. She pushed into the seat, hanging on, hearing nothing but the overwhelming din of the engine as they headed over Bristol Bay.

The changed noise of the engine woke her from a dream in which a gold star had been sewn onto her quilt. A gold star in the window meant a death in the family and Ellen shuddered, frightened of her dream until she remembered she had left the quilt safe in the attic bedroom at the hospital.

The pilot banked, made a tight turn into a broad harbor, and landed on a snow-packed runway gouged out of the side of a volcanic mountain. He skied to a stop and turned off the engine. "Dutch Harbor," he said, pushing his goggles onto his leather helmet.

"What are we doing here?" asked Ellen, wondering why they had detoured so far from Anchorage.

"We gas up here and check the weather out west. If it's no go, we stay the night."

"Out west?" Ellen's voice rose.

The pilot left the plane without replying. When he

returned, he motioned them all onto the ground. "Socked in down there," the pilot grunted to the assembled group. "We'll stay here until the clouds lift."

"The way I hears it, the fog never lifts in Adak," said one of the men.

"Adak?" Ellen's shock brought grins to the men's faces.

The pilot removed his cigarette to speak. "Military."

"But why Adak? I thought I'd be going to Seward or Anchorage."

"Can't say I didn't warn you," said the pilot.

"What do you mean, warn me?"

Ignoring Ellen, the pilot propped his cigarette back between his lips and motioned them to climb into a waiting jeep. The thrill of her first car ride paled for Ellen under the confusion of the pilot's remarks. Adak? That far out the Chain? Her mind raced as fast as the wheels and before she knew it, the driver had dropped her at a small open boat ferrying the short distance between Amaknak Island, on which the major portion of the base had been constructed, and the island of Unalaska, on which the established village of Unalaska tried to go about its daily business.

"There's the hospital." The jeep driver pointed across the channel to a two-story wooden building. The far end of the building had been destoyed by bombs. "Check in with the matron. I'll pick you up tomorrow."

"Ain't going in the fog," grunted the pilot.

"If you don't like the weather, wait ten minutes," said the driver.

"We'll be here forever," said one of the passengers.

Their voices faded as Ellen boarded the ferry and crossed to the opposite shore. Carrying her bag over her shoulder, she walked toward the hospital.

The matron, a broad woman with corseted hips that seemed to bludgeon their way down the hall, told Ellen she could sleep in the night nurse's bed after the night nurse got up for duty at seven o'clock. "Stay inside," she warned in a crisp voice. "The men here will pester a little thing like you to death. You can set in the kitchen. Clara will take care of you."

When the matron disappeared into the wards, Ellen slipped out the door of the hospital, desperate to stretch her legs and soothe her mind. She clomped over the stony beach, letting the cold salt air fill her lungs. Bald eagles flew overhead, the white tails a flash against the dingy sky. She walked past a large house and a larger two-domed Russian church. She passed a noisy saloon with her head down. The big harbor was packed with ships. But she ignored everything. Swinging her arms, feeling the free movement of her body in spite of the tightness of her sealskin parka, she followed the beach until she reached a graveyard perched on a small hill. Wrought-iron fences enclosed the graves and three-bar crosses held crowns of snow.

Ellen clambered partway up the hill on a snowpacked trail. She stood there, looking seaward. A familiar fishing boat bobbed at anchor. Only the color had changed. It was painted as grey as the sky and sea.

She cupped her hands around her mouth, but before she could draw a deep shouting breath, a man's voice behind her said, "Hello."

22

E~LLEN~ FOUND HER VOICE.

"Hello."

He smiled.

"Ted Kleet. I thought you were still in Arizona."

"And I thought you were in Harold's Point."

"You heard?"

He smiled again. "Through the bush telegraph."

He had a purple-yellow bruise around his left eye and a gash down his cheek. His prominent nose looked like it had been broken in the middle and the bone in that area had enlarged. He stood several inches taller than Ellen and seemed more imposing than she remembered.

"Where did you get this?" she asked, lightly examining the bruise with her fingertips.

"Out west. Got caught in a williwaw and got knocked around a bit." He looked at her, his eyes bright.

"In the *Yethl*?"

"Yes. The old man pulled us through. Myself, I wasn't sure we'd make it."

Ellen looked at the seiner. "The *Yethl*'s in better shape than you."

"We've been here a few weeks, working on her, getting her shipshape again." Ted stood motionless in front of her.

"You're still fishing with your daddy?" Ellen asked, thinking how lucky he was in his closeness to his father. If only Stewart and Angus had grown that intimate.

"We aren't fishing," Ted was saying. "We're part of a

local patrol organized by Squeaky Anderson. They call us Yippee Boats and we take supplies out west." Ted tightened his jaw. And we also search for lost Scouts, he wanted to add, thinking of Stewart. Three months ago, when he had been asked to join the search for the missing team, he had been sworn to secrecy. He considered breaking that trust for Ellen but thought it better, given the uncertainty of Stewart's whereabouts, to say nothing.

"I think Daddy mentioned Squeaky once," said Ellen thoughtfully, trying to remember.

"He used to be harbor master at Dutch," said Ted. "Now he's harbor master at Adak."

"What's at Adak? How come no one knows?"

"A military base."

"Why?" Her voice came out pitched and high.

"You haven't heard?"

"Nothing. We've heard nothing in Harold's Point except a few rumors."

"Nips occupied Kiska and Attu and the military is on Adak blasting the stuffing out of them."

Ellen knew now why the pilot had acted so strangely. An uneasy feeling began to plague her. Maybe there had been a mistake.

"What brings you to Dutch Harbor?" Ted asked.

Ellen heard him but so preoccupied was she that she could not register on the question. She stared at his bruised eye with blank eyes until he asked again. "How come you're here?"

"Dr. Constance sent me." She responded with a flat voice, a duty reply to a friendly question. Surely Dr. Constance didn't know about the war zone.

"He assumed I'd be sent to Anchorage, or to the Fort Raymond Hospital at Seward," she continued slowly, reviewing each word in her mind first, searching for the ones that would make the most sense, that might convince her to continue on to Adak. "We put in here because of the fog. But I heard them say we were going to Adak..." She paused, kicking the stones with her feet.

"Maybe there's a mixup," said Ted.

"Why do you say that?"

"They wouldn't send a woman to Adak."

"What's so different about being a woman?" Ellen stomped her foot before she realized what she was doing.

Ted laughed, throwing back his head until his black hair covered the wide collar of his new woolen pea coat. He searched her eyes.

"Lots of trouble there," said Ted. "Trouble here, too."

"Like what?"

"Outsiders not knowing what to do with themselves."

"It's not as if we aren't without problems," Ellen retorted and, holding her hands palms up, she studied the healing cuts, reminders of Abby's childbirth pains.

"Come to the *Yethl*," Ted said, his tone commanding.

Ellen felt uneasy with his imperiousness and wished he'd laugh again. He meant something to her, this boy who had changed into a man. It was he who had told her to make her own luck and who had given her the courage to go to Harold's Point. If she hadn't gone there, she wouldn't be here now. She smiled, wanting to tell him that, but something in his eyes stopped her. Ellen held back. There was an intensity about him that she did not understand and did not want to disturb. "Won't a ship sink with a woman on board?" she teased, hoping to change his mood.

"Let's find out!" With long strides Ted walked down the beach until they reached a skiff beached above high tide. He lifted one side and Ellen hoisted the other. It was like old times with Stewart, hauling the skiff to water.

Ellen jumped in the bow. Ted shoved and swung himself over the side, his knee-length boots dripping into the hull. Standing in the center, he rowed with long oars toward the *Yethl*. Ellen sat on a plank, licking the salt air on her lips. A whaleboat passed. It overflowed with navy men in round white hats.

"Give ya fifty bucks fer yer lady," someone shouted across the water.

"Make it a hunnerd."

"How much will ya take for the squaw, Injun?"

Ellen crossed her legs. She cupped her hands at each side of her face, shielding her eyes but looking at Ted. His jaw was clenched so tightly the soft area beneath his cheekbones quivered. He rowed in the same even rhythm, making as little splash as if he were paddling a canoe.

"Hey, pretty boy! Is she hot?" The lewd remarks seemed to feed on one another. Ellen tried to shut them out.

"This is the first time I've been in a boat since I don't know when," she said, glad to climb over the wooden guard rail and onto the deck of the *Yethl*. She kept her voice even, pretending the men had not disturbed her.

Ted flexed his fingers, unnerving Ellen with his steady gaze. The *Yethl* rocked in the wake of a passing launch. Ellen grabbed Ted's arm and, laughing with a falsity she had not known she possessed, said: "Are we sinking?"

A sailor's voice boomed across the water: "If you've bitten off more than you can chew, pretty boy, I'll eat her."

Ted put his head down and crossed the deck to the galley. Ellen followed. She slid onto the narrow bench between the table and the wall and tried to control her vexation. Those men! Is that what it would be like on Adak?

"Cup of joe?" Ted spoke in a voice that barely concealed his outrage at what they had heard.

Ellen nodded.

"Canned cow?" he asked.

Ellen nodded again.

Ted topped off two mugs of coffee with sugar and evaporated milk. The bittersweet, familiar flavor settled on Ellen's tongue as she forced the men's taunts from her mind. Soon her anger melted, and chattering like a small bird just out of the nest, she told Ted about leaving for Harold's Point, about Miss Long and the school, about working with Dr. Constance in the hospital. The boat rocked like her chair in the attic at Harold's Point and she thought of the time she had sat there, dreaming of Dr. West. She didn't tell Ted about that.

Darkness clothed the harbor. Voices, drunken, angry, lonely, fell over the water like rain squalls. Ted stood, setting the mugs in the enamel basin. "I have to get the old man. You better come. It's not safe to stay alone."

"I'll go to the hospital," said Ellen. "I'm sleeping there tonight."

Ted flexed his fingers. They were thick, worn square

with use. The nails were chipped and the thumbnail on his left hand was black, ready to fall off. "I want you to stay," he said in a husky voice.

"They'd worry," Ellen said, her words jumping ahead of her thoughts. "They told me not to leave the hospital and to stay away from town and anyway, I need to be there, in case we leave tomorrow."

"Stay with me," he said.

"I'm going to Adak," said Ellen.

"It's too rough."

Ellen stood up. Ted stretched his fingers wide, pressing them together while he tapped his thumbs against each other.

Ellen looked away, burdened by the feelings she saw in his eyes.

"Come on," she said lightly. "Let's go."

Ted washed the mugs and hung them on hooks above the sink. He blew out the candle and, striding onto the deck, lowered himself down into the skiff. As Ellen climbed over the gunwale she felt his hands holding her waist, steadying her.

The skiff rocked as he settled himself on the seat in the center, fixing the oars in their locks. He faced her as he rowed to shore. He did not smile.

Ellen felt jangled and upset. Why had she drunk so much coffee when she needed steady nerves to keep up her courage? No, she would not stay. Something pulled her to Adak, where she was obviously needed.

"Where is your dad?" Ellen heard a lightness in her voice and it sounded odd, as if she were trying too hard to avoid the real questions between her and Ted.

"He's at a funeral for one of our crew."

"Did he die in the storm?"

"No. He got in trouble in a bar." Drunken noises carried over the water. Ted held the oars. The boat drifted. Ted looked into Ellen's eyes, but it was as if he were talking to himself. "Our mate sparked one of the local girls, but she'd been bought off by a gold leaf major. The major called the girl his 'klootch' and our mate told the major he should at least treat her decently. The major called the girl a few other things and when our mate threatened to get his gun, the major shot him. A clear case of self-defense, they said, and shipped the major home for a rest with his wife and children.''

Ellen moved forward on her seat.

"It's that corn whiskey with the beer chasers.'' Ted pulled the oars with a vengeance. "Boilermakers and Apprentices, they call them. You won't catch me drinking that stuff. I'd rather take arsenic. Get it over sooner.''

On shore, Ted tied the skiff and walked beside Ellen to the hospital. When they entered the bright hospital kitchen, Ellen could see nothing for several seconds and stood beside Ted smelling the aroma of beans and stewed cranberries as if they had come from some imaginary source. When her eyes adjusted to the light, she noticed a very pregnant Aleut woman washing dishes at the sink. The woman looked radiant. Her joy was so obvious that Ellen wished there were some way to bottle it and send it to Harold's Point, as a tonic for poor Abby.

"Are you hungry?'' The woman moved toward the stove, already holding two crockery bowls.

"Yes," said Ellen, suddenly aware that she was starving.

Ted looked at Ellen. "Will I see you tomorrow?'' His right eyebrow seemed higher than ever.

"If the fog doesn't lift,'' said Ellen, feeling uneasy again.

"Will you change your mind?''

Ellen raised her hands, palms upward, and shrugged. She thought of Daddy, how he had held her so tight, and knew she had to go, had to keep moving for fear of getting stuck again.

Ted reached for her hands, held them between his own.

"I'm glad you were here,'' she said, smiling. "Now I don't feel like such a stranger.''

"Some people are never strangers.'' With a slight nod of his head, Ted dropped her hands and slipped out the kitchen door.

Ellen rolled out of bed at seven when the night nurse came off duty and shook her awake. She slipped into her grey skirt and brown sweater. Feeling as if she'd been tossing out one decision after another all night long, she carried her parka and mukluks down the hall to find a cup of coffee.

"Matron says you're off to Adak," said a pockmarked resident in white surgery garb. Ellen joined him at a table in the dining room. She nodded.

"Do you want to trade places? I'd give anything to get out of here."

"I'm tempted." Ellen smiled at the cook, who set a plate of herring and fried potatoes in front of her.

"Coffee?" the cook asked.

Ellen nodded. "I'll get it. You went to bed after I did last night."

"Let me," said the resident. He followed the cook to the kitchen and returned with two steaming mugs. "I hope you don't mind black," he said, putting one in front of Ellen. "Something happened to our shipment of milk and Clara's saving sugar for a birthday cake."

Ellen cradled the hot mug in both hands. She thought of Ted Kleet, how knowing he was here made her feel welcome, part of the place. It wouldn't be so bad to stay here. She didn't have to go to Adak, didn't have to go anywhere she didn't want to go.

When the sky lightened to a dull grey, they opened the blackout curtains. Ellen helped the resident change the IV on a man with a body cast. She helped with another patient who had a square patch of adhesive tape on a chest wound.

"Rip the bloody tape all at once," the soldier shouted. "It ain't going to hurt any more that way."

The resident yanked. The adhesive pulled a swath through the man's ruddy chest hairs and he yelled.

"Nice scar," said Ellen, looking down at his chest.

"The doc who did it got sent down to Adak," said the resident. "I'd give my eye teeth for a chance to work with him again. He's a swell surgeon."

"What's his name?"

"West. Sure you don't want to change places?"

Ellen gripped the blue and white ticking on the thin mattress. West? It could be Jason West! Nothing would keep her from Adak now.

The island of Adak appeared, a brush stroke against the grey background of sea and sky. Bald eagles appeared like sentinels on the headlands. Adak had a volcanic shape similar to the other islands they had passed en route, but was distinguished by a crowding of cruisers, minesweepers, destroyers, and battleships in a large outer bay.

The Norseman bounced on the metal runway as if it were iron bedsprings instead of Talley's brilliant invention of interlocking perforated metal plates. Built in record time on a lagoon drained for the purpose, the runway lay on the only continuous length of level ground in Adak. On one side of the runway, five GI's tossed a baseball back and forth. A group of flyers in layers of clothes of no particular design lolled against airplanes whose long noses were painted like tigers with snarling white teeth and bright red mouths.

The Norseman idled. The pilot shouted out the window to the grounded fliers. "Where do you want me?"

A man in green coveralls directed them to a pair of heavy oil drums. "Tie 'er down good," he shouted, "or the wind here will take the plane off without you."

Ellen stared out the window. A makeshift sign saying LAST CHANCE stood at the end of the runway.

Despite a cluster of circular tents dug into the hillside, a few metal buildings shaped like half moons, and a large square wall tent, the island looked bleak and deserted. Snow swept down off the volcano, covering the lower hills, filling the crevices in the cliffs. East, across the water, Ellen thought she saw through the mist an active volcano spewing steam. Gulls and ravens scudded downwind. Above everything, clouds the color of faded khaki blew across the sky.

Crushed by the overwhelming burden of the landscape, so different from her flat open tundra, Ellen could not move. Finally she clutched her carpetbag, squared her shoulders, and followed the Yup'ik man off the plane. When he and the others left to examine the squadron of P-40 Warhawks they called the Flying Tigers, she spoke to the nearest GI.

"Can you direct me to the hospital, please?"

"General ailments or surgery?" he asked.

"Surgery," said Ellen with her heart in her mouth.

"I'll take you," he said in a good-natured voice. "You're not safe alone."

Ellen stumbled over frozen mud and snow, past muddy snow drifts, over snowless patches of frozen tall grass, onto higher ground. She stopped, panting. Roaring in, a huge flying boat landed on its belly inside the breakwater that protected Sweeper Cove from the ocean swells of the outer bay.

The GI stood waiting with his hands clasped behind his back, his feet wide apart.

"What's that?" Ellen asked.

"PBY. Some folks call it a Catalina."

A man on the wharf caught the plane's overhead wing and guided it across the dock. The huge wing extended over the water on the other side.

"Where've they been?"

"Our planes bombed the smithereens out of Amchitka yesterday," he said. "But someone over there sent up a good old American flare just as we dropped our last payload. They went back today to check."

Ellen shifted her weight. Her eagerness to see Dr. West seemed irreverent. She watched intently as a man backed out of the door behind the gun turrets on the PBY. He hauled one end of a stretcher. Another man emerged carrying the other end. They laid the stretcher on the wharf.

"Looks like business for the doc." The GI beside her seemed to speak to the wind.

Hypnotized by the scene, Ellen watched the two men reenter the PBY and back out with a second litter.

"That must be them that set the flare, but they don't look like they're alive enough to strike a match," said the GI.

Ellen shivered, but not from the wind kicking past them on its way down the mountain.

"Everybody's at mess," the GI said, watching the struggle with the stretchers. "I better lend a hand." With a finger that had lost its tip, he pointed to four isolated tents further up the hill. "You'll be safe now. No one comes up this far unless they're carried."

Ellen slogged alone up the hill, holding her carpetbag with both hands. I wonder what Dr. West will say when he sees me, she thought, picturing the even smile on his perfect face.

A gust of wind whipped past. She leaned into it. And if it's not him? If it's somebody else by the name of West?

Pushing the unthinkable from her mind, Ellen trudged on, pausing only once to look back at the flying boat. They had gotten the two stretchers off the dock and were carrying them in her direction.

The wind died as quickly as it had started. Catching herself from falling face first onto the frozen ruts of mud and snow, Ellen hurried on. Breathless, her heart thumping so hard against her throat it made speech impossible, she approached the closest of the military tents. A strip of cardboard with SURGERY DEPT written in pencil flapped on the canvas door.

23

DR. WEST STOOD INSIDE. A white mask covered his nose and mouth. New rimless spectacles magnified his blue eyes. Holding the bridge of his spectacles with his middle finger, he held them onto his nose and peered down at her. She had forgotten his height, but no longer felt like a wee goose beside him. I've grown, thought Ellen, as she waited in anticipation of his response.

"Who have we here?" The mask muffled his speech but she still heard the unmistakable accent of what she had come to believe was culture, prosperity. How she loved that voice. The antithesis of fish and mud. She could not imagine anyone with a voice like that out on the tide flats, picking salmon from the nets. And how she loved him! Blushing with the recognition of the hidden thought, Ellen dropped her bag on the boards beneath her.

"This is Ellen," she said. "Don't you recognize me?"

"You can't mean it." His voice was a mixture of admiration and dismay.

"I cawn," Ellen said, mimicking his accent. "Dr. Cawnstance sent me."

"No!" Dr. West's voice rose several decibels.

"You can say hello, can't you?" she said, feeling the welcoming smile freeze on her lips.

"Did Dr. Constance know I was here?"

"No. Neither did I. Your letters were censored."

"Doc!" someone bellowed up the hill.

"There's two litters coming," said Ellen.

Dr. West hurried outside. Ellen shrugged off her parka

and hung it on a clothes tree near one of the two support poles. The tent boasted a kerosene heater, a metal stool, a metal folding chair, and a fifty-five gallon metal drum with a heavy linen cloth draped over the top. Bunches of dried grass filled the many cracks in the rough floor. Stacks of boxed supplies lent support to the sagging canvas sides. An autoclave for sterilizing instruments sat on a white enamel table. Two five-gallon cans of water stood over a coal heater. A basin lay underneath. Ellen turned a stopper on one of the cans and scrubbed her hands with green soap. She was just shaking them dry when Dr. West poked his head through the tent flap.

"Get on a gown," he said, pointing to a stash of white surgery garb, "and disguise your hair under a cap. We'll have a riot on our hands if the buck privates find out there's a woman on the island."

The thick linen gown hung to her ankles, covering her skirt and sweater. She secured the back flap with a blanket pin so there was no chance for her skirt to show. Did Dr. West really think she needed to disguise herself? Then she remembered the abrasive remarks of the men in Dutch Harbor and, braiding her long hair, stuffed it under a white surgery cap.

"Not a handsome sight out there," said Dr. West as he reentered the tent. "I'm not sure you want to see it."

"I'm not the innocent girl you remember," Ellen said, looking at him with what she hoped was a convincing maturity.

Dr. West's eyes seemed amused above the white mask and then troubled. "I hate to initiate you this way."

"I can stand the sight of blood."

"If this was blood we wouldn't have such a problem," he said.

"I came here to help," Ellen retorted, cross. What was wrong with him?

"In that case," he said, "come into the surgery and we'll see what we can do. Precious little, I'm afraid."

"How do I look?" Ellen asked.

A crease deepened in the center of his forehead. "Something's wrong." He took a white gauze mouth mask out of a box. "There's no man alive who has lips like that," he murmured as he tied the strings at the back.

Ellen forced her voice into its deepest register. "Thank you, Doctor." She did not know whether to be pleased or sad. Everything was wrong. He was acting peculiar, not at all like the gentle man she had cared about in Harold's Point, the man she thought would be excited and pleased to see her.

"Follow me," he replied. Shoving her perplexities aside, Ellen followed.

An overpowering odor saturated the close air in the adjacent larger tent. Ellen gagged, remembering the smell of rotten bear meat forgotten in the cache all summer. Her stomach assaulted the breakfast of herring.

Dr. West approached an emaciated Aleut. The man's eyes had rolled into his head until only a crescent of black iris showed. Dark rings circled his eyelids.

"Start the generator," Dr. West said to the GI standing by the door. "We've got to get heat lamps on. And El . . ." Recovering himself, Dr. West continued: "Mac, cook up some hot water bottles. I'll start the IV. This boy's in shock."

After setting a kettle to boil on a kerosene stove, Ellen joined Dr. West at the wash basin. The odor of the second patient cloaked her like a decomposing hide. Forcing a stiffness upon her face to conceal her disgust, she wondered if the patient smelled it too, or if he had developed an ability to protect his senses from the reality of his flesh's decay.

"Ellen," Dr. West said, his voice so low and gentle it felt like a lip brush against her cheek. "Have you ever seen a case of gangrene?"

"Once," she said, remembering Sour Pete's appendix.

"It's a dirty case," Dr. West continued, handing Ellen a glass bottle of denatured alcohol. "Can you help me scrub?"

Ellen poured alcohol over his hands. The fingers were long and thin, nails clipped and clean. There were no brown spots where a hammer missed a mark, no ragged lines where a fish hook had gouged deep into the flesh. The alcohol splashed into the basin. Dr. West turned his hands over. Ellen poured again, admiring the unscarred whiteness of his skin.

"Do a quick job on yourself before you put on my gloves," he said, holding his hands out in front of him like vestal virgins.

The cuts from Abby's fingernails stung. Ellen's eyes smarted with pain. But it wasn't just that. Something unexplained threatened her stability. She felt it in the air, swirling around her as if one of Mother's ghosts had come to haunt the tent. She slid the thick rubber gloves onto the doctor's hands.

"You better put on gloves too," he said. "If you get one of those little clostridia into a cut, there won't be anything we can do for you either."

The kettle boiled. Ellen filled two hot water bottles and tucked them under the armpits of the first patient. Then she pulled on gloves and joined Dr. West beside the second and obviously sicker patient. Avoiding the patient's face, she twisted her fingers into the corner of the army blanket covering him, trying to imagine it was the tartan tie patch on her quilt and she was in Harold's Point in bed with the smell of woodruff under the attic roof. She lifted the blanket and draped it over the rung at the end of the gurney.

The man wore wool trousers with the left leg pinned back at the knee. Ellen undid the fly buttons, moving the limp body to one side, then the other. The trousers were caked with mud and crusted with salt as if he were part beast from a cave at the ocean's edge.

"His shorts too?"

Dr. West nodded and since the rumble of the generator was now audible, he returned to the first patient and turned on the heat lamps. Light circled the tent. Ellen drew a deep breath and, keeping her nose snapped shut, breathing through her mouth, she undid the buttons of what had once been white shorts, navy issue. She slipped them off. The remaining stirrup of leg, now exposed, lay black and dead against the white hospital sheet. The groin area was swollen. When she undid his shirt she noticed streaks of blood poisoning blooming on his chest. An unhealthy shade of bronze colored his skin. Feeling the patient's eyes on her, Ellen forced her mouth to stay easy. She scoured her mind for something comforting to say but, finding nothing, didn't dare return the patient's gaze. In a voice stoppered against emotion she turned away from the patient and said to Dr. West: "What are you going to do?"

"Make him as comfortable as possible," Dr. West replied. "Get me the catheter equipment please."

The patient didn't move when they threaded the tube into his urethra and a gush of poisonous smelling blood-colored urine flooded the collection bag. Ellen clamped it off and connected a second bag.

Dr. West leaned over the patient with a stethoscope. Thinking the patient would be paying attention to Dr. West, Ellen stole a glance at his face. He was covered with black grease.

Dr. West took a syringe and filled it with morphine. "I'm giving you something for the pain," he explained as he jabbed the patient's arm, "but there's nothing else we can do."

A scream bottled itself into Ellen's throat at the brutal words. She suddenly wanted to dissect Dr. West with her bare hands.

The doctor removed the empty syringe and spoke to the man in a softer tone: "I'm sorry."

Ellen wanted to thank him for that, but heard herself challenge his diagnosis instead. "Can't you save him?" she questioned, the words tumbling out of her. "Can't you cut more off?"

"It's too late."

The patient dozed off under the effects of the drug.

"Maybe we should send him to Seattle," said Ellen, her voice rising.

"There's nothing they can do there, either."

"What about sulpha?"

Dr. West shook his head. He looked perturbed.

"I can drop ether."

"The infection has spread."

Despite her agony, Ellen sensed the doctor's composure.

"There's no reason to put him through the discomfort of an operation," said Dr. West, pulling off his gloves and dropping them into a bucket on the floor. "It's curtains for this guy."

Knowing she was in danger of committing the unpardonable sin of breaking down in front of a patient, Ellen ducked outside. The GI stood beside the tent smoking. "Don't know how you can stand it," he muttered.

Dr. West joined them shortly afterward. "Please get my dinner," he ordered the GI. "And bring a tray for my assistant. We'll eat up here."

Grateful to be gone, the GI bounded down the hill

toward the mess hall. When the GI returned, Dr. West and Ellen sat together in the first tent while the GI watched the patients. Ellen stared at the beets and Vienna sausage sitting on her tray. She could not eat.

"Never thought I'd see you lose your appetite," Dr. West said kindly.

"How long does he have?" Her hand froze into position above the plate.

"I've seen people with kidney damage go pretty quickly and I wouldn't be surprised, from the look of that urine, if his kidneys were shot. It's twenty-four hours, more or less."

"Will you tell him he's dying?" Ellen found the words choking her.

"I did, didn't I?"

Had he? Ellen tried to remember, but her mind refused to cooperate. She set her tray on the floor and looked at Dr. West with a blank expression.

"I'm bunking you in my tent," he said, standing. "I'll get it fixed up for you now. Don't worry," he patted her head, "you'll be safe with me until we figure out what to do with you."

"And you'll be safe with me," Ellen blurted, feeling annoyed.

The ridge between his eyebrows deepened.

"What about the others?" Ellen asked as he put on his army greatcoat.

"What others?" His weariness showed in his voice.

"The ones who flew west with me from Dutch Harbor."

"They have their own quarters down below. They're bunked at the first-aid station. The worst cases get up the hill to me."

"They know I'm here."

"I'll tell them you're on your way home, that it was all a mistake."

"Does this mean I can stay?"

"For now," he said and, dropping the tent flap behind him, took off down the trail toward the main encampment.

Ellen returned to the surgery tent, determined to bring comfort to the dying man. "I'll stay with him," she said to the GI in what she hoped was a male voice. He bolted away.

Ellen boiled water, cooled it with cold creek water and

added tincture of green soap. Wearing a fresh pair of rubber gloves, she squeezed a cloth and began to wash the gangrene patient's face.

"Are you hot?" Ellen asked, feeling the man's fever beneath her cloth.

He opened his eyes. Despite the blackened face and wretched greasy blackened hair, the eyes that stared back at her were as blue as Russian beads.

"Where's Sigori?" He raised his head.

"Do you mean the man who came in with you?" There was something in the way he spoke that sounded familiar. Ellen sharpened her ear to his voice.

"Yes," he said, dropping his head back on the mattress.

"Your friend's in shock," she answered, scrubbing his chin, "but he's going to pull through. He's already breathing easier."

Sparse blond whiskers emerged from the black tar as Ellen washed.

"He saved me life."

Ellen dropped the cloth into the basin, splashing her gown. What did this young man mean, saved his life! The strange feelings that churned inside her threatened to erupt. Ellen tugged at the neck of her gown, trying to loosen it. Agitated by the man's hypnotic stare, she yanked on Dr. Constance's gold chain, pulling the labret from the hidden cove of her breasts.

"Where'd ye get that?" The man's eyes cleared.

That brogue, that long roll of the tongue against the roof of the mouth sent shivers up her spine. She stared past the camouflage of tar on his face and deep into his blue eyes. "Stewart," she whispered. "Is it you?"

"Ach and it's ye, Ellen." He reached for the labret at the same instant she leaned toward him with a cry. When her wet face touched his fevered cheek, he wrapped his arms around her head. Safe, secure with her beloved brother, Ellen let her long-suppressed feelings rise. Her wrenching sobs filled the tent.

It was only when Ellen felt the bedrail cutting into her stomach that she stopped crying. She reached for Stewart's hands, released their grip on her head and pressed them against her cheeks. The hard callouses along the edge of his palms felt as rough as fish scales.

"Stewart," she said, her voice soft. "Whoever would believe it?"

"How did ye come here?" he asked.

"It was an accident. I got sent here by mistake. I thought I was going to Seward or Anchorage, but I ended up here. I'm really not supposed to be here, I know it, but I've been stubborn enough not to listen to anyone."

"Maybe ye are supposed to be here."

"What do you mean?"

"Maybe there be no accidents."

"Oh, Stewart," she said, bending closer, unsure that she had heard him. "If there are no accidents how come you're like this?"

"Donna be worrying all the time, Ellen. Ye'll ruin yer brains."

She smiled, remembering his frequent warnings when she was young.

"I'll be all right," he said.

"O Stewart! How can you be all right?" She heard the sad wail of her voice and closed her eyes, fighting for control.

"Where have you been?" she asked after a long pause. She had to know everything, to have something to hang onto later. Ellen dropped his hands and unhooked the bed rail. She sat on the mattress beside him. "Tell me everything."

Stewart struggled to speak. His chest heaved with the effort as he told her about Mutuk and the first day he left Unaganik. Listening intently as each labored word resonated in her ears, Ellen caught the gist of Stewart's journeys.

"Why didn't you stop and see Mr. Stokes in Anchorage?" she exclaimed when he drifted off. "Someone told him about you and he told Daddy when he came back to Unaganik. Daddy went looking for you."

Stewart stared at her with an expression that made her shiver.

"Daddy wanted you back, Stewart." She tightened her grip on his hands.

"Why?"

"For goodness sakes!" Ellen dropped Stewart's hands

and, forgetting the possibility of infection, pressed her own to her face, covering her mouth for fear she'd blurt out something useless, something hurtful.

"He didn't love me." Stewart searched her face as Ellen searched her mind for the right words. She was grateful when Stewart drifted off.

"It's all right, Ellen," Stewart said, coming back. "Angus doesn't have any power over me anymore."

Ellen wiped her eyes with her sleeve. Daddy was always considerate of Joe Stokes, she thought, why couldn't he have been that way with Stewart?

"My anger carried me a long time," said Stewart in a heavy voice, "but one day"—he struggled to breathe—"one day I looked over my shoulder, thinking I'd see it like a ghost, ready ta perch ag'in, but it was gone. I felt free fer the first time in me life."

"Where was this, Stewart?" Ellen felt uneasy, bewildered by what he was saying. Ghosts? Only mother saw ghosts.

"Dutch Harbor." His eyelids drooped. She noticed the rapid pulse of his temples and knew his heart struggled with the toxins in his blood. Anguished, Ellen reached over to the basin for the washcloth, but he put his arm out to stop her. "Stay," he said. "Please stay with me."

"I'm here, Stewart," she answered quietly.

"I met a woman." Stewart spoke with his eyes closed. His voice was labored. "She dug me out of a foxhole. Saved my life."

"Who is she?" Ellen leaned closer, straining to understand every word.

"It's hard ta know what love is when ye had so little of it in yer own life," said Stewart. He was drifting, Ellen knew, and she swallowed hard.

"I love you, Stewart," she said, determined not to cry. "I've always loved you." And she knew the feeling was different than anything she had felt for anyone else. It came from deep within her and harbored no conditions.

"That's why I left her ta rescue the platinum off the *Northwestern*." His voice reverberated in the old Scottish brogue he had picked up from Angus. "I wanted ta give ye the platinum fer yer school."

Ellen gripped his hands. "Stewart! You don't need to give me anything. It's enough that we're here together!" Her voice cracked and broke.

"It's gone," he said in a low voice, his eyes shutting. "Gone and I have nothing fer ye." His mouth hung open, and it sounded like he was snoring.

Feeling more sobs welling up like a flood tide at full moon, Ellen raced outside. Grief swam past her as she fought to stay in control. She breathed deeply, watching intently as each deep gulp of air left her body in a cleansing cloud of steam. So close was she to bottom, so determined to stay afloat, she did not notice Dr. West until he spoke.

"Get a coat on," he said. "You'll catch your death of pneumonia."

"He's my brother," she said, her voice flat.

"The gangrene patient?"

"How did you know?" Ellen looked at him, startled.

"The other one's an Aleut."

Ellen sunk into herself, thinking how often she took a feeling from a person rather than looking at their features. Why was it that she hadn't known it was Stewart right away? Had she not wanted to let herself know?

"Has it been a while since you've seen him?" Dr. West adjusted his spectacles.

"I don't know. A long time." And she didn't know, could not count. It seemed a lifetime he had been gone, a lifetime that they had been together. She trembled. Opening his greatcoat, Jason West enclosed the sides around her, clasping her to him. The labret pressed like a rock into her chest. She drew back to twist it out of the way. As if aware of what he had done, Dr. West drew back too. He took off his coat and draped it over Ellen.

"I'll give him another dose of morphine and check on the Aleut before we retire," he said, pulling up the tent flap, leaving her alone.

Ellen stood against the wind, hearing its hiss above the rumble of the generator, waiting for her strength to gather.

"How is he?" she asked when Dr. West returned. "I mean, how long..."

"He should be out of his agony soon," Dr. West said gently.

"How soon?" She wavered, clutching the coat around herself, seeking its protection. The coat seemed heavy enough to hold her up, but then she realized it was the doctor, steadying her with his arms.

"I gave him more morphine, Ellen. He should not feel anything."

I could kill him with morphine, she thought, put him out of his pain. The idea panicked her. She looked at Dr. West, wondering if he had read her mind. Her skin crawled. She lifted the heavy coat off her and swung it toward the doctor. He put it over his shoulders and said: "Come. I've got everything ready in my tent. It's the small one tucked behind this."

"I'll stay with Stewart."

"Do you want me to stay with you?"

"No." She straightened her back. "I want to be alone."

Ignoring the wretched odor, she slipped back into the tent to Stewart's side. He opened his eyes at the cool touch of her hand against his cheek.

"I want ye to have me watch," he said, moving his arm for her to take it off. "It's not the platinum, but it's something."

"I don't care about the platinum," she said, her eyes misting. A drop splashed on the clock face and he watched her wipe it off.

"Got damned bloody wet . . ." His voice drifted off.

"You learned to swear," Ellen said, wanting him to come back.

"I learned a lot," he said. "I learned to be me own person."

Ellen strapped the watch on her arm, pushing it up until it fit above her elbow.

"Lie with me, Ellen," Stewart said, his voice hoarse.

The circles from the heat lamps glowed through the linen cloth of the screen, throwing their shadows onto the curtain on the opposite side. Ellen felt as if she were in an amphitheater. At any moment one of the curtains would open and she would discover that this was a Greek play that Miss Long had given her to read. Was she going mad, like Mrs. Berglund? Was this how it felt?

Maybe it was a dream. She'd wake up, Stewart would be nine, she would be eight, and they would be sleeping in the same cot for the last time before he moved to his own bed and Bonnie moved in with her. They would live their childhood over only this time they'd do everything right. She kicked off her mukluks and lay beside him.

"How'd this all happen? How did you lose your leg?" If she kept him talking could she keep him alive?

"Didn't I get ta that?" His voice was slow.

"I need you in my life, Stewart," she said, speaking rapidly. "I've missed you so much. Did you know Baby Bruce died, and I worked for Dr. Visikov and then I went to Harold's Point and I lived with a crazy lady who shot herself?"

Stewart opened his eyes. "Angus sent ye?"

"He let me go," she said. "So I could go to school."

"And live with someone crazy," his voice slurred, "so ye'd lose courage and go back home."

"That's not true! Daddy wouldn't do that!"

"Ye know what they say about Angus?" His voice was weak. "Honest as the Arctic night is long."

Ellen strained to hear. She looked into the depths of his eyes where there was no color.

"With everyone but himself."

"What do you mean, Stewart?"

Stewart's mouth hung open. A gurgling sound rattled in the back of his throat. His chin dropped. Ellen knew there was no time. She crunched up on the bed, cradled his head in her arms, holding him as if to keep him forever.

"Come," Dr. West lifted her arms from Stewart's head.

Her cap had fallen off, the red ribbon had slipped off her braid, and her hair spilled over the doctor's coat. Ellen thought it was Stewart carrying her away from the incoming tide. She did not cry for her boots. Oh no. That had angered Daddy. No reason to have him scream down the cliff, his leather belt cracking Stewart's back so Stewart had to leave her.

Dr. West leaned over her. "Are you able to walk?"

"Certainly," she said in a clear and normal voice. "I can stand by myself." But when he set her down she crumbled to her knees. She remained that way while Dr. West pulled the sheet over Stewart, covering him. Then the doctor removed Ellen's rubber gloves, bathed her with alcohol. She felt no sting.

Dr. West put an arm around her and helped her into the grey morning. She heard the wind like the air in her lungs. It lifted the strands of hair that had strayed from her braid. Dr. West tightened his lips to keep her hair from catching in his mouth. He helped her onto the spare cot in his sleeping tent, behind the blanket he had hung from the center pole for privacy. Ellen clung to him. He lifted her onto the cot, humming a lullaby of Brahms that had always calmed him as a child.

The brass buttons on his coat dug into Ellen. She undid them and tucked her head against his chest. His heart beat strong and even, coursing with warm, clean blood.

24

"WE DON'T HAVE A Russian Orthodox priest on Adak," said Dr. West the next afternoon. "Would you prefer a Roman Catholic or an Episcopal to handle the service for Stewart?"

"I'm taking him home," said Ellen.

"To Unaganik?"

"Yes. It's a long time since he saw Daddy."

Drowning out the sound of the wind, a lone Warhawk roared to the base in the last tint of daylight. "Ellen," said Dr. West in the stillness that followed, "Stewart's dead. He can't see your father."

Ellen trembled like a scrap of paper in the breeze. She heard Stewart's voice. "I'm away," he said. "Away, away..." The wind carried it past the drifts of snow, down the cliffs, through the long rollers coming in from the ocean. "Away..."

"Why not let your father remember Stewart as he was?"

Ellen pulled Stewart's watch from the pocket of her white medical coat. She held it to the kerosene lantern, balancing it against the light. How did Daddy remember Stewart? She doubted if he talked about him with anyone, even Joe Stokes.

Dr. West held out his hand. Ellen gave him the watch. He wound the knob on the side. The watch ticked. Pushing up his sleeve, he checked the luminous dials on his own watch. "Send your father this instead," he said, adjusting Stewart's wristwatch to the correct Roman numerals.

"Can't," said Ellen.

"Why?"

"Because." How can I tell him, she thought. He'd never understand someone like Daddy.

"Because why?"

"Because," she blurted in a rush of emotion, "Daddy thought it was frivolous and useless when Stewart bought fine things. He swore at him and called him a dandy." Her voice rose, competing with the wind.

"Stewart not buy that." Ellen and Dr. West turned to the Aleut patient on the next gurney. "Colonel give Stewart that," said Sigori.

Dr. West turned the watch over and read the finely scrolled letters on the back. "*Virtus Millia Senta.*"

" 'Courage worth a thousand shields,' " said Sigori. "Colonel say."

Dr. West closed Ellen's fingers over the watch. She held it to her ear. In its tick tock, tick tock, images of Stewart passed before her.

"Thank you for saving Stewart's life," Ellen said in a slow voice.

Sigori looked at her and his eyes revealed nothing.

"Well, you did," said Ellen in a rush of words. "If you hadn't saved him, I might never"—she swallowed hard—"might never have seen him again."

"You see him again," said Sigori.

Ellen looked quickly at the roof of the tent, ebbing and flowing with the wind.

In preparation for the funeral, Ellen held a bowl on her head and cut her hair around it. The long tresses tumbled to the floor. She took them outside, lit a match, and burned them in the snow.

She put on the recruit's uniform Dr. West had given her and joined the funeral procession up a bleak, snowdrifted hill overlooking the harbor. The Roman Catholic priest walked with them, swinging a silver censer with incense that scented the wind. The priest wore a black cassock under a white ankle-length surplice. Under that the wore long red underwear, which showed every time the wind lifted his skirts. He did not wear a gold crown.

Three quarters of the way up the hill, a gust traveled so fast it smashed against Ellen, pushing her down. Dr. West ducked in front of her, shielding her. He extended a hand to help her up and as he did so Ellen noticed distractedly how handsome he looked in his official uniform with the medical caduceus on each lapel, the gold bars on his shoulders, the khaki tie.

They had told no one who she really was and how she was related to Stewart. In order to fulfill everyone's image of a man, she set her grief in a padded box to wait for the day she could take it out and carve her own private shapes. Inside she felt like a scared younger sister, desperate for the comforting presence of her older brother. Had she killed him?

Sigori, too weak to walk, traveled in a litter behind the coffin, swathed in blankets to fend off the cold. The GI's who strained with both burdens knew neither man. The secret whereabouts of the Scouts prevented Dr. West from contacting Colonel Kelly with the news of Stewart's death.

The procession stopped in a gully offering indifferent relief from the wind. Graves lay in scattered rows. The Roman Catholic priest swung his silver censer in a circle over a shallow grave. He spoke words in Latin that Ellen did not understand. She tried to recall the burial words of the Russian Orthodox service but her mind, consumed by the effort of controlling herself, did not oblige. She held her army cap over her left breast and stood at attention with the others, her tears drowning in her throat.

Dr. West led them in singing: "Oh God our help in ages past, our hope for years to come." Their voices rose with the churning wash of clouds. "Be Thou our guide while troubles last, and our eternal home."

They put him underground. A plain box. No three-barred cross. No flowers—not even a satin rose. When the bugler played taps, Ellen, ready to explode, climbed out of the gully and watched a narrow submarine slice through the busy harbor. The waves from its slender wake looked like white flags of truce.

The next days and weeks passed in a listless round of sleep and work. Ellen felt removed from everyone, a blank. She was dimly aware of Dr. West but her earlier feelings vanished in the effort of maintaining any semblance of normalcy. And normalcy, for her own protection, meant looking and acting like a man, meant pretending the wind was a friend.

Occasionally she felt blessed. Seeing Stewart had been a gift. The circumstances surrounding her arrival on Adak at precisely the right moment seemed foreordained, as if someone, somewhere, were watching out for her. At those times she felt she had tapped into another dimension of life, one in which Stewart had not died but merely taken a new shape, a spirit shape similar to the one Ellen had taken when she flew above her body on the mud flats. Cheok talked often about *chigiaks,* or spirits. Some native people said it was the work of the devil when a spirit returned. For Ellen, however, Stewart was not a devil but a presence of acceptance and lovingness. Sometimes she felt as if she could cuddle against him as she used to do when they shared a bed. Stewart's death was a mere metamorphosis of the connection that had existed between them since their earliest childhood.

It was during one of these good times, when she felt especially close to Stewart, that Dr. West broached a subject she had avoided all month.

"You've got to go home," he said in that paternal voice she hated so much. He sat in the tent on his own cot, on the opposite side of the blanket curtain he had hung between them for privacy. Until this evening, he had not spoken to her at night, maintaining, it seemed, a pretense that they did not sleep in the same place.

Ellen tiptoed past the curtain and curled herself onto the foot of his bed. "I don't want to go home," she said.

Dr. West tucked his spectacles into a net pocket hanging from the side of the tent. He put his book on the wooden crate underneath the kerosene lantern. "There's talk," he began.

"Why should there be talk?" Ellen asked, huddling into the oversized hospital pajamas she wore. "No one knows I'm a woman!"

"I don't mean—" he said, stumbling over his words. What did he mean? He frowned, trying to cover his confusion. "There's latrine rumors that an invasion is being planned for Attu."

"Why would they do that?"

"The Japanese have occupied Attu. The brass think they might use it as a foothold to get onto the mainland."

"Why don't they set up a blockade and starve them out?"

"Tokyo Rose says they'll fight until they eat stones."

"If Attu's anything like Adak, there's lots of stones," said Ellen in a hot-tempered voice. "It sounds ridiculous to fight for a place like this."

"War's ridiculous, but what are the choices?"

Noticing the flush on his face in the dull light from the lantern, and the tightening of his lips, Ellen stopped talking. She did not want to argue.

"You must leave," he said.

"Aren't you pleased with my help?"

"I am pleased, Ellen, but if I get sent with the troops invading Attu, you won't be safe." The crease between his pale eyebrows deepened. Leaning over, Ellen pressed her fingers on it, trying to rub it away. He removed her hand from his face and tucked it back in her lap.

"You'll be left here alone," he said, his voice stern.

"You mean I'll be the only person left on Adak?"

"The only woman."

"And it's no place for a woman," she said, flipping her hands up through her chili bowl haircut.

Dr. West's blue eyes, without the glasses, looked wearily from their lined sockets. "You learn fast," he said, grinning suddenly.

"It's no place for anyone," said Ellen, unnerved by his smile. It was the first time she had seen him smile since she arrived.

"Ellen! I can't stand it any longer! I'm worried about you!"

"I can take care of myself."

"You know I don't want you to go." Dr. West's voice dropped.

"How do I know that?" she asked, propping her chin on her knees, speaking softly. "You practically ignore me, except to order me 'Mac do this, Mac do that,' and now you want to order me home."

He closed his eyes. She stared at the shadow cast by the lantern across his face. It looked less perfect, more vulnerable in this light. The blond hair, a little too long, hung over the side of his high forehead. Her eyes misted. The blondness of his hair merged into an image of Stewart, and she remem-

bered how Stewart's hair had shone creamy white at the end
of a hot summer.

"Ellen," Dr. West said, opening his eyes. "It's part of
being a doctor, giving orders. I'm sorry if I offended you."

"It's not just that," she said softly. "I want to be with
you."

"God only knows," he said in an anguished voice, "I
want you too."

In the long silence between them, the wind increased in
intensity. Soon it was screeching like a wild beast pursued by
vengeful gods.

"Better be careful," Ellen cautioned in a teasing voice.
"That sounds like the laugh of the *yuilrig*."

"What do they do?" His voice was low.

"They reach down and pull out your guts." She pounced
toward him, playfully tickling his stomach.

Her grabbed her hands and, pressing her against him,
smothered her giggles with his mouth. Her lips softened
against his. "Ellen," he whispered, "you can't imagine how
I've longed for this moment. Some nights I've hardly slept,
thinking of you in the next cot. Have you thought of me this
way at all?"

Ellen's body grew heavy with warmth. She kissed her
answer into his chin, his cheeks, then kissed the deep crease
in the middle of his forehead. "You worry too much," she
whispered.

"I'm worried about what's going to happen next," he
said and, moving her to one side, he rolled out of the cot.
"Bedtime," he said in a husky voice.

He picked her up and carried her to her own bed, tucked
her in, and kneeling on the floor beside her, kissed her lips,
her eyes, her hair until she dissolved in the pleasure of it. She
yearned to drape herself around him, to feel his cool skin
against the fire of her flesh.

"Sleep well," he whispered, pulling away.

Ellen circled her arms around his head. "How can I
sleep," she asked, "when I feel like this?"

He stood up. "We mustn't, Ellen," he said, and
disappeared behind the blanket that hung between them.

Ellen squirmed under the covers, trying to get comfortable. Her body ached in places she had never known existed.

She longed to fling herself into his arms but felt laced to the army cot and its metal frame.

When sleep finally stopped the pain, she dreamed that someone stood above her, waiting to rescue her from the tide. She woke with a start and, looking up, saw not Stewart but Dr. Jason West. He was dressed and ready for work. He avoided her gaze.

All day Ellen, pretending to be Mac, dispensed brown bombers to a contingent of constipated GI's, picked cooties off a new recruit who was covered with the "shifting freckles," and lanced a boil on the bum of the skipper of the honey barge. She could hardly wait until evening.

She reached the tent early, slipped off her clothes, and did not put on pajamas. Her body burned with heat. She wanted to dig into herself, to stop the agony. Never had such sensations risen from such a private place. She tossed on the cot, trying to get comfortable. The bottom tuck of the blankets came loose. Cold blew on her feet. Ellen pulled the blankets around her, into a cocoon.

Looking for anything to distract her from this demanding heat, she imagined the cold wind blowing off Bristol Bay, blowing away the hot sun, the mosquitoes, the haze, so that the earth contained only light and scent.

But still her limbs felt charged with expectation. Why didn't he come? Maybe there was an emergency. I'll go and help, thought Ellen, dragging herself out of bed. The cold snapped against her as she stood stark naked, reaching for the pants and shirt in which she masked her womanness. At that moment Dr. West entered. The beam of his flashlight played across her breasts.

Ellen jumped. "Oh!" she said. "I didn't hear you coming."

"What are you doing here?" He swung his coat around her shoulders.

"Waiting for you," said Ellen and huddled into the greatcoat.

"I've been at the CO's," he said. "I've made inquiries to get you home."

"I'm not going."

"You can't stay here." He bent over her cot, straightening it.

"I'm not going."

"Ellen." His voice was too loud, and he peeked out the tent flap, to see if anyone lurked about. "Ellen." He led her like a sleepwalker to her cot. When she did not budge, he lifted her off her feet and shoved her into bed. The coat fell to the floor. Ellen shivered at the touch of his hands on her naked skin.

"I've already explained why you can't stay here." His voice shook.

"I can't go home," she said, too confused to argue. "I've already told you." What had she said? That Daddy would never let her get away again?

"Ellen," he continued, looking at her with a mixture of tenderness and admiration. "If anyone has the gumption, it's you."

"Gumption? What's that?" She tried to reach under the cot for the carpetbag where she kept Dr. Visikov's dictionary.

Dr. West held down the blankets. "Courage. It means courage."

Ellen thought of Stewart's watch wrapped in gauze, tucked under the corner of her bed. Curious he should say "courage," she thought, remembering the inscription on the watch. "I'm scared to go back to Unaganik," she said. "It will kill me."

He clasped her chin with his hand. "That's a dreadful thing to say!" He looked from one eye to the next, his concern obvious. "Home's a place you can always go. When I go home, I feel like a hero. Mater cancels her engagements and the maid fixes roast beef and strawberry tart."

"If I went home we'd have stinkyhead and *akutaq*," said Ellen. She felt, rather than saw, the grimace on his face. "You see, Dr. West," she added, "I don't want that. I want to go to the city and go to school."

"You need money for that!"

"Money?" Ellen stared at him. "Can't I go to school for free?"

"It costs a great deal of money to go to university," said Dr. West. "Besides, you'll have to pay for a place to live in Seattle, won't you?"

Ellen covered her face with her hands. Why hadn't she known?

"I'll see what I can do to help you out," said Dr. West, and without another word he ducked behind the blanket to his side of the tent.

Ellen heard him undressing, heard his cot creak as he lay down on it.

"Dr. West?" she whispered through the blanket. "What's wrong?"

He did not respond.

Confusion settled over her. She could not sleep. The night wind blew into oblivion as she replayed, over and over, the events of the past two days. I've done nothing wrong, she told herself as the roof of the tent lightened to grey and the wind veered, bringing ice rain. It doesn't rain in the Aleutians, they would say, it rains in Siberia and blows over.

Dr. West woke with his lips in a straight line and his shoulders stiff. Ellen, dizzy from the turmoils of the night, could not muster the courage to talk to him. When he left the tent without a word, she stuffed her pillow into her mouth and choked down a scream.

It grew bitterly cold. The Aleutians were experiencing the worst winter in fifty years, but it was nothing compared to the glacial formality with which Dr. West treated Ellen. She dared not mention her longing for him. As the days moved into weeks, her despair deepened. Over and over she reviewed what he had done, what she had done, why he had turned away from her, what had gone wrong. It's someone in New York City, she decided, but threw the idea aside like an undersized cod. He couldn't have kissed her if he loved someone else, couldn't have written all those letters to Harold's Point.

There was nothing specific in Jason West's behavior that Ellen could fault. He discussed cases, called her Mac, and kept up the pretense of her masquerade. He made sure that she had so many Vienna sausages they seemed to crawl like maggots across her plate. She never ate with him, eating instead with Sigori in the Quonset hut they had erected to replace the surgery tent.

She told Sigori that she was Stewart's sister. He filled her in on the events of Kiska, the Rat Islands, and how they had made their way to Amchitka, only to be bombed by American fliers making sure that no Japanese occupied the evacuated Aleut village. Sigori stayed on, waiting, Ellen supposed, for the Scouts to pick him up. She dreaded the day when he would leave. But no one arrived and no one left. The weather grounded all planes and anchored all ships. The Quonset hut filled with men who, crazy from the constant wind and the desolate landscape, sat motionless and unblinking with what they called the "Aleutian Stare." Aleutian malaria, the common head cold, was preferable. One got over that.

A GI got lost on a trail and when they found him, a fox had eaten half his face and his right leg. A buck private refused to leave the sack for six days and his kidneys became inflamed. A corporal broke his arm when the latrine blew over while he was reading Dashiell Hammett's column in the camp paper.

And always the wind cursed the treeless hills, the white volcanic cones, the fogged-in harbor with its toll of battered ships, the grounded planes. The land, the sea, the soldiers cursed back. The wind jostled the clouds, often pushing them into shapes that reminded Ellen of the lion staring off the page in *Our Wonder World*.

She clung to the knowledge of what had happened to her after Baby Bruce had died, the dead-end tunnel into which she had crawled. Over and over she said, "I'm sane! I'm sane!" It became a litany to keep herself grounded in the real world. She chanted it in time to the wind, faster when it blew at sixty, slower when it diminished to thirty. When it blew to a hundred miles an hour her mind was stunned to silence by the overpowering force of the gale.

Men fought over one up or five card stud. They lost interest in washing and fought for the honor of the worst body odor. They fantasized romance with Tokyo Rose, the Japanese broadcaster whose job it was to subvert the Allied forces. More than one GI arrived at Surgery with his penis stuck in a bottle after listening to her daily radio show.

"If these men knew I was a woman would they be more embarrassed?" Ellen asked Dr. West after they took care of one man with a grotesquely swollen organ that had turned purple within the tight neck of a bottle.

"They'd be standing in line!"

Shocked, Ellen looked at him and noticed that the crease in his forehead had deepened.

"I wish we could get you out of here," he mumbled, turning his back. His shoulders were stooped, and she longed to break through his reserve. Why couldn't they comfort each other in this awful hellhole? Most of the time, however, she was able to forget that she and Jason had once held and kissed each other. He was the Chief, she the underling, and that was the sum total of their togetherness. She gave up thinking there would ever be any love between them.

Ellen now longed to get off Adak, but as long as the bad weather held, all travel off the island was canceled. Whenever there was a brief lull in the storms, the flight jockeys took off to drop some "cheese," their word for dynamite, into a "rat hole," by which they meant a hole in the clouds. They dropped ash cans, what they called depth charges, and coke bottles full of gasoline. When the planes returned from bombing Kiska, the base held its collective breath, counting each landing. Not all of the planes always returned, and then there were more cases of depression, more fights.

One spectacular morning when the wind blew off the lower ceiling of clouds and the faintest rays of sunshine beamed through the high cirrus, Ellen, in her soldier's outfit, paused outside the sleeping tent. Sky-starved pilots swarmed to their planes. The lagoon on which the corrugated metal field was laid had been hurriedly drained by the ingenious system of locks and dikes designed by the engineers. The snarling jaws and painted tigers' heads of the P-40's sped down the runway one after the other and lifted into the air.

With noses pointed to the cove, propellers spinning, the fleet of B-24 bombers waited for the signal flag. The roar deafened the base. It buckled against the snowcapped mountains and returned to shake the canvas roofs of the partially buried tents.

Sigori, wearing a coat over his hospital robe and heavy boots on his feet, stood beside Ellen. The first bomber roared into the air, skimmed the dock, banked, and at two hundred feet shadowed the heavy navy muscle moored in the outer harbor. A second bomber followed in close succession.

"Off to Kiska," said Ellen.

Sigori grunted in reply.

The third bomber waffled on the makeshift runway, came down hard on a section of disconnected sheeting, bounced into the air and, in a blinding flash of light, exploded. Shards of wing burst like flak over the land and sea. The fuselage torpedoed into Sweeper Cove.

Sigori bounded down the trail. Ellen followed.

Gasoline coated the water. Men raced down the dock, heaved themselves into a lifeboat and cast off. One threw his cigarette over and a tongue of fire licked over the gasoline. With a quick suction of air, the fuel whooshed into flames. A shield of fire covered the cove. Ellen jumped back, her face amber hot. Peering through the blaze, she saw an arm emerge from the burning water, grasping at flames. As she watched, horrified, the hand sank beneath the surface and was gone.

On the next clear day a new bomber arrived. On the sixteenth of February eight new Warhawks arrived. The day following, under a rainless overcast sky, Ellen, without a word to anyone but Sigori, hiked up the hill to Stewart's grave. She carried a trench shovel called an idiot stick and a three-barred cross Sigori had carved out of wood from a packing crate.

"I miss you, Stewart," she said, after planting the cross in the bare earth that marked his grave. "But not too much. Not like when you were gone before and I was waiting for you to come back."

She squatted beside the grave, inhaling the cold air. "I hate to ask you, Stewart," she said, looking at the mound of dirt, "because I'm afraid you'll get upset again about the platinum. But I'd be grateful for any help."

Ellen slipped into a reverie where time and space merged. The endless wind pushed clouds down off the volcanic mountains, over the hills, shrouding the island. Just in the nick of time, the wind pushed the clouds aside. Taking advantage of the sudden visibility, a patrol plane roared to a landing on the drained lagoon. Hearing the noise, Ellen stood and stretched her stiff legs.

"As soon as the weather breaks, Stewart," she said, "I'll leave Adak. But I'll always remember this spot."

She impressed the gravesite into her memory, how the grave was a long perfect shape, obscuring for all time the one-sidedness of Stewart's body, how the cross stood against

the barren hillside and how the hillside lay against the sky.
Then she headed down the trail, swinging the shovel and
skipping in time to her song. "Oh Mary, don't you weep,
don't you moan. Oh Mary, don't you weep . . ." On the third
verse she saw Dr. West coming up the path.

"I came to look for you," he said in a tone of relief.

"Were you worried about me?"

"Of course I was." Suddenly he bent and kissed her
cheek.

"Don't start rumors, Doctor," Ellen teased. "Remember
I'm a man."

"I've been trying to," he said, "but it's difficult to
forget you're a woman."

Standing on tiptoes, Ellen pulled his head down. "I've
missed you," she whispered against his lips.

"You had a visitor," he said, holding her away.

"A GI to see me?"

"No. Someone off the Yippee boats."

Ellen moved off in a hurry. Dr. West held her arm,
slowing her. "Expecting another lover?" he asked.

"How dare you!" Ellen cried in anger.

"I'm sorry," he said.

"I hope so."

Ellen glared until he turned away, flushed from her look.
"What do you mean, 'another' lover?" she said. "Are *we*
lovers?"

"He brought you a letter."

Why doesn't he answer me? The old confusion returned.
Ellen closed her eyes and fought to keep separate of his
mood.

"Who is he?" Dr. West asked. His voice sounded
strange.

"Ted Kleet," said Ellen. "I don't know anyone else on
the Yippee boats."

"Is he a friend?"

"Since the very moment I met him," said Ellen, "and
don't you dare accuse me of anything else, because if you do,
I'll suspect *you* of having lovers."

"Me?" His voice rose. "Here? On Adak?"

Ellen couldn't help but laugh. "Dear Dr. West," she
said, touching his buttons. "Don't you want a lover on

Adak?'' He swerved away and all down the trail she wondered what she had done wrong.

The reached the hospital area in silence. And then Ellen asked, ''Why didn't Ted wait?''

''Two torpedo boats collided. He dashed off on a search and rescue. He said to tell you he'd be back soon.''

Inside, Dr. West handed her an envelope written in Dr. Visikov's unmistakable scrawl. She sat on a stool and, straining her eyes, deciphered the script.

> *Dear Ellen,*
>
> *I have set up a Trust Fund in your name. When you get to Seattle, and I hope you do, please contact my attorney, Mr. Rupert, who knew me long before I became the broken-down doctor you so kindly assisted. Now my dear Ellen, if you learn anything from this, that is to treat your own self with as much respect as you treat your patients, a lesson my former wife tried to teach me, but which I chose to ignore.*
>
> *However, if I had not been addicted, I would not have practiced medicine in Unaganik and would not have had the pleasure of knowing you. If there has been any comfort for me in my declining years, it is the knowledge that I may be able to offer you some assistance. It is for this reason that I am writing.*
>
> *The monies I have left will be adequate for whatever you decide to do. They were earned during my productive days in Seattle, before I fell from grace. While I hope you will use them to study medicine, I am too aware of your own independence to want to persuade you one way or the other. If you do study medicine, please remember this piece of advice from an old doctor: The patient who wants to get well, almost always will.*

Ellen checked the date. January 1, 1943. Six weeks ago. She tucked the letter into the pocket of her army greatcoat and left the office, unaware that a man in striped hospital pajamas followed.

25

WHEN HE FOLLOWED HER into the sleeping tent, Ellen screamed. Powerful hands spun her around. His mouth crushed hers, pushing her to the floor. Ellen drove her knee into his crotch. He gasped. Cupping his hands around his groin, the man slunk outside like an animal who had soiled his own nest.

Sigori punched him back into the tent. The man crumpled to the floor. "I kill you," Sigori said in a hard voice, pressing his full weight on the man.

"Don't!" The word burst from Ellen. She struggled to her knees.

"Not kill him?" Sigori looked up, surprised. He released his thumbs from the man's neck.

Ellen slumped onto the cot and gasped "No!" Her chest heaved.

The man leered at her. Sigori slammed down his boot. "You go in brig!"

The man was the rear gunner whose cheek had frozen when the gun door had fallen off during a bombing raid over Kiska. He no longer wore bandages and his recovery was due to Ellen's tireless application of hot water bottles to thaw his face. His striped pajamas were covered with mud, as if he'd been hiding in a foxhole, waiting his chance.

"If he's locked up," Ellen said, "he'll tell who I am and it'll get Dr. West into trouble for concealing my identity." She turned to the patient and spoke in a sharp voice: "Did you tell anyone about me?"

"No," he whined.

"How did you know I wasn't a man?"

The patient said nothing. Sigori smashed down his boot. "I guessed," the patient whined.

"He get ideas," said Sigori. "I been watching him."

"Why didn't you tell me?"

"I not scare you."

Ellen fell silent, wondering if she would have been scared. One thing she knew was that she'd never have hiked up the hill to Stewart's grave alone.

"I promise Stewart," said Sigori.

"You did?"

"He tell me to protect his woman."

"Me?" said Ellen. "When did Stewart say that?"

"When you out of tent. He wake up and tell me."

"He must have meant someone else."

"Who be that?"

Ellen ransacked her brain, going through each treasured word Stewart had spoken before he died. She found a clue. "He told me that a woman dug him out of a foxhole in Dutch Harbor," she said at last.

Sigori looked at her through hooded eyes and suddenly Ellen wanted it over, the whole horrid business. "Let him go! He's learned his lesson."

"You tell anyone and . . ." Making a gurgling sound with his cheeks that rattled like the last breath of air, Sigori twisted his fists and stood back. Clutching his private parts, the man snaked out of the tent. Ellen tried to push herself off the cot but fell back, dizzy.

"I get the doctor," said Sigori.

"No!" Ellen shook her head. "He mustn't know."

"You be pale." Sigori leaned over her.

Ellen concentrated on her breathing. Her pulse slowed. She felt overcome by weariness and cold. Above the tent, the never-ending wind blew across the canvas, over the barren ground, piling snowdrifts higher. Sigori lit the heater. The kerosene fumes filled the tent.

"Does anyone else know who I am?" she asked. "Did he tell anyone?"

"He not tell because he want you for himself."

"He might tell now."

"He not dare." Sigori twisted his fists again.

"What about when you go? You've been well enough to leave the hospital for some time."

"I know." Sigori nodded. "Dr. West say I go when I want."

"Why do you stay?"

"How I take care of you if I not here?"

Ellen tilted her head, letting the tears run into her eyes. Each muscle in her body seemed to be quivering independently of every other one, as if each muscle was responding in its own way to the separate events of her recent life: Stewart's death, Dr. West's baffling behavior, and now this.

"The cross looks good on Stewart's grave," she said after a long silence.

"That be good," said Sigori.

Then Ellen remembered the answer to her prayers: Dr. Visikov's letter. She quickly curved her fingers around it as if she were drowning and had just found a skiff. "You can go," she said, looking at Sigori. "I'll be fine."

"If you not," he said, lifting the tent flap, "holler."

"Thank you," said Ellen, trying not to shake. "Thank you very much."

Sigori left and Ellen reread her letter in the light from the heater. She was huddled by it when Dr. West entered the tent. He hung his greatcoat over the blanket separating their cots.

"Hold me," Ellen said, going to him.

His arms remained at his sides.

Ellen held her arms in front of her chest, trembling. "Please?" she said and fumbled with the brass buttons on his jacket.

"Not bad news in your letter, I hope," he said.

"Good news." She tried to sound cheerful, but the shock of what had happened weighed on her.

Ellen threaded her arms inside his jacket. Dr. West stood still. She tucked against his chest and heard the Gregorian chant of his heart as if she were back in the old church at home. How long ago that seemed.

Slowly his arms crept up her back. "Ellen," he cried and pulled her to him so suddenly the breath whooshed out of her lungs. Freeing her arms from the constraints of his jacket, Ellen raised her hands to his face. It was still cold from the wind. She rubbed the heels of her hands up and down his cheeks, feeling the bristle of his evening beard, the hard set of his jaw. Suddenly she stiffened at the sound of voices on the trail.

"I let a couple of the patients out to play panguini," he whispered into Ellen's ear.

"Don't, Dr. West." She twisted away from the tickle of his breath.

"What's my name?" He grabbed her hand. His voice was loud, angry.

"West."

"Do you call Ted Kleet, Mr. Kleet?"

"No." Ellen's voice fell. Why was everything so difficult? What was wrong with this man? On a whim she said, "Do you want me to call you Jason?"

"You make me feel like I'm about to buy favors when you call me by my last name."

"Favors?"

"You know," he stumbled, "favors."

"Is that why you've stayed away from me?"

"It just seemed," he said and before her unblinking stare he began to stutter, "I mean, it didn't seem right."

"My mother always calls my father Mr. MacTavish."

"Your mother doesn't call him that in the bedroom!"

Ellen undid Jason's shirt buttons. "Everywhere," she whispered.

"I don't believe you."

"Come home with me and find out."

"Will you come to Manhattan and meet Mater?"

"Yes!" Bunching up his undershirt, twisting his dog tag until it hung down his back, Ellen flattened her hands against his warm chest, playing with his nipples. They hardened under her fingertips and she felt the corresponding hardening of her own breasts. She nuzzled her lips against his throat.

"Ellen!" He drooped against her, anguish in his voice. "Do you know how hard it's been, sleeping over there"—he pointed to his cot—"with you here?"

"I know," she replied, reliving the nights when sleep was no comfort.

"I can't stand it!" He clung to her and she swayed under his weight.

"Let's sit," she said and inched him toward her cot. He sat on the edge and absently adjusted his pants.

Ellen took off her boots and sat crosslegged, facing his profile. His skin had the sheen of polished ivory and his features the perfection of an exquisite carving. She stroked her hand on the back of his neck, massaging the vertebrae at the top of his spine, moving her fingers up through his hair to the crown of his head. He trembled.

Ellen moved closer. Suddenly Jason swept out his arms and lifted her onto his lap. She felt his maleness between her legs, rocked back and forth against it. Her body felt fluid, as if she were a ribbon of light flicking against a night sky.

"Ellen," he said hoarsely, "you can't do this."

"Why?"

He grabbed her elbows, holding her still. "We're heading for trouble."

"Why?" she persisted and tried not to move.

Jason pushed her off his lap until her buttocks touched the floor. Her feet remained on the cot. Ellen felt heavy, as if the light had collapsed into a mass of atoms that needed only a paper match to explode. Holding the legs of Jason's pants, she tried to pull herself up. He lifted his knees and moved back on her bed. Ellen swung her feet around and stood. She undid her pants and shirt and dropped them to the floor.

"What are you doing?" Jason's eyes widened.

"I'm getting ready for bed." She swung the blanket from the rope that held it between their cots. Jason's greatcoat fell to the floor. Shivering, Ellen pulled the blanket around her and curled under it at the head of her bed.

"What time of the month is it for you?" His voice came from far away.

"I have something," said Ellen. She dangled sideways off the bed and reached into the pocket of her sealskin parka, bringing out a round package.

"Where'd you get that?" Jason sounded angry.

"I found it on the medicine shelf. You keep a stock of them."

"All military bases do. How'd you know what it was?"

"Dr. Constance explained birth control to Abby after she had her baby. I listened and, when I saw this, I thought it might come in handy."

Jason raised his eyebrows. "You mean you wanted to sleep with someone?"

"You," said Ellen, matter-of-factly. "But I didn't know if you wanted to sleep with me. If you did, I knew I didn't want to get pregnant."

"I don't believe this," Jason said. "I must be dreaming."

"You're not," teased Ellen and nuzzled her lips against his neck.

"You've done this before," he said, hollow, not moving.

"Why do you say that?" Ellen stiffened. She looked him in the eye.

"How do you know so much?"

"You learn a lot working around a hospital," said Ellen.

"Do you want me?" he whispered, his lips against her mouth.

Ellen felt a charge of electricity start between her legs and spread through her body, drawing all her energy to that one focal spot. "Yes," she said, aching for release from the overwhelming sensations, held so long they now seemed to erupt from her.

When Jason struggled out of his clothes, Ellen admired his whiteness in the blue light of the heater. He slipped his dog tag over his head and dropped it on the floor. She took off her jade labret and set it beside the dog tag.

When he took off his undershorts, she shivered with excitement at the sight of the long shaft jutting proudly between his white legs. He unrolled the condom onto his penis, dropped on top of her and, in a thrust of urgency, entered. Ellen gasped. Jason thrust in and out as if he had forgotten her. She dug her hands into his shoulders and bit her bottom lip to keep from crying out loud. Jason shuddered and slumped to one side. His fingers stroked her neck. "Darling," he sighed, "I don't believe this."

Ellen wondered again what she had done wrong, why she was left with this awful feeling of drowning in her own heat. She thought of the drowning pilot reaching through the water, grasping at flames. In desperation, she stroked Jason, wishing he would come to her again and solve this awful dissatisfaction she felt. But Jason slept.

In the morning, as soon as Jason awoke, Ellen said, "I have to go."

"I know," he said, stretching his arms, smiling broadly. "This bed's too small."

"I mean leave Adak."

"Go? Not now. Not after all the time we've wasted."

"You were right. It's too risky to stay."

"Oh God," he said, peering at her through eyes not yet fully awake to the world, "you can't go. Not now."

"You have to arrange it for me, Jason."

"No. I want you. I need you, Ellen, and I've been such a cad."

"Jason," said Ellen, hating what she had to say next. "Someone grabbed me in the tent yesterday. Sigori arrived in the nick of time."

"Oh God!" Jason leaned over her, pressing her to him so tightly Ellen could hardly breathe.

"I'll stay with Sigori while you find out when the next transport ship is expected," she said with her hands against his shoulders, shoving him off her chest.

"You'd never be able to keep up your disguise on board ship."

"A Douglas might be going to Anchorage. I'll fly."

"It would be difficult to swing a seat for a medical assistant."

"You have to," Ellen insisted.

"You astonish me!" Jason's frown deepened. He fell back onto the cot, scrunching himself within the narrow confines of the canvas mattress. "How can you be like this? After last night?"

"You think because a woman has a man she loses her mind?" Ellen teased, but inside she felt welts across her heart.

"I did think," Jason stuttered. "I mean . . ." He studied her closely, looking into her eyes, across her face, over her lips, across the blankets that shielded her naked body. He returned his gaze to her face as if he had discovered a secret. ". . . it was your first time and all."

Ellen forced herself to smile, to remain calm when she really felt like an outgoing wave bucking an incoming tide. "So you do believe me."

"Yes, my darling, and if I stay here much longer I'll never be able to get my clothes on."

Ellen dropped off the bed, pulling him with her. They tumbled to the floor. Ellen laughed out loud and Jason pressed his mouth against hers, stifling the sound. Ellen tickled him and he twisted away.

"Shh!" he said, pursing his lips.

"Shh!" Ellen mimicked, pressing her pursed lips against his. Their lips softened into each other and they played with each other's tongues until Jason pulled away. Ellen watched, heavy, as he stood up and reached for his clothes.

"I can't see the CO until I get a shower," he said, sniffing himself.

"Let the wind do it," said Ellen, wishing she had more than a wash basin for herself.

"I'll have to think up some cock and bull story to get you on a plane with the brass," he said, watching her with adoring eyes. "And that will only get you to Anchorage. You'll have to find your own way home."

"I'm not going to Unaganik. I'm going to Seattle."

"You can't go to Seattle by yourself."

"Why not?" Ellen planted her hands on her bare hips.

"Because."

"Dr. Visikov has left me a trust," said Ellen, mimicking Jason's paternalistic tone. "I'm going to Seattle to start school and wait for you to get off this rock."

"I've never met a woman like you," said Jason, shaking his head.

"You've never looked for one," Ellen said and drew his face down to hers and kissed him squarely on the lips.

When Jason departed for the showers, Ellen felt a desolation in her whole being. Her body, the secret parts, ached. She wanted to cup her hands over herself and press everything together. Was this how it was? How it felt? Was this why Mother moaned from the big bed sometimes in the middle of the night when they thought everyone was asleep?

While she waited for Jason, Ellen straightened shelves, removed instruments from the autoclave and laid them in kidney-shaped basins, and tried to sort through the conflicting feelings tormenting her body and mind. "What are you going to do next?" she asked Sigori.

"Go to Dutch Harbor."

"Maybe you could stay here and take my place."

"I go," said Sigori, "soon as you leave."

"If I can't get a plane," said Ellen, after a long pause, "maybe I'll get one of the Yippee boats."

"You could ride the *Yethl*," said Sigori. "Ted Kleet be glad."

"I should have thought of that myself," said Ellen, now wishing she hadn't told Jason to find her transportation.

"A C-47 is arriving with a new high-frequency fixed band direction finder," Jason said when he returned. "They hope to beat the fog with it. On its home trip, the brass are shipping some blokes out. I got you a place."

"Will it be easy to find another plane in Anchorage?" Ellen asked.

"This one's flying direct to Seattle," said Jason. "It's got extra fuel tanks in the cabin. You can thank your lucky stars."

But by mid-morning the fog coated everything. The C-47 with its special fog-proof instruments did not arrive. Jason spent part of the afternoon reading one of his medical texts while Ellen, after completing her regular routine of sharpening needles and sterilizing instruments, went from patient to patient, checking temperatures, pulse and respiration, giving medications, and straightening bedcovers.

She joined Jason for dinner for the first time in weeks and afterward watched him slip a condom into his coat pocket. She felt the stirring of her skin, the flush behind her ears.

"I never thought I'd thank the fog," Jason whispered as they lay together, naked, in Ellen's cot. The kerosene heater flickered. In the distance, they heard the clank of chains as a Liberty ship dropped anchor.

"How I love you," Jason whispered. He lay on his back, his arms pillowing his head. His blue eyes, like the flame in the heater, glowed.

Ellen lay on him, pressing her thumbs against his nipples. Laughing, she made kissing noises a handspan from his mouth. His responding laugh was a warm brush of air. Without moving his arms, he lifted his head until his lips reached hers. With the tip of his tongue, he traced the outline of her mouth.

"Did you ever think of me this way in Harold's Point?" he asked.

"No," said Ellen, smiling, "but I did think about being a doctor like you."

He grinned. "I'm glad I'm good for something."

Ellen took her right hand from his chest and, pressing it against his mouth, sealed his lips. "You're taunting me, Dr. West."

He sucked the tips of her fingers into his mouth. "What did I tell you?" he said, sounding as if he had a mouth full of coins. His teeth gnawed on her knuckles. "I'll bite these off and you won't be able to do surgery."

"I don't want to cut people!" Ellen said, drawing herself up, sitting across him so her knees pressed against his ribs and her labia pressed against his stomach. "I want to make them whole."

"You'll have to do some surgery, if you're going to be a doctor. It's in the training."

Ellen's eyes widened. Jason's tongue circled around and around her fingers. He clasped her to him, stroking his long elegant fingers along the nubs of her spine. Intoxicated with happiness, Ellen pressed her lips to his. Her skin seemed to slip off like one of Mrs. Meriweather's satin sheets, leaving her nerve endings wild with sensation.

She felt as wide as the tent, as formless as a wind-driven cloud. She rubbed against him, eyelids heavy over her partially closed eyes so that she was unaware that Jason watched with a pleased smile on his face. Her labia swelled. She found his sturdy shaft, centered it between her legs and, with both hands holding it, brushed the tip over her swollen clitoris.

"Mmm," she said, feeling the resonance in the back of her throat. Her pulse beat into her loins. She opened her legs and Jason slid inside. Her sensations exploded. Her fingers plucked at his nipples as if to lend reality to the rest of his body. She swam in her own juices. His shaft slipped deeper. She opened around it and felt the waters lap around him. He plunged in and out, up and down. Ellen lost herself in the union of their linked bodies, their melded flesh, as if they had escaped together into a warm and salty ocean. She let go and, arching her back, moaned over and over.

Ellen felt as if she were the whole Pacific Ocean. A palm tree swayed at the shore. Its leaves tickled the sky. She collapsed into the curve of Jason's arm and as the sensations eased from her body, she smiled at the memory of her mother's sounds late at night in the big bed off the kitchen. Now she understood their meaning.

Jason stroked her head and Ellen fell sound asleep, dreaming that she lay on white sand and watched naked brown boys tossing coconuts from tall palms.

"Let's pray for more fog," Jason whispered in the early morning when they awoke. Their sweet musty smell permeated the tent.

"Have you ever seen a palm tree?" Ellen whispered.

"Mater and I went to Florida when my father died. I saw them there."

"I thought they grew in Hawaii."

Jason brushed his fingers through her cropped hair. "You say so many funny things, Ellen. How do you know about palm trees?"

"The cannery bosses always sent Daddy a calendar from Hawaii," she murmured from the edge of sleep. "I would stare at that calendar in the middle of winter and pretend I was there."

"Someday I want to take you," Jason said, kissing her on the lips.

There were four days of fog, four glorious nights together on the narrow cot. Ellen felt changed forever from a child into a woman, felt the softness of her skin, the looseness of her mouth. How quickly Jason smiled at her now, how often they touched, sneaking contact when they thought the patients weren't looking. The fifth day dawned clear and bright. The sun bounced off the sweeping mountain snowfield and dropped onto the craggy cliff face, melting snow from the crevices. The drops trickled down like tears.

In preparation for packing, Ellen dumped her carpetbag on the bed. The matching ivory whale Jonah had carved at Jason's request fell out.

"Mater will be so pleased," Jason said, examining it closely. "Before the Great Depression, my father dealt in art.

She values fine pieces and had to sell most of hers in order to survive, you know.''

"I didn't know," said Ellen. The ivory matched hers and was for Jason, not his mother. She felt grumpy and out of sorts, and rushed to stuff her things into the carpetbag which Jason hid, along with her sealskin parka, in an army duffel bag. Wearing pants and shirt, a greatcoat and a soldier's folded cap, she darted into the Quonset hut to see Sigori. The patient who had grabbed her faced the curved metal wall.

"Sometime again," said Sigori, smiling. "*Elanigulu*."

"*Elanigulu*," said Ellen and tried to smile back.

Jason walked her to the metal runway. "I've a second cousin in Seattle," he said. "Please look her up. I've asked her to help you." He handed Ellen an envelope with the address on the front.

"Shall I tell her we're lovers?"

"My God, Ellen!" Jason's forehead wrinkled in annoyance.

"Don't swear," snapped Ellen.

"I've got some money for you," he said, handing her a roll of bills.

"Is this pay for my favors?"

"You astonish me!" Jason's voice exploded. His eyebrows rolled over his glasses.

Ellen laughed at the shocked expression on his face. As if thawed by a ray of light, the unspoken tension between them broke. She barely resisted the impulse to put her hands on his cheeks and pull his face toward her own.

"It's your salary from assisting in the hospital," said Jason. "It'll tide you over until you get your trust fund."

Ellen slipped the money into the pocket of the greatcoat. The C-47 loomed before her. She closed her eyes, trying to stem an almost uncontrollable sense of panic. Her leaving was suddenly real.

PART
THREE

26

"HUT-SUT RAWLSON ON THE rillerah and a brawla, brawla sooit" . . . Voices banged out the lively march rhythm of a favorite Aleutian song. "The brawla is the boy and girl, The Hut-Sut is their dream," the soldiers sang. Ellen, with hands clenched and her heart pounding, forced herself to stay in the plane. "A boy would sit and fish and dream," the soldiers sang, "when he should have been in school." She had longed for school, but if that patient hadn't gone off the beam, if Dr. Visikov hadn't written, and Ted Kleet hadn't brought down the letter, she might never have left Jason, never have trusted her life to the anonymous pilot of this C-47.

Beaches lined the sides of the plane. The GIs, many of them glassy-eyed from too many wind-howling days in the Aleutians, huddled together, bound by canvas straps. Stashed and tied down in the center of the plane were eight fifty-gallon fuel barrels with a web of interconnecting tubes designed to extend the range of the engines and avoid the triangular route to Seattle via Anchorage.

A man in denims scrambled past them. "Chow," he said, handing out C-rations for the long flight. He checked the seat straps.

"Where's our 'chutes?" asked an ensign near Ellen.

"We dump in this water and you might as well pack it up," the man in denims replied. "You got fifteen minutes at the most."

"Got any battery acid?" asked another GI, meaning coffee.

"Have to wait till you hit the pavement," answered the man in denims.

"Talk like foreigners up here," said the man on the other side of Ellen. He wore a cap that said BLENNIES TRACTORS and looked like a feather merchant—a civilian brought up to repair some machinery.

Ellen kept quiet. She distrusted her voice and disguise and imagined that she oozed with the smell of love-making.

The man with the Blennies cap introduced himself. "Smitty's the name," he said. "What's yours?"

"Mac," said Ellen in her deepest voice.

"You don't look old enough to be in the service." He turned his head and studied her closely. "Are you Aleut? You with the famous cutthroats?"

"Cushy!" said an ensign on the other side. He scrunched around in his seat and stared at Ellen. "Where's your necklace of Jap ears?"

Someone shouted, "Farewell to the chamber pot of the gods!" as the earsplitting roar of the engines obscured all conversation. The C-47 pitched over the perforated metal runway. It rose into the air, roared over the battleships, cruisers, and destroyers anchored in Kuluk Bay. Ellen tried to breathe. Gas and sweat fumes filled the compartment. Her whole life, it seemed, remained back on Adak.

"*Bei Mir Bist du Schön . . .*" Soldiers sang above the airborne throb of the engines.

Smitty spoke in Ellen's ear. "Is it true the sharpies got the blokes to blow their whole pay at panguini or four-five-six?"

Ellen nodded, but inside she was remembering the beautiful time with Jason and wondering how she could survive without him. She felt tortured on the one hand, but fulfilled on the other, as if their love could last a lifetime of war.

The engines droned. Smitty started to snore and the ensign read a thin paperback titled, *See Here, Private Hargrove*.

Hours later, the man in denims opened the fuel lines leading from the drum that lay in the belly of the plane. The engines spluttered while the tanks were switched. Ellen stiffened. She twisted around and through the frosted window saw the reassuring presence of snowcapped mountains on the eastern horizon.

"How do you like that?" said Smitty, next to her. "Land."

"We've had a tail wind," said the ensign, checking his pocket watch.

Stewart's watch, thought Ellen in horror. I've left it. Her mind reeled. She tried to relax. Jason will find it. And if he doesn't? It doesn't matter, she tried to convince herself. Remember what happened when you cried about the boots? She shoved the watch out of her mind but could not push away the longing for Jason that persisted, despite her best efforts, to occupy her thoughts.

She pictured his symmetrical face, his blue eyes, how the glasses fitted around them—when did he get those? she wondered. I never asked! She saw how he looked without them, when he slept on his back with his hand pillowing his head. I love him, she thought, and her stomach knotted with the fearsome chance that they might never find each other again.

When the nine-hour flight ended in Seattle, she jumped out with the rest. The night air felt warm and the greatcoat oppressive. There was no wind.

"Move!" A GI bumped against her as she hesitated before hauling the duffel bag up the steps into the waiting bus.

The bus bounced over dark roads, past dark shapes that loomed against the sky. Ellen felt as if she were hurtling overground at hundreds of miles an hour, faster than the dog team when Wolff was at his best, faster, definitely, than in the Jeep at Dutch Harbor. The brakes on the bus squealed. Ellen was thrown against the seat in front of her.

"Shee-it," said a GI. "We're going to cash in our chips right here."

A car roared past them. Ellen stuffed her hands in her pockets and went rigid. Eventually their bus driver pulled to a stop.

"You've got two hours at the USO Club before I have to take you down to the depot," shouted the driver, turning in his seat.

"Shoulda worn me liberty clothes," said a GI.

Ellen followed the soldiers down the aisle. Despite her short hair and the coat that obscured her breasts, she felt as if a gong were about to ring and she would be jumped, not by one crazed patient in pajamas but by a whole mob.

The mob burst into the USO Club. The Andrews Sisters sang: "Don't Sit under the Apple Tree . . ."

Smitty strode away. Ellen entered the bright room, her bag bumping against her. Her senses, so long atuned to the wilderness, were assailed by the sounds. Even the roar of Aleutian wind had less effect than this noise.

"Need help?" asked a matron with three chins and a tiny dark moustache.

"Yes, please." Ellen unfolded Dr. Visikov's letter. "Could you tell me how to find Mr. Rupert, the attorney?"

The matron led Ellen into a back room, and spoke instructions into a telephone. She handed it to Ellen.

Ellen heard ringing in her ears. She clutched the black piece the matron had given her and heard a disembodied voice say: "Yes! Who's calling at this hour?"

"Is this Mr. Rupert?" Her voice quavered.

"Speak up! I can't hear you," a gruff voice answered.

"I'm Ellen MacTavish," Ellen shouted back. "Dr. Visikov sent me."

"Yes, yes. We've been expecting you. Come to my office tomorrow. The Arctic Building. Tenth floor. Ten o'clock."

There was a sharp click and a female voice said, "Operator."

Bewildered, Ellen dropped the earpiece and let it dangle. She left the small back room and sidestepped to avoid couples on the dance floor. The music played from a brightly flashing jukebox and the couples danced in a way that Ellen had never seen in Alaska. They moved toward and away from each other, holding opposite hands with their arms extended as if they were all being introduced at the same time. Suddenly, beside her, a GI flung a woman over his head. The woman's full skirt flew open, showing her many ruffled petticoats. She landed right side up on her feet and kept jitterbugging. Astonished, Ellen made her way to the door.

Outside, the strange smells of city streets assaulted her nose. But within the unfamiliar odors, there was the tang of salt water. Ellen followed her nose to the waterfront, to a building where she saw a welcoming sign: ALASKA STEAM-

SHIP TERMINAL. She pulled open a door and entered a dingy room.

On a back bench, an old woman slept under a pile of *Life* magazines. Pushing aside an urge to find the next boat heading north, Ellen stretched full length on another bench and closed her eyes. "You can survive a night," she told herself, glad for the first time that evening that she had the warmth of the greatcoat. "Daddy and Mr. Stokes survived worse than this and you can too."

She dreamed that she wandered alone on an ice floe in the farthest reaches of the northland. The kayak on which she'd reached the floe had drifted away. Why hadn't she tied down her sole means of escape? Clutching her fists even in sleep, she wandered over the barren ice, searching for a solution. A green plant poked through the turquoise blue crystals. Something lived. Crouching on all fours, she poked her nose into its center. Above her she heard the song of sparrows.

Ellen opened her eyes, found herself crouched on the wooden bench. A man snored opposite her. A wine bottle lay on the floor beside him. In the corner, the old woman had not changed position under her blanket of magazines.

The cavernous waiting room danced with dust motes. Ellen read the sign LADIES and headed toward it. After changing into her grey skirt, brown sweater, ribbed stockings, and mukluks, she draped the sealskin parka over her shoulders like a cape. She had finally outgrown it.

Returning to the large room, Ellen laid the army greatcoat over the sleeping woman. Beside the man she laid the hat, pants, and jacket in which she had disguised herself for so long. Dropping the duffel bag into the trash can by the door, and swinging the carpetbag with the dictionary, Jonah's ivory, Miss Herringbone's uniforms, and Jason's letters, she hurried outside.

Dense fog obliterated Seattle's waterfront. At regular intervals a horn sounded its melancholy warning to ships creeping across Eliott Bay. Invisible in the fog, the world's only streamlined ferry, the *Kalakala,* waited as workers boarded for the trip across the bay to the naval shipyard in Bremerton. In a hurry to catch it, a young woman wearing a scarf knotted at the top of her head bumped into Ellen.

"Gee, I'm sorry!" She pushed her face close to Ellen's.

"Where is the Arctic Building?" Ellen dared to ask this stranger.

"Haven't the faintest." The young woman dashed off.

Ellen hitched her parka over her shoulders and trudged on. The pounding of shadowy running feet sounded like shamans exorcising the spirits. Overcome with the strangeness of everything, the lack of visibility, Ellen closed herself off. It felt as if parts of her were shut down in the same way one turned off the kerosene heater, or the spigot on the water cans.

Rumbling noises joined the foghorn. Dazed, Ellen balanced on a flat iron rail and looked around. To her left, a circle of light burned through the fog like a fallen sun. A whistle blew. A bell clanged.

"Idiot!" said someone and snatched Ellen's arm, pulling her forward. Her parka flew off.

"Augh!" She fell onto her hands and knees, her breath gone. Behind her, massive iron wheels pounded on the rail on which she had just stood, pounding the parka to shreds. Her muscles convulsed in spasms. Ellen pressed against the wet ground. It was solid. Safe. The clank and rumble continued behind her.

"Nice going," said the man who had grabbed her. "You almost got yourself killed."

"Was that a train?" Ellen's voice shook. She looked at a bow-legged shipyard worker standing above her.

"How do ya like that!" he exclaimed to the small crowd that had gathered. "She ain't never seen a train."

The ferry tooted its intention to leave. The man plunged into the fog. Ellen hugged Mrs. Meriweather's carpetbag. She rocked on her heels for a long time. The foghorn guided the ferry across the bay. People swirled in and out of the fog. One of them, a very tall man wearing thick leather gloves, offered Ellen his hand. Ellen let him help her up.

"Are you just off the reservation?" he asked kindly.

"No," said Ellen, surprised. "I'm from Alaska."

"Oh," he said. "Then you're Eskimo."

Ellen shook her head slowly. "My daddy's white."

"Won't make no difference downtown," he said, " 'specially if you're sprawling on the railroad tracks."

"I'm not sprawling," Ellen said and felt like stomping her foot. "I—"

"Let me give you some advice," the man continued. "Stay away from the bars."

Ellen straightened her shoulders. "Can you please tell me how to get to the Arctic Building?" she said in a firm voice.

"Come along," said the man. "I'm going right past it."

They climbed a steep hill in silence. The man opened the door to a tall building whose height disappeared upward into the fog. "Here you are," he said and continued down the street.

The marble lobby glared with light. When her eyes adjusted, Ellen started up a mountain of stairs. At the tenth round, she pulled open a door.

"Mr. Rupert, please." She spoke to a young lady with short, sun-colored hair pinned on either side of her face with two green bows. The bows matched her green-dotted dress. She was tall and thin, about Ellen's age, and for the first time in her life Ellen felt squat and unshapely. She set down the carpetbag and tried to straighten her skirt.

"Hello, Miss MacTavish," the lady said. "Do you mind if I call you Ellen?"

Ellen stared uneasily at the stranger who knew her name.

"I'm Mr. Rupert's secretary, Jill Hall," she continued. "He has business at the courthouse and won't return until ten o'clock."

Ellen caught sight of a clock on the wall. It was eight-thirty.

"Please take a seat," said Jill, pointing at the couch.

The leather couch emitted a gust of air. Perching on a metal chair behind her desk, Jill was saying, "Are there really Japs in Alaska?"

"Yes." Ellen crossed her legs. Adak seemed stark and unreal in the warmth and comfort of this office. She did not want to think about it, or to think about Jason still being there. Why had she left? The question troubled her and she tried to fix her attention on the hexagonal clock, watching it tick off the minutes, the years, until she and Jason would be together again. Part of her seemed to die with each movement of the hands—she felt halved, quartered, as if her whole self were incomplete without him. As longing swept over her, she saw his dog tag on the floor, her jade labret beside it. Fingering the labret under her brown sweater, she closed her eyes and let the images engulf her.

"Mr. Rupert will see you now," someone said.

Ellen woke with a start. Jumping up, she followed Jill into another room.

"Mr. Rupert," said Jill, "this is Miss MacTavish from the Territory."

"Greetings," boomed a short man who looked as if he'd been stuffed into his white shirt and striped vest. His neck bunched around the tight collar and his round face was florid. "So you knew my friend Aleksandr Visikov."

"Yes," said Ellen, shocked to think that Dr. Visikov, who always seemed so detached, so alone, had friends in the city.

Mr. Rupert cleared his throat. "Did you know that Aleksandr passed away on January second?"

Ellen blinked hard. She sniffed, trying to avoid wiping her nose on her sweater, as Miss Long had taught them. Mr. Rupert removed the white handkerchief from his breast pocket and pushed it across the table. He swiveled his chair and looked out the window for many minutes.

When she stopped blowing her nose, he swiveled back to the desk. "You have five thousand dollars in trust," he said, taking a pad of lined yellow paper out of a side drawer. "With care, that will be sufficient for your education."

Ellen leaned forward in the chair. Five thousand was more than Daddy had seen in his entire life.

"Where are you staying?" asked Mr. Rupert.

"At the steamship terminal," said Ellen, thinking of the hard bench and hoping she didn't have to spend another night there.

Mr. Rupert's face flushed a deep purple. "I wish I'd known," he said, tapping the tips of his fingers together for many minutes. "I think I have a solution. A client of mine might be interested in boarding you."

"I want to live alone."

"There's no rooms available unless you want a hot pillow arrangement."

" 'Hot pillow'?"

"An innovation of the war. A day worker sleeps the night in the same bed in which a night worker sleeps the day."

"No thank you," said Ellen.

Mr. Rupert looked at her. "My client, Mrs. Ardley, is a widow. She has a large house to maintain and we could offer her financial compensation. In addition, of course, I am sure she'd enjoy your companionship."

"I won't live with a lonely old woman," Ellen retorted, her mind ablaze with images of Mrs. Berglund.

"Why don't we invite Mrs. Ardley and her butler to join us for dinner at my club," Mr. Rupert continued in an even voice. "You can meet them and decide for yourself."

At the mention of food, Ellen's stomach growled. "Fine," she said, "I'll meet them."

While Mr. Rupert wrote on his pad, Ellen twisted the handkerchief between her fingers, wondering if she should give it back or keep it. Finally he looked up and called, "Miss Hall!"

Jill poked her head in the door.

"Go to the Bon Marché and buy Miss MacTavish as many pot pies as she can eat and then help her shop for clothes. I want her at my club at five o'clock. We'll eat with Mrs. Ardley."

He smiled at Ellen and reached a hand across his desk. Ellen offered him the handkerchief. "You're welcome to keep that," he said and motioned them out the door.

Jill tucked the carpetbag in her desk well and took Ellen's arm. "Sometimes I go with Mr. Rupert when he plays his cello at Mrs. Ardley's," she said. "I know you'll just love her."

How do you know? thought Ellen, as she headed for the stairs.

"Over here," called Jill. "Let's take the elevator."

Her jaw set and feeling very much at risk, Ellen followed Jill into a small cage. A man in a brown uniform with a gold stripe down his leg closed the gate. He moved a brass lever and Ellen found her stomach dropping out of the center of her body. She held her breath. Outside, the fog had thinned. The streets were weighted with people and she saw several who looked as if they might have been born in Alaska.

When they sat down to eat at the restaurant in the basement of the Bon Marché department store, Ellen tried to remember everything Miss Long had taught her about holding a fork and not talking with her mouth full, but the hole in her stomach nearly forced all manners from her mind. She dove into her chicken pot pies.

"What's your favorite color?" Jill asked when they had finished eating and stood in front of a dizzying array of dresses. The overwhelming variety of colors and styles flabbergasted Ellen. She plucked at her brown sweater and felt like a faded spruce chicken scurrying through the pages of a Sears catalogue that had miraculously come to life.

"Red?" asked Jill, pulling out a slim-fitting red wool dinner dress.

"Yes," said Ellen.

"Try it on," said Jill.

While Jill looked for more clothes, Ellen waited in the dressing room with her eyes closed, her mind blurred.

In addition to the dress, Ellen tried on and bought a blazer, a skirt and sweater, two blouses, two cotton dresses for the summer, underwear, and shoes.

"I wish I could buy you silk stockings," Jill said as they waited to buy cotton lisle. "But all the silk's gone for parachutes."

"They could think of the women once in awhile," a lady next to them grumbled.

Jill's eyes flashed. "Don't you know there's a war on?"

The lady looked at her feet.

Laden with bundles, Jill led Ellen to a drugstore for a Coca-Cola. Then they walked to another department store where she showed Ellen a window display of a single-story house they were calling "The New Post-War House."

"When I have a baby," Jill was saying, "I don't want to live with my mother and grandmother. I want my own house, even if it is this small."

"Are you pregnant?" Ellen asked, thinking the post-war house looked three times as large as the house in Unaganik.

"Good heavens, no. I'm not married. Not like some of these Allotment Annies." Jill's eyes looked troubled. "Do people in the Territory get married?"

"Yes." Ellen looked away from the window. Near them

a blind man with an accordion played the same apple tree tune that had blared from the jukebox in the USO club the night before. It seemed like a very long time ago and Jason, beloved Jason, seemed a million miles away. Would they ever have a chance to marry?

"In a church?" persisted Jill.

"If there is one."

"And if there isn't?"

"A sea captain might marry you or someone like Father Hot Whiskey might come along. He used to travel to the villages."

The accordion tunes swung over the pavement and Ellen thought of the time she and Jason had danced when the winterman played. How grand that had been.

"And if there isn't a minister?" Jill poked her head into Ellen's face.

"We have a fish wedding."

Jill wrinkled her nose as if she had smelled something. "What's that?"

"That's when the Fish Commissioner marries you and the witnesses are a can of salmon and a keg of herring."

"Did you ever!" said Jill and, looking up, pointed to a huge clock across the street. "Look at that! We better rush. You've got to change and get ready for dinner." She dropped a coin into the blind musician's cup and grabbed Ellen's arm.

Breathless, her feet blistering from the new saddle shoes, her face flushed and sweaty, Ellen followed Jill up several streets and finally into an ivy-covered building. Jill led her into a tiled bathroom and showed her how to put on the garter belt and stockings. She rummaged through the packages, uncovered the red dinner dress, and shook it at Ellen. Ellen dropped off her clothes, slipped into the dress, and before she could protest, Jill held something to her face.

"Like this." Jill tightened her lips.

Dizzy and faint from the day's events, Ellen copied Jill's expression without protest. Jill pressed something on her mouth and then pointed Ellen in the direction of the mirror. A bizarre image looked back. The mouth seemed to bleed with red paint, the eyes were rimmed with dark circles and looked haunted. Ellen pinched her sallow cheeks, doubting whether she was real. Had she flown from Adak today or yesterday?

Was her name Ellen or Mac? Had she known someone named Jason West? Was that man at the train tracks right? Did she look that different?

"You look divine," Jill insisted, "simply divine." She yanked a comb through Ellen's bowl-shaped haircut. The comb broke. "Damnation," Jill said, throwing it in the garbage.

"Don't swear," said Ellen and straightened her shoulders.

"Sorry," said Jill.

Ellen raked her fingers through her hair. It looked like a squirrel's nest.

"We forgot to get you a pocketbook," Jill whispered as she hurried Ellen across a plush patterned carpet.

"What's that?" Ellen asked, but Jill had already opened a heavy oak door.

Ellen teetered on the new high heels and, feeling like the red light on a harbor buoy, she lurched forward.

Mr. Rupert rose to greet her.

27

"PLEASE EXCUSE ME FOR being late," Ellen said as she entered the lounge, proud of herself for remembering Miss Long's lesson in manners. "We were unavoidably detained."

A tiny white-haired lady looked up from a brown leather chair that enclosed her like a jewelry box. A diamond brooch in the shape of a *V* glittered from the *V* of her white neckline. Diamonds dangled from holes in her ears and glittered from her veined hands. She wore a silk dress as blue as Alaskan forget-me-nots and her grey eyes had the peacefulness of an early dawn.

A man as old as the lady stood tall and regal behind the chair. In contrast to her thick white curls, his head was bald except for two tufts of white hair that bracketed the shiny pate and muttonchops that widened his thin face. He wore white gloves and a black jacket that buttoned to his neck.

"Mrs. Ardley," said Mr. Rupert, extending his hand toward the elegant little lady, "may I introduce Aleksandr's protégée, Miss Ellen MacTavish."

Feeling like a salmon heading up the wrong river, Ellen jutted her hand forward and wobbled off balance. Before she knew it, the man with the white gloves had caught her elbow and was helping her to a chair.

As if from a distant hill, Ellen heard a genteel voice saying, "Are you all right, dear one?" For the slightest fraction of an instant Ellen doubted whether she'd ever be the same again.

"Can you walk to the Bentley?" asked Mrs. Ardley. "Butler and I will drive you home and put you right to bed. Anything we need to discuss can wait until tomorrow."

"Indeed," added the man with the gloves.

"I heartily agree," said Mr. Rupert and he and the man with the gloves escorted Ellen outside to a black car. It was square, with jutting headlights and a silver insignia on the sides. Ellen slid into the backseat and inhaled the aroma of polished leather.

Butler drove through darkened streets, across a bridge, and down a wide curving street along the shores of a large lake. He parked the Bentley in a building that was the same size as the MacTavish homestead on Bristol Bay.

Ellen followed Mrs. Ardley into a large stone mansion. She caught sight of her matted hair, her flushed cheeks, and hideous painted lips in a beveled mirror at the end of a long hall. I look like an *angalkuk,* she thought, but before she could frown at the grotesque image of herself, Butler had her elbow and was leading her up a curving flight of stairs.

"I think the southwest room, don't you?" said Mrs. Ardley, behind them.

"I do indeed," said Butler and led Ellen down an upstairs hall and into a large room papered with tiny yellow flowers. Arched leaded windows faced Lake Washington and square windows faced blossoming trees separating them from another mansion to the west. The trees looked like tethered clouds.

But then Ellen caught sight of Mount Rainier in the darkening violet sky. She stood at the arched window staring at its majestic beauty while Butler and Mrs. Ardley turned down the bed behind her.

"Let me show you the lavatory," said Mrs. Ardley after Butler left. Ellen pulled herself away from the window and followed Mrs. Ardley into a black and white tiled room with a sink, an enormous bathtub, and a commode.

"I'll draw you a bath," said Mrs. Ardley and, bending over, turned the taps. Water crashed into the tub. "Do you like bubbles?"

Although she had not the slightest idea what they were, Ellen found herself nodding. Mrs. Ardley left the room, and

Ellen, feeling a rush of pain in her abdomen, sat on the commode. She had not gone since early morning.

When Mrs. Ardley returned, Ellen pointed to the covered toilet. "Where do I take that? At home we took the honey pot to the outhouse."

Mrs. Ardley's responding smile was so untroubled Ellen felt a burden shift off her. Mrs. Ardley pulled on the chain dangling from a box on the ceiling. A crash of water cascaded through. Ellen realized, embarrassed, that she should have done the same at the steamship terminal that morning.

Water continued to fill the tub. "Lavender," said Mrs. Ardley as she added bathsalts, foaming them with a jeweled hand. Then she turned off the taps. In the sudden quiet Ellen realized her exhaustion.

"Now, dear one," said Mrs. Ardley, "soak as long as you want. I've left a nightgown for you on the bed and there are towels here." She tapped a small door beside the sink. "When you're ready, we'll bring up a bowl of soup. You can eat in bed."

Ellen felt as if she had just crossed a rickety wooden bridge above a raging chasm. She lowered herself into the warm scented water, so different from sponge baths and steams. She slid lower and lower until only her nose poked above the surface. Ellen soaked until it seemed as if everything that mattered would be taken care of and everything that didn't matter would disappear.

Mr. Rupert enrolled Ellen in a special program that had been designed to upgrade the education of rural students. Six days a week she walked from Mrs. Ardley's to classes at Pacific Northwest University. She studied math, biology, chemistry, physics, English, history, and Latin. She returned in time to eat with Mrs. Ardley and Butler and listen to the war news on the Philco radio that dominated the sitting room. Riveted to the broadcast, Ellen waited, in vain, for word of the wind-blown, fog-riddled island of Adak where Jason remained. Lowell Thomas reported from Europe, but no one reported from the Aleutians.

After the news, Butler, wearing the white helmet and armband uniform of an air raid warden, inspected the sand buckets in the neighborhood, kept in the events of fires from a Japanese attack.

Mrs. Ardley played the grand piano. Ellen, alone in her bedroom above the music alcove, studied with Beethoven sonatas wafting through the heat vents in the floor. Often she dropped her pencil and covered her eyes, overcome with sadness at the poignancy of the music.

In addition to the heat vents, Ellen's large bedroom held an electrical heater that resembled a small log fireplace. Mrs. Ardley had given her a woven shawl bought during a visit to Tibet. With that draped over her shoulders, Ellen huddled over her books long after Butler damped the coal furnace and shut off the downstairs lights. She studied until her eyes spun with black dots.

When she closed her books and lay in the warm tub, her fingers slipped between her legs to become a separate entity, pressuring, insistent, while her mind fondled the memory of Jason in the tent. Released, Ellen climbed out of the tub, dried herself with the thick towel, and crawled, naked, under the sheets. She never wore the nightgown.

On her study table Ellen had placed Dr. Visikov's dictionary with the gold-edged paper and the ivory whale from Jonah. She wore Stewart's labret on the gold chain from Dr. Constance. During the day she tucked it under her sweater, but at night she hooked her finger around the chain and, holding the labret, felt that Stewart was near. Sometimes she talked to him. I'm worried about Jason, she would say. Take care of him, Stewart, if you can.

Other times, after a day at school when her brain felt taxed to its limit, she worried about Bonnie's schooling. Once she started worrying, it kept her up all night. She worried whether Charlie had learned to sleep through the night without wetting his bed, if Cheok would have another baby like Flora, and whether anyone had sent word of Stewart's death and how Daddy had taken it. Mr. Rupert had mentioned that he had written to Mrs. Meriweather and told her that Ellen was safe at Mrs. Ardley's. Satisfied that Daddy knew where she was, Ellen wondered what he thought of her living in Seattle. But she wrote no letters and none arrived. It was as if that portion of her life were folded like nets during the winter, stored for a future season.

Sometimes when the waves lapped the lake shore and the wind gnawed the windows, she missed the bay, the tundra. But all in all she felt comfortable in Seattle and she loved going to school. Although there were other Alaskans in her class, Ellen felt closest to her lab partner, Reginald Beck, a farm boy from God's country east of the mountains, as he described it. Often they discussed assignments during lunchtime. Other than that, Ellen kept to herself, spending every spare minute at her books. And feeling that she had bought enough clothes to last a lifetime, she had no trouble resisting Jill's friendly invitations to take her shopping again.

By late April, when the Seattle rains caught their second wind, Ellen felt as if she had found hers. In all her classes except physics, she ranked near the top of the class, competing with Reginald Beck for first place. Her feelings of strangeness had dimmed, somewhat, as had her fears for Jason. But then one day in early May, she awoke screaming his name. Jabbing her fist into her mouth, she dug her elbows into her stomach, terrified. Was he in trouble?

Slowly the morning noises trickled into the bedroom. Butler cooked in the kitchen. Mrs. Ardley set the table in the dining room. The grandfather clock ticked in the front hall. Ellen's bedroom, with its high ceilings and floral wallpaper, took on a softness, a normalcy. Ellen rolled out of bed and grabbed her clothes. A button flew off the blazer. Clutching it in one hand, she darted down to the kitchen, yanked on her saddle shoes which Butler had polished the night before, and broke a lace. She threw it to the floor.

"Maybe you need to stay home today," said Mrs. Ardley.

"I can't," said Ellen.

"Will it matter if you miss one day?"

"Yes." Ellen grabbed the new shoelaces that Butler handed her and, with trembling hands, threaded them through the eyelets.

Mrs. Ardley sewed the button on her blazer while Ellen gulped down her cod liver oil and a few spoonfuls of porridge. Butler backed the Bentley out of the garage and insisted on driving her. And Ellen, dashing out the kitchen door, forgot her homework.

* * *

"That's a stupid thing to do," said the physics professor. "Especially since you're doing so poorly in physics."

"I'm not stupid," Ellen stormed at him. "I can understand. You're not—" When she realized that she almost said "not teaching properly," she bolted for the door. The professor, a nimble man in a black professor's gown, jumped in front of it. His arms, like black crow's wings, stopped her.

"We'll discuss this in my office at five, Miss MacTavish," he said.

Ellen slunk back to her seat.

"You're in for it," Reginald Beck said during chemistry lab that afternoon. Reginald had a body that no amount of food shortages had diminished and a brain from which no information seemed to escape.

" 'He is a dull observer whose experience has not taught him the reality and force of magic, as well as of chemistry,' " Ellen retorted, quoting a line from their study of Emerson.

"You think you can get out of this by magic?" Reginald laughed.

"What do you know?" Ellen said, although her insides roared with a mixture of mortifying embarrassment and bewildering confusion.

"Simmer down," Reginald added. "You're turning into a witch."

Ellen's hand trembled. The match she had struck to light the bunsen burner went out. It reminded her of how Jason could never light the kerosene heater, how she always had to do it. Fear for him pestered her like a drunken wasp. She spent the remainder of the day trying to control her panic.

"Tell me about yourself," the physics professor said when Ellen entered his spotless office. He motioned to her to sit. "Where are you from?"

"Unaganik." Ellen perched on a stiff wooden chair across from his desk.

"Do you live in a boarding house? Do you get enough time to study?"

"I live with Mrs. Ardley," said Ellen, and as if to explain her bewildering behavior, added, "She wanted me to stay home today."

"If Mrs. Ardley told me to stay home I would," the physics professor said with a grin.

Ellen looked at him in astonishment, unsure she had heard correctly.

"That is," he said, "if it's the same Ananda Ardley who used to teach metaphysics?"

"META-physics?" said Ellen, her voice strained. "What's that? I'm having enough difficulty with plain old physics." She pronounced it "diffoogulty," with Angus's Scottish accent.

The professor laughed. He leaned back in his chair. "My graduate student, Mrs. Van der Voewn, might tutor you," he said. "Shall I ask her?"

"Yes, thank you," said Ellen. She could not leave the office and the building fast enough. She raced home and dashed to the Philco. As usual, there was no news about the Aleutians. So agitated it was useless to study, Ellen spent the rest of the evening rolling bandages with Mrs. Ardley.

Ellen's odd feelings of dread continued to surface at unpredictable times throughout the month. Once, in the wee small hours of the night, Ellen woke in a sweat, her heart beating with such passion she wondered if it would beat itself to death. When the circles beneath her eyes became puffy and black, Mrs. Ardley prescribed valerian root tea. It tasted vile, but it helped Ellen sleep.

Thursday morning at the end of May, Ellen woke with an excruciating headache and a burning fever. She tossed in bed, too ill to care whether she went to school or not. Butler and Mrs. Ardley hovered at her side for days. Then she dreamed that Stewart stroked her forehead. She reached for his hand and instead grasped a wet rag. Ellen stuffed it into her mouth, muffling her sobs.

"I'm wondering what's been going through your mind," said Mrs. Ardley.

"Nothing," said Ellen in a voice raw from fever.

"Something's bothering you."

"What do you know?" Ellen rasped, angry, wanting to be left alone.

"You're worrying yourself sick," Mrs. Ardley persisted.

Ellen raised herself onto one elbow. "I am not making myself sick," she said loudly and then dropped, exhausted, onto the pillow and closed her eyes.

"It will help to talk about it," Mrs. Ardley said in a quiet voice, "to bring it up out of the dark."

Ellen rocked sideways onto her stomach, her back to Mrs. Ardley. The pressure in her body suddenly exploded through her arms. She found herself pounding the pillow with her fists. Great gulping sobs burst from the depths of her being and filled the corners of the big house. Butler, wearing a tartan housecoat, hurried into the bedroom and cradled her in his arms. Mrs. Ardley stroked her head.

Ellen returned to school, and every day at five Mrs. Van der Voewn, a buck-toothed woman with a sad mouth, tutored her in physics.

One afternoon at the end of May, someone banged on the scrolled glass on the top half of the classroom door. Startled, Ellen jumped up. An older gentleman stood at the threshold in a Western Union uniform. He held a telegram.

Static sparked along Ellen's spine. Behind her, chalk scratched against the blackboard.

"Mrs. Van der Voewn?" asked the messenger in the uniform.

The chalk hit the floor. Limply Ellen waved toward her physics tutor. Mrs. Van der Voewn gripped the blackboard ledge with tight fists.

"I'm sorry," said the messenger, handing the telegram to Mrs. Van der Voewn.

Mrs. Van der Voewn remained motionless. The man wrote in a black book and left. Ellen found herself holding the hateful piece of paper.

"Read it!" Mrs. Van der Voewn's voice snapped against Ellen's ears.

She tore open the seal. "The Secretary of War desires to express his deep regret that your husband, Private First Class N. Van der Voewn, died May 30, in Africa." Ellen watched the message spin through the room like a symbol of infinity.

Mrs. Van der Voewn dropped into her chair and in a strange inhuman voice grunted, "Go!"

Ellen hesitated, then picked up her books and raincoat. She shut the door softly behind her. Her feet echoed down the hall as she ran from the building. Outside the light was silver-grey. Above, a sunbeam the color of a goldfinch pushed through the tangled nest of rain clouds.

Ellen knotted the belt on her reversible raincoat. Turning east, she raced toward home. The spring wind lifted her hair, dried her eyes.

Red-winged blackbirds sang like a church choir. Cherry blossoms and new grass scented the air. In a break between the houses, she stopped suddenly to watch a cloud lift off Mt. Rainier and rise like an arm in salute to the sky.

Ellen raced to Mrs. Ardley's, threw open the front door and flung her books onto the hall table. From the Philco a broadcaster announced in a ringing voice: "Japanese Imperial Headquarters concedes loss of Attu in the Aleutian Islands."

28

ELLEN SLUMPED TO THE floor beside the arched rose-wood box with its fifteen tubes, its four broadcast bands, and its ominous black dials.

"The American army invasion that started May 11 on Attu in the Aleutian Islands," the broadcast continued while Ellen's stomach lurched, "has been successful. The Japanese have surrendered."

"Was May eleventh the day you broke your shoelace?" Mrs. Ardley asked.

"I don't know." The air waves crackled. Ellen felt as if she were sitting on a beach in a lightning storm.

"Compared to 2,351 enemy dead," the broadcast continued, "only 549 American soldiers lost their lives."

Ellen jerked her head toward Mrs. Ardley's chair and for a split second saw a tern spinning to the sky above the mud flats.

"Where are you, dear one?" Mrs. Ardley asked in her quiet voice.

Ellen stared at her, unseeing.

Mrs. Ardley got up from her chair, knelt in front of the stool and held Ellen's burning cheeks between her cool hands. Something clicked inside Ellen, as if a rock were tumbling over an Aleutian hill and turning into a waterfall. She saw Jason. He was climbing a cargo net onto a navy transport ship.

There were times in the days that followed when Ellen felt desperate to see Jason, to really believe he was all right. Other times she felt as if she were a spectator watching her own life pass before her like ciphers on a page. Those days when she sat in front of her books, she had to force herself to concentrate until the brain cells ground into gear. No further news of the Aleutians was broadcast on the radio.

Four weeks later, on an unseasonably hot day in July, Ellen sat in the shade of a campus chestnut tree with Reginald Beck. They had just finished comparing Latin translations for their exam that afternoon when Stephanie, the overweight secretary of their special program, puffed down the path. Her braided red hair stuck to her head like hawsers to a capstan.

"Telephone call for you, Miss MacTavish. Urgent."

Ellen's heart stopped. Somehow she scrambled to her feet and ran up the stairs two at a time to the office in the turret of Ainsworth Hall.

"Yes," said Ellen, picking up the phone.

There was no answer.

Ellen shouted, "Yes!"

"Ouch!" said a familiar voice.

"Jason!"

"You just perforated my eardrum," he replied.

"Where are you?" Ellen talked as if she had to be heard in Adak.

"Seattle. I've had the devil's own time trying to find you. What are you doing? Hiding from your old lover?"

"I'll get the jitney and be right down." Her heart racing, Ellen dropped the phone onto the hook. Before she reached the top of the stairs, it rang again. Stephanie was nowhere in sight. Annoyed at the delay, Ellen dashed back and picked it up. "Yes," she said.

"Wait!" said Jason.

Ellen sagged against the desk.

"Where did you think you were going to meet me?" Jason asked, his voice not concealing his annoyance.

"I'm sorry." Ellen's voice quivered.

"Seattle's a big place," Jason said. "And let me tell you, I've telephoned every last school just to find you. So don't hang up again."

Ellen's hand tightened on the telephone.

"I'm stuck at Fort Lawton for a couple of hours but I've got a Jeep later on the pretense of talking to Dr. Goodman at the med school. Can you meet me inside the front doors of the med building at three o'clock?''

In a daze, Ellen wrote her Latin exam, told Mrs. Van der Voewn she had to miss the physics tutorial, handed in a paper on "Emerson's View of One Mind," and rushed to the med school building. She waited in front of a Norman Rockwell war poster, in which a mother and father tucked two children into bed. OURS TO FIGHT FOR was printed across the top and FREEDOM FROM FEAR across the bottom.

That could be Jason and me, thought Ellen, and she smiled, imagining the stories she would tell their children about Unaganik. Ellen was still smiling when Jason burst through the front doors.

He wore his dress uniform with the caduceus on the lapels and the stripes on the sleeve. His trousers were pressed. His khaki tie was knotted perfectly at his neck. His billed overseas cap sat above his high forehead. Ellen ran to him. He scooped her into his arms. Ellen closed her eyes, feeling the surety of his body within her grasp. He trembled and she held on, tighter.

"Your hair's grown," said Jason, smoothing it against her neck.

"Yes," said Ellen, searching his eyes. They looked as if he'd fallen off a steep cliff and still didn't know whether he'd landed on his feet at the bottom.

A delivery girl elbowed past them with a large bouquet of roses for the small hospital adjoining the medical school. The scent engulfed them and Ellen looked up and realized that they were blocking the doorway.

Jason straightened. "I've been drinking battery acid for so many months I forgot what good old American coffee tastes like. Is there any around here?"

The coffee in the cafeteria was made of cracked wheat and roasted soybeans. It tasted charred. The donuts were dry and sugarless. Jason tossed his into the garbage.

"If you throw food away," Ellen teased, "when you're out hunting, a bear will throw you around."

"You and your superstitions," he said sarcastically.

"They're not mine," Ellen retorted. "They're my—" She stopped in mid sentence. What would Jason think of

Cheok? She dunked her dry donut into the coffee and watched the crumbs float to the surface.

"What do you think about being the only Eskimo at school?" Jason seemed to hurl the words at her.

Ellen looked up at him. He was staring into his cup. "What do you mean?" she asked, curious, realizing that she didn't think of herself as Eskimo and didn't particularly notice features on anyone else either. She usually got an inner sense of a person more than any idea of what they did or didn't look like.

"Well," Jason said, stuttering, "has anyone been rude to you?"

"Of course not," she said. "What are you talking about?"

Jason gripped the cup so hard his knuckles whitened. The soft white fingers were chapped, the fingernails broken and ground with dirt. He forced a smile and Ellen, alarmed by the insincerity of his expression, bit her tongue. Uneasiness surged over her. Jason didn't seem that different from soldiers who'd been Z-I'd home, the expression the military used when a GI had gone crazy and was sent home in a strait jacket. "What happened up there?" she asked quietly.

"Sigori left."

"With the Scouts?" asked Ellen, trying to appear normal, to converse as if no murky backwaters ebbed between them.

"He caught one of the Yippee boats to Dutch Harbor. A boat called the *Yethl*." Jason looked at her with a peculiar expression. "Your friend Ted Kleet came to see you again, and Sigori left with him. I knew Sigori was malingering, but he was such a help, I didn't care."

"I guess the Scouts just needed him for Kiska," said Ellen, troubled by the strange look in Jason's eyes.

"They could use him again," Jason said and his voice was hard. "There's a major attack being planned for Kiska in August."

"Loose lips sink ships!" Ellen looked furtively around the cafeteria. A retarded man removed dishes from an empty table. A group of doctors discussed a case at a table next to the high windows.

Jason took off his lieutenant's cap and pushed back his

hair. His frown deepened and when Ellen reached up to smooth it, he caught her fingers and crushed them between his own.

"You're hurting me," she said, trying to keep her voice soft.

He held her fingers to his lips but did not kiss them.

"I heard about Attu on the Philco," she said, wanting him to talk.

"Did you hear about the thirty-eight hundred American and Canadian casualties?"

"I heard five hundred and forty-nine," said Ellen, surprised. The broadcast was imprinted on her mind. She could have repeated it word for word. "Were you there?"

"General Wise Guy brought the Seventh Infantry up from the south in dress uniforms. He refused to send in our Thirty-seventh with their cold weather gear and winter training." Jason's voice drifted off.

"As Emerson says, 'Nothing astonishes men so much as common sense,'" Ellen said, wanting Jason to continue, wanting to generate some spark in those beloved blue eyes.

Jason laughed, a raw sound that scratched the ears. "Common sense would tell you that May in the Aleutians isn't exactly sunshine and forget-me-nots." Ellen heard deep bitterness seething in him and felt frightened.

"Most of the casualties were frozen feet, and I got dragged in at the last minute to help their medics deal with them. It's no fun knowing a man has to lose his feet, let me tell you, especially if you know it could have been prevented."

So he *was* on Attu, Ellen thought, wriggling her toes as if they were a luxury. "But you'd be safe in a hospital tent," she said, "wouldn't you?"

He laid his glasses on the table. The frame was wound with adhesive tape. "A swarm of Japanese attacked us," he said, rubbing his eyes, his voice full of pain. "Carved up my assistant while he was dressing a wound."

Ellen's shaking hand rattled the coffee cup. Had that been when she got sick? Had she sensed something? She touched Jason's sleeve. "You got away," she said. A statement of fact, the truth—he was there in front of her, in one piece.

"They screeched 'We die! You die,' " Jason said, his voice low.

Ellen strained to hear.

"Their bayonets were all they had," Jason continued. "They had no ammunition left."

"And they killed your assistant? Where were you?" Ellen had to know what had shocked him into this odd behavior.

"I crawled under the tent. Some of the patients, those able to move, followed me. We got away."

Jason seemed not to notice Ellen. "And the Japanese doctor on Attu," he continued as if speaking to himself, "killed his patients with morphine and gave grenades to those who could pull the pins. If a doctor does that, what will a regular soldier do?"

"How did you know about their doctor?" Ellen struggled against her own emotions, building on top of his anguish.

"Their physician trained in America. Wrote his diary in English, down to the last detail of . . ." He stared at her, his eyes darting from one side of her face to the next. "Am I crazy, Mac, or is that crazy?"

Ellen looked at him, hard-pressed to find an honest answer.

"You don't understand," he said, squeezing her hands until they hurt.

"I don't understand what?"

He paused, holding her hand to his cheek and looking into her eyes. "What's to become of us?" he asked, his voice urgent.

"If it's about us," said Ellen, her voice firm, "then it's up to us to decide."

"If only it were."

"What do you mean?"

Abruptly Jason dropped her hand. He pulled up his sleeve to examine his wristwatch. "Oh my God," he said, replacing his glasses, jerking up suddenly from his chair. "I've got to talk to Dr. Goodman. He's developed a treatment for frostbite and I want to hear about it before I get shipped out."

"Shipped out?" Alarmed by Jason's erratic manner,

Ellen rose from her chair. "You're not going back to the Aleutians already!"

"I've got ten days' leave and I wangled a flight to New York. I fly tonight. Then I'm off to Great Britain with new orders."

"Please, Jason," Ellen found herself pleading. "Let's take your leave together."

"Don't you have classes?"

"It's you that matters."

"Good God, Ellen. Are you ready to throw it all over after such a short time? You won't make it through medical school that way."

"Don't swear," said Ellen, stunned at his vehemence. She rode up in the elevator with him. She held his hand and did not let go when the elevator operator stopped at the top floor.

"Jason," she said, as they entered the hall, "come home and spend the night with me. Please?"

"If only I could."

"I'll call Mrs. Ardley and explain."

"You haven't told her about us!" Jason's voice rose. "Why?"

"Oh, Ellen! I'll never understand you. There's some things people aren't supposed to do!"

Ellen stared at him, alarmed. "What do you mean?"

He looked so angry Ellen wished she could gulp back her words. "Don't worry about it, Jason dear," she said. "Mrs. Ardley knows things about people without them even telling her." Ellen paused and then continued. "When I get home too exhausted to speak, she never pesters me to talk, or makes me feel like I should even say hello. Sometimes I think she reads my mind but—"

"That's a little different than the two of us sharing a bed, Ellen. We aren't married!"

"She wouldn't care," said Ellen. "She accepts people the way they are and she'd accept us the way we are."

"If I'd known where you were I'd have stayed," he said in a cold voice. "Then I could have met this Mrs. Ardley and judged for myself."

"Change your plans," Ellen pleaded in spite of herself.

"Mater's expecting me."

Ellen felt as if her insides had dropped with the departing elevator.

"Why didn't you write?" Jason said angrily.

Ellen looked at him in surprise. "I didn't know how to get a letter to you," she said.

"You put a stamp on it and it goes through the postal service and into the military pouch," Jason explained in an amazed voice. "How can you act so smart and be so stupid?"

Ellen stared up at him, her eyes glazed. "The letters you sent me in Harold's Point were censored," she said, "and I thought I had to get my letters to a censor, too. I didn't think—"

"You're right there," said Jason. "You didn't think."

Ellen bit her bottom lip, trying to control its trembling.

"The mail goes *through* the censor," Jason emphasized. "He blacks out the parts that would aid and abet the enemy and then sends it on."

"Oh," said Ellen and felt the donut spin in her stomach.

"You should have contacted my cousin," Jason continued.

"How could she have taken you a letter?"

"Don't be so stupid," said Jason. "If you'd told her where you were I wouldn't have had such a devil of a time finding you and I wouldn't have made plans to visit Mater."

"I left her address in the pocket of the coat when I gave the coat away," Ellen said, feeling angry with herself. "That's why I couldn't call her." Ellen stiffened her jaw. She felt the muscles in her arms tighten.

Jason looked at her with a bemused expression on his lips. "You look so cute when you're mad," he said.

"I'm not mad," said Ellen but felt like punching him.

"I barely have time to talk to Dr. Goodman," Jason said, standing.

"I'm coming with you," said Ellen, "and I won't take no for an answer."

Jason took her elbow, gripping it too tightly as they moved down the long corridor, looking for Dr. Goodman's name on a door.

Dr. Goodman was a man of medium height, with solid features that had collapsed from overwork, a thick shock of salt and pepper hair, a nose that bunched upward, holding his bifocals. He looked sixty, but his voice had the firm tone of a younger man. When he finished explaining the hydrotherapy unit, he turned to Ellen. "What is your interest in this, Miss MacTavish?"

"Miss MacTavish is hoping to attend medical school," said Jason.

"How interesting," said Dr. Goodman, looking her up and down through his bifocals. "We've been encouraging women to apply since so many of the male candidates are being drafted overseas."

"Does it make a difference that I'm not a man?" asked Ellen, surprised. The thought had never occurred to her.

Dr. Goodman smiled at Ellen, his tired eyes alight with good humor. "To some people," he said, "but I think that's a lot of rubbish. I think it's high time we realized that the fair sex have brains too."

Jason cleared his throat. "I think Miss MacTavish would be a credit to the profession," he said in the pompous style that Ellen hated. She tried not to wince.

"Have you heard of our new program?" Dr. Goodman addressed Ellen at the same time he drew a prescription pad and pen from his upper pocket.

"No, sir." Ellen squared her shoulders, eager to hear more.

"The War Office has asked us to step up our training of doctors. The wheels are in motion to start an accelerated pre-med/medical program in September and to go full time for five and a half years. Are you interested?"

"Yes, sir!" Ellen barely concealed her excitement.

Dr. Goodman wrote something on his pad. "How old are you?" he asked, looking up.

Ellen thought for a moment. "Eighteen," she said at last. "And a half."

He replaced his pad in his pocket. "We're particularly looking for candidates with prior medical experience."

"Miss MacTavish assisted in our small hospital in Harold's Point," said Jason. "I can recommend her without qualification."

Dr. Goodman studied Ellen as if he had not heard Jason.

"I started in Unaganik," said Ellen. "I worked for the doctor there."

Dr. Goodman took off his glasses and wiped them on a

tissue pulled from a box in the disheveled bookcase behind his desk.

"I assisted a physician named Aleksandr Visikov."

Dr. Goodman returned his glasses to his nose and, lifting his chin, looked at her through the bottom halves. "I consider myself fortunate to have known Dr. Visikov in his, shall we say, better days."

"He left me money for school," Ellen added in the relaxed presence of the older doctor. "If it wasn't for him I wouldn't be here."

"I don't believe that," said Dr. Goodman. "You look to me like the type of person who would get on with what you wanted, no matter what."

"I need to get on too," interjected Jason with a sharp laugh. "Thank you for your time."

"Please let me know if I can be of further assistance." Dr. Goodman shook Jason's hand and turned to Ellen. "See me next week, Miss MacTavish. I'll do what I can to get you into our program."

"Thank you," said Ellen and felt as if she were walking with wings.

"I don't want to butt into your affairs," said Jason as they rushed down the hall to the elevator, "but you might be biting off more than you can chew. Med school at a normal pace keeps you plenty busy."

"I'd be able to join you in the medical corps sooner," said Ellen, smiling up at him.

"Let's hope the war's over by then," said Jason. He sounded mad.

Outside the sky spat rain. Ellen ignored the drops splattering her cotton summer dress and clung to Jason's hand as they walked to the open army Jeep.

"I'll drive you to your boarding house," he said when he started the Jeep.

"Let's go to a hotel," said Ellen.

"I'm going to see Mater," said Jason.

Ellen felt her nerves string into a cat's cradle. She told him the directions through campus, around the lake, past the large mansions with their well-groomed lawns and patches of Victory gardens. Butler was at the side of the house, covering his tomato plants with storm glass windows. "Here," she said.

Jason stopped the Jeep. "What kind of an establishment is this, anyway?" he said, his tone provocative.

"It's just me living with Mrs. Ardley and her friend Butler."

"I thought butlers were servants." Jason's tone didn't change.

Ellen thought for a minute. "He and Mrs. Ardley take turns cooking," she explained in a careful voice, "and I help clear the table and do the dishes. And we all eat together. Don't servants eat in the kitchen?"

"Does Butler have a name?"

"I don't know," said Ellen, surprised. "I thought that was his name."

"You Alaskans. You're all the same. Make up names."

"Ted Kleet hasn't a made-up name."

"The hell he doesn't!" stormed Jason. "He's known up and down the Chain as Torpedo Ted."

"That's news to me!"

"I thought he'd have told you."

Ellen pursed her lips. They were getting nowhere. "Please," she said, laying a hand on his arm. "Let's not fight."

Jason gripped the steering wheel. "What is he to you, anyway?" He turned toward Ellen, his eyes darkening.

"He's a friend," said Ellen, feeling frightened with the intensity in Jason's face and voice.

"A boyfriend?"

"What's this about?" Ellen tucked her feet underneath her and crouched on the seat, as if to protect herself from his wrath by curling into a ball. Overhead the sky rumbled.

"Maybe I'm being ridiculous," he said as Ellen turned sideways and stared at him, "but when he came that day with the letter, and that second time, it seemed as if he had his mind made up about you, as if—"

"What are you saying, Jason?" said Ellen, her voice cool.

Jason laid his head on the steering wheel. "I can't help feeling there's something between the two of you."

"Maybe it's because we're the same kind of people."

Ellen spoke slowly, thinking out each word with care. "We understand certain things about each other because we come from the same kind of places. But that doesn't mean we're anything. I'm in love with you, Jason."

"It can't work, Mac," said Jason, his voice pained. "We've got to forget each other, because there's no way I'm ever going back to Alaska. The experience on Attu has cured me of any romantic notions about wild country."

"You're upset," said Ellen. "You don't know what you're saying."

"Are you suggesting I'm suffering from shell shock, Dr. MacTavish?" Jason looked straight ahead. His knuckles whitened on the steering wheel.

"There's no reason for us not to be together," said Ellen and her whole being ached. "I know that. Don't you?"

"I've got to get the Jeep back and get to the airplane," said Jason abruptly. "What's your address? I'll write and maybe you'll figure out how to put a stamp on an envelope and write back."

Ellen ripped a sheet from her looseleaf notebook and handed it to Jason.

"Four-one-three-seven," Jason said, copying the brass numbers on Mrs. Ardley's door. "Now what street is this?"

"Lake Washington Drive."

He scribbled it down. Pins and needles prickled Ellen's legs. She clicked open the door of the Jeep and slid to the grass boulevard, stomping life into her feet. She felt on the verge of hysteria. Jason was leaving and everything between them was wrong. Controlling her voice against the spasms rising from the pit of her stomach she asked, "When will I see you again?"

"I don't know," said Jason.

"I love you," said Ellen and, with more strength than she knew she possessed, she shut the car door.

"'Wish Me Luck as You Wave Me Good-bye,'" said Jason, quoting the title of a popular song.

Ellen watched him spin the Jeep in the middle of the road and return the way they had come. She held up her arm, to wave, but he did not look around.

There was no point pretending hunger. Ellen went straight upstairs. She lay on the bed and stared through the high clerestory windows, watching the black clouds. There was a loud crash of thunder and the rain fell. The drumming on the roof dulled her thoughts. Feeling sodden with her own hidden tears, she fell into a troubled sleep.

Sometime in the middle of the night the rain stopped. Ellen awoke. She slipped out of her dress, her underthings, and walked naked to the arched window. The dark lake lapped at the beach in front of the house. A moist breeze blew through the window vents and brushed her skin. She rubbed her hands down her breasts, her thin waist, her rounded hips, stroking her skin in an effort to find herself.

Ellen felt as she once had when she watched a King salmon thrashing the set net, full of life one minute, in death throes the next. She had felt caught then, as if she were the salmon, as if she'd never get out of Unaganik. Now she was free, going to school, but caught in another way, caught by her feelings for Jason, by the magic of their caresses under the billowing tent on Adak.

Searchlights cut the black sky into geometric pieces. Jason had flown through that sky to see his mother. It's my own stupidity for not calling his cousin and letting her know where I was, or figuring out how to mail a letter, thought Ellen. And anyway, no wonder he wants to go home. He almost lost his life and he's going home to the person who gave it to him. I had no right to ask him to stay.

Try as she did to see Jason's side of it, doubt burned around her like votive candles in a bed of straw. What's wrong with me that I couldn't comfort him? Why wouldn't he cancel his plans once he found me? Ellen snuffed her doubts out until not a single spark remained. She stood by the window a long time, feeling the breeze, seeing nothing, thinking nothing. Her head cleared. She knew Jason was alive, and someday they would be together again.

29

A MONTH LATER JASON wrote. "Darling Ellen, Please forgive me for being such a cad when I saw you. I was not myself. Now I've had a good rest, good food, and am off to Great Britain, which, they assure me, is heaven compared to the Aleutians. I do love you . . ."

Ellen put the letter under her pillow. "I love you," she wrote back, "I'll be waiting for you when the war is over." She gave the envelope to Butler to mail and then tucked Jason into a warm corner of her thoughts and forged ahead at school.

True to his word, Dr. Goodman arranged for Ellen to apply for the wartime medical program that was to start in September. Ecstatic, Ellen told Reginald Beck, who also applied. After an extensive interview in which Ellen told of her experiences in Unaganik, Harold's Point, and Adak and convinced one particularly obnoxious board member that she had no intentions of quitting halfway through to get married, and after a thorough appraisal of her grades, Ellen was accepted.

Reginald was also accepted. It spurred their enthusiasm for studying throughout the long hot summer. Rather than joining their classmates for ice cream in the Arboretum, or rowing on the lake, they stuck to their books.

One twilight evening in early July, Jill Hall telephoned. Ellen and Mrs. Ardley were in the kitchen flattening tin cans for the neighborhood scrap drive.

"I've joined the Minute Maids," Jill said in a bubbly

voice. "We're selling war stamps at a rally on Sunday. Will you join us?"

"Yes," said Ellen and on Sunday drove downtown with Butler and Mrs. Ardley to Victory Square. The sun shone, Mount Rainier stood silhouetted against the blue sky, and the war seemed very far away. A tall cardboard statue of Uncle Sam stood next to a concrete replica of the Washington Monument, on which were inscribed the names of local servicemen killed in action. Ellen found the name of Mrs. Van der Voewn's husband.

A swing band played on a platform festooned with red, white, and blue bunting. "We're off to see the Wizard . . ." sang a man in a striped suit. "Buy war stamps," he exhorted through a loudspeaker when the music ended. "Raise your arm and a Minute Maid will be right over."

An enormous cardboard thermometer stood next to the platform. A boy on a stepladder painted in the red mercury as the sales increased. Jill rushed up to Ellen, gave her a basket, and told her how to sell stamps. Ellen hung back, intimidated by so many strangers. An Indian man with a long, black pony tail approached her and held out a two-dollar bill.

"I know how it feels," he said as she counted out stamps for him. "When I first came to the city, I felt awkward around so many people for the longest time."

"Where are you from?" Ellen asked, feeling less shy.

"Arizona," he said, smiling. "And I never thought I would, but I've even gotten used to the rain."

Laughing, Ellen handed him his stamps. She hadn't minded the rain.

When Bing Crosby strolled onto the stage with a straw panama supported by his big ears, she stopped any pretense at collecting. So this was the singer from east of the mountains, whom Reginald Beck always raved about.

Bing Crosby crooned through the microphone. He sang "When You Wish Upon a Star," and "My Blue Heaven," and when he sang "Ol' Man River" Ellen thought of Harold's Point, and dear Dr. Constance, and how he used to hum that tune as he made his rounds at night in the small hospital.

When Bing sang "The Very Thought of You," Ellen's thoughts switched to Jason and of how missing him had become such a part of her everyday life. She looked away from the stage and between the tall city buildings to Eliott Bay, where the ships docked. It would be so easy to get on one, to go back north. But for what? Ellen found Mr. Rupert's handkerchief in her pocket and blew her nose. She hated this betwixt and between feeling, as if once again she were on that rickety bridge, not knowing whether to turn back or move on.

"Hello," said a voice.

She looked into a rugged face with a whitened scar striking up through the right eyebrow. He wore a cotton shirt rolled to the elbows, exposing thick forearms muscled from years of hauling gear. The prominent veins on his arms looked like branches of a blue spruce.

"Ted Kleet," she said, catching her breath.

"I had a feeling I'd find you here," he said. "The sawbones said you'd come to Seattle to school."

Ellen laughed, thinking of Jason as a sawbones. "I am at school," she said, "and I'm usually studying on Sunday. It's lucky I came downtown today."

Ted grinned back and Ellen thought of the time, long ago, when they had talked about luck. "What brings you here?" she asked.

"I was ordered down to bring back a power scow." He smiled and she laughed, noticing that he was looking at her bobbed hair. She pushed her fingers through it, fluffing it up.

"Where did it all go?" he asked, his voice solemn.

"I cut it when I was on Adak. It was lots shorter than this."

Ted's hair was cropped close to his head, navy style.

"Did you join the navy?" Ellen asked. They walked to a row of folding chairs and sat next to a sailor in dress whites. A girl hung on his sleeve.

"Never! I'd have been court-martialed if I'd joined the Regulars."

"Why?" Ellen asked, feeling easy beside Ted, feeling as if she had seen him yesterday and no time or trauma had intervened.

"A four-striper ordered me to anchor off one of the Rat Islands and row him and his two brown-nosers ashore. I told him he might be a captain in the navy but I was captain of the

Yethl and I wasn't getting off the *Yethl* and neither was my skiff.''

"He wouldn't like that," said Ellen.

"You bet! When we got back to port he demanded I be put in the brig." Ted chuckled. "They couldn't do a thing since I didn't come under their jurisdiction. I was sure glad the old man convinced me to stay with the Yippee boats."

Bing Crosby left the stage and the man in the striped suit returned. The Minute Maids moved through the crowd with their baskets. The boy climbed higher on his ladder, painting the mercury higher in the fake thermometer.

"That same captain got tamed later," said Ted, warming to the subject. "I took him to another island. This time he had his own skiff so he could go ashore in his own way. I studied the water and found a streak where the waves didn't break. I told him to go in that way, but he knew all there was to know about landing a skiff through the surf. Trouble was he got swamped and lost two guys. He didn't complain to anyone about that!"

Ellen saw the soldiers on Adak, the ships in the harbor, the plane exploding over Sweeper Cove. She remembered thawing the rear gunner's face and felt the fear when he jumped her. "I'm glad I'm not up there," she said at last. "I'm glad I left."

The band broke into music and more couples joined the dancers in front of the bandstand. "Mairzy Doats" sang the man in the striped suit. The sailor in dress whites and his gal started to polka.

"Come on!" Ellen needed to move. "I'll teach you. It's like the schottische only you hop after each step."

"Do you remember that time at Mrs. Meriweather's?" Ted asked.

"Yes," said Ellen and grinned to see the sparkle in his eyes.

Ellen put her hands on Ted's shoulders and bobbed from side to side. Ted's feet tangled. Giggling, Ellen held him up. Soon they were circling the whirling mass of dancers. Ellen tossed her hair, happy to feel the music lift her feet and clear her head after so many long hours glued to the books.

They danced until the band started a slow waltz. "I don't know this one," said Ellen.

"I'll learn it and teach you next time," said Ted. He bought two Coca-Colas and they returned to their seats sucking on paper straws. Beside them, the sailor and his gal shared one Coke with two straws.

Ted looked as carefree as a kid. It reminded Ellen of the time she had first met him and they had whirled over the tundra. "Where's the old man?" she asked. "Did he come down with you?"

Ted held the empty bottle on his knee and went very still. "He's dead."

Ellen's heart leapt. She bit her tongue, wishing she could swallow her question.

Ted looked straight ahead. His cheeks hardened and there was an indentation where he held his jaw too tight. "We were lightering to Amchitka, keeping just outside a fog bank," he said. "We spotted an enemy mousetrap rising out of a southeast swell. I was at the wheel and spun us around, to hightail it into the fog. The old man was on the stern. A Nip on the sub's conning tower shot him through the chest with a semi-automatic."

The band sounded like drunken wireless operators tapping an SOS. Ellen took the bottle from Ted's knee and set it beside her own on the pavement. They sat together and said nothing until much later, when Ellen caught sight of Jill at the corner of the platform.

"Will you come and meet my friends?" she asked, touching his arm.

"I'd like to," he said.

"Jill," said Ellen when they walked over. "Guess who I bumped into?"

"Hi," said Jill and a cute smile covered her pert face. Ted's rugged face blossomed into its lopsided grin.

"Ted Kleet," said Ellen, "Jill Hall."

Mrs. Ardley and Butler joined them and Ellen again introduced Ted.

"Will you join us for dinner?" Mrs. Ardley asked.

"I've got work to do on the scow before we head north tomorrow," he said. "I planned to work all afternoon but something drew me to the square." He looked at Ellen. "Now I know why."

Mrs. Ardley's eyes lit up. "It's so nice to meet people who pay attention to their inner voice," she said.

Ted looked at her for the longest minute. Behind them the band played "Begin the Beguine." "Sometimes I don't have time to listen to it," he said, and Ellen thought of him turning the *Yethl* around, avoiding the Japanese submarine and exposing his father to danger.

"There's no such thing as accidents," said Mrs. Ardley quietly.

Ellen gulped. She had heard something similar before, on Adak. Stewart, she thought, blinking rapidly. He said that, too.

Ted looked from one old face to the other. "Meanwhile it's back to America's Siberia." He held out a strong hand. "Pleased to meet you."

"And you," said Butler, returning Ted's handshake.

"Go with God," said Mrs. Ardley.

"Indeed," said Butler.

Ted turned to Ellen. Their eyes locked, and she remembered Emerson: "A friend is the hope of the heart." Then Ted tilted his head and was gone.

"Where's he going?" Jill asked.

"Adak. In the Aleutian Islands."

"Gee whiz," said Jill. "Are you kidding me?"

"No," said Ellen, "I'm not."

"Aren't you scared for him? With the Japs there?"

Ellen shook her head. No. She wasn't scared for Ted. He was like her, a survivor. But she was scared for Jason, and whether he'd come out of this war the same as he'd gone in.

Back at the mansion, Jill changed into a turquoise bathing suit and swam in the lake while Ellen watched in envy. "Come on in," said Jill.

"I can't swim," said Ellen.

"I'll teach you," said Jill.

"I don't have a bathing suit," said Ellen, admiring Jill's trim, well-proportioned figure. "And my legs don't look like Betty Grable's."

"You're kidding me!" Jill laughed, holding one leg.

"I look dumpy, that's why."

"What's with you, Ellen? You've never cared about how you looked."

Ellen plopped to the grass. She looked across the lake, watching the long twilight dapple the water. A woman with three children paddled toward them in a wooden canoe. On the opposite shore, other children splashed one another. Their laughter echoed over the lake. "I'm worried about everything," said Ellen quietly, "not just how I look."

"I think you're in love," said Jill.

"I am," said Ellen.

"He's simply divine," said Jill. "I'm glad I got to meet him today."

"It's not Ted Kleet," said Ellen. "It's Jason West. Dr. Jason West. You haven't met him."

"I hope I do," said Jill. "He's a mighty lucky guy."

Ellen grinned and for a moment felt better.

In the fall, Ellen and Reginald and forty-eight other students started the probationary period of the accelerated medical training program. They studied biology, botany, organic chemistry, Latin, and English. By Christmas 1943, Ellen was ready for a break and was pleased when Mrs. Ardley planned a musical party.

"We haven't had Mr. Rupert and his cello over for a long time," Mrs. Ardley said.

"Let's invite Jill, too," said Butler.

I wish Jason could come, thought Ellen, and fingered the letter from him in her pocket. He had also sent a bottle of Chanel Number Five. "So you won't forget you're a woman," he wrote.

"Do you want to invite anyone from school?" Mrs. Ardley asked.

"Yes," said Ellen and put reveries of Jason aside.

A week later, Reginald arrived with red-haired Stephanie in her father's Plymouth. He brought a record of Bing Crosby singing "White Christmas." Jill arrived with Mr. Rupert and his cello in a 1941 Ford.

Ellen followed Mr. Rupert into the music alcove. "Boeing needs women to work on the Flying Fortresses," she said.

Mr. Rupert loosened the end pin on the cello, pulled it out and tightened it into the down position. "Do you want to be a Rosie the Riveter?" he asked, looking at her as he hit low "C" on the piano and tuned his string.

"Maybe I should quit school and go to work for the war," Ellen said.

Mr. Rupert leaned over to the piano and hit the "D" note. He tuned his second string.

Ellen paced back and forth while he continued tuning his cello to Mrs. Ardley's grand piano. "It doesn't seem fair," she said when he finished, "for me to go to school when they're desperate for people to work on the airplanes."

Mr. Rupert played a few stanzas of music and then spoke. "Are you finding the school work too difficult?"

"No." Ellen stopped pacing. "No," she repeated. "I love it, it's just that I wonder if I should quit school now, work for the war effort, and go back later. The money from Dr. Visikov will still be there for me, won't it?"

"Did you hear that appeal for workers on the news last night?" Mr. Rupert laid his cello on the waxed oak floor and stood up.

Ellen nodded.

"Do you want my opinion?"

Ellen nodded again.

"The money is there for you whenever you want it, but in my opinion it would be a cockeyed shame for you to quit school. The war isn't going to go on forever." He held open the music room door and Ellen went into the hall, relieved.

"Sometimes I wonder if I'm going to go on forever," she said when he took her arm and led her to the dining room, where Butler and Mrs. Ardley were serving dinner.

"You can get through anything you put your mind to," said Mr. Rupert. At that moment he sounded just like Daddy and Joe Stokes when they talked about climbing the Chilkoot Pass Trail and hauling up fifty-pound loads day after day until they met the RCMP requirement of a year's supply of grub, clothing, and equipment, totaling almost two thousand pounds each.

In June 1944, right after the news of the Normandy invasion, Ellen, Reginald, and their classmates Emmett Nash, Will Green, Bob Waller, Thornton Percival, and Hannah Finch were among the thirty accepted to medical school at the end of the probationary period. Giddy with the good news, they crammed into Bob's Model T Ford and rattled downtown to celebrate at The Dog House. To her surprise, Ellen met Jill there with a young man.

"Nils Lund," Jill said, introducing a man who wore dress blues and naval insignia. "Are you on your break now?" Jill continued.

"A whole week," said Ellen, grinning. "Can you both come to the house some time? I've bought a bathing suit and I can't wait for swimming lessons."

"Gee whiz," said Jill, laughing. "We'll come tomorrow."

By late November 1944, Ellen forgot that she had learned how to swim. She clung to her books as if they were Mae Wests, the overstuffed life jackets named for the famous actress. Buoyed on by Reginald's joking remarks about "hen medics," she studied hard to stay afloat.

"You are remarkable," Reginald teased one dark damp November afternoon when she told him her secret code for remembering the twenty-seven bones in the skeleton of the foot, "and you're only a woman."

"I can pass as a man any day," said Ellen, tossing her hair, which had now grown past her shoulders. She closed her osteology text and opened her chemistry book.

"You think like a man," said Reginald. "I'll admit that."

Ellen laughed, disturbing Thornton, who was manipulating his slide rule next to them, figuring out a problem for biostatistics class. "And you look like a man who eats too much," she whispered. "You should tell that friend of yours not to bake so many tortes."

"That friend is Stephanie," said Reginald. "Or do you only remember the names of bones?"

Ellen laughed again. "I thought I saw you with your arms around another redhead," she said.

"That was Stephanie." Reginald blushed slightly. "She's losing weight."

"Really?" said Ellen, surprised that she hadn't recognized the secretary of the program Mr. Rupert had enrolled her in when she first came down from Adak. "I could have sworn..."

"I thought you never swore," said Reginald.

Thornton tapped his slide rule on the table, and said in a loud voice, "Will the meeting please come to order!"

Usually Ellen and Reginald studied until midnight. Then Ellen walked home in the dark and sat in the kitchen and ate the soup Butler always left simmering on the stove. She loved those moments, when her mind and body, numb with exhaustion, were revitalized by the soup and the thought that bed was a flight of stairs away.

One soggy black afternoon near Christmas, Ellen noticed her physics tutor trudging across campus. Mrs. Van der Voewn's shoulders curved as if she were bent under the weight of the world.

"How long does a person grieve?" Ellen asked Reginald when they talked on the front steps of the library the following evening.

Reginald rolled a cigarette before replying. "I think some people enjoy being unhappy," he said at last.

"How can you say that!" Astonished, Ellen raised her voice. "You can't help it if you're unhappy."

"I've been reading William James," Reginald said, blowing smoke.

Ellen groaned. She held out her hand and took his hand-rolled cigarette, puffing so deeply that she started to cough.

"James says the greatest discovery of our century is the discovery that people can change their lives by changing their attitude of mind."

"Penicillin is the greatest discovery of our century," retorted Ellen.

"Do you know if it cures VD?"

"For goodness sakes, Reginald, are you kidding me?"

"No," he said. "Bob Waller was attacked in his Model T and came down with the clap. He asked me if I thought it would help."

"Tell him to go to a doctor."

"Between you and me, he's afraid he'll get kicked out if anyone knows."

"Dr. Goodman's decent," said Ellen.

"He'll turn into a syphilitic maniac if he's not cured," said Reginald.

"He's already a maniac," said Ellen, laughing.

"Not compared to that mad German Schicklgruber," said Reginald. He stubbed out the cigarette and, silent with thoughts of war, they headed back into the library.

30

"**H**ITLER'S DEAD."

Ellen dropped her fork at Mrs. Ardley's bald remark. She stared at the tiny lady with the snow-white hair, the diamond *V* pinned, as always, to the *V* in her white-collared dress and glittering in the dinner candlelight.

Mrs. Ardley smiled. "The BBC picked up Hamburg radio's announcement that he died defending Berlin on the first of May."

Ellen looked back and forth between Butler and Mrs. Ardley, her mind a mixture of disbelief and hope. Was it true? Was Hitler really dead?

"Too bad FDR couldn't live to see the end of Hitler," said Butler.

"I suspect he's working hard on a solution from the other side," Mrs. Ardley replied.

The next day, Wednesday, Ellen walked to her classes slower than usual. She savored the spring air in her lungs, the tap of rain on her umbrella, the hyacinths like purple crowns poking up through the waterlogged earth.

When she entered anatomy lab that morning she felt the grey pall of the room, as if spirits hovered in dismal observation of the laborious dissections of their vacated bodies. Ellen pulled on her lab coat and rubber gloves and walked across the room behind Emmett Nash, who performed evenings as a magician to put himself through school. Emmett was running his scalpel around his nimble fingers as if it were dull as a coin.

In a corner of the room, their heads bent under the metal

droplamp that hung above the slate-top cadaver table, Hannah Finch and Will Green studied their dissecting manual. Thornton Percival stood at the sink, scrubbing his hands with antiseptic.

"Nicked yourself again?" asked Ellen.

He grinned sheepishly.

Ellen joined Reginald at their table and yanked the yellow oilskin drape off the cadaver. They stared in shocked surprise at its penis, standing in full erection. A small American flag waved from the end.

"A little sexual preoccupation?" she said to Reginald.

He wiped his laughter off his face. "Wasn't me," he said, pointing in the direction of Bob Waller.

Bob Waller ducked as Ellen plucked out the flag and pretended to stab him with it.

"Come to my office and I'll analyze your libido," joked Reginald.

"You must be currently out of red-headed women," said Ellen and picked up *Gray's Anatomy* to better memorize the muscles they were currently exposing.

On Sunday, May sixth, at five-forty-one P.M. Pacific War Time, the war in Europe was over. A bugler played taps across the lake. Fireworks shot from rooftops. Jill telephoned and asked if Ellen wanted to join her at the USO club. Instead Ellen stayed home to listen to Mr. Rupert and Mrs. Ardley play Liszt's transcription of Beethoven's Fifth Symphony. Tears streamed from their eyes.

"I've been assigned to a displaced persons camp," Jason wrote. "You can't imagine the poverty. No Kotex for the women and their blood just runs down their legs. Thousands of homeless people. It couldn't be worse. I can't wait to get out of here."

The pressure of beginning second-year labs in bacteriology, anatomy, and clinical pathology, with additional lectures in pharmacology, physiology, pediatrics, and surgery, kept Ellen's mind off Jason's return. He seemed to be hovering over her shoulder, however, when they were introduced to the stethoscope. She remembered with nostalgia how he had taught her, in Harold's Point, to distinguish the normal "vesicular" breathing from the "rales" of their tuberculosis patients. She sighed for those naïve days when it seemed as if all her problems would be solved by going to school.

Jason was not back by August when the big news in the Pacific broke. DAZED JAPS ADMIT WIDE ATOM DAMAGE, the headlines read Tuesday morning, August seventh. Ellen dished out five cents for a copy of the newspaper and read it on the way to the medical buildings. Instead of rushing into anatomy lab, however, she went to find her physics tutor, who briefly explained the splitting of the atom.

"What does it mean?" Ellen persisted.

"It's the beginning of the atomic age," said Mrs. Van der Voewn. "And the end of the war. At least for some people."

"You should see her," Ellen told Reginald as they bent over their cadaver that morning. "Her skin hangs on her cheeks. She looks emaciated."

"Maybe she should see a psychiatrist," said Reginald.

"The solution to the world's problems," said Ellen.

"There's going to be lots of need for them when the soldiers start coming home," said Reginald. "Mark my words."

But Ellen had other things to mark, and by the end of August and the beginning of a week's break, she was so tired she had to think to stand up. Ellen had slept almost all of three days when a letter arrived from Unaganik.

"Dear Ellen," the priest wrote, "Things are not well with your daddy but Cheok has everything in hand. You're not to worry."

"What do you mean?" she wrote back, giving Butler the letter to mail.

"Dear Ellen," the priest wrote again, "I would have written sooner but mail was sporadic during the war, with very few planes coming by. We've been very isolated and last week the cannery burned to the ground. Talk has it that the bosses lit it in order to get the insurance. Times are tough but you're not to worry about anything. Mrs. Meriweather, Joe Stokes, the wife, and I all hope you are doing well."

For several days after the priest's letter arrived, Ellen felt lonely for Unaganik, for the little house on the bluff, for wide open spaces, the wind in her hair, and the rich flavor of Daddy's smoked salmon. I should go and see Daddy, she thought, knowing she could visit him without feeling pressured to stay. But she only had a one-week break at Christmas, and if the weather was bad, the plane would be grounded and she'd miss getting back to classes on time. Finally Ellen put the whole idea of going home for a visit out of her mind. She concentrated on her studies with only an occasional daydream about Jason settling in Seattle after his discharge from the army.

Jason did not settle in Seattle. "I've had enough ugliness with this war," he wrote Ellen. "I want to make people beautiful. Luckily I've been offered a residency in plastic surgery at Columbia and am getting credit for my wartime surgery. I'll be finished before you're due to graduate. Then we can make plans."

Ellen tucked the letter under her pillow. If Jason was going to stay in New York, why hadn't he visited her before starting his residency? Still unaccustomed to using the telephone as a means of communication, especially long distance, it never occurred to Ellen that she could telephone Jason or that he could have called to explain what he was doing. Her feelings were chaotic enough as it was, and it was days before she sorted them out enough to write Jason back.

After much debate during the fall of 1945, the medical school elected to continue the accelerated program of training they had started during the war. Ellen finished her second year of classes with distinction and started her first clinical clerkship in June 1946.

Dr. Goodman, her preceptor, instructed her to take a history of an Oriental woman running a fever. The woman spoke no English and her husband, an American who had married her in Japan after the war, spoke no Japanese. With a great deal of difficulty that taxed her patience, Ellen took a history and afterward drew several samples of blood.

"What do you suspect?" asked Dr. Goodman when they consulted in the hall beside the examining room.

"Typhoid," said Ellen. "She's had a high temp, swinging from a hundred two to a hundred five for over a week, the lymph glands in her abdomen are swollen, and there was evidence of a nosebleed when I examined her. She seems to be complaining about a headache. Her husband believes she's had diarrhea, although we've been unable to substantiate that since she looked blank when I attempted sign language.''

''How do you sign for diarrhea?'' asked Dr. Goodman. Ellen saw his eyes tease behind the bifocals. She smiled.

''What about a rash?'' he continued in a serious tone.

''There's no rash,'' said Ellen, ''but the rose spots don't show until the second or third week.''

''Have you looked at those under the microscope yet?'' he asked, pointing to the vials of blood she was holding.

She shook her head, embarrassed. Mrs. Meriweather had sent down Dr. Visikov's microscope and Ellen had left it in the histology lab at school.

''Better get a stool sample too,'' he said.

Ellen nodded.

''Let me know immediately if you find any *Salmonella typhosa*,'' he said. ''We'll have to tell the public health people. They'll want to make a thorough investigation. Now who's next?''

''I've only taken one history,'' said Ellen, surprised.

''We've a waiting room full of patients,'' he said. ''Lesson number one—keep moving.''

Ellen kept moving. All that day, and the next, until vacation at the end of August. One day Jill came over and Ellen took a break to swim and splash in the lake and to talk about Jason and Nils, who had just returned from the South Pacific. But then classes began again and Ellen realized with a start that another summer's salmon season had come and gone and she had not noticed.

One day in early December, Ellen arrived home to find Joe Stokes sitting with Mrs. Ardley in the room with the Philco. The initial sight of his grossly disfigured hairless face and bald puckered head shocked her. She had forgotten his accident and remembered him as he used to look, with a full beard.

Ellen looked quickly at Mrs. Ardley, wondering what this gracious white-haired lady must think of her friend. Mrs. Ardley smiled, as composed as usual, and Ellen, grateful, darted into Mr. Stokes's arms.

He held her, trembling.

''How'd you get here?'' Ellen asked, finding her voice.

He cupped a hand around his ear and she spoke again, louder.

"Rode the steamship from Seward. Won't catch me on one of those new-fangled flying machines again." Without lips, his speech was odd. But Ellen understood, especially when his eyes watered. They looked rheumy and old but were still green and still reminded her of the color of a deep river.

Ellen smiled at this man who had first helped her to leave Unaganik. "How's everyone at home?"

"Did the priest write?" Joe's eyes had taken on a distant look, as if he were remembering old times.

"Yes," said Ellen. Her feeling that she should go home to Unaganik surfaced. But she didn't want to go. Not yet. The reason bubbled within her. She had promised to visit Jason in New York over Christmas.

"Are you a doctor yet?" Joe asked, breaking into her thoughts. "Can I ask you about my pains and achements?"

"What seems to be the problem?" Ellen asked, worried that this friend who had survived so much was finally breaking down.

"Old age." Joe chuckled and Mrs. Ardley laughed too.

" 'We do not count a man's years until we have nothing else to count,' " Ellen quoted, looking from one to the other of her beloved friends.

"You'll have to forgive her," said Butler, who had come to the door to tell them dinner was served. "She can't stop spouting Emerson."

"Emerson," said Joe after Butler repeated himself in a louder voice. "Did I ever meet him up north?"

"No," said Ellen, laughing. "He lived in Boston."

"Met two *cheechakos* from Boston once," said Joe. "They had the bad fortune to get lost with Spit 'n' Polish Patty."

"Dinner's ready," said Ellen, taking his arm and not wanting to hear the familiar story before they ate. "You can tell us later."

Joe told many stories later, and for days Ellen laid her books aside in the evening and stretched on the carpet next to the Philco, cushioning her head with her arms, dozing as Joe recounted the highlights of his life to Mrs. Ardley and Butler. She felt like a child again, listening from her cot as Joe and

Angus, thinking she was asleep, wove yarns about their days on the trail.

Two weeks after Joe left on the train for Minnesota to look for his long lost son, Ellen found herself in front of the hall mirror, waiting for Butler and Mrs. Ardley to drive her to the airport. She wore a stylish new coat with wide lapels that buttoned at her waist. A red silk scarf flowed and rippled as she paced the floor in her new high-heeled shoes with the open toes.

"That's not going to be warm enough for an Eastern winter," Mrs. Ardley fussed, adjusting the veil on Ellen's new pillbox hat. "You need something to cover your ears."

"Indeed," said Butler, who was searching for his driving gloves.

When they finally got into the Bentley, Butler discovered it was almost out of gas. Ellen was frantic when they had to stop at a gas station, but they still arrived at Boeing Field in plenty of time for her to catch the Pan Am DC-3 for New York City. Butler and Mrs. Ardley stood side by side, the one tall and thin with white muttonchops that widened his narrow face and the other petite and jeweled and looking as if a light wind could blow her away. They did not smile.

"I'll be back the fifth of January," said Ellen.

"Go with God," said Mrs. Ardley and Butler nodded.

Ellen boarded the plane, and then it hit her: she was finally going to see Jason. She tried to memorize pages in her *Gray's Anatomy*, but could not concentrate. The country passed beneath the small window and, as she watched it roll by, she could not help hoping that it was only miles that had come between them.

When the plane landed and she entered the terminal, she did not see Jason. Her head spun. Picking up her carpetbag from the baggage claim, she started to pace. People surged through the terminal, jostling with packages and suitcases. A kid held up fingers sticky from candy cane. A matron adjusted a hat that looked like a raven sitting on a nest. Ellen put her hand to her head. She had forgotten her new hat on the airplane. Her glance fell on a tall man in a brown coat and brown felt hat. He entered through the revolving doors, leaning at an angle peculiar to Jason. Ellen rushed to him. The man backed off, tipping his hat. He was completely bald.

"I'm sorry," said Ellen. "I thought..." The man vanished before she could finish her sentence.

Fifteen minutes. Thirty. The carpetbag was heavy on her arm. The terminal was too hot and the coat too warm. Taking her return ticket from her pocketbook and clenching her jaw, Ellen headed for the airline office to see if she could get reservations to go home.

"Miss MacTavish. Miss Ellen MacTavish." A voice came from the ceiling. "Please come to the information booth."

Her bag banging against her legs, Ellen reached the booth at a run.

"Miss MacTavish?" said a young woman wearing a blue suit with a snowman pin on the lapel. "There's a message for you from the hospital. There's been an accident."

Ellen seized the counter and held her breath.

"A hospital clerk called to say Dr. West has been held up in surgery and wants you to meet him at the Monarch Hotel. He'll be there as soon as he can get away."

Ellen began to breathe again.

"Here." The clerk handed over a pale green slip of paper.

"How do I get there?" Ellen scrunched the note into her fist and stuffed it in her pocket.

"Out those doors," the woman pointed, "you'll find a taxicab. He'll know where to take you."

Ellen hunched in the backseat of the vehicle. They crossed a lighted bridge, entered streets of buildings so tall there seemed to be no sky above them. Her ears ached with the jumble of noises. Her eyes felt gritty.

The taxicab driver screeched to a halt in front of a hotel. A portly man in a red uniform with gold braid across his chest stood beside a marble statue of a lion. A man and woman, both in fur coats, strolled into the building, arm in arm.

When Ellen paid the driver the amount shown on the meter, he glared at her, his eyes full of hate. Shuddering, she yanked her carpetbag from the seat and hurried into the hotel, terrified that the taxi driver was crazed and might follow her. Entering a lobby paneled in dark mahogany, she walked up and down a plush red carpet searching for Jason. A man in a gold uniform carried a silver tray above his shoulder. He offered a sherry to Ellen, but she shook her head and sank into an overstuffed chair beneath a painting of Queen Victoria. Red and gold Christmas lights flickered on a small tree standing in an alcove opposite her. For a moment they seemed like her encounters with Jason: on again, off again, on again. Determined to enjoy their reunion after such a long absence, Ellen shut her eyes and concentrated on composing her unsteady nerves.

31

ELLEN DREAMED THAT PALM leaves tickled her cheek. When she reached to brush them away, someone pulled her hands. Her eyes flew open. "Jason!"

"Darling." He pulled her into his arms. The trauma of their long separation vanished. She clung to him.

"I'm so sorry I'm late," he said. "Got held up by a nose."

"What a blow!" joked Ellen.

"My patient stuck his nose into someone else's business," said Jason, "and went down swinging."

"Who knows what will happen next," Ellen said, smiling up at him, her eyes sparking in remembrance of old times, her fingers playing with the buttons on his overcoat.

Jason's face was drawn and grey, his eyes pulled down by the dark circles beneath them. "Are you getting fresh with me, Miss MacTavish?" he said, his voice deep and suggestive.

"Fresh as the wind on Adak," Ellen replied, grinning with remembered pleasure.

Jason grimaced. He said nothing about her long hair, about the rouge that accentuated her broad cheekbones, the mascara that Jill had taught her to brush on her dark eyelashes. His eyes looked distant, as if he were again falling down that cliff on Attu. "Have you checked in?" he asked.

"I was waiting for you." Ellen felt uneasy. Was he unchanged from the last visit?

"Stay here," Jason said briskly, "I'll be back in a flash."

Jason got a key and, carrying the carpetbag himself, led

Ellen onto the elevator. Except for the ancient elevator operator who acted as if he were deaf, the elevator was empty.

"I've been thinking a lot about Alaska lately," Jason said as the elevator rose. "It's such an emotional place to live, it keeps you on your toes just to avoid going nuts."

"I'm afraid I'll go nuts in New York," said Ellen. "Butler doesn't drive half the speed of the taxicab I took in from La Guardia."

Jason laughed and Ellen looked up at him, happy to see the brooding slide from his face.

The elevator stopped. The old operator opened the doors and a small boy in short pants, a tartan jacket, and a red bow tie looked at them in surprise.

"Going up," said the operator. The boy darted away. The doors closed, the inside gate clanged, and they continued upward.

"It's not as if it's easy living up north," Jason continued. "Especially with all the problems you see as a doctor."

"Poor Mrs. Berglund," said Ellen, thinking back to that awful scene on the kitchen floor and shuddering. "She had a terminal case of cabin fever."

Jason put his arm around her shoulders. "I'm sorry you had to see that," he said. "I wish I could have been more help."

Ellen relaxed against his arm.

"I've thought often about what you said," she replied.

"What was that?"

"That ultimately each person is responsible for himself."

The elevator stopped on the twenty-third floor and they walked into an empty hall. "My uncle said that to me after my father died," said Jason, taking Ellen's arm. "It helped me to stop feeling guilty."

With a jangling of the key in the lock, they entered a room carpeted in green. Candle-shaped lamps hung on the gold-and-white striped walls. There was a double bed covered with a gold bedspread. A bedside table held a Gideon bible and a lamp with a pleated shade. Beneath the high windows stood an oval table with two curved back chairs covered in the same glossy material as the spread.

"Do you know," Jason continued after he hung their coats in one of the four closets, "I can't think of Christmas without thinking of that picture Jonah drew for you. It haunts me.''

Ellen said nothing. Through the high windows, she saw lights rising up from the city like ladders to the black boat above. Taking Jason's hand, she led him to the window and stared out.

''Manhattan's full of buildings that go up and are torn down, people who come and go, and everything's busy and lively and full of life. I think that's why I like it so much. Something's always happening.''

''Compared to Manhattan,'' said Ellen, ''Seattle's a village.''

''Don't you like those lights, Ellen? They make me think of gypsies dancing around a campfire.''

''My mother likes to talk to the sparks in the fire,'' said Ellen quietly, absorbed by the view and the thought that as many people as there were lights lived in this place.

''Do they talk back?''

''Sometimes.'' Ellen felt as if she'd come not just two thousand miles across the country but from another continent, a different civilization.

''What do the sparks say?'' Jason asked behind her ear.

''Sometimes they say I'm cold, put on more wood.''

''Are you cold?'' Jason stood behind her, his arms enfolding her. Ellen leaned into him, feeling the soft wool of his suit jacket and feeling she belonged there, fitting as she did so easily under his chin.

''I'm fine,'' she said, disliking the intrusion of language.

He held her tight, his lips pressing against her hair, his hands pressing underneath her breasts.

''Have you seen the famous Torpedo Ted?''

Ellen jerked away from the window and stared up into Jason's eyes. They looked like cracks in a glacier. ''For goodness sakes, Jason, what's the matter? Why are you always so silly about Ted Kleet? Why do you always bring him up?''

''I'm nobody's fool, Ellen.''

Ellen felt as if a sack of meal had been offloaded directly onto her back. She could not understand Jason, could not get through to him. He seemed as deaf as an old dog with frozen ears. Ted Kleet was a friend, nothing more. She moved away from the window and dropped into one of the matching chairs.

"I can't stand it," said Jason, still looking out the window.

"Sit then," retorted Ellen. "You look dog tired." As if I'm not exhausted myself, she thought, feeling not only the strain of the ten-hour flight creeping up on her but the past several months of intensive study as well.

"I feel like I'm going off my nut with jealousy."

Ellen pushed off her shoes and curled her legs underneath her on the chair. She could think of nothing to say, nothing to ease Jason's mind. Talk seemed to get in the way of their true feelings for each other and she longed for what Emerson called "a wise silence."

"You know," Jason continued, "I feel like such a cad saying that."

"Reginald says we're better off if we talk about our feelings."

"Who's Reginald?"

"My lab partner. If you want to be jealous of anyone you should be jealous of him. I see more of him than I ever see of Ted Kleet."

Jason stiffened.

"I'm sorry," Ellen said quickly. "I don't know what made me say that. I'm in love with you and I always will be. Why can't you believe that?"

Jason walked over to her chair and stood behind her, stroking her jaw. Ellen tilted her head back until it rested against his pelvis. He seemed drained, as if all the strength she had known in him before had run out.

"I think I made the right choice," he said, "getting this hotel. I didn't want you to have to sleep in the Murphy bed at Mother's and you certainly don't want to stay in my basement room at the hospital. I didn't think you were hurting for money. You've got plenty, don't you?"

"Yes," said Ellen. "And I'll have the hotel bill sent to Mr. Rupert."

Jason pulled away. "We can't! Oh my God!"

"Don't swear," said Ellen.

Jason dropped into the adjacent chair and gripped his hair with his fingers. "I signed us in as Dr. and Mrs. West."

"For goodness sakes, Jason, it doesn't matter. Jill knows I'm coming here to see you and she pays the bills. I'll explain what happened."

"She knows?"

"Of course."

"Didn't she ask if you were going to have a chaperone?"

"Why should she? It's none of her business."

Jason shook his head.

"Why, Dr. West?" Ellen said, leaning forward, knowing she was pressuring him. "Why can't I send the bill to Mr. Rupert?"

"What did I tell you?" he said, sticking her fingers between his teeth. "What did I tell you I'd do to these if you called me that again?"

Ellen pulled her hand away and tucked her fingers underneath her thigh, rubbing the teeth marks. "I thought maybe you'd changed," she said softly.

"Have you?" he asked.

"I remember saying I didn't want to cut people," she said, trying to rekindle those wonderful days in the tent. "I surprised myself. Dr. Goodman had me excise a cyst during my first clinical clerkship and I didn't have as much diffoogulty as I thought."

Jason laughed as he settled into the chair.

"How about the other students?" Jason asked. "Any women?"

"One. Hannah Finch. There was another, but she dropped out."

"Do they treat you like one of the boys?"

"Yes," said Ellen, smiling. "And some of them call me Mac."

"Mac," said Jason, patting his lap. "It's been such a long time since I called you that."

"It has been a long time." Ellen unwound her legs, stood, and resettled herself on Jason's knees, curling against his chest. She loosened the double knot on Jason's wide dark tie. "Why don't you move to Seattle? Start a practice there," she said, her voice soft, her fingers unbuttoning his vest.

"Darling, I would if there was anybody worth specializing under. You know I'm taking a residency in plastic surgery."

"Hmm," said Ellen, biting her tongue, remembering her feelings when she received the letter explaining his decision.

"There's no place like New York to get the training I want. They've pioneered the use of refrigerated skin grafts here, for one example."

"Will you ever move to Seattle?" Ellen tried to sound calm, to force her voice to remain even.

"It's easier for you to move here than for me to go there."

"I can't!"

"Do it, Ellen, I need you here. I need a wife. Mater's driving me crazy with her plans to get me married."

Ellen waited, hoping for Jason to say more. When he didn't, she lifted his hands from her shoulders and clasped them between her own, holding them, prayerlike, in the narrow cleft between her breasts. "When I was interviewed for medical school," she said slowly, "I told the board I had no intentions of quitting school to get married."

"You don't have to quit," said Jason. "You can finish your training here."

"I can't," Ellen said. "Especially since I'm in this program. I'd lose time, probably have to add another year to my training, and what would I do in the summers if I moved here?"

"You could work."

"At what?"

"Some of the med students get orderly jobs."

"Do they hire women?" Ellen asked, surprised. "They don't in Seattle."

"Do they hire women as doctors? We don't have any at our hospital."

Ellen laughed. "I suppose I could get into the Public Health Service."

"And see charity patients?"

"Doesn't matter to me," said Ellen, looking at him curiously. "A patient's a patient as far as I'm concerned."

"I used to think that too." Jason leaned back and closed his eyes.

Ellen rubbed the deep lines in his forehead, trying to flatten them. "I suppose I could go back to Unaganik in the summers and pick fish," she said.

"You haven't been back since you left, have you?"

"No."

"How long is that?"

Ellen counted in her head. Normally she never thought about how time passed. She was too busy.

"How long?" Jason repeated, opening his eyes.

"Oh," said Ellen, swinging herself back through time to the muddy beach at Unaganik, the tide rising and fish still to pick. It seemed like yesterday she had flown to Harold's Point with Joe Stokes. "Four years. Exactly four years and three months."

"That's a long time," said Jason.

"You people in the Lower 48 are always talking about time," said Ellen. "It really doesn't mean anything, you know, it doesn't mean a thing. My mother never uses the word tomorrow. It doesn't exist for her. There's only today."

"You astonish me, Ellen. If you could see my schedule, you'd realize how screwy that sounds. I had to plan weeks in advance to get four days off. And for that I have to be on duty Christmas day."

"I'm glad you did, Jason," she whispered against his Adam's apple.

"If I could," said Jason, "I'd invent an eight-day week."

"Mrs. Ardley thinks people invented time when they became separated from the earth."

"She sounds like a real lulu, Ellen."

Ellen sat up straight on his lap. "I don't know when the fish run anymore or when the bull moose calls his mate," she tried to explain. "Even the seasons escape me."

"I know this season is winter," said Jason, his voice so tired it sounded as if he were dragging the words out of a frozen river, "and I know I'm beat. Let's go to bed. What do you say?"

"I was wondering when you were going to ask!" Ellen said, laughing.

She kneeled on the floor, helping Jason off with his socks, his trousers. Underneath his white undershorts, his penis was flaccid.

"You know one of the things I like about you?" said

Jason as he stood above her, stroking her scalp with his fingers.

Ellen rubbed her hands up his legs as she stood up against him, her body pressed against his, her fingers cupping his buttocks.

"What?"

"You have no shame."

Reaching on tiptoes, Ellen kissed him quickly, then darted into the bathroom. "I'm going to have a bath," she called over her shoulder. "And you're welcome to join me."

"Let me know when it's drawn," said Jason. He moved to the bed and lay down, crossing his hands over his stomach.

Turning on the taps in the clawfooted tub, Ellen removed her skirt and stockings. Wearing only lace underpants, feeling the tantalizing brush of warm air on her bare skin, she returned to the bedroom to tell Jason the tub was full. His eyes were closed. He was sound asleep.

Ellen soaked in the hot water and felt the discomfort of the long flight ease from her. But Jason's discomfort remained in her mind. He seemed tense, dreadfully tired, and more complicated than she had remembered, as if there were hidden rooms inside him that would never be opened. Had she changed so much that she noticed things about him she hadn't understood before? Ellen lathered her body and wondered if it had been the war that had affected Jason or just the long strenuous residency that had sapped the tenderness and compassion she remembered.

We're both sharp tempered, she decided, rubbing her back with the thick white towel. And we haven't seen each other for so long we have to be patient.

Ellen tucked Jason, still sleeping, underneath the covers. She wrapped her legs around his, reveling in the feel of his body. He did not waken and she, after a struggle to subdue her yearning flesh, finally dropped to sleep.

Sometime in the middle of the night Ellen awoke. Jason's breathing had changed. He did not move but she knew, as if their souls had communicated, that he wanted her. Ellen lowered herself onto him, gripping his sides with her knees. An image of a hot day on the muddy beach, Joe Stokes carrying her on his shoulders, the sun beating on her bare back and the feel of her legs around his neck flitted into her mind and she rocked on Jason, luxuriating in the growing sensations. He pressed his hands on her buttocks, drawing her to him.

Outside there was the noise of cars, the clank and clatter of a garbage truck. Distracted, Ellen tried to focus again on her body, on how it had been on Adak. She rolled off Jason and he crouched down in the bed, suckling her. Her whole body seemed in motion, the nerve endings catching long dormant feelings and playing them against the excited onslaught of brand new sensations.

From the depths of her being she seemed to speak to him, this beloved man of her heart. Moving again, he entered her. She opened to meet him until they joined as a beacon of light across a barren landscape where only the wind howled.

In the late morning they heard noises in the hall. "Maids," Jason said, and he slipped a DO NOT DISTURB sign on the door. The made love again, and it was slow and sweet and Ellen kissed him and he kissed her in places the writers of medical texts would never have thought suitable for kissing.

It was early afternoon when they awoke again.

"Let's order room service," suggested Jason.

"Let's walk," said Ellen. "I need to feel the ground under my feet."

"I've been dying to show you my city," Jason said.

Ellen smiled.

They strolled arm in arm past men selling roasted chestnuts from carts, past Salvation Army Santa Clauses ringing bells and clanging pots of coins, past carolers singing "Silent Night, Holy Night," past wooden reindeers. Jason bought Ellen a gardenia for her hair. "Since you aren't properly dressed in New York without a hat," he said. Ellen laughed and did not tell him that she had forgotten her hat on the airplane.

They stopped for a soda at a lunch counter and an early dinner at a tiny candlelit steak house on Forty-ninth Street. At dinner, Jason put two theater tickets in front of her. "For *Annie Get Your Gun*," he said. "We're going the night before Christmas. I've wangled the time off."

"I've never been to the theater," said Ellen, smiling at him, thinking of the first time she had seen *Gold Rush* in Harold's Point. "Will it be anything like the moving pictures?"

Jason laughed. "You're in for a treat," he said. "Wait and see."

After dinner, on the way back to the hotel, they detoured in the direction of the hospital so that Jason, even though he was off duty, could check on the patient with the broken nose.

"Will you come and do your internship at a hospital in Manhattan?" he asked Ellen.

Ellen watched the cars bumping one another down the street, the dirty papers lining the curb, the pigeons pecking at peanut shells. She breathed deeply and smelled dirt and exhaust and the sweat of rushing people.

"Do you think you could live here?" he persisted.

She looked at him, stopping so suddenly in the middle of the sidewalk that a man bumped into her.

"Pardon, ma'am," he said in a deep Southern accent and backed away.

"Maybe I'll never feel at home anywhere," she said slowly, staring after the man, thinking he looked exactly like Dr. Constance, and how did a man from the Deep South find himself so far north?

"If you aren't going to feel at home anywhere," Jason said, guiding her to the globed lamppost and out of the way of the pedestrians, "then you might as well live here, with me." He kissed her, right there on the sidewalk, and Ellen thought, what does a place matter as long as I'm with you?

After two of the happiest days of her life, days in which the pressures of medical school were almost forgotten, Jason took Ellen to meet his mother. Mrs. West lived in an apartment on Lexington Avenue. A large handsome woman with blue tinted hair and lines scraping from a tight-lipped mouth, she seemed as guarded as a she bear protecting a cub. She wore a black rayon dress, belted below her abundant breasts. Her black shoes reminded Ellen of Miss Long's, although the similarity between the two women ended there.

"How do you do," said Mrs. West.

"Pleased to meet you," said Ellen.

While Jason and his mother hung up the coats, Ellen walked to the corner of the room. A large glass cabinet had caught her eye. Squatting down, her hands on her hips, she examined, shelf by exquisite shelf, a collection of jade that bore the sheen of adoring centuries. Ellen fingered her simple jade labret, tucked safely beneath the buttoned jacket of her checkered wool suit, and could not believe the beauty before her eyes. Gradually she stood up, shifting her weight until she gazed at the top shelf.

"Mater had to sell most of her collection," Jason was saying behind her. "This is all she's got left." He spoke under his breath, and Ellen almost didn't hear him for there, between two intricately carved jade elephants, was Jonah's beautiful ivory whale.

A petite Negro woman appeared from a nook around a corner. She stood with her hands tucked underneath her starched triangular apron.

"Please serve our sherry," said Mrs. West and placed herself on a sofa. "Sit here, Jason," she said, patting the cushion beside her.

The maid returned with a lacquer tray holding three crystal glasses and a plate of fruitcake. "Will that be all, ma'am?" she said.

"You may go now," said Mrs. West.

Still stunned by the sight of Jonah's carving in Mrs. West's apartment, Ellen barely registered that the maid had served the sherry. Jason touched Ellen on the arm. "Sit here," he said, pointing to a brocade chair opposite the sofa. Ellen sat down.

"Birdie fell off her horse, Jason darling," Mrs. West was saying. "She says she's got a terrible bruise on her back and she wants you to look at it."

"Bruises aren't my specialty," Jason replied. "If she needs to see a doctor, she should see one in Riverside."

Mrs. West passed the fruitcake.

"No thank you," said Ellen, feeling too tense to eat. Her hand jiggled on the sherry glass. Something was going on between Jason and his mother that had nothing to do with words. She watched them talking and wondered, if she did move to New York, if she would ever feel like she belonged in Jason's life.

32

On CHRISTMAS DAY, JASON was on duty at the hospital. He had persuaded Ellen to spend the day with his mother, "to get to know her better." After Episcopal services at the Cathedral of St. John the Divine, Ellen and Mrs. West traveled on the train to the home of her brother, Dr. Harshorne, in Connecticut. Mrs. West wore an ankle-length black lace dress and a black hat with a feather that curled under both chins. She talked pleasantly of the symphony concert she had heard George Szell conduct at Carnegie Hall and the Henry Moore exhibit she had seen at the Museum of Modern Art.

"I found Moore's sculptures remarkable," she said. "But of course I'd seen some of his work at the Buchholz when he exhibited there in Forty-two. I don't understand why he diminished his show by including drawings of London air-raid shelters. We've all had quite enough of the war."

Yes, thought Ellen, wondering what Mrs. West knew about Jason's experiences on Adak and Attu.

"Did you enjoy seeing *Annie Get Your Gun?*" Mrs. West asked Ellen after the train had clacked over several more miles of track.

"I loved it," said Ellen, "but I can't sympathize with that line in 'Doin' What Comes Natur'lly' about not needing school when I wanted so much to go to school. I guess that's true, isn't it?" she finished in a rush. "When you want something so badly, you think the whole world wants it too."

"I have never approved of the celebration of ignorance," said Mrs. West, smoothing her dress. "That's why I insisted Jason go to medical school."

"The problem I'm having now," Ellen said, "is the more I learn, the more I want to know. There seems no end to it. Of course in medicine you're so scared, at first, that you'll make a mistake, that you want to study everything! I was just so lucky I got to work with Dr. Visikov and Dr. Constance and Jason. I learned so much from them before I even started medical school."

Have I said something wrong? Ellen wondered when Mrs. West tightened her lips and the conversation abruptly stopped. But the words of the song "Doin' What Comes Natur'lly" popped into her head, and she hummed the tune under her breath, remembering the feeling of holding hands with Jason in the theater and feeling transported to the life on stage.

A man driving a limousine met Ellen and Mrs. West at the train station. He drove down long winding streets bordered by high hedges. He turned between stone gates, drove down a wide curved driveway to a wooden house three stories high and three wings wide. In front of the house, a bird bath spilled water into a circular pool. The driver parked under a covered porch in the center of the middle wing. On either side of the porch stood two Chinese statues, hands folded under ornately carved robes. Ellen thought of the Chinese workers in the Unaganik Cannery and saw no resemblance.

Inside, in a hall as big as the house in Unaganik, another man in a shiny black uniform took their coats. Along the walls hung Chinese scrolls depicting scenes that looked like foggy days on Adak. Ellen blinked, and tried to visualize the hill where Stewart was buried. It seemed so long ago and so far away.

Straight ahead, through leaded glass doors, they entered a large room punctuated by a tiled fireplace in the center of the right wall. A woman wearing a skin-hugging dress of white satin leaned against the mantle. The sleeveless dress showed off her long arms, her small pointed breasts, straight hips, and tiny buttocks. A spray of gold sequins glittered from her slim high waist. Straps of gold sandals circled her trim ankles and were just barely visible below the hem of her dress.

Mrs. West went directly to her. Ellen, shy, stood by the door, worrying that her new red silk dress with the pink rose pattern and square neck was too short for the party. Except for the lady in white, everyone else wore dresses that reached the floor.

Ahead, on her left, was a ceiling-high fir tree, so emblazoned with green lights, tinsel, and red balls, it took Ellen's breath away. I wish Jason could see this, she sighed to herself, remembering the little toothpick tree he had made on Adak when she was too consumed by grief over Stewart's death to care about Christmas or that she was missing the old Russian traditions.

Playing quietly near the tree were two small children. Ellen sat down on the floor beside them. The little girl played with a doll with glass eyes that opened and closed. Ellen thought of the long-forgotten wood and fur doll in Unaganik that Bonnie used to play with, and wondered if Bonnie was now too old for such pastimes.

The little boy wore a blue sailor suit and appeared the same age Charlie had been when they walked to Beaver Lake. "Who are you?" he asked.

"Miss MacTavish," said Ellen.

"Where are you from?"

"I'm from up north," said Ellen, smiling. "From the Territory of Alaska."

"Are you Eskimo?"

"My mother is."

"Do you rub noses?"

"No," said Ellen and thought of Jason's insistent lips on her own.

Jason's uncle, Dr. Harshorne, a man as large as his sister, Mrs. West, and with the same tight mouth, introduced himself. Ellen stood and he took her around the room, introducing her to his guests.

There was his wife, Mrs. Harshorne, their married daughter and her husband, that husband's brother and his wife, another daughter, unmarried, wearing a pink, green, and black striped dress that Ellen had seen in Saks Fifth Avenue and thought hideous. Seeing it worn did not change her opinion.

There was a bachelor neighbor named Mr. Achity the

Third and Dr. Harshorne's young assistant, a Dr. Thorpe, and his wife. The two children, Trixie and David, were the Thorpes' children. Then there was the woman in the white dress who still leaned against the mantle.

"Miss MacTavish," said the host, "may I introduce Bernadette Rockport."

"Birdie," said Miss Rockport. Her blond hair capped a lean athletic face and was short enough to show off two gold nuggets in her pierced ears.

"Ellen," said Ellen, and felt her own weariness beside the radiating good health of this exotic woman.

"Did you come with Mabel West?" Birdie asked, lowering her chin to peer curiously into Ellen's eyes. Birdie's eyes were a golden shade of brown.

"Yes," said Ellen.

"Mabel told me all about you." Birdie spoke in a voice used to commanding large beasts to jump high fences. "What brings you to New York?"

"I came to visit Jason," Ellen said.

Birdie's eyes narrowed. "Jason?"

"Didn't Mrs. West tell you?"

"Why, no," said Birdie, and fingered her gold nugget earrings.

"I met him in Alaska," said Ellen. "In Harold's Point."

Birdie inched away from the fire. "I should adore to go to Alaska," she said. "My grandfather went there in 1898. Did you ever hear about a dog with a gold tooth?"

"The one they called Goldfang?" said Ellen.

Birdie burst into laughter. Ellen noticed that Mr. Achity the Third had shifted closer to the fireplace and was watching them.

"Do you have dogs?" Birdie continued. "My grandfather swore by the huskies. Myself, I prefer my hounds. You don't hunt, do you?"

"My mother hunted ptarmigan with a .410," said Ellen. "She taught me, but I never shot anything."

Birdie laughed again. "I don't mean that kind of hunting," she explained, her eyes amused. "I mean with the horses."

"No," said Ellen and, infected by Birdie's light-hearted manner, laughed at their misunderstanding. "I don't ride."

"I should adore to teach you," said Birdie.

"Thank you," said Ellen, smiling at the impossible thought of her on a horse. "I don't really have time this visit. I'm too busy studying."

Birdie raised one of her finely plucked and blackened eyebrows. "What are you studying in New York?"

"*Gray's Anatomy*." Ellen tried not to groan out loud over the seventeen hundred anatomical terms they were supposed to know. "I've got an exam two days after returning to med school."

"How divine that you're going to school," said Birdie. "My horses are going to school too, but not me! To tell you the truth, I never liked it much."

"To tell you the truth," said Ellen, "I'm afraid of horses."

Birdie laughed. Her throaty voice was rich and uninhibited and Ellen tried to relax, feeling how carefree and easygoing Birdie was when she herself felt so serious and dull.

Dr. Harshorne's son-in-law, a man whose myopic vision was not improved by the thickness of his eyeglasses, joined them. The man in the uniform passed a tray of martinis. Birdie and the son-in-law both took one, but Ellen declined. She already felt as if she were in danger of falling flat on her face and needed all the presence of mind she could muster.

All afternoon when Ellen was not trying to keep up her end of a conversation, she pondered about the name Rockport. It had a familiar ring, a flavor of stories by the fire, nights when Angus and Joe talked late into the night of creeks panned and nuggets overlooked, of the nefarious doings of Soapy Smith and the goodness of Diamond Lil, of survivors like Spit 'n' Polish Patty.

But at dinner, at a long table covered with a linen cloth and decorated with glittering pine cones a dozen times larger than spruce cones, Ellen concentrated on her table manners. Dinnertimes with Mrs. Ardley and Butler were so relaxed, Ellen had slipped into her old eating patterns, established before Miss Long had instilled in her the importance of good manners. Ellen felt stiff with the effort of holding her fork in her right hand instead of the left, as Angus had taught her, and at one point her elbow nudged Dr. Thorpe, sitting next to her. Another time, some peas landed in her lap. Ellen folded the linen napkin over them and hoped no one had seen.

She did not look up from her plate until Cora, a heavy black woman with tight black curls, a shiny black dress, and a red satin apron set a flaming plum pudding in front of Mrs. Harshorne.

"Now," said Dr. Harshorne after the pudding was eaten. "I'd like to invite the gentlemen to my billiard room to assist me in giving a speedy dispatch to a shipment of Courvoisier and Havanas from the Rockports." He smiled at Birdie, who was sitting next to Mrs. West. "As you all know, they're spending the winter in Nassau."

"Come, ladies," said Mrs. Harshorne, "we'll take our tea by the fire."

The ladies disappeared behind the glass doors of the Christmas tree room. Ellen remained in the dining room. "Can I help you?" she asked Cora.

"Laws no," said Cora. "That wouldn't be right."

"Then I would like to use the facilities," Ellen said.

"The ladies' room is right here," said Cora and bobbed down the hall to a closed door. Ellen entered a black and white tiled bathroom. She sat on the lid of a white commode with her legs crossed, her eyes closed. Covering her cheeks with her hands, with the tips of her fingers Ellen gently smoothed her eyes, ran her fingers over her cheekbones, under her jaw, as if checking that she had not, in the duration of dinner, become faceless.

Calmed, resolving to be friendlier, less shy, she straightened her dress, the seams of her nylons, and checked her hair in the mirror. It lay thick and glossy down her back, and she was glad she had not let Jill persuade her to cut it again and get it styled.

Ellen walked down the hall and met Cora standing outside the glass door with a silver tea tray. She reached forward to open the door and at the same moment they heard Mrs. West, in a loud voice, say, "Of course being a half-breed, she wouldn't know any better."

Cora winced. She backed away from the door.

"She means me," Ellen whispered between clinched teeth. No one in Seattle had ever called her that.

"She sho' do," Cora whispered back.

Laughter from the men ricocheted up from the basement billiard room. Ellen wished Jason's voice was among them and she could run to him and be protected as she was when Mrs. Berglund threatened her. She felt utterly abandoned until there seemed to be a hand supporting her elbow as if Butler held it, helping her to stand. "Do go first," she said to Cora. "I'll hold the door."

"Laws no," said Cora. "It wouldn't be right."

"Then I'll go," said Ellen, and she entered the room. The tree blazed with light. On a sofa in front of heavy velvet drapes sat the sisters-in-law. Birdie stood as if she had never moved, leaning on the mantle as she might lean on the saddle of a horse. The unmarried daughter stood beside her. Mrs. West, Mrs. Harshorne, and timid Mrs. Thorpe, who looked utterly embarrassed, sat on the sofa near the door. Cora set the tea tray in front of Mrs. Harshorne and, scowling, left the room.

In the far corner the two Thorpe children were soundlessly tugging on a pack of cards. Ellen walked over to them, sat down on the floor and said, "Can I play?" David dropped the cards. It was a game of Fish.

When the men appeared, smelling of cigars and brandy, it was time to leave. The limousine drove Ellen and Mrs. West to the train station. On the long ride back to the city Ellen pondered where she had heard Birdie's name before. "I think my daddy might have known Birdie's grandfather," she blurted out loud.

"Is your father a banker too?" Mrs. West asked.

"No," said Ellen. "He's a fisherman and he works at the jailhouse. There are no banks in Unaganik."

"And are you planning to go back there?"

"I don't know where I'll go when I finish medical school," said Ellen, wondering how much Jason had told his mother.

"I hope you're not planning on moving to Manhattan."

"Why?" Ellen bit her tongue and tried to control the trembling in her stomach.

"My son has a brilliant career ahead of him and you wouldn't want to hold him back, would you?"

It was not a question, but Ellen answered it anyway. "I'd never hold him back," she said, her pulse quickening. She looked straight into Mrs. West's eyes, at the white thickened to bluish grey, at the darkness of her pupils that looked like knots in an outhouse wall. Beneath her, the wheels of the train seemed to be saying over and over: half-breed, half-breed, half-breed.

On her last afternoon in Manhattan, Ellen attended a lecture on the medical effects of the atomic bombings of Hiroshima and Nagasaki. A team of doctors from University Hospital presented their findings. The series of slides that ended the program sickened Ellen so much that, had Jason not been sitting beside her, she would have left.

"I'll wait for you at the Monarch," she told him afterward when he was called to an emergency on the fourth floor.

She bought a package of Players at the tobacconist on the corner and now sat in the hotel room, lighting a cigarette with matches provided by the hotel. With a deep puff that caused her to croak like a spring frog, Ellen settled into the curved chair, determined to relax. Behind her the floral drapes were drawn tight in an effort to seal off the street noise. The room lay in semi-darkness, with the glow of the cigarette the only visible light.

"Dear Jason," Ellen said out loud, practicing for that evening, "I can't live here. I don't care whether your mother likes me or not, but I feel disoriented and uprooted more than I ever felt in Seattle. I've discovered that the feeling of a place matters to me—more, even, than you do right now."

From the distant street a siren wailed. Ellen thought of the years she and Jason had spent studying to save people's lives, of the satisfaction of that, and she felt guilty wishing Jason had not gone to the emergency, had stayed with her this last day. Surely she, as a potential doctor, should understand his priorities.

Ellen took another drag on the cigarette, another exhalation of smoke until her lungs felt as gritty as her body. Stubbing the end in a red glass ashtray, stubbing the turmoil out of her system, she rose from the chair and drew a bath. She lowered herself into the steaming water and, resting her head on the back of the tub, closed her eyes.

"Darling!"

Ellen woke with a start. She splashed to a sitting position. "You should thank your lucky stars you didn't drown!"

Ellen bent forward and turned on the tap. Fresh steaming water filled the tub, warming the lukewarm soup in which she had fallen asleep.

"Wash my back, will you?" She handed Jason a wash-cloth and scrunched forward, hugging her knees.

"Darling," he whispered against her ear. "I wish you didn't have to leave tomorrow. Please stay."

"I wish I could, Jason." Ellen hugged her knees tighter to keep them from shaking and tried to remember the speech she had rehearsed for this evening.

"You could go to Columbia University. You've met my uncle, Dr. Harshorne. He has contacts there and might be able to pull some strings to get you in."

Ellen thought about what Jason's mother had said on the train and wondered what kind of a recommendation Dr. Harshorne would give her. But the gentle stroking of Jason's hand on her back, the temperature of the water, made her think instead of palm trees and warm salty oceans and the delicious feeling of making love to this wonderful man.

"Please?" Jason tickled her neck with his kisses and Ellen, aroused, hesitated. Could she really say no?

She leaned back in the tub, searching for his lips. "Are you getting fresh?" she asked, trying to joke.

"I'm all wet," he answered.

Ellen's mouth went dry. She tried to speak, but the words were lost in the sensations aroused by Jason's gently probing and insistent fingers.

"Take off your clothes," she said instead. "Dive in."

After long lovemaking in the bath, they lay in bed, plans for the evening forgotten. Ellen's thick hair was still wet, but Jason's thinner, finer hair had dried in four directions. Ellen styled it with her hands, trying the part on one side, the other, down the middle. His hair refused to settle.

"Bad case this afternoon," he said.

"Mmm," Ellen replied.

"Four-year-old's nightgown caught on fire."

"Third-degree burns?"

"Over her legs and back."

"How'd you treat it?"

"Tried a technique I learned in the army from a St. Louis plastic surgeon. Cleaned her up and put her in a light body cast. First time I got a four-year-old plastered," said Jason.

Ellen's laughter was stopped short by Jason suddenly slapping his forehead. "Oh my God!" he said.

"Don't swear," said Ellen.

"I almost forgot. Mater asked me to stop in."

"Let's stay here," pleaded Ellen. "Just the two of us this last night."

"Please, darling," said Jason, laying back on the bed after examining his watch. "She's counting on it. She complains that she doesn't see me enough."

Ellen bit her tongue and kept quiet.

"You've had it easy," he said, shifting onto his stomach, studying her face. "People help you, make things happen for you, but my poor mother has had nothing but hardships."

"Mrs. Ardley says life is easy," said Ellen. "It's only hard because we make it that way."

"It's as easy as falling downstairs," said Jason, his voice dripping sarcasm. "That is, if you don't break your tibia or fibula."

"Not to mention the patella or femur or tarsals, metatarsals or phalanges," said Ellen, making her voice light and teasing, wanting to change the mood.

"Have you learned—'Never Lower Tilly's Panties, Mother Might Come Home'?" he asked with his mouth against hers.

"Do you mean the bones in the wrist?" Ellen asked, teasing. "Or—"

"Be nice to Mater," Jason said, standing up, grabbing Ellen's wrists and pulling her up too. "She'll get used to you and everything will be perfect."

"I feel perfect when I'm with you," she said.

Jason lifted her high off the floor. "I love you," he said, his voice hoarse. "I only wish . . ." He kissed her and it was many more minutes before he looked at his watch again. After quickly finishing their dressing, he searched distractedly through the four closets, looking for Ellen's coat. He found it in the last closet and held it out for her. "Ready?" he asked.

Ellen slipped her arms into the sleeves and leaned

against Jason for a minute, letting the longing for him surge over her. Then she tied the silk scarf around her neck, dabbed Chanel Number Five on her wrists, picked up her pocketbook and tucked it under her arm. When they reached his mother's apartment, Jason lifted the brass knocker. It was still in his hand when his mother unlatched her door.

"Come in, my darling, come in, how cold you must be," she said, presenting her cheek for Jason to kiss. "How do you do, Miss MacTavish," she said, her voice formal.

Jason poured brandy into snifters and served it over cups of boiling water.

"Have you missed the ice and snow?" said Mrs. West in a charming voice.

"It rarely snows in Seattle," said Ellen, "but it rains all the time. I don't miss that!"

"I read in the *Times* that it might snow tomorrow." Mrs. West spoke as if she had savored this tidbit as something she and Ellen might have in common to talk about.

"Maybe the plane won't be able to leave," said Jason, and his voice sounded wistful.

Mrs. West sipped her brandy. Ellen felt hers rush to her head. Through the mists of the brandy and her own strange thoughts, Ellen thought she saw gelatinous strands joining Jason and his mother, binding them. It was certain they would stretch, but stretch enough to include her?

By the time they left the apartment, flakes of snow were drifting between the tall buildings, coating the dirty sidewalks. Ellen opened her mouth and caught one on her tongue. It was icy cold.

"Will you move to New York?" Jason asked when they reached their room on the twenty-third floor of the Monarch Hotel.

"Jason." Ellen sat on the bed. "Why can't you move to Seattle when your residency is finished? They need plastic surgeons there, too."

"My roots are here," said Jason. "I love Manhattan. I'm at home here, and besides, there's Mother . . ."

"You don't have to live your life for her."

"I'm not, Ellen. You must believe me. It's what I want to do. The least you can do is try to understand." Jason sat on one of the upholstered chairs, his legs crossed. The blue package of Players sat on the table and he pulled one out, lighting it with a new mother-of-pearl lighter. His hands shook.

"What's the matter?" Ellen joined him, sitting on the second chair.

"I decided a long time ago, long before I met you, that I would make it up to Mother for all the disappointments she's endured."

Ellen reached for a cigarette and struck a match. The room was dim, lit only by the bedside lamp. The drawn curtains cut out the city lights behind them. "What did you tell me before about being responsible for another person's life?" Ellen asked quietly.

"I can't just go off and leave Mater," Jason said, his voice harder. "She nearly died when I went to Alaska, Ellen, and I wouldn't do that to her again, not for anything."

Do people use illness to manipulate others? Ellen wondered, and took a deep puff on her cigarette. The smoke swirled into the room.

"I haven't told you this," Jason said, and his voice sounded strange, "but my father lost all his money during the Depression, he was overextended financially with his art collection and he hanged himself. That's why I can't leave Mater."

Ellen stared at him. He was looking at his hands, those slim unscarred hands that had filled her with such awe when she first saw them back in Harold's Point. Slowly her cigarette burned down, unsmoked. There has to be another way, Ellen thought, stubbing out the cigarette in the red glass ashtray. We can't give up!

"Couldn't your mother move to Seattle too?" she asked. "Live with us?"

"I can't ask her to leave Manhattan," Jason said, shocked. "To her mind, this is the center of the world. Can you imagine a cultured person like her in a backwater like Seattle?"

Ellen got ready for bed. Jason joined her and when they were under the covers, he laid his head on her naked breasts. Ellen soothed his forehead, combed her fingers through his hair, and felt his pain sink through her until she, too, felt as if everything were hopeless, as if there were no future for them at all.

Suddenly Jason burst out crying. His uncontrolled sobs echoed eerily around the dark room. Ellen held him in her arms and found nothing to say.

33

DESPITE A CASCADE OF snow, the DC-3 left La
Guardia on time. It refueled at Washington, the capital city,
but Ellen, in a stupor from leaving Jason, didn't take advantage of the opportunity to get off and stretch her legs.

She hunched down in her seat, feeling as if her heart had
exited her body. Someone sat down beside her. She inched
away, pressing her shoulder against the tiny window and
closing her eyes to avoid conversation. The only solution for
her and Jason was for one of them to change. Meanwhile they
had agreed not to argue about where to live until he finished
his training in plastic surgery and she finished medical school.

Over the middle of the continent, after their third stop,
Ellen opened her eyes and noticed something familiar in the
hands resting palm down on the legs next to hers. Large
knuckles with distended thumbs, they were obviously hands
accustomed to hard work, despite their present clean and
unbroken nails. The man wore a stylish suit and gave the
impression of great physical strength.

Sitting beside him, watching the peace with which he
held himself, Ellen thought of Jason, of Jason's constant
disquiet and how it spilled over into her life, making her so
agitated and sharp-tongued that she overreacted to everything.
It was as if, when she was with Jason, her good nature would
change into something she didn't like but couldn't control.
Ellen sighed out loud.

"Hello," said the man next to her.

She turned sideways. "Ted Kleet!"

He grinned lopsidedly above a starched white shirt and

plain blue tie. His eyes were clear and obviously happy to see her.

"Strange that we meet in such odd places," said Ellen.

"Looks like a pretty normal airplane to me," said Ted.

"Where have you been?"

"Pentagon. The navy took out a petroleum reserve north of the Arctic Circle and my uncle sent me to bid on the construction contract."

"Does that mean you've given up fishing?"

"The fun's gone out of it since the old man died."

Ellen noticed that his face changed slightly when he mentioned his father, like a second of grief before the world chugged on.

"How's your mother?" she asked quietly.

"My mom's taken a job at the Mount Edgecumbe Sanitarium," said Ted. "She loves being around children."

"Those are pretty sick kids," said Ellen, thinking of the bone tuberculosis patient she had seen with Dr. Goodman.

Ted nodded. "Mom says that's all the more reason for her to be there."

The stewardess, wearing a linen apron over her grey suit and white tailored blouse, brought their meal. She hooked the trays onto the sides of their armrests and Ellen, starving, dove into the beef stew. A potato landed in her lap and she picked it up with her fingers and popped it in her mouth.

"I still have the *Yethl*," Ted said between mouthfuls. "I've moored it in Anchorage but it's a real problem with those thirty-foot tides. I keep planning on selling her, but somehow I don't think I ever will."

"What's happening about a union?" Ellen dunked her biscuit into the stew.

"The fishermen have organized one, but they still don't have much say in what happens. Last summer there were eight drownings with those Bristol Bay sailboats. There's nothing much the fishermen can do with those double enders when the weather comes up, but the people in charge still believe that gas boats shouldn't be allowed on the Bay."

"I suppose it's one way of controlling the number of salmon that are caught."

"They say that on the one hand," said Ted, after he

finished swallowing a spoonful of stew, "but on the other they allow the huge traps."

"There're no traps in Bristol Bay," Ellen reminded him.

"Some people think the traps are catching salmon on the Pacific side and curtailing the runs into the bay. In the southeast we have them right on the fishing grounds."

Fishing seemed so foreign to Ellen all of a sudden. She had to think hard to remember how it had been, picking salmon from the nets in the twilight of midnight, in the gumbo of the mud flats. "It's funny to talk about fishing," she said, feeling pensive. "I don't even know how many salmon Daddy's catching in the set nets anymore."

Ted turned very still. "Did anyone write you from Unaganik?" he asked.

Ellen's spoon stuck in the remains of cooked dessert. "Yes," she said. "The priest wrote." She felt Ted looking at her and turned to meet his eyes. He looked as if he expected her to say more. "He didn't mention Jonah," she said. "Is he all right?"

"He's at art school in Chicago." Ted spoke slowly, as if reluctant to change the subject. "I saw him. He seems very happy."

"I'm glad." Ellen thought about describing to Ted how Jonah's ivory whale sat between two jade elephants, but changed her mind. It just seemed too difficult to explain.

They finished eating in silence. After the stewardess removed their trays, Ellen slipped out of her shoes and tucked her feet underneath her, adjusting herself in the narrow seat. Clasping her hands together, she placed them on the armrest between them and faced Ted. A quotation from Emerson popped into her head: "A man's friends are his magnetisms," and it seemed as if she had drawn Ted to her like a magnet, to help her over this long lonely flight away from Jason.

"Are you happy?" Ted turned toward her and his face was very close.

"Yes," said Ellen a little too quickly.

"Did you like New York?" he asked with the slightest change of tone.

"I have to feel a place in my bones," she said, returning his gaze. "In order to be comfortable. And I don't know if I can live with so many people."

Ted's jaw had tightened. Ellen noticed the indentation above the mandible.

"The old man used to say he could live anywhere," he said, noncommittally, "as long as it was on the *Yethl* and on the water."

At the fourth stop, in Salt Lake City, Ted and Ellen walked around the terminal, stretching their legs. When they walked across the tarmac to the DC-3, Ellen blurted out: "You know, on the outside, it looks just like the C-47 I flew in the first time I left . . ."—she paused before saying Jason, and added lamely—"I mean when I left Adak."

Ted followed Ellen up the stairs into the plane and with each step she wondered why she didn't tell him about Jason, why she wanted to keep her love for Jason a secret.

On the last leg to Seattle, Ellen and Ted settled into a comfortable silence. When the lights of Seattle glittered below the airplane, the stewardess checked their seatbelts and asked people to put out their cigarettes. The flaps vibrated. Ellen clung to her armrest.

"Are you going to settle in Alaska when you get your MD?" Ted asked.

"Maybe I'll go to Unaganik." Ellen listened to the roaring noises of the landing plane and realized that she could not separate them from her own noises roaring inside of herself. Jason was now a continent away.

"Since the cannery burned, there aren't enough people to justify a doctor," Ted was saying.

Ellen closed her eyes. "I have a long way to go before I'm a doctor," she said, thinking of Jason, of how long they had to wait.

"Time goes fast when you're doing what you want to do," said Ted.

Do I know what I want? she thought as the DC-3 skidded down the runway. Do I want to move to Manhattan? Do I want to go to Alaska and give up Jason?

The plane pulled up to the terminal and they stood up and crowded into the aisles. Ellen remembered her coat, her pocketbook, the rolled prints from the Metropolitan Museum of Art.

"Would you like to spend the night?" she asked as they

moved down the aisle. "Mrs. Ardley and Butler will be glad to see you again."

"I've an early flight in the morning," said Ted.

"Butler won't mind driving you to the airport."

"Why don't you drive me?"

"I've never learned to drive a car, and to tell the truth, I don't know that much about living in a city. I go to school and I study and that keeps me so busy I don't have time for anything else."

They walked down the stairs and headed through the dark starlit night to the terminal, glowing like a welcoming cottage at the end of a long tiring trip.

"Your sister Bonnie is engaged to marry a man who flies a plane and runs a boat but can't drive a car," Ted said as they walked side by side across the tarmac.

"I can't believe Bonnie is old enough to be in love," Ellen exclaimed.

"True love can happen at any age."

Ellen was silent. Was it true love that she felt for Jason? And if so, why didn't she give up everything to be with him? Her thoughts dissipated in the flurry of getting her carpetbag and the joy of seeing Butler and Mrs. Ardley. Neither Mrs. Ardley nor Butler asked her any pointed questions about the trip except to say, "How was it?" to which she was able to reply in all honesty, "I'm glad to be back."

Soon they were at the stone house on Lake Washington Drive. They sat in the sitting room dominated by the large Philco. Butler sat in his favorite wing chair, Mrs. Ardley in hers, Ted Kleet, Junior, on the gouty stool, and Ellen tucked her legs under herself and sat on the floor. A bouquet of holly stood in a mauve vase. The hard red berries shone like merry faces peering through the prickled glossy green leaves.

Ellen listened as Ted explained his business in Washington. Her head dipped. Her chin touched her collar bone.

"Here, Missy," said Butler, rising with difficulty from his chair. "I'll help you up to bed."

"Let me," said Ted, and Ellen, hearing through ears muffled by dreams, jerked up her chin and opened her eyes. Ted held out his hands and Ellen let him pull her up. Her legs, numb from sitting on them, did not hold her weight. When Ted let go of her hands, she crumpled to the floor.

"Oh!" said Ted, "I'm sorry," and with one motion he scooped her up in his arms.

"Up the stairs and to your right," said Butler.

"Everything's ready," added Mrs. Ardley.

I can walk, thought Ellen, but felt dizzy from the long journey and the exhausting week in New York. Ted started up the stairs and she relaxed against him while memories raced back of Stewart saving her from the tide.

Ted carried her into the familiar bedroom and lay her down. Her eyes barely opened. He was at her feet, slipping off the brand new heels with the open toes. "Tch," he murmured, seeing the blisters on her pinched feet.

Gently, with no hint or suggestion of anything other than helping her into bed, Ted undid her hosiery from the garter belt. Ellen stirred. "It's okay," he whispered, his voice soothing, "I'm used to my sisters."

Of course he would be, as she was used to Stewart. But still, she was a grown woman and it wasn't right. Hadn't someone said so? Ellen tried to rise. When she did, there was Ted's arm at her shoulders, slipping off the sweater, unfastening the skirt. Overwhelmed with the confusion of it all, the mixed-up feelings warring with logic, she let him help her as if she were a child. He lifted her again, pulled down the covers, and tucked her into bed.

"I'm leaving my card on your table," he said softly. "Call me when you come to Anchorage."

"Hmm," Ellen murmured, thinking of Jason, thinking she'd take the next plane to Manhattan.

Ted had left by the time Ellen awoke. It was Sunday and she wandered onto the soggy lawn between the house and the lake, desolate. Standing there watching the desultory clouds scrub against each other, she did not notice a dog swimming, head high, toward her. He climbed onto shore and shook Lake Washington off his black coat. He stood medium height, a mongrel with Lab and German shepherd mix with white fur in the shape of a diamond on his chest.

"Here, boy," said a voice. Mrs. Ardley approached with a large bath towel.

The dog wagged to the sun porch as if he owned the place. He allowed himself to be dried off and, with an abundant wag of his tail, followed Mrs. Ardley into the kitchen.

"Has he been here long?" asked Ellen, joining the procession.

"Never saw him before," said Mrs. Ardley. "Not in this form."

Ellen laughed. How good it was to be home with her old friends, protected by the stone walls of this big house, the warmth of the feelings contained between their uncluttered corners.

"I've missed a dog," she said. "We always had so many."

"He's come to see you," said Mrs. Ardley as the mutt placed a paw on Ellen's foot.

Ellen laughed again. She sat on the floor and hauled the dog onto her lap, fondling its ears as she used to do with Wolff's.

Butler set a bowl of leftover porridge on the floor. The dog gobbled it up and sat back, looking at the bowl with an expression that seemed to say, "Why isn't there more of that?"

"My second husband said porridge makes a stronger animal," said Mrs. Ardley.

"That's what my daddy used to say," said Ellen and buried her head in the dog's damp coat, thinking of Unaganik.

When Jason wrote, Ellen answered immediately. She told him about Sirius, the dog, but did not mention Ted Kleet.

Jason wrote by return mail but gradually time lapsed between their letters. Ellen, busy with classes and her clinical clerkships at the hospital, tucked Jason back into that small corner of her mind, waiting for graduation and the opportunity to resolve their plans for a life together.

By the end of 1947, Ellen understood the integration of the body as a unit, combining her studies in anatomy, histology, embryology, physiology, and biochemistry. She had seen the effect of digitalis on a beating heart, of quinine on malaria and how too much produced toxicity and killed the patient with drug poisoning. She had learned to cross-match blood samples and to use a blood pressure machine.

Her brain became a repository of facts and it amazed her, sometimes, to dip in and pick out the right answer to a professor's question. She moved into high gear, doing clerk-ships in surgery, internal medicine, pediatrics, neurology, obstetrics and gynecology, and radiology. Often she worked late at night in the morgue with Reginald. On one occasion they performed an autopsy on a man who had bled to death from an ulcerated gastro-intestinal tract. They discovered cirrhosis of the liver. "An alcoholic," Reginald said. "He needed a psychiatrist." Ellen was too tired to disagree.

In early January 1948, when she made the rounds of the hospital with Dr. Goodman, her attention was drawn to a young boy with an indeterminate diagnosis. Leaning over the hospital bed, she smelled the boy's breath and remembered something Dr. Visikov had told her. "I bet it's his appendix," she suggested.

"Is there any pain in the right lower quadrant?" Dr. Goodman asked.

"No," said Ellen, "but his breath smells of rotten apples."

"Get the platelet count," ordered Dr. Goodman, "and if it's normal, schedule the operation."

"You saved this child's life," Dr. Goodman said later when they had found a gangrenous appendix abnormally high in the abdomen.

"Dr. Visikov did. He taught me that trick." Ellen wondered, not for the first time, if he was watching her from wherever it was he had gone.

A few weeks later she was sitting at the table in her bedroom, reviewing the cranial nerves. On Old Olympus's Towering Top, A Finn And German Viewed Some Hops. She wrote the standard mnemonic on one side of the page. Down the other side she listed the corresponding nerves: olfactory, optic, oculomotor, trochlear, trigeminal, abducens, facial, acoustic, glossopharyngeal . . . when someone knocked. "Come in," Ellen called.

"Dear one," said Mrs. Ardley. "Excuse me for disturb-ing you, but I've something to talk about."

Ellen looked up, her eyes glassy, her mind in another gear.

Mrs. Ardley pulled up a boudoir chair and sat opposite Ellen at the study table. "Ellen," she said, "I'm concerned about you. You're working too hard."

Ellen laid her pencil on the table. She stretched her arms toward the ceiling and, clasping them, rested them on top of her head. She leaned backward in the chair. "If I don't work hard," she explained pleasantly, "I'll never get through."

"You'll get through," said Mrs. Ardley, "but you'll do much better if you take some time each day to relax."

Ellen sighed. It seemed as if she hadn't relaxed since Christmas.

"If you don't pay attention to your body, dear one, you're going to get sick." Mrs. Ardley picked up the green vest pocket dictionary and settled back in the boudoir chair.

"The doctor in Unaganik gave me that," said Ellen. "He drugged himself so he didn't have to pay attention to anything."

"He chose that path," said Mrs. Ardley. "You don't have to."

"Why would anyone choose to be a drug addict?"

"Who are we to judge what one soul chooses for its learning?"

Ellen bumped the two front chair legs back onto the floor. She planted her elbows on the table and leaned forward. "Can you prove the existence of a soul," she retorted, thinking of the years she spent studying the human body, memorizing the names of the multifarious parts. "I've never seen it."

"You're seeing one way. With your intellect."

Ellen stared at her medical text. "You sound like an Eskimo shaman healer," she said. "Everyone knows that's cockeyed nonsense."

"Do you believe only in logic?"

"Yes." Ellen spoke emphatically, but her mind drifted to that experience of soaring above her body on the mud flats. Could that be what Mrs. Ardley meant by the soul?

Ellen looked at her. Since the war ended, Mrs. Ardley no longer wore the diamond *V* brooch. But in other ways she had not changed. In fact, it seemed that Mrs. Ardley had not grown any older than she had been when Ellen arrived in Seattle, five years ago.

"When Dr. Visikov wrote to me he said that the patient who wants to get well almost always will," Ellen said slowly. "Is that what you mean?"

"That remark gives me a great deal of comfort," said Mrs. Ardley. "I didn't know Aleksandr had starting thinking that way."

In Mrs. Ardley's grey eyes with the dark violet rims, Ellen saw the reflection of her own frustration. Then she felt a rush of warmth, as if someone had covered her with a well-loved quilt. "Aleksandr?" she said, surprised that Mrs. Ardley knew his first name. "Did you know him?"

Mrs. Ardley stroked the embossed leather cover of the dictionary for some minutes before she replied. "Yes."

"Then tell me why," said Ellen, "why did he do that to himself?"

"His wife left him for another man."

"Why did she do that?"

Mrs. Ardley's eyes seemed to lose their glow a little, then catch light again.

"Oh I know," said Ellen sarcastically. "He worked too hard. Spent too much time with his patients and not enough time with her. He behaved with logic instead of passion. He believed only what he saw with his own eyes and knew with his own mind."

"Perhaps," said Mrs. Ardley. "But his wife was a young woman, wanting adventure. She's to be forgiven."

"Nobody understands, do they," said Ellen. "They expect the physician to be all things to all people and to forget living his own life in the process."

"That's why I came in here." Mrs. Ardley set the dictionary on the table and stood. "I don't want you to forget that you're human too."

"Where did you meet Dr. Visikov?" Ellen picked up her pencil.

"I was his wife," said Mrs. Ardley and tiptoed out of the room.

Ellen stared at the doorway for a long time before she finally forced her attention back onto her book. She studied all night and at dawn stood by the arched window watching a spray of yellow in the eastern sky, a reminder that the sun was beyond the clouds, waiting for a chance to break through.

No one needed logic to know that something was wrong with Mrs. Van der Voewn. Her eyes, dark and empty, looked as if they had ended a journey her body had not yet begun. They seemed disconnected to any will or soul. Ellen saw her several times on her way through campus to the medical school, and although she had invited her to Mrs. Ardley's Christmas Party, Mrs. Van der Voewn had declined.

"I think she's still grieving for her husband," Ellen said, discussing it with Reginald.

"Maybe she doesn't want to live without him," Reginald replied.

His remark shocked Ellen. Would she have wanted to live if Jason hadn't returned from the war?

It did not shock Ellen to meet Mrs. Van der Voewn one day during regular rounds at the hospital. She was in a private room and the physics professor was visiting.

"Our lives have come full circle," he said, following Ellen into the hall. "Mrs. Van der Voewn helped you once and now you're in a position to help her."

"I hope there's a something I can do," said Ellen, and when Mrs. Van der Voewn died of hepatocarcinoma in March, she could not shake a deep feeling of inadequacy. She felt completely unprepared to be a doctor.

"Dear one," said Mrs. Ardley one Sunday evening when Ellen sat morosely at the dining room table, unable to eat. "It was Mrs. Van der Voewn's decision to cross over. You mustn't hold her."

"How can you talk like that!" Ellen barely had enough energy to raise her voice. "What do you know?"

"I know she was ready to leave," said Mrs. Ardley. "Would you have her stay just because of you?"

Leave, stay, death, life, comings and goings—Ellen's thoughts warred. "Why be a doctor, then," she asked, "if people want to die?"

"Illness can be a warning, and you can make a person well enough to change whatever it was in their life that created that illness for their learning."

"But why me?" said Ellen.

"Your soul chose that path."

"How," said Ellen, seeing the reflection of a tern in a pool of water, "can you say that?"

"The world opens its arms when the pathway of the soul is followed," said Mrs. Ardley, "and I have seen how it has opened for you. Therefore I know you are doing the work your soul wants you to do."

What about Jason? thought Ellen. Are our souls making it hard for us to be together? "You make it sound so easy," Ellen said, trying not to sound sarcastic.

"It's thinking it's hard that makes it so."

Despite their conversation, despite Butler and Mrs. Ardley's solicitous but unobtrusive concern, Ellen felt weighted with the inadequacies of her profession. Mrs. Van der Voewn's death bothered her more than she logically knew it should, and she was grateful when Jill invited her to watch the blessing of the halibut fleet before its departure for Alaskan waters.

She stood on the bridge of Nils's father's halibut boat at the Ballard fishing docks, listening to the priest's invocation and wishing she could stay aboard and forget the whole business of making people well. But by the time the boat returned in October, from a successful season up north, Ellen had put not only Mrs. Van der Voewn's death behind her but the deaths of several other patients besides.

Nils bought a small house in Ballard, near the docks, and spent his time remodeling. Jill spent her time planning a Christmas wedding. The morning of the big day, Jill sat on Ellen's bed. She was dressing at Mrs. Ardley's because her mother disapproved of Nils. "Don't you wish we could be married in a double ceremony?" Jill said.

"When I get married," said Ellen, "I'll get married by the priest in Unaganik and wear a gold crown." She dabbed Jill with the Chanel Number Five that Jason had given her so many Christmases ago. "Wear a little bit when you go to bed tonight," she teased. "It will drive Nils crazy."

"Tell me," said Jill, "what's it like to be married?"

Ellen went to the window and watched, smiling, as Butler tried, for the umpteenth time, to teach Sirius to fetch a stick. The interminable rain had stopped and a wintry sun was negotiating passage with the clouds. A single red apple hung from the bare limbs of an apple tree in the orchard next door.

"Tell me," Jill pleaded.

"I've never been married," said Ellen.

"You know what I mean."

Sirius had arrived two years ago, the Christmas she had spent with Jason. Ellen had not seen Jason since then, but yesterday she had received a letter telling her he had finished his plastic surgery residency and was going into private practice in Manhattan. Nothing about moving to Seattle. Nothing about coming to Seattle for Christmas. Pensive, her mind elsewhere, Ellen returned to her study table next to the electric fireplace.

"Please," said Jill, pulling the boudoir chair up to the table across from Ellen.

Ellen looked up. There wasn't the magic between Jill and Nils that there was between her and Jason, but Nils was steady against Jill's flighty, bubbly personality. While he bored Ellen, she wondered if being bored wasn't better than always being in turmoil.

"You know," Jill was saying, "you aren't telling me anything."

"Oh," said Ellen, trying not to sound surprised as she finally got the drift of what Jill needed to know. "Here, let me draw you a diagram," and with a piece of school paper and her new Parker pen, which Jason had sent as a Christmas present, she explained the details of married life.

"Does everybody know this?" asked Jill shyly.

"Everyone but you," said Ellen with a straight face, "and now you know."

Jill clapped her hands and laughed and Ellen smiled, relieved to see the tension fade from Jill's face.

"I hope I'm not being nosey," said Jill, leaning across the table to Ellen, "but how come you've never gotten pregnant?"

"I always use a condom."

"What's that?"

Ellen explained.

"You mean Jason uses it," said Jill.

Ellen smiled, but inside felt a painful yearning for the love between her and Jason.

After the wedding in the Lutheran church in Ballard, and the reception in the little house Nils had remodeled, the newly-weds flew to Hawaii for their honeymoon.

"Lie under a palm tree," Ellen said when she hugged a radiant Jill good-bye.

"Maybe you and Jason will have a honeymoon soon too," Jill whispered.

Ellen shrugged, wishing she could put the hope out of her mind.

As she raced through the final days and weeks of her training, however, Ellen forgot about palm trees and thought only of the state boards, which were to be held in conjunction with their final medical school exams. Reginald lost weight, Emmett Nash gave up his magician's act, Thornton Percival stopped tinkering with test tubes, Bob Waller gave up sex, and Hannah Finch got a new, third pair of thicker glasses. Will Green seemed the only relaxed person in the group.

After five hours of exams on each of five successive days, they all piled into Bob Waller's Tin Lizzie and headed for The Dog House.

"Those blokes asked questions they couldn't possibly know the answers to themselves," Reginald complained.

"What an ordeal," moaned Emmett as he pulled a dime from behind Hannah's ear.

"What are we supposed to do for the next two weeks while we wait for results?" grumbled Hannah.

"I've got me a cute red-headed woman to pass the time," said Reginald.

"I've got free lab space," said Thornton. "I'm going to test some chemicals on tumor growth."

"I'm checking out graduate schools," said Will. "I want a Ph.D. next."

"I'm going to drink and be merry," said Bob Waller. "What about you, Ellen?"

"I plan to sleep, play with Sirius, and read Emerson," said Ellen.

"When are you going east?" Reginald asked.

Ellen shrugged. Two months ago she had written to Jason about her decision to move to Manhattan and do her internship there. She was still waiting for his response.

34

HAS ANYONE SEEN REGINALD?'' asked the lady who was dispensing gowns and ticking off names in preparation for the graduation ceremonies.

"I'll look for him," said Ellen and slipped outside, glad for a chance to be alone. She'd thought that today, of all days—the culmination of her studies, the successful end of pushing her body and brain past the point of exhaustion—she would feel better than she had ever felt in her life. But she felt unsettled, as if she were in a low-pressure zone and the wind was about to shift to the southeast, bringing bad weather. She had made up her mind to move to Manhattan, but Jason had not yet responded to her letter. She didn't know what to do next.

By the horse chestnut tree she saw Reginald with a tall, slim woman.

"Doctor Beck!" she shouted. He came running. "Is that redhead number four or five?" Ellen asked as they hurried back to the hall.

"Number one."

"You're kidding me."

"Stephanie's dropped some more pounds."

"Maybe I need glasses," said Ellen. "All that studying has ruined my eyes."

There were only twenty of them to graduate from this special wartime experiment, along with other graduates from the regular medical program. The hall was full of parents, relatives, and medical staff. Hannah Finch and Ellen, as the sole women graduates, marched together at the head of the group.

Ellen saw Mrs. Ardley, Butler, and Mr. Rupert sitting together. Jill, looking very happy and very pregnant, sat on the aisle. Down another row sat Dr. Goodman. There was Mrs. Snodgrass, the starched head nurse whose kindness and extra time had made such a difference to all the students. Franklin, the deener who ruled the morgue, sat beside her.

Was she seeing right? Jason? Ellen stopped and looked at the familiar yet unfamiliar face on the center aisle of the fourth row. Jason smiled. His eyes were as blue as she remembered. The eyeglasses were different. His hair was styled straight back off his high forehead.

Reginald nudged her forward. She moved on, taking her place in the front row, remembering to breathe. Jason. He had come.

The preacher started the ceremony. He extolled the virtues of Church, God, and doctors. Then Will Green, who had driven a jitney to earn enough money to pay his way through medical school and had still received the highest honors, spoke. Ellen thought she saw Dr. Visikov up on the stage. He wiped his glasses and stuck them back on his nose. She blinked and he faded from view.

Then the president of the university stood at the podium. "By the authority of the Board of Regents of Pacific Northwest University and your having successfully completed the prescribed course of study, I confer on you the degree of Doctor of Medicine, with the rules and dictates of the American Medical Association."

"We did it," Reginald whispered beside Ellen. Then there were the diplomas. One by one the names were called. Reginald went up and returned with his diploma. Hannah went up and returned with hers. Ellen thought of Jason sitting behind her and wanted to twist in her seat to see him. She heard her name.

"Miss Ellen MacTavish." Beside her, Reginald coughed. Hannah, on her other side, tugged on Ellen's gown.

Ellen walked onto the stage and felt the sea of faces, the storm of applause. She looked for Jason, but her eyes were too full of tears. Ellen took her diploma and left the stage.

When she sat down, Reginald pulled out two handkerchiefs and handed her one.

After all the diplomas had been given out one by one, the dean of medicine began the Hippocractic Oath. Their voices rang out: "...while I continue to keep this Oath unviolated, may it be granted to me to enjoy life and the practice of the art respected by all men in all times. But should I trespass and violate this Oath may the reverse be my lot."

Ellen felt a wave of goosebumps travel up her spine. It was over. She had done it.

The graduates paraded down the aisle and onto the lawn outside. The sun shone and between the brick buildings where she had spent so much time, Ellen saw Mount Rainier like an altar against the sky.

"Can we have dinner together?" Jason whispered in her ear.

She rubbed away the tickle and looked around, wanting to collapse into his arms. Instead she smiled and said, as if they had just parted yesterday, "If you'll come with me to Mrs. Ardley's for a little celebration first."

"I finally get to meet that lulu of a boarding house lady," said Jason.

"Jason," said Ellen, feeling the whirlpool of turmoil inside him, "relax."

"Congratulations, Dr. MacTavish," said Dr. Goodman, coming toward her. "I had hoped to be the first to wish you all the best, but I see your old friend has beaten me to it. How do you do, Dr. West."

They shook hands, and Dr. Goodman added, "Congratulations on your upcoming marriage are in order, I understand."

Ellen's mouth flipped open in surprise. But before she could say anything, there was Jill, waddling toward her. We're getting married, she wanted to whisper to her, to shout to the world, but the words were so new, so special, so long awaited, she couldn't budge them from her lips. Marriage, Dr. Goodman had said. How did he know? Ellen rubbed the fourth finger of her left hand, then looked at it, wondering how it would sparkle with a diamond. Probably not one as big as Mrs. Ardley's, she thought, and I'll have to hang it on Dr. Constance's gold chain, with the labret, when I scrub.

"Hi, Dr. MacTavish," said Jill. "I have a problem here, and I wonder if you could help me?"

Laughing, Ellen patted Jill's stomach. "There's someone I want you to meet."

"Gee whiz," said Jill when Ellen approached Jason, who was still talking to Dr. Goodman. "Am I seeing things?"

"No," said Ellen, "this is Dr. West."

"How simply divine to meet you," Jill said, holding out her hand.

"Pleased to meet you," said Jason, offering his in return.

"Her husband, Nils, is fishing up in the Bering Sea," said Ellen. "I wrote to you about their wedding."

"I remember," said Jason, and for the slightest fraction of an instant Ellen thought she detected a flicker of embarrassment in his eyes.

They gathered on the sun porch at Mrs. Ardley's and drank a bottle of champagne that Butler brought up from the cellar. The lawn glistened green in the June sun. Spring flowers bloomed in the patch where Butler had grown vegetables during the war. Song sparrows chirped from the apple trees next door. Just offshore, a young couple rowed a wooden boat and in the middle of the lake the wind filled a red and yellow striped spinnaker.

Mrs. Ardley's rings sparkled across the tile floor and Sirius, thinking he was chasing a star, knocked over a heavy glass ashtray.

"Get out, dog," said Jason, but Mrs. Ardley bent down and picked up the thick shards of glass. "We permit him a few indiscretions," she said. "After all, he's part of the family."

"And I've stopped smoking," said Ellen, feeling Jason's nerve endings as if they were tied to her own, "so I don't need an ashtray."

Mr. Rupert gave her a medical bag, well used. "Mrs. Meriweather sent it down with Dr. Visikov's microscope," he explained. "I've been saving it for this occasion."

More tears sprang to Ellen's eyes.

"Open Nils's and mine," said Jill, and Ellen pulled away the bright yellow ribbon and green paper to find a wide-brimmed hat. "A big one," Jill explained, "so it won't get lost."

Jason threw back his head and laughed. It sounded so good to hear him laugh, and later, when they excused themselves to go to the Olympic for dinner, Ellen found herself laughing until tears rolled down her cheeks.

"It's the champagne," said Jason.

"No," said Ellen. "It's you. It's you being here just when I finally knew I could live in New York. I've got to go back to Unaganik first, to see my family, and then, Jason, I promise to join you."

"Ellen," he said, "I've got something for you. Will you join me in my hotel room?"

"You know I have no shame," said Ellen, laughing.

Jason took her arm and led her to the elevator. "Darling," he said when they entered his room. "I've got something to tell you."

"Are you kidding?" Ellen teased, feeling coy and giddy.

"First of all," said Jason, "I've brought you something." He opened a closet door and brought out a white silver fox fur. "This is for you," he said. "I decided to bring it out myself. In fact I promised myself when I was being overrun on Attu that if I ever got out of it alive I'd attend your graduation. And this is your graduation present."

Ellen stared at the coat, at Jason. The coat was beautiful. Luxurious. But not her. He must have an image of her that didn't fit. It wasn't her kind of a coat. It was too impractical. Something was wrong. How could he . . .

"Do you like it, darling?"

"It's beautiful, Jason, but you shouldn't have. Honestly."

"Try it on."

Ellen held out her arms. He slipped it over her and kissed her neck. "Oh, Jason," she cried, turning to him, clinging to him, "how I've missed you."

"And me you, darling," he said. "And me you."

He pushed her onto the bed, yanked off his trousers and Ellen's skirt. She pulled down her lace panties and opened her legs. Her slip bunched up around her waist.

With the silk lining of the luxurious coat beneath her, the pressure of exams, patients, diagnoses, and treatments behind her, the long suppressed desires erupted and she shuddered over and over in exquisite release. "Well, Dr. West!" she sighed. "That certainly makes up for lost time."

He took her hand and she waited for him to put her fingers into his mouth.

"Ellen," he said, "I'm sorry this happened."

"I'm not," she said, closing her eyes.

"I'm getting married," he said.

"Why don't we go to Unaganik together?" she said. "I'm sure the priest will forgo some of the reading of the bans for us."

"Ellen," said Jason. "I won't be able to see you again."

She sat up. Her skin crawled.

His frown deepened. "I'm sorry, Ellen. I'm sorry it's worked out this way." His eyes were clouded. Blue-grey thickening over the whites. Why hadn't she noticed it before?

"What way?"

"It just wouldn't work, Ellen," he said, and she saw a small boy towered over by a mother whose iron will extended over years and continents.

"We can make it work," she said. She crossed her legs, concentrated on breathing steadily, on Jason's thumbs twirling around and around each other in front of her, on keeping her growing panic from exploding through her arteries.

"I'm marrying Birdie Rockport."

"No."

"Yes, darling, and I'm sorry. I really am, but there's no other way. You and I are too different, we'd have a battle with each other, destroy each other. I admire you so much, Ellen, if you only knew. But I don't have your strength. Mater . . ."

While she could still function Ellen slipped on her panties and linen skirt. She straightened her stockings and slip. She pinned on the new hat from Jill and Nils.

"You don't have to let your mother run your life," she said, cold.

"Listen to reason, Ellen. Don't leave like this."

"Good-bye, Jason."

"*Elanigulu.*"

"No," she said. "Good-bye."

Ellen opened the door.

"Wait." Jason slipped the fur coat over her shoulders. "I love you," he said.

Ellen did not wait for the elevator. She walked down the four floors, past the uniformed man in the lobby, past the buckets of fresh flowers at the side of the entry. She saw them all, clearly, saw everything, until she hit the street.

Night had fallen. Overhead, somewhere, stars twinkled. On the buildings neon glinted on and off, on and off. Ellen sniffed a familiar smell. She walked toward it, toward the waterfront. Down the steep streets, her stupid high-heeled shoes sticking in the cracks of the sidewalks. She felt perfectly calm. No tears blotted her eyes. Oh no, not her, not Ellen MacTavish. Why had she done it? Why hadn't she followed Jason to New York and stayed there with him. What was it that made her stay in school, struggle so much? Make life hard for herself?

Ellen stopped at the railroad tracks and looked left to right, right to left. She could not move.

Yes, she thought. Mrs. Ardley has a point. I make everything hard for myself. Life is so easy, it's as easy as falling downstairs, as easy as lying on a railroad track.

"Easy, lady," said a man in a brown felt hat.

"I'm fine, thank you," said Ellen and lifted her feet and with great agility marched over the tracks and across the street. There was the Alaska Steamship Terminal. The door was open, and Ellen stepped inside. The pale yellow light glittered in the corner. On one of the scarred benches, an old woman snored under a heavy army greatcoat. A *Life* magazine lay open on the floor beside her.

Pacing from one end of the terminal to the other, Ellen passed the open magazine. It tugged at her. She picked it up. JUNE BRIDES, the title read.

Not me, she thought, and was about to lay the magazine back beside the old woman when it fell open to a page of photographs. Ellen moved to the yellow light. "Our first bride, Birdie Rockport, granddaughter of well-known banker, will marry Manhattan's brightest plastic surgeon, the man who intends to reshape America's nose . . ."

Ellen stared at the page. There was a black and white photograph of Jason and of a tall blonde woman, a statue of

a woman, a horse-riding woman in a skin-hugging white
dress . . .

"'Will marry . . . '"

The words stuck out like brambles on a rose bush. The
old woman snored. Ellen stared at her under the old coat,
stared back at the page. Her mind sought meaning. He was
not married. She would not let him go.

She dropped the magazine. Racing in the high heels, her
fur coat flapping, her purse bouncing across her side, her hand
on her hat, she retraced her path to the hotel, rushed past the
doorman, up the stairs, down the hall, panting, her heart ready
to explode.

"Jason!" She burst into the room.

A bouquet of blue forget-me-nots stood in a water glass.
A note stood against them. In Jason's carefully formed
handwriting, so unlike a doctor's illegible scrawl, it said:
"I'm sorry."

PART
FOUR

35

F AR TO THE EAST, a gun-grey wall of water loomed against the sky. A freak wave, the fishermen called it, and knowing its import headed into it, the better to ride it out.

Ellen imagined that she saw such a wave. She prepared for its onslaught. There was the carpetbag to pack. First she removed Jason's letters and dumped them into the trash can, along with most of her school papers. Stuffing the fancy city clothes into the carpetbag seemed foolish, but Mrs. Ardley stood at her elbow, encouraging. "You'll need them, Ellen, I promise you."

What she needed was rubber boots, pants, a slicker, a fish pick. Not a red dinner dress, a linen suit, and several winter wools.

Reginald dropped by wearing a new worsted suit. He looked slim and handsome and had changed his hairstyle so it was now parted on one side instead of down the middle. "I'm going off for a vacation and then to the Menninger Clinic," he said, pushing his horned-rimmed glasses up on his nose. "I've been accepted for psychiatric training. This is good-bye for now."

"I never say good-byes," said Ellen.

"Ellen," he said, and his eyes seemed to waver as if they, too, had seen the terrifying wall of water. "What's wrong with you?"

"I'm fine."

"I know that you aren't."

"You don't know anything."

"Listen, Ellen, come with me to the lake. My relatives have a place there. We can talk."

"There's a lake here and we can talk here."

It was pouring. A June deluge. Only the slugs, who were busy devouring Butler's flowers, enjoyed the weather. Certainly Sirius did not. He lay at Ellen's feet on the sun porch and whined, often in a tone as wretched as if he had a nose full of porcupine quills.

"I mean Lake Chelan. God's country, east of the mountains."

"I'm going back to Unaganik to fish for the rest of my life."

Reginald took off his glasses and polished them with a crumpled handkerchief. "You seem to me," he said, "to be disassociating. It's a classic reaction to stress."

"Don't pontificate," said Ellen.

"Then I'll say it straight, for God's sake." Reginald readjusted his glasses. "You're cracking up."

"Don't swear."

"Listen, Ellen, let me help you."

"Forget it, Reginald. You don't understand."

"Tell me so I can understand."

She laughed. A false laugh that trilled over the tiled floor of the sun porch.

"Will you write to me?" he asked.

"I never write letters."

"That's not true. You told me you wrote to that bloke in New York. What was his name again?"

"I don't remember," said Ellen.

"Reginald," said Mrs. Ardley, entering the sun porch, wearing a blue dress with a wide white collar edged in lace, "I didn't get a chance to talk to you after the graduation service. Congratulations."

"Thank you," Reginald said, standing.

Reginald came with them the next day to the airport, along with Jill, who looked like she wanted to cry. Reginald and Jill drove with Butler and Mrs. Ardley in the Bentley. Ellen drove with Mr. Rupert in his brand new burgundy MG-TC sports car, with the top down.

"There's money left," said Mr. Rupert while the breeze

rushed past them. "You can use it to set yourself up in practice."

"I'm not going to practice medicine," said Ellen.

"I'm sorry to hear that. After all your hard work."

" 'One of the benefits of a college education is to show the boy its little avail,' " retorted Ellen.

" 'Marriage signifies nothing but a housewife's thrift,' " rejoined Mr. Rupert, who had also studied Emerson.

Ellen twirled her hat in her lap. "I'm not getting married," she said, her voice precise.

"Of course not. Why get married when you can support yourself in a civilized fashion?"

"I can support myself fishing," retorted Ellen.

"I thought you planned to be a doctor," said Mr. Rupert.

Had she? Ellen couldn't remember. All her ambition seemed to have disappeared with Jason's departure.

"I've always wanted to go to the Territory," said Mr. Rupert. "Ever since Aleksandr left. Maybe I'll take the car up on the new highway."

"You can't drive to Unaganik," said Ellen. "There's no road."

"How do you get there?"

"Boat. Or plane."

"I don't relish the thought of being in a plane," said Mr. Rupert.

"You used to be able to take a boat down from Seward to Dutch Harbor and cross to the Bering Sea and Bristol Bay from there. Before ice-up."

As if considering this option, Mr. Rupert continued on to Boeing Field in silence. "Let me know when I can do anything for you," he said when he parked the MG in front of the terminal.

"I can take care of myself," said Ellen.

"Of course," said Mr. Rupert and tossed his car keys up and down while they waited for the Bentley to arrive.

Mrs. Ardley patted Ellen's arm. "Go with God," she whispered and Ellen was not surprised to see her violet-grey eyes sparkle like diamonds.

There were things Ellen wanted to say but did not dare.

If she dropped anchor now she might get beached and never ride out the approaching storm.

"Cry," Reginald whispered into her ear after kissing her on the cheek. "Find a private place and cry your eyes out."

"It won't work," said Ellen.

"How do you know unless you try?"

She moved to Jill, patted Jill's stomach, looked up into her tear-filled eyes. "I'm going to miss you so much," Jill said, sniffing openly.

Ellen could not say good-bye. There had been too many good-byes, too many hellos, too many strange events, too many strangers who turned out to be friends, and a friend who turned out to be a stranger. Whatever possessed her to think she'd get used to their ways? Mrs. West had said it all. Half-breed. A bit of here and there, of this and that, half of a whole.

"Ellen," said Mrs. Ardley in her clear voice, "remember you are loved."

Had Mrs. Ardley seen it too, the wave?

With the carpetbag checked through to Anchorage, the wide-brimmed hat on her head, the heavy fur coat a burden on her shoulders, Ellen, by some miracle, found herself on the plane with the seat belt snapped around her. She unpinned her hat and laid her head on the white cloth covering the backrest. Dr. Visikov's old medical bag lay under her feet.

"Let's get the damned sails off those coffins and get us some kickers," said an angry male voice behind her.

"Why not own our own boats?"

"Pay by weight, not fish," said a rough Italian voice.

"Get rid of those traps down the Islands. They're catching all the Reds meant for us."

"If it wasn't for traps, where'd they get wood to burn for winter?"

"If people were meant to live in that region, God would have given them trees."

"Are we talking about trees or fish?" said the Italian.

Some things never change, Ellen thought, and even though she could see the wall of water racing closer, she knew she'd make it to Unaganik before it caught her.

*   *   *

In Anchorage, Ellen found a Grumman Goose loaded with tanks of diesel fuel for the generator at Harold's Point. The pilot agreed to drop her off at Unaganik en route. The Goose roared down Merrill Field toward the Chugach Mountains, went into a climbing turn over Cook Inlet, and flew over glaciers and mountains blistering white in the June sun. Like a malevolent predator, the plane's shadow pursued them, following Ellen's misery to the far corners of the earth. Was there no escape?

They descended over the vast parabolic bowl of Bristol Bay, landing with a rush of water over the window that made Ellen wonder if they had sunk. An Eskimo boy rowed toward them in a skiff. Ellen climbed out of the plane. The pilot tossed her the carpetbag and the silver fox fur.

"My medical bag," she called over the roar of the engines, which looked like two bug eyes protruding from the overhead wings.

The pilot disappeared, returned with the bag and her hat, and slammed the door. He was winging over the bay while Ellen bobbed in the stern of the skiff, being rowed toward shore.

"You must be Ellen MacTavish," said the boy.

"Who are you?" said Ellen, her voice sounding much too loud and surely carrying far across the water.

"Henry," said the boy. "My father is Shushanuk."

The boy eyed her while he rowed against the pull of the river. Across the opposite bank, Ellen looked for the cannery and saw only the rusted remains of an Iron Chink, the machine that cut the salmon heads off and split them open, and the charred remains of heavy beams. The boy pulled her up to a near-empty dock. Nobody was bluestoning their linen nets and laying them out to dry.

"Where are the boats?" Ellen asked.

"At Harold's Point," said the boy. "Since the cannery burned, everybody's fishing down there."

Ellen climbed out of the skiff, thanked Henry, and headed for the Mud Dog Saloon carrying the heavy weight of her accumulated city life. Mosquitoes and the hated white sox battled for supremacy on the exposed layers of skin. She had forgotten them. A chained dog stiffened and snarled. Ellen thought of Sirius and his welcoming wag.

A door flapped against an abandoned cabin. Next to it,

the jailhouse stood empty, its windows nailed, its lack of stairs forgotten. Dr. Visikov's quarters at one end, the school at the other—how often Ellen had run between the two of them, both now abandoned.

Where do the kids go to school? she wondered, and shrugged, not caring. If she had never gone away to school, she would not have met Jason, would not have had such grief.

The door to the Mud Dog was open. Mrs. Meriweather stood behind the bar. Her back reflected in the big mirror, pieces of which had been pocked with gunshot, a corner of which had broken away.

"Ellen." Mrs. Meriweather unhooked the countertop and rushed forward. Her hair was grey without a hint of color around the edges. "How are you?"

"Fine," said Ellen and dropped her cases, her coat.

An old man in the corner lifted his head from the table and stared. "You gonna give me a whiskey chaser?" he called, banging his glass on the old table.

"Aren't supposed to serve liquor during fishing season," said Mrs. Meriweather. "But there's nobody around here to say yea or nay."

"The place has changed," said Ellen.

"And so have you."

"Have I?" said Ellen.

Mrs. Meriweather raised her eyebrows. "Are you all right?"

"Yes." Ellen picked up the fur coat, the hat.

"I suppose you'll be wanting to go home," said Mrs. Meriweather.

"How do I get there?"

"Same way as always."

"Any bears?"

"They're all up river. Or so they say. Say, why don't I close up and come with you. Burley," she turned to the man with the glass. "Get out. This here's Ellen MacTavish and I'm going home with her."

"Burley," said Ellen, thinking. "Isn't he the man whose son died of rat poison?"

"One and the same," said Mrs. Meriweather.

"Where's Robertson Sharpe?"

"He's gone to Cold Bay. Got a desk job with the DEW line."

"Where's the priest?" Ellen asked as they passed the boarded-up church.

"He was transferred," said Mrs. Meriweather. "Down to Unalaska."

"I'm sorry to miss the priest," said Ellen.

"Did he write to you?"

"Yes." The old suspicion loomed its ugly head. "Is everything all right at home?" Ellen stopped walking and looked inquiringly at Mrs. Meriweather, whose flushed face and short breath indicated that she did not make this trip often.

"Bonnie's moved," said Mrs. Meriweather between puffs. "You knew that."

"Oh," said Ellen, puzzled, wondering if she'd heard.

The ground was soggy. Ellen's feet were soaked. At least she had had the good sense to wear her flat shoes, which were well worn from running up and down hospital corridors. Mrs. Meriweather wore shoepacs beneath her long full skirt. They looked as old as the skirt and as comfortable.

"Bonnie married Brick Tandy, a big game guide."

"I heard," said Ellen. "Ted Kleet told me."

"Ted flies in occasionally. En route to here and there. He comes to check on Angus. He didn't mention that he'd seen you."

It was of no interest to Ellen. They passed the willows, the spruce, there was the smell of smoke, there was someone sitting in front of the cabin.

"Where are the dogs?"

"It was too difficult to keep them up and Charlie wasn't interested. He had too much else to do taking care of everything."

"Where's Charlie now?"

"On the bay. He'll be back when the season's over. He's deckhand on a monkey boat."

Ellen stopped in her tracks. "How old is he?"

"Seventeen," said Mrs. Meriweather.

Have I really been gone that long? thought Ellen.

"Charlie's grown into a clever lad," continued Mrs. Meriweather. "He has Stewart's watch, by the way."

Ellen stopped walking.

"A watch?"

"A gold wristwatch. They sent it up from Adak. With a letter about Stewart."

Jason, thought Ellen. He did that.

"That's when your daddy's trouble started," Mrs. Meriweather continued. "He was so proud of Stewart and felt so terrible that he'd never been able to tell him. He was never that kind of a man . . ." Her voice stopped and Ellen faced the older woman, waiting for answers.

Mrs. Meriweather's eyes scanned the horizon like an Arctic explorer searching for a thread of smoke from a hearth. "Come on," she said in a voice husky with emotion. "You're almost home."

"I feel as if I've never left," said Ellen.

It was Angus in the chair. Unmistakably. "Daddy!" Ellen shouted. "Daddy!"

He didn't hear.

As deaf as Wolff before he crashed into the cabin, she thought. Deafer than Mr. Stokes.

"Ellen," said Mrs. Meriweather, laying a hand on her arm.

But Ellen was running. Racing the last hundred yards, she flung herself at Angus's feet. "Daddy!"

There was no response.

36

ELLEN FELT SIX YEARS old. Her hair was in pigtails with red ribbons, and Daddy sat outside waiting for her to come home from her first day of school. But she grabbed his head in both hands and forced him to look at her. "I'm home, Daddy. Your wee blue goose is home. I've graduated, got my diploma, and see, I came back. You never thought I would, did you?"

There was no response.

Ellen dropped her head onto his knees.

The balloon of sun seemed so close Ellen wanted to jump and catch it, give it to Angus to play with as he sat, caught in some halfway world that made him burst into chuckles from time to time.

"He had a stroke," said Mrs. Meriweather.

"Where's Mother?" Ellen said angrily. "Why isn't she here taking care of him?"

"She's probably down on the beach. She keeps a little net out for herself. You know your mother."

I don't, thought Ellen. Don't know her at all.

"He's not getting into any trouble," said Mrs. Meriweather.

Angus sat in a high-backed wicker chair with large rubber wheels and ample footrests. He looked clean, well shaven, although a few nicks of blood telltaled someone's inexperience with a razor. His hands were scrubbed clean and looked like well-kneaded sourdough.

"How is his bladder functioning?"

"He wears a diaper."

Like a baby. The word hit like an axe on dry wood.

363

Ellen felt split in two. She wanted him to take care of her. *She* wanted to be the baby.

"There's no hope for it," said Mrs. Meriweather.

"It!" stormed Ellen. "You mean him. *Him!*"

"Yes," said Mrs. Meriweather, "I mean him."

Cheok approached finally, carrying a Red salmon for dinner. It was cleaned and split and plenty for the four of them.

Ellen stood up from the wheelchair where she had been kneeling beside Angus. She faced the squat robust woman who had given her birth twenty-four years ago.

"Hello, Mother," Ellen said, trying to get a sense of this shy stranger.

"My smart girl come home now?" said Cheok.

"Yes, Mother," Ellen answered. "I'm home."

Cheok fed Angus first and then they sat down to their meal.

"Do you have that little old piece of paper that say you're a doctor?" Cheok asked while they ate.

Ellen rummaged in her medical bag and produced the sacred diploma. Beside her, Angus burst into laughter at some private joke.

Cheok rubbed the embossed seal.

"I'm so proud of you I could spit," said Mrs. Meriweather.

"Only spreads disease," muttered Ellen and stuck the diploma back into the bag.

"Bonnie's man Brick said there's a sanatorium outside Seward. They used the old army hospital. I bet they need doctors," said Mrs. Meriweather.

Ellen said nothing.

"There's a Health Ship going around the coastal villages," continued Mrs. Meriweather. "You could doctor on that."

"If I wanted to," said Ellen, "but . . ." She stopped speaking. She looked at her plate and realized that the wall of water had crashed beyond her. She had survived it and was back in Unaganik, safe.

All summer Ellen sat with Angus, swatting mosquitoes and white sox who penetrated the thick *buhach* smoke meant to keep them away. Occasionally she read to him from *Our*

Wonder World. Once he seemed to respond to the sound of her voice and Ellen, encouraged, tried to teach him to speak. There was no response again.

Cheok picked, cleaned, split, and hung to dry the salmon she caught in her small net. Charlie, deckhand on a monkey boat used to tow double enders back and forth between the bay and the canneries, heard that Ellen was home. He sent a message via Shushanuk asking her to wait until September before she left. I want to see you, his message said.

Ellen sent a message back: "I'm not going anywhere."

At the end of the summer Charlie, a short lad with black hair and eyes as black as the oil Cheok burned in the converted wood stove, came home. Stewart's watch glittered on his wrist. Ellen told him about it, how she had met Stewart, and a little about her life in Seattle. She didn't mention Jason.

When Charlie had been home a week, Cheok insisted Ellen accompany her on a berry picking trip to Nachook.

"Charlie he take care of your daddy. You come with me."

"No," said Ellen.

"You come," said Cheok.

"No."

"Go," said Charlie. He had a manner that demanded response. Ellen went.

"No," said Cheok when Ellen wanted to stop at the nearest bush. "Not here. We go farther."

Cheok carried two buckets and Ellen carried two. These were oil buckets that had been scrubbed and cleaned in the creek which still ran with fresh water at the end of what had been a dry summer.

After a long day, they entered the village of Nachook. Dogs howled from their chains, kids played baseball in the twilight, and a line of salmon hung next to blue jeans on rope strung between the row of squat houses. Ellen and Cheok slept together on a reindeer robe in the *maqi* of a longtime friend of Cheok's from the orphanage.

The next morning, Cheok dragged Ellen by the hand to another house. "This here my daughter," she said to a stocky Eskimo man. He wore a cloak, invisible, but Ellen could see its white sheen nevertheless. He studied her from behind its protective folds and then threw it off, his face like the glow of moonlight on a dark trail.

"Hello, Ellen," he said.

"How did you know my name? Who are you? What's going on? I want to pick cranberries."

"Those little old berries can wait," said Cheok. "This here's Paul."

Hanging from a leather thong around his neck, he wore a whalebone carved in the shape of a salmon and curved to represent the wheel of life. Carved on the dorsal fin was the face of the Creator.

Of square build, Paul stood with his legs wide apart, his hands easy by his sides.

"I've been asked to take you down into the earth," he said, looking at Ellen with an implacable expression on his face.

"Who asked you?"

His responding smile reminded her of Mrs. Ardley. "Would you like to go?"

It was the perversity in her that said yes. Wouldn't her professors laugh? Maybe not all of them, she decided. Maybe Dr. Goodman wouldn't.

She suddenly burst out like a lost child from a thick woods. "You've planned all this," she stormed, looking at Cheok. "You came up here . . ."

There was no evening that Cheok had not been home. It must have been Mrs. Meriweather. No. Mrs. Meriweather, even in the best of health, could not have walked this distance.

"I was spoken to," said Paul, "by my spirit guides. They told me you were coming and that I should offer you the opportunity to go to the center of the earth. Now that you've accepted, we'll get ready."

He spoke with such authority that Ellen was reminded of the many times she had prescribed medicines and treatments and given the patient no reason to doubt her ability to make him well.

Paul tied a red bandanna around his forehead. He undid leather ties that held an Indian blanket rolled into a bundle. Tying the leather around his waist, he unrolled the Indian blanket, which opened to reveal a wolfskin, a pile of stones, and a braided crown of sweet grass. He smoothed out the blanket, with the skin on top of it. Picking up the stones, he circled the blanket. Each stone seemed to tell him where it wanted to go, and soon there were eight stones placed variously at the edges of the blanket. Ellen rippled with curiosity even as she scoffed.

There was a noise in the windbreak and a large man entered the small room. "You call me?" he asked.

"Tiny," said Paul. "Go get old Mrs. Beedle and Beartooth Tom."

"Tom's upriver," said the large man.

"He's on his way back," said Paul.

Beartooth Tom was a legend Ellen had heard about but did not believe until she saw him enter the cabin. He had a fine set of false teeth that clacked, and he said, in answer to her question, that yes, he'd used bear teeth after his own rotted, boiling up gum boots to get enough stickum to make them stay in. "Lady wouldn't marry me until I got store-boughts," he grinned.

"Sit here, Tom," said Paul. "At Ellen's feet."

"Mrs. Beedle," he said to an older woman who had just entered. "Please sit at her head."

Mrs. Beedle smiled and her face crinkled into a million wrinkles.

Tiny sat on Ellen's left.

Paul sat on the right with a stick of yellow Alaskan cedar and a hunk of wood that looked like an old fire log. "Ready?" he asked.

Ellen saw her head nod in the lacquered surface of his eyes.

"Lie down. On your back."

Ellen lay on the wolfskin with the sweet grass between her legs.

"If an animal bares its teeth at you," he said, "turn the other way."

She closed her eyes.

"Listen to the drum," said Paul and beat with the stick on the log. "Allow yourself to be accepted by Grandmother Earth."

The methodical one, two, three, four rhythm beat across Ellen's pulse. She felt her mind untangle and soon found herself in a valley between purple mountains scalloped against a pale blue sky. A kingfisher flew through the valley. Soaring above him, a bald eagle sang in a high-pitched voice.

Below her the earth rumbled with the roar of drums. The mountains moved. With the softness and comfort of silk, they enclosed her, covering her until the sky disappeared and she found herself deep underground, swimming in black oil. A salmon arrived. Huge, silver, each scale perfectly outlined against every other scale, it swam ahead of her, beckoning her.

Somewhere out of hearing the drumbeat skipped. Ellen popped like a bubble onto dry ground. The salmon and black oil disappeared and she breathed sweet grass deep into her lungs. To her left, suddenly, a huge brownie reared on its hind legs, teeth bared. Ellen turned quickly to her right and walked to the beat of the drum through tussocks of grass that tickled her knees. It was then that she saw a family of lions. The male stood guard. Two tawny cubs played while the mother rested, her plump nipples full of milk.

The drum continued. Ellen reached a brick wall enclosing a city so ancient the sun had faded the bricks to pink. Through an arched doorway, past domed houses curved against the swept dry earth, she entered an open courtyard where the same lion lounged on a golden throne, his front paws resting on the red upholstered arms of the throne. Ellen sat in his lap. The mother licked her feet and the cubs tumbled over each other in play. In front of them, an enormous diamond burst into a million stars and she heard from the sky above, "It's time to come back now. I'll bring you up."

Ellen opened her eyes. Paul crouched on his haunches to her right. At her feet sat Beartooth, at her head old Mrs. Beedle. Tiny, the large man to her left, Paul's young assistant, held out his hand and helped her up.

"You have your strength back," said Paul. "And whenever you need assistance, you can ask your animal helpers."

"My lions," said Ellen. Her voice was hoarse.

"Know that you are not alone in this world," said Paul as he pressed his palm between her eyebrows.

Still in the netherworld of illusion—or was it reality? —Ellen sat in the hot steam of the *maqi* with Cheok and Cheok's friend from the orphanage days. "My half-breed *maqi*,'' laughed the friend, because the roof was higher than tradition and there was a wooden floor.

Half-breed no longer held any meaning for Ellen.

They patted their backs with bird wings. They dipped ladles made of cans into cold spring water containing the pronged leaf plant Cheok called her Eskimo medicine and poured water over their heads. The steam rose and they laughed and talked in the old way.

"I fell once and burned my meat," said Cheok's friend.

"You live long time if you take *maqi*," was Cheok's reply.

"Old Mrs. Beedle she live long time," said the friend. "She live so long she know the old old dances."

That night old Mrs. Beedle, waving ptarmigan feather fans in her gloved hands, wearing a calico *qaspeq* over her slacks and shirt, danced on the flat land above the river. Ellen lay on her side on the ground. Next to her a toddler gnawed on a hank of dried salmon. Across from her, on a stone, sat ninety-year-old Mr. Kesianek. He spoke no English. When he was young, the chief of his village had posted sentries to keep out the priest and keep his people from attending the new church. Anyone who left was not permitted to return. The people of his village survived the flu and the children kept their traditional language and learned the traditional ways.

Old Mrs. Beedle bobbed up and down, moving her arms and knees, waving the ptarmigan feather fans she held in her gloved hands. Paul beat the drum. Ellen thought of the earth she had entered and from which she had returned. Up river a loon called into the golden evening. Farther north a family of wolves foraged for dinner.

The sky changed from summer gold into autumn red into evening purple. And old Mrs. Beedle, without moving more than six inches in any direction, danced the story of Angalkuq the shaman, who freed the world from despair.

37

A FLOAT PLANE CIRCLED the bluff at Unaganik. Ellen, who was on the beach packing dried salmon for the winter, waved. The wings dipped in answer. When it came in for a landing, she knotted the straps of her boots over her shoulders and waded through the mud to greet the visitors. A lumberjack of a man jumped from the pilot's seat and Ted Kleet jumped from the passenger side. He wore gum boots and suit pants rolled to his knees. A thin black moustache dotted his upper lip and his eyes, as dark as ever, shone at Ellen.

"I'd like to introduce my friend Brick Tandy," he said, grinning. "I believe you've heard of him."

Brick jutted forth a paw of a hand. "I belong to Bonnie," he said.

Grief rippled over Ellen like creek water over a fingerling. Was it because she no longer belonged to Jason? After the visit to the shaman, she had started feeling restless again, caught in a fathomless net strung between Unaganik and some unknown place.

They pulled the plane up onto the mud, slogged to shore, and climbed the trail to the cabin, carrying bundles of dried salmon.

"How are you?" Ted asked when Brick charged ahead. "I've been wanting to get over before now, but we've been swamped with work on the petroleum reserve."

"So your trip to the District of Columbia was worthwhile," said Ellen.

"More ways than one." Ted smiled, looking at her.

Ellen looked over the edge of the bluff, avoiding his eyes.

They reached the top, where Brick was speaking as if Angus were deaf. "Howdy there!" he boomed to the drooling man in the wheelchair. "Y'all better know I've come to take Ellen."

"You have?" Ellen felt disconcerted by this abrupt news.

"Where're your things?" Brick ducked into the cabin.

Charlie handed Brick the carpetbag. All summer it had lain unpacked beneath the canvas cot on which Ellen slept. She had worn a pair of Stewart's pants and a shirt of Charlie's until no amount of Fels Naphtha got out the smell of *buhach* and salmon.

"Angus doesn't need you here," Brick said as he balanced the bag on his shoulder. "Cheok and Charlie take perfect care of him and my Bonnie needs help."

"What seems to be the trouble?" Ellen asked, pushing aside her own inner struggles.

"Bonnie's big as a beluga with the baby and I've got two dudes from D.C. that Ted here set me up with to take out for trophy bear. Bonnie needs you."

"I'll only be a minute," said Ellen. She took her bag and hurried into the *maqi* to wash. She shook out a cotton dress she had worn in Seattle and slipped it on. Unaware of the appreciative glances of Ted and Brick when she returned to the cabin, she went to the kitchen area, where Cheok stirred beans on the stove.

"You go be my smart girl," Cheok said, wiping her eyes with the back of her hands. "They needs you at that San more than we needs you here."

"I'm not going to the sanatorium," said Ellen. "I'm going to Bonnie. Shall I give her a message for you?"

"You tell my girl she have good baby," said Cheok.

"Will you come over to Seward when the baby's born?" Ellen asked.

"A mother don't like them little old ducks," said Cheok. "She stays with Mr. MacTavish, and you tell Bonnie to bring that little old baby here."

Ellen touched her mother's arm and turned away from

the stove. *Our Wonder World* lay open on the table. The photograph of the lion stared up from the page.

"I ask him to take care of you," said Cheok, moving to Ellen.

"How is it that I have a lion?" Ellen asked the question that had perturbed her ever since that day with the shaman. "When I live here?"

"Your spirit part of the whole wide earth," Cheok said. "This be too small a place for your spirit. Your lion tell you that."

"Mother," said Ellen, facing the roly-poly woman who had borne her first child at the age of fourteen and had never been more than a day's journey from home, "how did you learn all this?"

"Some people just know things," Cheok said, patting Ellen on the shoulder like a benediction. "Some people have to learn them from books. You go on now. You got work to do."

Ellen looked into her mother's eyes, seeing her wisdom for the first time. She turned away and went slowly to Angus. Kneeling in front of him, she took his hands and said, "Your wee blue goose is leaving, Daddy."

Angus only drooled.

Charlie picked up the medical bag and the silver fox fur.

"I don't need that coat," Ellen said.

"You going to throw out a good fur?" Charlie raised his thin black eyebrows. "That not be right."

Ellen sighed. Was she never to be rid of reminders of Jason? She took the coat, her wide-brimmed hat, her medical bag, and was glad when Ted took them from her and carried them to the plane.

Soon they were flying over the mud flats, where Charlie grew smaller and smaller in the distance and eventually the tiny cabin with the soot-colored smokestack disappeared. Ted Kleet sat in the seat behind her with her things. No one spoke above the noise of the engine.

Brick put down at Taryaqvak to refuel. Ellen turned around in her seat and noticed Ted absently stroking the silver fox. He caught her gaze and opened his mouth as if to speak.

"It's a stupid gift," said Ellen before he could ask. "Just stupid."

He removed his hand from the coat, and reached toward her, tracing his finger along her chin until he reached the dimple in the center of it. "Did the tern hatch any eggs this year?" he asked quietly.

"I didn't notice," Ellen replied in an equally quiet voice. "I didn't notice anything this summer except..." She stopped speaking. Except my own pain, she was going to say, but it was over, she suddenly knew. Had it really happened that fast or had it been happening all along and she hadn't recognized it until she went down into Grandmother Earth? Could she keep the coat and not think of Jason, of their past or their unfulfilled future? The realization came like the roar of a lion in her head and she smiled at Ted, her old friend, and swiveled back in her seat, waiting for Brick to take them up in the air again.

They flew through mountains so magnificent Ellen clapped her hands together and forgot to breathe. She felt as free and unencumbered as a bird. On the other side of the mountains, above Shelikof Strait, a puffin, like a wooden wind vane, flicked its wings over the water, leaving a trail of drops. Ellen laughed as it plopped down onto the water again, giving up its attempt to get airborne.

They entered the glacial green waters of Resurrection Bay. Brick flew low, pointing out sea lions resting on the edge of black rocks. A freighter loaded with barrels of oil was heading for the port of Seward, the city named for the far-sighted secretary of state whose foolish spending of 7.2 million dollars resulted in the purchase from Russia, in 1867, of 375,296,000 acres of wild and rugged land.

The town itself was a triangle of land between sea and mountains. The mountains felt too close and Ellen wondered at their stability. What was it that made her fear their falling? Was she afraid that her own foundation was loose and would tumble to pieces?

Better mountains than skyscrapers, she told herself, and by the time Brick landed behind the breakwater and docked in the small boat harbor, she felt calm again.

Carrying Ellen's things, Brick strode ahead down the waterfront street that paralleled the railroad. All freight to

Fairbanks and Anchorage was shipped from Seward's famous ice-free harbor on those tracks.

"Anyone ask you where you live," said Brick when they turned away from the tracks, "y'all tell them you're halfway between St. Peter and Standard Oil."

He strode up the street to a brand new Willys station wagon parked in front of a Quonset hut. Bonnie stood at the door. Long hair brushed to her waist, darker-skinned than Ellen, she had inherited Cheok's flat face and squat figure. Beside the lumberjack shape of Brick, she looked the size of a spruce cone.

"Forty dollars we paid for the house," Brick was saying, but Ellen barely heard, so overcome was she with the sight of Bonnie grown up after so many years.

"Thanks for coming," Bonnie said, drawing Ellen through the arctic entry, Seward's name for a windbreak.

And Ellen, standing beside her sister, felt Bonnie's deep pleasure that she had come to their cozy home.

Inside, the concrete floor was covered with a mottled green and brown Olson rug, made from recycled wool. A cook stove stood in the middle of the room with an oil attachment. On one side stood a bed, a bureau, and a mooserack holding trousers and jackets. Spread out on the table near the stove were boxes of L.L. Bean dehydrated potatoes, a pint bottle of 6-12 insect repellent, boxes of bullets and Kleanbore .30-06 Remington Express cartridges. The room smelled of Alaskan perfume—Hoppe's Number Nine, evidence that Brick had been cleaning his guns. Along the back of the Quonset hut, beneath a window, stood a sink and counter. A fat tawny cat slept on the counter next to a pot of pink geraniums.

"We have running water," said Brick, "and an inside privy." He pointed to an area partitioned off with cardboard walls.

"It's lovely," said Ellen, wondering where she was supposed to sleep until she noticed the single bed along the back wall, behind her.

"You don't mind, do you?" asked Bonnie with a timidity that Ellen suspected concealed a lot more strength than she ever let anyone know.

"No," Ellen said slowly. "But I'm fine, you know. I

wasn't, but I am now. I feel much better and I don't need any shoves to get going again.''

Brick slapped his thigh. ''Y'all have a mind like a steel trap,'' he said. ''Y'all saw right through this right along.''

''I can see Bonnie's not as big as a beluga,'' said Ellen, ''and I can bet no big game hunt is going to keep you away when that baby's ready to come.''

Everyone laughed and Ted looked relieved.

The kettle on the stove boiled. Bonnie went to the counter and reached above the sink to a bouquet of needle-nosed leaves hanging overhead. She broke a bundle into a brown teapot and filled it with boiling water. Ellen sat on the floor and listened as Ted and Brick discussed the possibilities of statehood. During dinner Ellen answered, as best she could, Brick's barrage of questions about Seattle, her school, how it was to be a doctor. She was glad when the conversation switched to the DEW line, the Distant Early Warning system being built as part of the Cold War.

It was dark when Ted left to stay at the Van Gilder Hotel. He returned Sunday morning for Bonnie's famous sourdough pancakes with cranberry syrup, and then the four of them flew out to Montague Island.

Ellen found herself laughing at Brick's bawdy jokes, found herself skipping rocks over the water with Ted, trying to beat his score of eleven, found herself sitting quietly beside Bonnie, getting to know her sister again without the bother of words.

Ellen ate too much smoked salmon, too many beans cooked over an open fire, and drank too much tea. She disappeared into the bushes with a paper napkin. Returning to the beach, Ellen paused and in the quiet of the moment realized that it had been years since she had really enjoyed herself and had plain old fun. Was it the weight of studies that had held her down, or had she used them as an escape, as a way of not facing her feelings of always being out of place? Whatever it was, something had changed and she felt so contented she never wanted the day to end.

When clouds started to pile up in the sky, they took off for Seward. They spotted a cluster of mountain goats, white and nimble, perched on a steep ledge. As they skimmed in low over the water, they spotted an otter floating on its back, holding its paws on its chest. Back in Seward, Ted drove off in his paneled Willys to Anchorage, with promises to return soon.

Monday morning Bonnie left early for her job at the Jessie Lee Home, the orphanage that had been started in Unalaska and moved to Seward in 1925. Brick left to meet his two "dudes," who were expected to arrive from Anchorage by chartered plane. Ellen, wearing a loose pair of overalls from Bonnie and a silk blouse from the carpetbag, cleaned the house. Before noon she found herself on the floor by the stove, the cat on her lap.

"My little lion," she said, laughing. "Where did you come from?"

The cat jumped off her lap, stretched one foot after the other and mewed loudly until Ellen let her out the door.

Ellen swung a wool jacket of Brick's off the moose rack and walked along Railroad Street, past the breakwater, and out on the wooden dock. Brick was loading the plane. The two clients held .375 H. and H. magnums. Lying on the dock beside them was a pile of sheets and blankets.

"Mr. Barnes and Mr. Elgin," said Brick. "Meet my sister-in-law, Dr. Ellen MacTavish."

"How do you do," said Ellen and, turning to Brick, asked, "Where's the sanatorium?"

Brick pointed northeast to where a glacier sparkled between two mountains. "Look for Women's Christian Missionary Society," he said.

"Have a successful hunt," said Ellen, nodding to Barnes and Elgin.

"We'll be back Saturday," said Brick. "Weather permitting."

The autumn rays bounced against the overlay of clouds and reflected onto Resurrection Bay. Ellen walked inland. A magpie cackled past. Overhead she heard the sound of a plane. Brick disappeared into the horizon.

The sun, higher now, sprayed the cloud patches with light. Abide with me, Ellen hummed to herself, fast falls the eventide. She passed a sign saying WOMEN'S CHRISTIAN MISSIONARY SOCIETY, HOME IN THE WOODS, and turned west, walking down a narrow road until she reached a spread of buildings nestled among the evergreens.

There was no mistaking a laundry building with its billow of steam, and Ellen walked toward it. Inside the door of the steam-filled room a man slightly taller than Ellen and about twenty years older lounged against the wall. He had an abundant black moustache garnished with streaks of grey tucked beneath a large nose, a set of wrinkles that bridged bushy eyebrows, greying hair that curled back from a high forehead, and bright curious eyes. He wore a red plaid wool shirt, and red suspenders held up baggy wool pants that had been rolled at the cuffs to conform to his short height. He looked like a maintenance man.

"We're waiting for the plumber," he said. "That isn't your occupation by any chance?"

"No," laughed Ellen, thinking of all the plumbing jokes that had amused them in medical school. "I can't help you there."

"Dr. Milligan," he said, holding out his hand. "People sometimes think I'm the janitor but I'm medical director of the sanatorium. Welcome."

"Ellen MacTavish," said Ellen, shaking his hand, feeling the firm warmth of his grip and wondering what it would be like to work with him. "I'd like to look around," she said, "if you don't mind."

One of the laundry workers approached with a starched linen medical coat. Dr. Milligan slipped it on. "You're in luck," he said. "I've got time to give you the tour."

Separate ward rooms, joined by a long drafty corridor, housed women and children in varying stages of tuberculosis. Another long draft corridor ran like the cross of an *H* between the women's and children's wards on the one side, and the men's and boys' on the other. Off to one side of the center of this corridor was the surgery and Dr. Milligan's office. To the other side was the laboratory and the classroom.

"We give bedside teaching as well," said Dr. Milligan. "We get our patients started on an education just as soon as possible."

At wards five and six, housing the men, they turned right past medical staff quarters and down one arm of the *H* into the kitchen–dining room.

"That's my house," said Dr. Milligan, pointing through the window to the well-kept two-story house adjacent to his surgery and office. "And I can't let you leave until I show you the rehab unit." He took her to a Quonset hut set apart from the main cluster of buildings. "My pride and joy," he said holding the door. "Better than the new wonder drug."

"Better than PAS?" Ellen asked. "Are you using those big horse pills here?"

Dr. Milligan chuckled. "We combine them in various amounts with streptomycin, but we're waiting for the boys back east to give us something that will knock the you-know-what off those damn little bacilli."

They entered the Quonset hut. Women of all ages, colors, textures, and sizes were writing in notebooks. All but one looked up and smiled.

"Getting them ready to go back to their villages and be health aides, teacher's aides, bookkeepers, and what have you," he said when he shut the door. " 'Course I get away with it because there's no old goats looking over my shoulder telling me I can't do it."

"What about the Dall sheep?" said Ellen. "They ever come down from the mountains and butt into your business?"

The doctor laughed.

"How many patients?" Ellen asked.

"One hundred and fifty-five. Thirty are children."

"You wouldn't have a position for a new doctor, would you?" Ellen asked. "I have my Washington State boards and have had lots of hospital experience at Harold's Point and in Seattle, although I haven't done my internship yet."

"Are you the young lady Dr. Constance told me about?"

"I might be," said Ellen. "But how did you meet Dr. Constance?"

"He retired and came through Seward on his way south by steamship."

"Did he mention Miss Long, the teacher at Harold's Point?"

"I believe she accompanied him."

Ellen smiled.

"When can you start?"

"Tomorrow," said Ellen without batting an eye.

"You can have your own quarters, eat in the dining

room, run your feet off and cry your eyes out when we lose someone, all for the princely sum of seven hundred and fifty dollars a month.''

"I'll live with my sister Bonnie until her husband returns," said Ellen, "and then I'll move to the San."

"We'll cure those lungers yet," said Dr. Milligan, shaking her hand.

38

On SATURDAY AFTERNOON, AFTER an exhausting week, Ellen and Bonnie napped together on the double bed. Suddenly Bonnie screamed. Ellen, sitting up in alarm, reached over to comfort her sister.

"We have to hang it on the line," Bonnie said, her eyes wild, her hands clutching Brick's blue and white striped nightshirt, which had been tucked under the pillow.

"Why?" said Ellen, trying to be calm.

"So we know," said Bonnie in a distant voice, "whether he's alive."

"He'll be home tomorrow," soothed Ellen, but Bonnie had darted outside in her bare feet and was pinning the nightshirt to the rope tied between the birch tree and the kitchen window.

Although there was not enough wind to move the dried leaves hanging precariously from the birch, the heavy flannel nightshirt hung still on the line for only half a second before drifting back and forth.

"He's alive," said Bonnie and returned, triumphant, to the house.

Brick did not return Sunday. Ellen and Bonnie sat on the floor by the stove, and Ellen stroked the cat. Bonnie stared into space.

Monday, Bonnie went to her job with the orphans at the Jessie Lee Home and Ellen caught a ride in a Hudson with a crack in the windshield and a stuffed coyote in the back seat. The orderly who drove had trouble keeping his hands on the wheel, and had Ellen not been so concerned about Brick, she would have moved immediately into her own quarters at the San to avoid riding with him.

She checked with the night nurses coming off duty, made her rounds of the patients, then hurried to the regular Monday morning conference where Dr. Milligan discussed the latest cases and planned the next protocols.

Ellen was leaving the conference room when the desk clerk called to her from the end of the hall. "Telephone, Dr. MacTavish. Long distance."

She picked up the phone, her pulse racing. "Yes?"

"Ellen." It was Ted Kleet. "Is everything all right down there?"

"No." Ellen sat on the edge of the desk, crossing her legs. "Brick's not home. We expected him yesterday."

There was a long pause. "I have a feeling he's not injured," said Ted, "but just in case, we'd better get someone out looking for him."

"Maybe we're being overly anxious," said Ellen, standing now, wishing she hadn't been so forthright. Brick could return by dinnertime.

"How's Bonnie?" Ted asked.

"She's convinced he's alive."

"She'd know, wouldn't she." It was a statement.

"How?" Have I been gone too long? thought Ellen. Am I a city person after all?

"Her intuition's better than mine and mine's pretty reliable."

Ellen took a deep breath.

"I'll telephone you tomorrow," Ted said, and as Ellen replaced the receiver she wondered how on earth Ted had known she was at the San. She joined Dr. Milligan in wishing godspeed and good health to a lucky patient who was being discharged after four years and whose sendoff was the occasion for a party and cake.

Her day continued at a hectic pace until she finally slid into the Hudson for a ride to Bonnie's. Brick's plane was not behind the breakwater. Bonnie spoke little when they sat down to dinner, and they went to bed in silence. Tuesday morning Ted called the San on the dot of eight.

"How's the weather down your way?" he asked.

"The mountains are clear," Ellen said, "the water's calm, and the mockingbirds are singing."

"I've arranged for Gus to fly me down the Peninsula in his Pilgrim," said Ted. "We'll see if we can find Brick before organizing an all-out search."

"Good luck," said Ellen. She put down the phone and joined the social worker who was helping a new patient, Nina Johns, who had just arrived from Sandbar, on the Yukon River. Eight years old, forty-three pounds and four feet tall, the child's opaque skin hung on her frail bones. When she looked up, Ellen thought of Emerson: "He became all eye."

"Nina," said Ellen, holding a wrist as thin as a matchstick, "welcome to your Home in the Woods."

Nina convulsed into a spasm of coughs, hawking blood into the sputum cup the social worker held for her.

"Let's get her scrubbed and into pajamas," Ellen said to the nurse, "then I'll check her over."

When Nina was tucked into bed in the children's ward, Ellen tied on her own mask and tied one on Nina as well. She examined the sick girl's ears, nose, and eyes, felt nodes in her neck and, examining her throat, saw enlarged tonsils. There were no nodes in the axilla or groin, and no soreness in the back. Ellen warmed the stethoscope in her hands and listened to Nina's chest. When she finished, she wrote on the chart: "Heard crepitant rales weaving in the bronchial tubes and bubble-like sounds of gurgling."

After writing down orders for a blood count and urine analysis, Ellen tucked the crisp white sheets up to the little girl's neck. "You can slip your mask down as soon as I leave," she said, "and here's some tissue. Don't forget to spit in your sputum cup."

"You make me well, Missus Doctor?" Nina pleaded in a thin voice. Her eyes burned from her thin wasted face.

"If you work with us," said Ellen, stroking the child's forehead. "We need your help."

"I help," said Nina and her big round eyes drooped shut. "I help."

"I'll be in to see you later," Ellen whispered and, hanging the chart on the end of the bed, pulled the curtains around Nina.

She examined several children and then stopped between

the beds of two Yup'ik girls who looked the picture of health compared to Nina. They were complaining about their empty stomachs.

"*Ciin kaigpakarcit?*" Why are you so hungry? Ellen asked.

"*Nereksailama-wa,*" replied one. Because I haven't eaten.

"Are you going to see Dr. Milligan in Surgery?" Ellen asked.

The two little girls nodded solemnly.

"Do you want *akutaq* when you're finished?"

The children's round faces unraveled into huge smiles and Ellen made a mental note to ask the cook to make them Eskimo ice cream after they had had their bronchoscopies.

On the ride home in the Hudson, the orderly said he'd seen a red Pilgrim buzz the hospital but Ellen, busy with patients, had not heard Gus's plane.

Wednesday, the weather turned sour. Winds blew in from Resurrection Bay and clouds toppled over the mountains, settling like hats on bald Mount Marathon, which stood on the edge of the town. When Ellen arrived home in the dark, Bonnie was untwisting Brick's nightshirt from the line.

"He wouldn't fly in this weather anyway," Ellen said when they stood inside by the hot stove.

Bonnie did not respond. She had shut herself off and said nothing.

Thursday morning, driving to the San in the dark, the Hudson hit a deer. Its eyes, burning in the headlights, reminded Ellen of Nina and she hurried into the children's ward as soon as she could slip on her white linen coat. Nina slipped her mask over her mouth, reached out a thin hand and touched Ellen's.

"She seems a little better," Ellen said, consulting with Dr. Milligan.

"We'll schedule a bronchoscopy for next week," said Dr. Milligan.

"Do you have to?" said Ellen, shuddering, thinking of the trauma it might cause their little patient.

He snapped his suspenders. "I'll have it over and done with before she knows what's happening," he said. "Don't you fret."

But it was a week of fretting about Brick, about the

dudes from the east, about Ted and Gus, and by Saturday morning, Ellen wondered how Bonnie could keep going in the face of Brick's continued absence.

"He's got lots of ammunition," said Bonnie as if they had been speaking of him. "He can shoot enough food."

"Food," said Ellen, and opened one of the cupboards. "We need to shop."

"I don't feel like eating," said Bonnie.

"Ahlingnakfar," said Ellen. "Think of the baby."

Bonnie rubbed her stomach. Her eyes brimmed with tears. "Do you think," she asked, her voice plaintive, "that he'll get to see his daddy?"

Ellen tossed Bonnie her parka and, avoiding an answer, said, "Let's go!"

At the grocery store, Ellen picked up a fuzzy stuffed lion and was considering buying it for Nina when Bonnie tugged her arm.

"Someone I want you to meet," Bonnie said.

"Who?" Ellen tucked the lion into the basket with a can of Libby's beans, two cans of Campbell's tomato soup, and a box of Pilot bread.

"One of Dr. Haverstock's snowballs."

"Are you feeling okay?" Ellen asked, wondering if Bonnie had cracked up.

Bonnie nodded and dragged Ellen to the end of the aisle where a man reeking of winters past stood in white bunny boots, knitted watch cap, and hooded parka to his thighs. When they approached, he held a new wool union suit behind him and looked embarrassed.

"My sister," said Bonnie. "Bob."

"Hello," said Ellen. "Where's the snowball?"

The old man laughed so loudly the cans rattled on the shelf. "Dr. Haverstock tol' me I had as much chance of recovering as a snowball in July," he said when he had caught his breath. "They calls all his successes snowballs."

Ellen grinned. "What did you recover from?" she asked.

"That's when I cut meself to kill the snakes crawling on me," the man said, obviously relishing another opportunity to tell the story.

"Snakes?" said Ellen. "In Alaska?"

"You know them kind you get when you drunk too much

Aqua Velva,'' he chuckled. "They crawls up from your stomach and like to eat you alive.'' He pulled aside his well-worn shirt, undid the buttons of what shards remained of his union suit, and exposed a scar running three inches up and down his gullet.

"You are lucky you're alive,'' said Ellen.

"Coast guard come for me,'' he said, "and Doc sewed me up real good.''

"What about the coast guard?'' Ellen asked as they walked back to the house. "Would they send out a search for Brick?''

"I doubt it,'' said Bonnie and looked up. Overhead a Widgeon Bush plane wagged its wings, circled Resurrection Bay.

"Who's that?' Ellen asked.

"Lucky Ronston,'' said Bonnie. "He's a friend of Ted's from Anchorage.''

"Is he coming to see us?'' Ellen found herself hoping for some diversion from the sense of panic she felt over Brick's continued absence.

But Lucky in the Widgeon, obviously having seen that Brick's plane wasn't back, headed southwest. Bonnie sat in front of the stove the remainder of the day without saying a word. When she got up to go to the bathroom, Ellen sat on the same chair and noticed that, if she looked through the kitchen window, she could see the nightshirt moving gently in the cold wind.

On Sunday, Ellen, wanting to bring Bonnie out of the trance she seemed to be falling into, suggested church.

"You go,'' said Bonnie. "I don't want to.''

In the end Bonnie accompanied Ellen to St. Peter's Episcopal, holding onto Ellen's elbow to keep from slipping on the frosty streets. The small wooden church was warmed by six pews of worshippers. The minister's wife played the pump organ and while they sang from the hymnal, Ellen studied the painting behind the simple altar. Grouped around the open tomb from which Christ had risen into the heavens were fishermen, trappers, and pioneers on the one side, Eskimos and Indians on the other.

"Sing!'' Bonnie shoved her hymnal in front of Ellen.

Their voices joined in "Rock of ages, cleft for me, let me live, in harmony."

When they arrived back at the house Ted Kleet was sitting by the stove. Ellen noted his calm hands, relaxed shoulder, his tiny black moustache, and felt a moment of relief until she looked into his eyes. Then she knew, despite his manner, that he had not found Brick and was becoming concerned. Bonnie lay on the bed with her shoes on, saying nothing.

"Where's your pilot?" Ellen asked finally.

"He had to go to McGrath. He'd promised to pick up a miner's wife and bring her to Anchorage to have her baby. He'll be down again if we need him."

"Did you see Lucky in the Widgeon?"

"No," said Ted. He pushed his fingers up through his hair, stroking it back off his forehead. Ellen noticed how contained he looked, even after what must have been a disappointing search for Brick.

"Glad to know Lucky's out looking," Ted said, clasping his hands on top of his head and leaning back in the chair. "He'll radio the office and keep tabs on what's happening."

Bonnie suddenly rolled off the bed and peered past the geranium in the kitchen window. Then she started bustling around the kitchen, making lunch.

"How's the Home in the Woods?" Ted slipped off his chair and resettled himself on the Olson rug beside Ellen. "Do you like it there?"

"Yes," said Ellen and, remembering her puzzlement when he had telephoned, asked, "How did you know? Bonnie said you didn't call her first."

"Mom still works at Mount Edgecumbe," Ted explained. "They heard about the new Missus Doctor when an icepack of ribs arrived for their bone grafts. She told me about you when I called her last Sunday."

Ellen laughed for the first time since Brick had left. "Dr. Milligan did an extrapleural thoracoplasty last week," she said. "I'd forgotten."

"Folks at Edgecumbe are saying you've a mind like an elephant," said Ted, grinning, his black eyes lighting up. "They say you know everyone's name and where they're from and how long they've been hospitalized and you've only been there a week.''

"Two weeks now," said Ellen. She looked at the amount of food Bonnie had set out. "And if I eat my share of that, I will turn into an elephant.''

Bonnie napped in the afternoon and Ellen and Ted walked southwest of the town, past the railroad tracks, along a trail that fronted the water. They chatted of this and that until it felt to Ellen as if their lives had blended, as if they had caught up from their first meeting in Unaganik. It was strange, but with Jason she had never talked that way. Was it because he wouldn't understand, because they were so different and had no way of relating to each other's backgrounds? It seemed like a pattern of her mother's that she had repeated. Loving a man so totally and completely different than herself didn't make sense, although it made sense to Cheok, had been a means of escape for her. Mr. Rupert, or was it Emerson, was right. There was no need for her to marry. She could have a happy and complete life alone.

She knew the opposite was true for Bonnie. Ellen stopped walking and turned around to face Ted. "Do you think Brick took a chance?" she asked.

"You don't have to worry about him," said Ted. "He knows his plane like a mother knows her child. He doesn't take any more chances than anyone takes, flying into the bush.''

"It's like pushing destiny, isn't it," said Ellen.

Ted rubbed his fingers over his scarred eyebrow, as if trying to straighten it. "To me it's more like facing myself," he replied and, taking her arm, continued down the trail beside her until the bushes closed in and it was impossible to walk two by two.

"I'm sure Brick's prepared for an emergency in any case," said Ted, dropping behind.

"He may be prepared," retorted Ellen, "but those dudes were packing blankets and sheets and looked like they'd never been off the pavement.''

Monday, Bonnie stayed at home with Ted. As soon as Ellen got to the San and got her white coat and mask, she took the lion into Nina. "Thank you, Missus Doctor," said

Nina. For the first time since Nina had arrived at the Home in the Woods, Ellen saw her smile.

Dr. Milligan presented Nina's case at the regular Monday conference.

"We'll bronchoscope this afternoon," he said when he finished. "Would you be interested in attending, Dr. MacTavish?"

Ellen nodded slowly, unsure of her emotions. Nina looked so frail and bronchoscopy seemed so intrusive. She felt that even more when Nina, dulled by the Nembutal and codeine sedative, was wheeled into surgery.

"Remember, Dr. MacTavish," Dr. Milligan said as they scrubbed in surgery. "Save your pity for after the patient is well."

The doctor's technique was impressive. "Nice work," said Ellen when Nina, groggy, was wheeled back to her bed.

"A lot of necrotic tissue in there," he said. "When she's stronger, we'll ask her parents for permission to operate."

The next patient was wheeled in. When he was taken to recovery, a new patient, a man who had ruptured himself by coughing, was wheeled in.

"Feel this," said Dr. Milligan, indicating the area of the stomach.

Gently Ellen prodded. The stomach was up in the diaphragm.

"What would you do?" the senior surgeon asked.

"I don't know," said Ellen.

"I like you," he said. "I've always distrusted a man who wasn't in charge of his own ignorance."

Ellen grinned to herself and did not remind him that she wasn't a man. They finished late and Ellen nearly missed her ride in the Hudson. Bonnie was standing by the clothesline, watching the nightshirt, when Ellen arrived.

That night the geranium wilted near the window and outside the ground iced up. Ice crystals glittered like jewels from the evergreens as the Hudson pulled into the San parking lot Tuesday morning.

On Wednesday, at lunch in the cafeteria, Ellen heard the roar of a plane. She rushed outside. Skimming over the trees was a high wing plane on floats. Brick's plane. The orderly sped her to the harbor and by the time they reached the dock,

Brick and the two dudes were standing there with two brownie skins.

"How . . . ?" said Ellen, breathless from running down the dock. She stopped and looked at the plane. The left wing was covered with a bed sheet.

"Caught a branch when I landed in a bad gust," Brick said. "Took the cloth clean off the wing. One of these dudes here suggested I freeze on a bedsheet. Had to wait till the weather changed, but damned if it didn't work."

"Did you buzz the Jessie Lee Home?" Ellen asked, feeling the wing in amazement.

"Y'all bet I did. The little woman ran out. She knows I'm here."

Ellen returned to the San and called Ted's office, leaving word that Brick had arrived. She was still at the San when the phone rang at eight that evening. It was the Signal Corps, relaying a message from Ted, who called from Taryaqvak. He had not heard the news. "Brick's safe. He's back," Ellen told the operator. "Over."

"Roger, roger," said the operator. "Over and out."

Ellen spent the night at the San, letting Bonnie and Brick enjoy their reunion without her. She was awakened after midnight by a drunken brawl in the men's ward. Dashing down the hall in her fur coat, she entered in time to hear Dr. Milligan harangue one of the patients for getting chummy with a bottle.

"I warned you," stormed Dr. Milligan. "Next time this happened I told you I was sending you to a government hospital. You'll leave for the Lower 48 on the steamship tomorrow."

Ted called late the next day from Anchorage. "I'm heading back up north," he said. "I put it off until Brick got back. Is everyone in one piece?"

"Yes," said Ellen and when she told him how they had fixed the wing, Ted laughed. "That'll be one to tell the grandkids," he said.

Ted needs to meet someone like Jill, Ellen thought after she put down the phone. Someone who wants a husband, a house, some babies, and some grandbabies.

39

FOR THE FIRST TIME since she left Seattle, Ellen fully unpacked Mrs. Meriweather's carpetbag. After her red dinner dress, skirts, and blouses were hung in the narrow closet, and the sweaters and undergarments arranged in the oak bureau, she discovered, at the very bottom of the bag, a blue velvet box. It held Mrs. Ardley's diamond *V* pin. Quoting Emerson, Mrs. Ardley had written: " 'The only gift is a portion of thyself,' but I want you to have this as a reminder of all we've been to each other."

The diamonds burst like phosphorescence in a black sea. Ellen stared at it and through her tears she thought she saw Mrs. Ardley tucked into the wingback chair on one side of the Philco. Butler sat in his chair on the other.

"I miss you," she wrote in a quick note, knowing words didn't, and could never, convey what she really meant. "But I'm fine and I've found the pin. Thank you."

Of her other treasures, she had given the ivory whale to Jill and Nils for a wedding gift and had left Dr. Visikov's vest pocket dictionary with Mrs. Ardley. She still wore Stewart's jade labret around her neck on Dr. Constance's gold chain.

Unpacked and established in her own place, Ellen felt that her restless spirit had finally found a home. With work that she loved, people to care for and assist to health, a challenge to her mind and energy, winter wound its dark path through ice and snow and gales off Resurrection Bay without her giving more than a moment's thought to sunshine, palm trees, or Jason.

Families of the patients brought game to the sanatorium

that Dr. Milligan, with his dedication to a high protein diet, eagerly accepted. They ate moose, caribou, duck, goose, smoke salmon, halibut, and once a fifty-pound lake trout caught by the husband of a patient from Glenallen. Hating to cook, Ellen ate all her meals in the general dining room.

One evening as she was walking on the snowy path from the main dining room to her apartment in a separate building, a figure stepped out of the shadows.

"Are you that lady doctor?" asked a voice.

"Yes," said Ellen, turning toward the voice and making out the large shape of an older woman.

"I'se Irish Flo and I'se got troubles," said the woman.

"Come to the examining room," said Ellen. "I'll look you over."

"Oh no," said Irish Flo. "You don't want me in there. Will you come to my place?"

Ellen hesitated and then said, "Just a moment. I'll get my bag."

A silent man drove them in a white Cadillac to a large house with gables, a tower, and carpenter's lace along the steep slanting roof line.

"It's okay," said Flo as they got out of the car. "Tonight's my night off. There's nobody here."

Curious, Ellen entered the house and followed Irish Flo to her boudoir. Pink feathers fluttered from the walls, dark magenta satin drapes swayed from a curtained bed, and pale lights flowed under purple-tasseled shades. A hairless pink dog snored on red satin pillows embroidered with cupids. A pungent scent of jasmine perfumed the room.

"Are you having any chest pains?" Ellen asked after examining Irish Flo from top to bottom and listening, for the second time, to her labored heart.

"Some nights I feel as if the house is falling on me," said Irish Flo.

"I'd like you to see a heart specialist." Ellen examined Flo's hands, noting the bluish nails and the bulbous ends of her fingers. "Any chance you can get down to Seattle?"

"No," said Flo, "and besides, it ain't my heart, it's my back."

Ellen studied Flo's eyes. She looked worn out. "I want to caution you," Ellen said, trying not to alarm the lady but at the same time make her aware of the risks. "Don't overexert yourself. No running up and down stairs. No sudden movements."

Irish Flo gave a rich, deep chortle. Ellen found herself laughing too. "Try to get Outside," she said, "and if you can, take a long vacation in the sunshine."

"I might go to Hawaii next spring," said Flo.

"Good," said Ellen, but doubted if Flo would last a busy winter.

That winter Bonnie did grow as large as a beluga. In February she gave birth to a seven pound, nine and three-quarter ounce baby boy called Sonny. She quit her job at the Jessie Lee Home and Ellen, on her Sundays off, walked the two and a half miles into Seward to play with her new nephew. In March, a month after Sonny was born, Ted Kleet drove up in his Willys.

"You certainly look like a businessman!" said Ellen. She had not seen him since Brick's return from the bear hunt. Laughing, she pretended to examine his clean nails and scrubbed knuckles.

Ted smiled. "Do I pass inspection, Doctor?" he teased.

"You certainly do," said Ellen and, letting go of his hands, looked at his face. "You've shaved off your moustache," she added, surprised.

"I took it off up north. The icicles loved it."

"Didn't freeze your lips, did you?" Ellen asked, touching them with a gentle finger and noting that the lower lip wasn't distended, which usually happened as a result of being frozen.

"No," said Ted and seemed to grow very still.

Ellen removed her finger. "You look in perfect health," she said and stretched out on her back on the Olson rug. Bonnie tossed her a pillow for her head.

"I hear your company's doing well," said Brick.

"We've negotiated to build an apartment house in Anchorage," said Ted, not acknowledging the praise, as was the custom among his people. "We'll work 'round the clock and have it ready by September."

They discussed the business and politics of the DEW line and the pros and cons of statehood until Bonnie tucked the baby into a cradle Brick had lined with foxskins. Bonnie yawned. Knowing she was getting up nights to feed Sonny, Ellen stood.

"Are you hungry?" Bonnie asked. "I can cook something for us."

"For goodness sakes," said Ellen, putting her arms around her sister. "Go to bed. I can find something to eat at the San."

"Can I drive you back?" Ted asked.

"Yes," said Ellen, smiling. "I've been running on the wards all week and my feet would love a rest."

Bonnie handed Ellen her silver fox. "Will we see you next Sunday?"

"I'm on call," said Ellen. "I'll have to stick around the San."

"The weekend after that's the Firemen's Dance," said Brick. He put his arm around Bonnie. "The little woman and I are aiming to do some two-stepping."

"I'd like to come down for the dance," Ted said as he and Ellen walked to his car. Mounds of shoveled snow packed both sides of the path.

"Should be fun," Ellen said.

Ted opened the door and Ellen tucked herself in, gathering the heavy fur around her. "What do you think?" said Ted, climbing into the driver's seat.

"Think of what?" Ellen asked, trying to bring her thoughts back to the present. Since the baby had arrived, when she visited Bonnie and Brick she ended up missing Jason. She didn't feel incapacitated as she had after the shock of his engagement to Birdie, but she had thought she was over him, done with him altogether. Sometimes when she wrapped the fur coat around her, it seemed as if she were cuddling in his arms. It felt as if she had reached a level of grief that was tied to the very core of her being. Without it she could not survive. It reminded her of a Burmese tribeswoman she had once seen as a patient in Seattle. The woman had worn rows of gold bands around her neck for so long that to take them off and relieve the pressure would endanger her capacity to hold up her head. She needed the pain of the gold bands in order to stay alive.

"Shall we go to the dance together?"

Ellen turned sideways and sat crosslegged on the leather

seat. She studied Ted. He turned his head and smiled at her. His hands rested easily on the steering wheel.

"Are you asking me to the dance?" she said, surprised and yet not surprised, either, that he wanted her to go.

"Yes," he said. "I'm inviting you to go with me to the Firemen's Dance."

"Is this what they call a date?" Her voice had an edge of teasing.

Ted laid his hand on the seat and stroked the fox fur.

"I guess I've never been on a date before," said Ellen, surprised at how strange she felt, as if she were off at a distance, watching herself. "Not in the strict sense of the word."

"We can call it what we want," said Ted, his voice steady, warm.

Ellen remembered other dances with him. "Yes," she said suddenly. "I'd like to go. We always have fun when we dance, don't we?"

Ted's face lit up. He turned away, started the Willys and drove out of Seward. Just past the lagoon he asked, "Would you like to eat out?"

"Yes," said Ellen, and was pleased when he turned right and drove to Gabe's Restaurant. Exotic spices filled the log house. Ted led her to a table covered with a gingham cloth. Irish Flo sat at the next table.

"Hello," Ellen called over.

The old whore's face was puffy. The man who was with her looked as if he were counting the squares on the tablecloth and Irish Flo, with an embarrassed wave, turned away from Ellen. Even from the distance her fingers looked blue.

Ted seemed comfortable eating in silence and Ellen, who had been with patients all week, felt talked out.

"I'll see you in two weeks," he said, letting her off at the Home in the Woods after their spicy paella.

"Until then," said Ellen. Crunching through the snow, her coat bundled closely around her, she hurried, head down, to her quarters. It was noisily warm with the clacking of the radiator. The bed was soft. She burrowed her head into the pillow and fell sound asleep.

*   *   *

"The TB Division of the Alaska Native Health Services needs someone to visit the villages to isolate cases that can be treated in a sanatorium." Dr. Milligan looked directly at Ellen. "Can you start in two weeks?"

"Yes," said Ellen, without pausing to consider the implications.

The plan was, Ellen found from reading the correspondence between Dr. Milligan and the chief of the Tuberculosis Division, to base her at the Log Cabins Motel in Anchorage and fly her to the villages, particularly in the Kuskokwim–Yukon River Delta, where tuberculosis was rampant.

"You can't leave," said Bonnie when Ellen stopped by to tell her the news and to see the baby. "You promised to go to the Firemen's Dance."

"The train leaves Friday," said Ellen. "If I don't go then I'll have to wait until the Tuesday train."

"Isn't Ted Kleet coming down Friday for the dance?"

"Yes."

"Can't you ride back to Anchorage with him in the Willys?"

"I never thought of that."

Ellen lay on the floor with the baby on her chest.

"Weren't you planning on going to the dance with Ted?"

"Not really," said Ellen, tilting the baby over her head as she used to tilt Baby Bruce. "We were going to go together, that's all."

"Ellen, sometimes . . ."

Ellen nuzzled the baby. "What?"

"Do you ever plan to get married?"

"No."

"Have you told Ted?"

"What business is it of his?"

"Oh, Ellen, how can you be so dumb?"

The baby strained, screwed up his face, and started on an activity that Ellen fully understood and wanted nothing to do with. She handed him back to his mother and went into the kitchen to wash their dinner dishes.

Brick had gone to Anchorage for his guide business and Ellen decided to spend the night. She slept with Bonnie in the double bed. In the morning, Ellen caught a ride to the San with the orderly in his Hudson with the cracked windshield.

"Has the permission letter for Nina John's surgery come yet?" Ellen asked Dr. Milligan after she made her rounds.

He handed it to her and Ellen read, "I guess you got civilized down there," the priest from Sandbar wrote. "We don't know who Nina's father is but folks around here all call me Father so I'm assuming responsibility. Couldn't get her mother to sign inasmuch as she's been hitting the bottle. Let me know if I can help again."

"To whom it may concern," the priest had written, "As her Father, I hereby give permission for Nina to have whatever surgeries she needs in order to get well." He scrawled his name so that it would be impossible for anyone to know whether it corresponded to Nina's last name or not.

"I bet the authorities won't even notice that the *F* is capitalized," said Ellen. She handed the two letters back to Dr. Milligan with a grin. "I'm going to see Nina. She'll want to hear the good news."

"Tell her *Our Gang* arrived in the same mail," said Dr. Milligan. The film was part of his laughter-is-the-best-medicine philosophy.

Ellen sat on the bed beside Nina. "You are looking so much better," she said, tucking the stuffed lion next to Nina's cheek. "When I come back to visit you I'm afraid I won't recognize who you are."

"I be the same person here," said Nina, patting her sunken chest.

Ellen thought of the millions of bacilli destroying Nina's lungs and hoped she would not be the same in there next visit. "Monday is your surgery," she told Nina. "Your letter came."

"You not be here."

"No," said Ellen, patting Nina's wrist, noticing how it had filled out. "But I'll come to see you before *Our Gang* tonight."

That afternoon, in the two-hour lull when all the patients had enforced rest, Dr. Milligan motioned Ellen into his cramped office next to the surgery. The office was piled with X-rays, books, journals, case histories, and a speech he was preparing for his next money-raising trip Outside to the headquarters of the Women's Christian Missionary Board. Ellen moved aside a tiny shell bird that had been made by a patient and sat down on a metal stool left over from the military days in the building.

"Friend of yours died last night," said Dr. Milligan.

Knowing how he loved to joke, Ellen wondered if she should laugh or cry.

"Irish Flo," said Dr. Milligan. "Someone who shall remain nameless was with her and got one of the Seward doctors, Dr. Ham."

"I'm not surprised," said Ellen.

"A lot of people are going to miss her," said Dr. Milligan.

"Where'd they take her?"

"She'll be lying in state in the funeral parlor until the ground thaws. The gravedigger refuses to work in the winter."

Three days later Ellen caught a ride into Seward to pay her last respects. She stared with a mixture of awe and amusement at the carrot-haired lady of the night. Irish Flo wore a purple velvet dress that exposed much of her bosom, had bright red cheeks, paler skin than Ellen had seen on her alive, and huge red lips looking like they were ready to say, "Aw come on, pucker up, Babe." She lay in a red satin-lined casket, looking for all the world as if she were ready for another trick.

"I guess the undertaker had an old debt to repay," whispered a man next to her.

Ellen laughed and was positive she saw Irish Flo wink.

For the Firemen's Dance, Ellen wore her red wool dinner dress. She pinned Mrs. Ardley's diamond *V* on the right side of the bodice and then, examining the effect in the bathroom mirror, repinned it in the center. It sparkled in the glass and Ellen smiled at her own reflection above it. Then she pulled the jade labret from its customary place between her breasts and let it hang outside the dress for the first time in many years. Taking the fox fur, she shut her door, left a message with the desk clerk for Ted Kleet, and made a final round of the wards, saying good-bye to the patients. Finally she joined Nina in the children's ward for the last time.

"Oh you look beeeootiful, Missus Doctor," said Nina, gazing at Ellen with a rapt expression on her pale face.

"Thank you," said Ellen.

"Do you think I'll look as beeeootiful when I grow up?"

"Yes," said Ellen, "I do." The door opened and Ted entered. He waited by the door as Ellen stood.

"Can I ask you something else?" Nina whispered.

"Yes you may," said Ellen.

"Are you in love?"

"I'm in love with you."

"I know that," said Nina. "I mean him. That man."

"Ted Kleet is his name," said Ellen, "and no, I'm not in love with him."

"How come?"

"Because he's a friend."

"Don't people love friends?"

"I'm going to miss your questions, Nina," said Ellen. "Especially the ones I can't answer."

"I'll see you again," said Nina with a voice so old and grown up it made Ellen want to cry. "I know I will."

It reminded Ellen of Mrs. Ardley saying, "If we don't see you in this life, we'll see you in the next."

A small Yup'ik boy came up to her and tugged her hand. *"Yruingcaristenguyugtua,"* he said in a whisper. I want to be a doctor.

Ellen bent down. "If you want to be a doctor," she answered him seriously, "you have to stay with your studies. Teacher tells me you don't want to do your lessons."

The small boy hung his head.

"You study hard now," she said, "and when you're ready to be a doctor, you come and let me know. I'll help you go to school."

"School?" he said, his voice high pitched and incredulous.

"Yes," said Ellen, taking his hand and leading him back to bed. "Lots and lots of school to become a doctor."

"We could stay here all night," Ted said when she joined him at the door.

"It's my last day," said Ellen. "That's why the fuss."

"I bet they fuss over you all the time, Missus Doctor," he said.

Ellen didn't answer. There was a new job ahead of her and she didn't want to think about what she was giving up at the San. By the time she had finished telling Ted about her new position, they had reached the old wooden hall and the Firemen's Dance.

Light and fiddle music spilled out over the snow. Crepe paper streamers, balloons, bunting, and townspeople dressed in their finest greeted them as they entered. Ted paid the two-dollar entrance fee and signed up for the door prize. "May I have the first waltz?" he asked Ellen after hanging up her coat.

She stared at him. "I don't know how to waltz," she said.

"I promised to teach you the next time we danced."

Ellen looked at his light-hearted face, his easy smile. It seemed such a long time ago, and a time when she, too, was lighthearted and full of fun. "I remember," she said quietly.

Bonnie and Brick joined them at that moment, and Ellen was grateful. Too many things happening too fast. She could not think.

"Don't think," a voice said inside her. "Feel!" She let the music fill her and let herself be guided around the room by Ted, whose waltzing, as Jill would have said, was simply divine.

There were four men to every woman. They cut in on Ellen, and she danced a few rounds, stepped on several toes encased, luckily, in heavy boots, and was glad when Ted cut back in on her. She danced with Brick and Dr. Milligan, with the grocery clerk who was also the gravedigger, with the taxi driver, and several of the school teachers.

"If you ever need a job . . ." said Dr. Ham. He was one of the town bachelors and Ellen was trying to follow his version of the waltz.

She laughed. "Are you offering me yours?"

"I'm thinking of getting married and settling down," he said.

"Anybody in mind?" Ellen asked.

"Are you interested?"

"Haven't you heard?" she said.

"Heard what?"

"I plan to be an old maid."

Ted cut back in. "Not if I have anything to do about it," he said.

Ignoring his remark, Ellen thought of the tern soaring over the mud flats. How easy it was to fly.

"Where are you?" Ted asked, lifting her chin.

She blinked.

"You don't need to drift away from me."

Distracted, Ellen stepped on his feet.

"Don't you know the way I feel about you?" he asked, quiet, his eyes intent on hers.

Ellen searched for words but found only music flowing through her. She looked into Ted's eyes. At that moment Snowball Bob, smelling of his new union suit, swung her away and romped her around the room.

40

MONDAY MORNING, WHEN ELLEN walked into the Health Services Building in Anchorage, the chief of the TB division was waiting. An ex-army surgeon, his jaw had been shattered during the First World War and replaced by steel. But his eyebrows compensated for the lack of mobility on the lower half of his face.

"Hope it won't disrupt you," said the chief, eyebrows raised, "but in this business you get used to plans being changed. There's an emergency up in Sandbar. Someone's stuck a bottle up his ass." His eyebrows dropped over his eyes, rested a second, and returned to his forehead. "We need a doctor up there PDQ to take it out. The priest will put you up for a few days, and you can examine the rest of the villagers while you're there. We've arranged for Gus, one of the best bush pilots, to fly you up."

Ellen filled Dr. Visikov's medical bag with supplies, including bundles of vitamins a drug company had bequeathed to the Territory when it cleaned out its shelves. She walked across Merrill Field to an old red Pilgrim with an even older pilot. Sprigs of grey stuck out of his ears and chin, and his grey hair stuck up to the sky like a handhold for God to pull him into heaven.

"I'm looking for a ride to Sandbar," Ellen said. "Are you Gus?"

The man shoved a wad of snuff between his teeth and gums. "That's what they call me," he said, grinning.

"Looks like you've put this bird together with bailing

wire," said Ellen, wanting to shake the wings to see if they stayed on.

"Nothing wrong with wire," said Gus, "S'long as your brains aren't short-circuited by it. Now take some of these youngsters. They come out of the war thinking they're flight jockeys, but they know from nothing about how to use packing tape or wire when you're stuck in the bush."

"Or bed sheets," said Ellen.

Gus snapped his fingers. "You aren't that lady doc, are you? Friend of Ted Kleet's?"

"Did he tell you how Brick Tandy flew out of the bush?"

"We call him Bedsheet Brick," Gus said and laughed so hard his snoose almost fell out of his mouth.

The Pilgrim headed north, rattling and shaking. Ellen was surprised to find her teeth still stuck in her head when they refueled at Fairbanks. They flew on to a small village nestled in a grove of tamarack trees. The weather landed behind them. No sooner was the Pilgrim tied down than the rain clouds broke in a deluge that would have sent Noah whistling for twins.

The priest, who had been notified of her anticipated arrival by radio telephone, met the plane with a big black umbrella. "How's my daughter, Nina?" he asked, his expression worried.

"You wouldn't recognize her," Ellen answered with a grin.

Obviously relieved at the good news, the priest led Ellen down dirt roads already muddied from the rain, past log houses and caches roofed with sod and reinforced by moose racks. In a cabin the patient with the bottle crouched on all fours. Ellen pulled on rubber gloves and extracted the bottle with as much dispatch as she could muster. Blood spurted from the rectum. She grabbed a towel and, after soaking it in antiseptic solution, applied pressure on the anal area until the bleeding stopped and she could put on the dressing. Then she got on with the rest of the patients waiting in the schoolroom, explaining the principles of sleep, fresh air, good food, exercise, hygiene, and sanitation.

Three days later, on her way to the airfield, Ellen noticed a woman slouched against the side of a low shack. Bottles littered the ground. Sucking in her cheeks, the woman looked Ellen in the eye and spat. Ellen hurried on.

Gus waited beside the Pilgrim. The rain had stopped, the clouds had cleared, and he pulled up over the broad, flat meandering river. A muskrat scampered along the edge of the fallen bank. Fish wheels circled in slow motion like water wheels, catching salmon in their bucket traps as they dipped one after the other, endlessly, through the river. In the holding pen, Ellen saw several large salmon cresting the surface, looking for escape.

"Mr. Kleet left a message for you to call him," said the owner of the Log Cabins Motel when Ellen reached the row of small cabins across from the airfield. The health service had arranged for her to live in one while she was in Anchorage.

"Thank you," said Ellen but wanted nothing more than a hot bath and a solitary night to herself. She could call Ted in the morning.

She entered the narrow living room of her cabin. It contained a plaid couch, an easy chair, a coffee table with an ashtray the size of a dinner plate, and a rug braided from men's ties. A framed print of Mount McKinley, painted in pink and blue, hung on the wall. There was a cramped kitchen with a table, chairs, hot plate, and small refrigerator. The bathroom and bedroom lay to the rear. Ellen headed to them and, stripping, lowered herself into a hot soapy tub.

"Mr. Kleet's busy in a meeting all morning," Ted's secretary said when Ellen called the next day. Before she could reach him, she had left Anchorage again, flying east with Gus to a small village circled by sage bushes, spindly trees, and mountains. After three and a half days in the village, she had examined everyone. Not expecting Gus until the following morning, she took advantage of the extra time to explore. Ellen walked up one of the mountains to an old valley glacier that the villagers had told her was receding farther up the mountain every year.

Soil-embedded ice lay like a dirty ear against the turquoise-white face of the glacier. The silence was palpable. Thoughts of long-extinct mastodons displaced Ellen's concerns about the tuberculosis problems in the village. She remembered Gus saying he had found a mastodon tusk on a glacier. She remembered a night Angus and Joe Stokes had spent arguing about the existence of mammoths and whether Spit 'n' Polish Patty could have dug one up from the ice and survived on that.

"It'd be tens of thousands of years old," Joe had scoffed.

"An Eskimo up north told me he'd found one under the ice," Angus insisted. "The meat wasn't spoiled."

"How do you explain," Joe replied, "that they never found hide nor hair of those weather dudes Patty got lost with. It weren't no mammoth or no mastodon she ate, and that's my final opinion."

"Just think," Angus continued, changing the subject, "the north all used to be grassland."

"Were there lions here then?" Ellen remembered wanting to ask, but she was supposed to be asleep on her cot and hadn't.

Now she wiped her eyes and stepped away from the dripping shelves of ice as if she were backing away from times too painful to remember.

Back in Anchorage Ellen discovered that Ted had gone north on a job. She passed a busy month flying, usually with Gus, to places with names like Twisted Creek, Dredge, Unionsuit, Jade, Ukuut (You here), and Mumigtaq (Flapjack). She fixed her graduation hat from Jill and Nils with mosquito netting as protection against the bugs, which were hatching in record numbers, especially in the Kuskokwin River delta.

In that area, in Navtuli, she learned that every newborn in the past five years had died. She visited with the women, speaking Yup'ik, until she discovered that the elder everyone called Uncle Jordan insisted on helping feed the babies. He chewed the babies' food, as was the custom, and well chewed, removed the food from his own mouth and mushed it into the babies'. Without needing a laboratory analysis of his blood-soaked sputum, Ellen knew the cause of the babies' deaths. Uncle Jordan had tuberculosis.

"We can't hurt his feelings," said the young mother Ellen talked to about the need to keep him away from her newborn.

"But—" Ellen bit her tongue.

"He love babies," said the young mother.

"That's a great idea," said Ellen. "But where's the telephone? I haven't seen one since I've been here."

"We get ACS in Cold Bay, at the DEW line site, with marine radio," Sigori explained, enunciating his words with care. "And ACS relays up the Chain to Anchorage."

"What we need," Ellen said, thinking of all the possibilities, "is a code, so all the operators up and down the Chain won't find out who's got gonorrhea, who's pregnant, who's flat on their back."

While Sigori looked up hepatitis in the *Merck Manual,* Ellen pondered the idea of a code. "I've got it," she said finally. "The health aide can make a preliminary diagnosis using the *Merck Manual* and say, for example, 'I think I have a chapter such and such, page such and such, paragraph such and such, and these are the vital signs.' That can be relayed up to a doctor in Anchorage without anyone along the line knowing what they're talking about. The doctor can relay back. 'Does the patient show such and such symptoms?'"

"If I say no?" asked Sigori.

"The doctor can say: 'Turn to chapter so and so, page so and so, paragraph so and so.'"

"What if patient has none of those what you call symptoms?" Sigori replied.

"The doctor would know if those symptoms were really pertinent," said Ellen, remembering the Japanese patient with typhoid who had no rosy spots. "Or the doctor might ask the health aide to look at another page. They'd do that until the diagnosis could be made and then proceed to the PDR."

"How?" Sigori asked, turning to the thick green book.

"Same way. Except it would be easier. The doctor would have an inventory of the drugs on your shelf and would prescribe according to page and paragraph number."

Sigori smiled at her. "I understand."

"We'll need to get all the health aides together for a training period." Ellen suddenly realized that she had found a job for herself. She could staff the Anchorage line and at the same time have Jimmy with her.

When the weather cleared, Ellen reluctantly left Jimmy and flew back to Anchorage with promises that as soon as she found a place of her own and as soon as she could stop flying to the villages, she'd send for him. When the plane landed, she telephoned Ted from a small building beside the field.

"I've missed you," he said.

"I have to talk to you," said Ellen. "When can we get together?"

"What about right now?"

"If you've time," said Ellen, feeling too excited to sleep despite her long day. She walked across the field to her cabin and was admiring the delphiniums that grew under her window when Ted arrived in the Willys.

"You sound like you've got good news," he said, following her into the dark living room.

"I met Stewart's son," said Ellen. Her voice bubbled with enthusiasm. "His name's Jimmy and he's agreed to come to Anchorage to live with me. I thought you could help me find a place to live."

Ted flexed his fingers. Ellen noticed he was wearing a wide silver ring. She reached for his hand and was examining the raven's head carved on silver when the door opened and the owner poked his head inside. "We don't allow single ladies to have male company," he announced.

Fuming, Ellen dropped Ted's hand.

Ted stood. "What say I pick you up tomorrow. We'll go out in the *Yethl* and there will be no one to interrupt. We can talk about a place then. And I have something I've been wanting to ask you."

Ellen stood beside him, her enthusiasm turned to annoyance at the interruption. "I don't care what anyone thinks," she said. "You don't have to run off."

Ted held her by the shoulders and looked at her with an expression she remembered from way back. "Don't let him ruin your mood," he cautioned in a quiet voice.

Ted might have said "ruin your luck," for all I know, Ellen thought later when she tossed and turned in bed, unable to sleep for the plans jamming her mind.

Next morning, Ted picked her up in the Willys. Except for his clean hands and nails, he looked like a fisherman. He wore knee-high rubber boots, baggy dark pants, suspenders, a heavy checkered shirt, a red fisherman's cap with EAT FISH FOR HEALTH on the insignia above the brim.

"Let me check in at the office first," said Ellen. "I've got something to tell the chief."

It was Saturday, and the building was closed. Ellen laughed. "I have no idea what day it is anymore," she said.

"You're losing some of your city ways,"said Ted.

"I'm not sure I ever had any," she replied, grinning broadly.

Ted parked the Willys at the pier, launched his dinghy, and rowed out to where he had anchored the *Yethl*. "I'm tired of fighting these thirty-foot tides," Ted said. "I'm taking her down to Seward in a week or two and mooring her there. Do you want to make the trip with me?"

"If I'm not stranded out in the bush," said Ellen, thinking how much fun it would be to see Nina and her friends at the San, to see Bonnie, Brick, and Sonny and tell them about Jimmy.

Ted raised the anchor, and they headed down Cook Inlet. Clouds parted. The mountains shone in the sun, and the water sparkled. Ellen, standing on the foredeck, thought of how perfect her life would be when Jimmy arrived.

After putting the wheel on automatic pilot, Ted joined her. Above them, a flock of geese circled.

"They're getting ready to go south," said Ellen. "And I feel like I haven't even had a summer yet. Do you know I almost regret not fishing?"

"I always loved the smell of salmon," said Ted. "I miss that the most."

"Maybe next year I'll take a month off and take Jimmy fishing at Unaganik," Ellen mused, thinking of how she and Stewart had batted fish at each other when they were picking the nets. She almost laughed out loud, thinking how time dulled the pain of hard work and left only the fun.

"You look so happy," said Ted as he moved toward her. Suddenly his lips, soft and warm, touched hers.

She felt his gentleness, his patience for her response. For a moment she let herself feel the comfort of his arms. But as soon as her mouth started to soften, a stab of pain shot up from the soles of her feet. She pulled away. "I can't," she said.

He went very still. Ellen looked away, to Mount Susitna.

The sleeping lady seemed to be banging her white head against the wall of sky.

"No," she said, "I can't."

"I want to marry you," said Ted. "I have known that forever."

Ellen turned from the mountain and stared at him. "Why?"

"I love you."

"Love? What's that?" Her voice was hard. She thought of Jason. He had loved her too. Where did that leave her?

"You love Jimmy."

"Yes, but that's different."

"Doesn't it come from a place beyond knowing?"

Ellen paused. "Yes," she said, softer, "you're right. There's more than reason in it."

"So why do you ask me why I love you?"

It had been a long time since she'd thought of love. There had been bacilli to think of, collapsed lungs, medications, X-rays, and percentages. She had discovered that ninety-two percent of the children in the Kuskokwim–Yukon River Delta between ages seven and eight were infected with TB and had that to think about.

"Where are you?" Ted asked. He lifted her head, held her eyes with the magnetism of his own.

"I can't," said Ellen.

"I never thought of you as someone who used that word," said Ted.

"I just can't. That's all there is to it."

"Are you living in the past?"

"No."

"Each season brings new growth," he continued, speaking like an elder.

Ellen closed her eyes. He still held her head.

"You change when you take on something new," he said. "I know that, and I also know very well that the old ways are gone. We have to move ahead."

Ellen saw them, the old ways of her mother, of his family, as if they drifted like cloud shapes past her closed eyes.

"Keep what's good of the old times," Ted said, "and discard what isn't of value."

She opened her eyes. How much did he know of Jason? "Do you know," she said, some dark force burning her tongue, "that I have had a lover?"

"Does it matter?"

"Yes."

"Clara had a lover before Sigori."

"Yes."

"Is that so different?"

"But Stewart's dead."

"Your lover is dead for you, and now you have me."

Ellen felt as if a string had snapped on Mr. Rupert's cello and twanged in her face. The music stopped. The sawing of the bow sounded like the clatter of old bones. She pulled away from Ted, frightened, and leaned over the rail. The peaked mountains to the north, still snow-covered at the end of summer, seemed to fade through the bleached sky. The autumn air hinted of cold.

"No," she said at last, turning to Ted. "I can't be a wife."

"I don't want a wife," said Ted. "I want you."

41

"**B**OOTLEGGERS' COVE," TED CALLED from the wheel and pointed toward shore on their port side. "Rum runners used to hide in there when the patrol boats were looking for them."

Ellen joined him in the wheelhouse. "I wish we could keep liquor out of the villages," she said.

"It's a terrible problem in the Southeast," said Ted. "The elders say it's multiplying like mosquitoes."

"There doesn't seem to be any solution," said Ellen, her voice sad.

"It's like luck." Ted smiled at her. "Most people have to find their own."

Ellen avoided his gaze, knowing they had been the lucky ones. They had not let their will and spirit be broken.

The *Yethl* continued down Knik Arm.

"Fish Creek." Ted pointed to the chart. His voice was light and Ellen noticed an eagerness in it. "That's where I want to build a house."

"It'll be nice to be out of the city," said Ellen, looking at the spikes of mauve fireweed coloring the distant shoreline. The yellowing leaves of aspen trees flickered like gold dust on the hill rising above the water.

"We'll still have moose in our yard, eagles in our trees, and look," Ted pointed at the water. A silver salmon leaped, flashing in the sunlight, heading for the creek.

My salmon, thought Ellen, and remembered her trip to the center of the earth. What had Paul said about having her strength back?

"I have come to be my own person," she said quietly. "I can't ever, ever again, be beholden to someone else."

"I never will ask that of you."

"But that's not being in love," she said. "Not to feel tied to someone."

"If you're tied, you can't breathe."

What he'd said startled Ellen. Was that why Jason had left? Had she stifled him in some way she didn't know? Some way that Birdie did not? Maybe I'm too much like his mother, she thought with sudden clarity. Stubborn!

"When you are no longer half a person," said Ted, "you don't need another person in order to feel whole."

Half? Half-breed? Her mind ran faster than the engine. Was that why Jason's leaving had hurt so much, because she was halved, incomplete within herself? Had Mrs. West only voiced that incompletion? It had nothing to do with Angus and Cheok, with who they were. Ted had a point—she was not a fraction of a person waiting for the right equation to make herself whole. She was herself, in all her stubbornness or determination or persistence, or whatever one called it.

Ted said nothing. In the long silence she thought of how tied she had been to Angus, breaking from him like a chopped limb to go to Harold's Point and how, having broken, she dared not return, fearing she would be grafted back on and never have the strength to leave again. But instead she had grafted herself to Jason. Was Jason's marriage to Birdie a blessing? Had it forced the final plunge out of the black oil and onto the dry sunny plain, where she sat with lions?

Ellen felt Ted in her thoughts unobtrusively, not judging or pressuring. "You are a fine person," she said, watching the wash of water caress the boat. "If I were going to love anyone again, I would wish . . ."

He stopped her. "Wishing," he said, "is waiting for the future. It's tomorrow. We are alive today."

It was true that she had spent much of her life waiting for it to begin. Waiting to get out of Unaganik, waiting to get to school, and then to get out of school, to be with Jason. It had occupied her, waiting for this and that. It had kept her mind busy, as if it had not been busy enough.

"Jimmy can come to live with us," Ted continued. "My

mom might be willing to live with us too, take care of Jimmy, cook for us."

Mom? It was Jason's mother who had ruined everything. "I've had enough of mothers," said Ellen. "Especially other people's."

"My mother is not like that." Ted's hand brushed the side of her cheek, brushed the long hair drifting down her back, and was gone, back onto the wheel, turning the *Yethl* toward the harbor.

"What I do need," said Ellen, joining him, "is a place to live. If Jimmy's going to live with me, I don't want to be in the motel."

"I'll show you our apartment building."

After they anchored the seiner and rowed to shore, Ted drove west on Eighth to a tall, square building, which looked modern and uninspired compared to the old brick and mountain-shaped buildings of Seattle. I could have stayed in Seattle, thought Ellen. If only Jason . . .

A polished brass elevator took them to the eighth floor.

"I'm not sure I can live among the clouds," said Ellen.

"A big risk," said Ted, "getting your feet off the ground."

"Us tundra people don't have tall trees to climb," Ellen laughed. "We aren't used to it like you are."

"But you hang over bluffs."

"That's still keeping your feet on the earth."

He opened a door. There was a narrow hall with two small but adequate bedrooms off to the left. Ellen stood in one of the rooms, wondering how Jimmy would feel sleeping alone for the first time. I'd never have met Jimmy if I hadn't been sent to Adak, she thought, and wished she could stop thinking how it had been there with Jason, stop this tug of her mind toward him.

Ahead was a living room the size of Mrs. Ardley's Philco room. Windows faced the mountains to the east. An *L*-shaped kitchen nook extended to the right, where windows faced the inlet to the west. Ellen leaned on the window ledge and felt the spread of earth and sky. Yes, she thought, I could adjust to being up here. Looking down, she saw the yellow bloom of wild snapdragons and the creamy white tufts of Alaska cotton.

"Do you prefer this to a house with me at Fish Creek?"

She heard him behind her, felt his breath flow against her hair. His arms, she knew without looking, remained by his side, waiting for her response. She thought she heard him flex his fingers.

"Yes," she said and, crossing her arms, faced him.

"What are you afraid of?"

Ellen closed herself off. Language meant nothing. All the words that needed to be said had been said.

"Then," he said, his tight jaw the only indication that his emotions had changed, "you must see my building manager and arrange with him to lease this apartment."

"I've got to talk to the chief about my idea for a telephone doctor," said Ellen. "Can't I make arrangements with you?"

"No," he said.

"Can't you tell the business manager?"

"Do you expect him to return to you?" he said.

"What? Who? Your business manager?" asked Ellen.

"The one you loved."

Loved. He said loved. He's right, I loved Jason, past tense. And if he returned? Could we really break with the past in order to have a life together?

Ellen looked at Ted and found herself shaking her head as if in answer to her own inner question or his spoken one, she wasn't sure.

"I won't bother you again," Ted said, turning abruptly, striding down the narrow hall. "I promise."

Like her, Ellen knew he always kept his promises.

Ellen signed the lease. She shopped for furniture in the Sears catalogue, gave the motel owner notice that she would move as soon as the furniture arrived from Seattle, and talked for days to the chief about her new idea for village health care.

"I think it can work," he said. "Why don't you take two weeks and write a proposal, outline it in detail, and we'll look for funding."

After two weeks, Ellen had developed a plan for further training of village health aides, incorporating a telephone doctor service.

"I'd like to apply for the job," she said, handing the sheaf of papers to the chief.

"Don't you enjoy going out to the boondocks?" he asked.

"I've had enough bush flights," Ellen confessed, "to last a lifetime."

"The first doctor we had went through the Kilkwim Mountains in a cloud bank," said the chief, his eyebrows gusting to sixty. "Hit it at the narrowest part of the pass. It wasn't wide enough for the pilot to turn around. He headed into the soup and flew blind to the other side. They made it, though."

"Only one pilot I know could keep his nerve doing that," said Ellen.

"Snoose-chewing Gus," said the chief, and his eyebrows hit Aleutian gale force as he slapped his knee and laughed.

"One time we hit a crosswind and Gus tilted the plane in at a forty-degree angle," Ellen said. "The right wing was getting ready to plow a furrow on the ground."

"Why don't you take flying lessons? Might make a difference to how you feel up there."

"I know how I feel," said Ellen. "I don't like it."

The chief guffawed. "Do you know what Will Rogers said on his fatal flight with Wiley Post?"

Ellen shook her head, wondering if the chief was taking yet another of his long-winded conversational detours.

"'Won't feel like a sourdough until I Siwash it'!"

"And look what happened to them," she said, trying to control the sharpness of her tongue, remembering how many times she had thought she might have to make a primitive camp in the bush. "Besides," she added in a quieter tone, "I want my nephew to come and live with me in Anchorage."

"Well, you don't want to be gone all the time then."

"No," said Ellen, "I don't."

"Will you take one more trip to finish your rounds in the delta?"

"I don't know if I can survive another bug bite," said Ellen.

He laughed. "Let's hope the heat has got the mosquitoes, and if it hasn't, the cold soon will. Winter's on its way."

Ellen restocked her medical bag. She replaced the *Merck Manual* and *PDR* she had left for Sigori to study, and the bottles of vitamins she had given away. Then, after much debate with herself, she decided to telephone Ted and see if they could remain as they always had been, as friends. His secretary told her that he had flown to the petroleum reserve.

"I hope he's with a good pilot," Ellen said.

"One of the best," said the secretary.

Probably Gus, Ellen groaned to herself the next morning when she walked from her cabin to Merrill Field and noticed that the red Pilgrim was missing.

A man leaned against the nose of a brand new Aeronca, chewing a toothpick and looking as if no one could tell him anything he didn't already know. His hair, the color of a fox, stood up from his high forehead in a brush cut. He wore baggy black pants tucked into shiny jackboots and a World War II jacket, although he didn't look old enough to have been in the war.

Oh, oh, thought Ellen, her senses alerted by the sad plights Angus and Joe had told her about know-it-alls on the Gold Rush trail. Doubting her instincts, she tossed her fur coat behind the seat.

"You don't need that," said the pilot. "It's summer."

"It's the middle of September," said Ellen, "and I don't need your lip."

"I wouldn't mind yours, baby!" he laughed, shoving the toothpick to the other side of his mouth.

Ellen bit her tongue, berating herself for her fast mouth. She put her medical bag and shoulder bag into the rear compartment before she could change her mind.

The pilot checked the plane over, as Gus always did, wriggling the ailerons, elevator and rudder, before climbing into his seat.

"Where'd you come from?" Ellen could not help herself from asking as she buckled herself down.

"All over." The pilot turned the radio on. It clicked and he turned it off. "You name it, I been there."

"How long have you been in Alaska?"

He adjusted his altimeter to the field elevation and made a quick adjustment of the directional gyro.

"Where'd you learn to fly?" Ellen persisted.

He unlocked and pumped the primer four times, locked it, adjusted the throttle, turned on the master switch, then the ignition key with his left hand. His right hand cupped the throttle. The starter groaned.

"Is the battery low?" Ellen asked, just as the engine charged into life.

"Don't worry, Doc," he said in a cocky voice, "I know what I'm doing."

Ellen saw the ammeter needle swing to the right when the engine surged and kept her concerns to herself.

The pilot filed their flight plan over the radio and headed through Rainy Pass to McGrath. They fueled up and spent the night in a roadhouse. The next day, flying along the wide delta of the Yukon River, they reached St. Theresa's. The health aide, who was expecting Ellen, had everyone prepared. Ellen finished her TB examinations in record time, identified three children she wanted sent to Seward and another, with TB of the bone, to be put on the waiting list for Mount Edgecumbe. She became reacquainted with Denny, a seventeen-year-old who had been in the sanatorium with bilateral cavernous TB. Dr. Milligan had done a pneumoperitoneum on him, pumped him with streptomycin and whatever else the doctor managed to infuse into his patients, and Denny had recovered and was home a year later.

While they were in St. Theresa's, a squall blew inland from the Bering Sea. They spent two extra days sitting out a deluge that Gus would have pushed the Pilgrim through. Relieved at the pilot's caution, and relieved that a bad head cold kept him out of her way, Ellen took the added time to examine a newborn and two women who were pregnant for the first time, and to talk to the health aide about the plan for consultations by radio telephone.

While they talked late one afternoon, an old-timer hobbled in with a chunk axed out of his skin. Ellen dulled his pain with morphine, cleaned him, and sewed him up.

"Come here, baby," he said, when she was through. "Come sit on me."

"Don't mind him," said the health aide, hustling the prospector out the door with a crutch. "He's so bushy he'd go for a walrus."

"We're a long ways from walrus," said Ellen, laughing to herself.

"Not in winter," said the aide. "We take the dogs and go all over."

"Anyone get lost?"

"You ever hear the story 'bout Spit 'n' Polish Patty?"

"Yes," said Ellen, laughing. Sometimes the world seemed so small. "Do you travel much in summer?" she asked.

"Only on the river. And that's not too reliable 'cause it's always changing course. This area's one big marsh. When the ground freezes is our best time."

When the weather cleared, they radioed their flight plan and left St. Theresa's, flying low over a river that wound, lazy and slow, through swamps and pools and flat barren tundra. The sky had a silver-gold light. A flock of snow geese skimmed the tundra pools below them, settling on the rim of a mirrored pond, where they looked like drifts of snow.

The pilot, studying the map, said, "Here's a place called Jolly. Let's put down there."

"Never heard of the place," said Ellen, pulling the map from his lap. "It's not Jolly," she said. "It's Golly. You mixed *J* and *G*."

"We've got just enough jas," he said. "Or maybe I mean gas."

"For goodness sakes, didn't you fill up before we left St. Theresa's?"

"Forgot." The pilot blew his nose with a grey handkerchief.

"I don't like going too far off our flight plan."

"Not that far off."

"In this country . . ." Ellen bit her tongue and looked at the fuel gauges. The left was pinned at empty. The right bounced. Who knew how much remained?

"It should be here," he said, circling lower until they saw a dirt strip outside yet another isolated village. They taxied to a large tank mounted on a wooden frame. A hose dangled from it.

"Wait," said Ellen. "Someone's bound to come."

"Don't got all day." The pilot's nose was plugged and he spoke with a twang. "We gotta get to McGrath before dark."

"They'll be here."

"I'll fill up and leave them some coin. I'm not going to cheat them. I've been warned about how long a memory these Eskimos have."

The pilot climbed onto the wheel and unscrewed the gas cap on top of the right wing. "Hand me the funnel, will you?" he said.

Ellen handed him a funnel and the chamois cloth that had been tucked in it, to filter the gas. Then she handed him the hose hanging from the raised drum. When he had fixed it in the wing tank, she turned the petcock and the fuel started to run.

Hoping to meet someone halfway, Ellen took off in the direction of the single-story cabins lining an eddy of the river. One lone mosquito buzzed at her. Stopping to swat it, she noticed bright red nagoonberries ripening low to the ground. Ellen stopped to eat her fill of the treasured fruit. Too soon the pilot shouted, "Done!" She returned in time to see him stick a roll of bills between the crossbars of the wooden structure supporting the fuel drum.

When they were airborne, Ellen looked back at the field. A man stood at a second tank at the other end of the strip, scratching his head beneath a green peaked cap.

"I hope he finds the bills at the other end," she said as the village disappeared into the haze of the horizon. Below them, the flat soggy land spread in all directions. Tiny tundra pools overlapped one another like circles from a stone thrown in a pond. In between the pools, seams of red bushes were turning brown. Tussocks of grass had turned yellow and dry from the hot summer sun, which was sinking lower and lower down the sky.

The pilot blew his nose. He turned on the radio but there was no sound. "There's a loose wire," he said, tapping it with his finger. Nothing happened. "I can't give a position report."

The right gauge now pinned empty.

"When are you going to switch over?" Ellen asked, feeling wary of the pilot's attention to the dials. Maybe his cold was worse than it seemed.

The engine sputtered and stopped. In the sudden silence, the wind seemed to caress their wings. The pilot switched tanks, the engine caught and sputtered.

42

W HITE SMOKE POURED OUT the side as the Aeronca's engine coughed.

"The smoke should be black," said Ellen.

"Those damn eskeemosquitoes," the pilot fumed. "They done me dirt."

"You sure you got the right"—there was a deadening calm as the engine stopped—"fuel?"

Ellen gripped the sides of her seat, jammed her feet on the floor. The wind raced past them while the pilot trimmed into a glide.

The pools filling the tundra loomed larger and larger. They skimmed water, bounced over a rock, slowed. The plane plunged ahead. The speed—what principle?—Ellen thought, seeing Mrs. Van der Voewn explaining physics on the blackboard.

The wheels hit the moss and stuck. The nose dug in. The plane flipped. Then there was silence. Overpowering, lonely silence.

Ellen was upside down, shaking. Next to her, the white-faced pilot gripped his seat. There was a creaking, groaning sound as the plane started to settle.

"Breathe," Ellen croaked, her voice raucous as a crow's.

The blood slowly circulated through her body, pooling at her head. Ellen pressed the palms of her hands on the creaking canopy, taking her weight.

"Unbuckle me," she said to the pilot.

He did not move.

"Listen," she said, feeling as if she were being sliced in two by the safety belt. "Help me out and I'll get you down."

"We've bought the farm."

"For goodness sakes," Ellen hissed. "We're alive. Get my buckle open and then I'll help you out."

His eyes rolled. His face flushed red.

"Do it," Ellen ordered, using her best hospital voice.

He unhooked her. Unable to hold her weight, she crumpled into a heap on the ceiling of the cockpit. Catching her breath, feeling the blood resettle in the proper places in her body, she unhooked his buckle and held him while he fell. He was thin, much lighter than he looked in his baggy pants. They opened the doors and crawled on the ten-foot patch of tundra. It was a sponge. They sank up to their calves.

The pilot shook his fist. "You should have told me."

"Told you what?"

"About the fuel."

"What about it?"

"Diesel. We put in diesel, or maybe kerosene. Christ! How were we supposed to know?"

We? thought Ellen, saying nothing. *We?*

A few lazy bugs, survivors of the summer heat, whined toward them. The pilot started swatting. Ellen retrieved her medical bag and brought out a bottle of citronella.

"Help yourself," she said, after dabbing her hands and face with the strong-smelling repellent.

He dowsed half the bottle on his head.

"For goodness sakes," said Ellen. "We might be here awhile. Go easy."

"I hope you brought a lunch," he said.

"I have vitamins," she answered. "And we can find food."

"We better start walking."

"In this?"

"Just because you're a doctor, you think you're so smart!"

Ellen chose to ignore his remark. They may have a day, days, who knew how long, to live together before they were found. The sedge and lichens, so gold and red from above, looked old and brown, lacking in life. The pilot sloshed off, stepped into the surrounding circle of water, sunk to his waist on the fifth step, crawled out, sunk again to his hip. The wet land curved away from them in all directions.

"It's safer to stay here," Ellen tried to reassure the pilot. "The plane's easy to see from the air and we can have signal fires ready."

She searched for a screwdriver and found a wooden box of tools under the pilot's seat. "Gus told me once that he soaked these with oil and lit them as soon as he heard a plane overhead," she said, starting to unscrew her seat. "They'll flare at night and smoke in the day and a search party won't miss us."

"If you're sure someone's going to come," the pilot said, gripping her arm, "why wreck my new plane? I'd never have gotten this job if I didn't have a plane, and I ain't got the dough to buy another."

"What do you suggest we use as a flare?" Ellen said, facing him, trying to keep her voice calm. "It's not likely they'll fly over this spot and be able to see us from the air."

"How will anyone land?" Since the pilot sounded rational at that moment Ellen removed her arm from his grasp and continued working to remove the seat.

"They can drop us food until it freezes," she said. "Then they'll come in on skis."

"We can flip this baby over and take off ourselves if the ground's hard."

Ellen realized that the pilot had already forgotten why they'd gone down. The worst part of it was, she'd known he was a greenhorn, a *cheechako*. She had gotten herself into this jam by her own impatience to have the last flight over. She jabbed the screwdriver into another screw and loosened it from the frame.

He pushed on the rear of the plane, shoving it two feet into the air. "You going to stand there?" he called, his face flushed. "Or you going to help?"

Ellen ignored him. He dropped the tail and, kicking furiously at the plane, started shouting obscenities. Ellen dragged her seat out of the plane and onto the marshy ground. Sloshing around the marsh, she found her eyes changing, found herself remembering plants she'd seen as a child walking with Cheok on the tundra. She returned to the plane,

pulled the cowling off the engine, banged it into the shape of
a pot and scooped up tannin-stained water from the stagnant
pond. Something underneath stirred. A blackfish. The inde-
structible tundra fish. Later she'd figure out how to catch
him. Meanwhile she had tundra tea.

Using fuel drained from the wing into a second pot of
cowling metal, Ellen heated the water in the first pot with the
thick and slightly sticky leaves of tea. The pilot circled her,
watching but saying nothing.

"Here," said Ellen, handing him a vitamin.

He reached for the tea.

"Wait," said Ellen. "It's hot."

They used the chamois to take the makeshift pot off the
heat and let it cool on the spongy moss.

Ellen took a vitamin, sipped her share of the tea, and
watched the flickers in the pond where the blackfish stirred.

Now if it had been Gus . . . She forced the thought away.
It was not Gus, it was . . . ? She looked at the frantic eyes of
the pilot.

"My name's Ellen," she said quietly, trying to soothe
him, but he did not respond.

Later, he tossed all night in the cockpit where they slept
with the silver fox fur as a cover. All the next day, without
talking, they watched the skies. The sunset burned violet and
orange, turning the barren tundra into a vast splendor.

No one brings you peace but yourself, thought Ellen at
the end of a second day with no sign of aircraft. Who had said
that? Not Daddy. He was, she realized now, anything but
peaceful. Stewart had been right. Daddy had run from himself, had hated Stewart because Stewart represented parts of
him that Daddy didn't want to acknowledge in himself. Ellen
wondered how much of Angus was in her—his restlessness,
his intensity, his disconnection from his feelings.

Her thoughts seemed to run in circles, without rational
form. Had Mrs. Ardley said that about peace? She wondered
about this for days, coming back often to the same subject.
Mrs. Ardley was always talking about feelings. If someone
asked Mrs. Ardley where I was, would she be able to tell
them?

Emerson. In a vacant moment, his name popped into her

head and Ellen was so surprised her face creased into a smile. Of course. It's Emerson. I'd almost forgotten him.

"Ain't funny," said the pilot, frowning at her.

"We've got to make the best of it," Ellen said, seeing his fear festering like pus in a boil, ready to burst.

The pilot's fear continued as the days shortened, one after the other in an unbroken pattern of tea and vitamins, vitamins and tea, blackfish caught with a net Ellen made from surgical gauze. She picked black crowberries, lichens, moss, and *kuagtsik* as she was able to range farther and farther over the gradually hardening tundra.

The pilot's eyes emptied. He seemed like a carcass rotting on the wing, where he lay endlessly watching the sky. Ellen felt her own skin hang over her bones, felt her pulse lag. She dug into the tundra, looking for mouse food. She watched the shrews and voles and, using the wooden tool box, set a trap to catch them as they left their holes.

The pilot did nothing.

Hunger amused her. One minute it was like a frisky dog, snapping at her legs. The next, it was a pursuing wolf, culling the most vulnerable from the herd.

Greyling, she thought, remembering Cheok's favorite fish. Salmon. She remembered the new potatoes from Butler's garden, the greens. Unused to fresh leafy vegetables, which had always bothered her stomach, she thought even lettuce would taste good now. There was the beef stew she'd had at The Dog House. The steak with Jason in New York. Ellen laughed out loud. It seemed so far away, another planet. Oh I loved him, she thought, hugging herself, staring at the sky. Then a startling thought occurred to her. She could still love him, as she had loved him all those years when they were apart. Living *with* him didn't matter. Living did—being alive, being.

Cranes darkened the sky. Their large wings beat high in the air, their legs trailed, necks extended like arrows pointing south. They came on and on, hundreds of them, calling to one another, urging one another on in their raspy voices. Ellen crawled into the plane and lay down on her coat, trying not to think of winter.

Frost hit the ground like a show of stars. The dying brown of the tundra showed a new face and Ellen, crawling

over it, found a patch of tiny red cranberries she had missed.
They were mushy from the frost and the tart juice started
contractions on the walls of her stomach. She saw a ptarmigan and fell on him, killing him with her whole weight. She
left two tail feathers in the spot where she had killed the bird,
so that his spirit might use them to fly away. They cooked the
bird in the pot. There was plenty of fuel.

"You have more," said the pilot, jabbing a finger at her.
He grabbed her share of the bird, shoving her against the door
handle of the cockpit where they were sitting, not an arm's
length apart.

Ellen kicked him and he threw the bird in her face. It
surprised her to discover how much strength she still had left,
and how fragile he appeared to be.

The pilot's eyes darted here and there as if he were
searching, always, for her to be off guard. Ellen never turned
her back to him.

"The side fell off the sun," he shouted one day, sitting
bolt upright in the cockpit, where he huddled to keep warm.

"That's a sun dog," Ellen explained, warming her
hands in her pocket. A prism of rainbow light separated from
the round disc low in the southern sky.

"Don't have them anywhere I've been," he said, distrusting
her.

Winter. It means winter, and she thought of how Sirius
had come to her one winter when she needed a friend.

She watched her shadow lengthen across the hardening
ground and thought again of Emerson: Many of the shadows
of this life are caused by standing in our own sunshine. Or
was it Emerson? Maybe Reginald had said it. Maybe she had
made it up.

The aurora started. The days shortened. They ran through
a bottle of vitamins each. Ellen tried to focus her mind on the
figures. A month's supply. How many days did that mean
they'd been here without any sign of rescue? We are encamped
in nature, not domesticated, she thought, positive that she
read that in Emerson. Where was her book? She'd forgotten it
somewhere.

"We're getting out of here," said the pilot, looking at
the frozen ground. "We'll walk to a village."

"No," said Ellen. "They'll see us easier here. We don't

even know the direction of the nearest village. We have a shelter here and our flare." She pointed at the pile of seats and canvas, and the fuel ready to be poured over and lit at a moment's notice.

"You're afraid to go because of bears."

"There's not likely to be bears on the delta." Ellen saw her vision in the center of the earth, remembered the bear Robertson Sharpe had shot, the spruce she had climbed, remembered Brick's bear hunt. She saw Brick's nightshirt flapping in the breeze. Had she left anything at Bonnie's? Was it on the clothesline? Was Bonnie watching it flap? And knowing she was still alive, would Brick search? Ted? Ted was off at the petroleum reserve. Who knew when she'd see him next. And Jimmy . . . how she longed for the time when they could live together.

Ellen tired of thinking, enjoying not thinking, enjoyed feeling the changes in her body, feeling the pulse and breath of the earth. Her senses sharpened. She felt parts of her open that had shut down like faucets in a sink. One moment moved gently into the next, and the next. She felt things slide away from her, events she had been carrying despite her resolve not to let "things" matter. More energy flowed through her, and her body, tightened against the hunger, sharpened into the season. She felt Cheok in her thoughts, saw her drawing pictures in the snow with her story knife. What stories will they tell about me, Ellen thought, and surprised herself with the tears that dampened her cheeks.

The pilot rarely left the plane. He lay inside, wrapped in the fur coat, staring into space. They slept longer, crowded together under the coat, the cold creeping up beneath them, the confining space of the cockpit forcing them to lie within inches of each other.

One morning there was a dusting of snow as light and fine as Mrs. Ardley's face powder. Ellen saw a hare, half grey, half white.

"As soon as there's enough snow," she told the pilot, who stared at her with vacant eyes, "we can pack it around the plane. It's good insulation."

The following morning, there was a sudden drop in temperature. At the edge of the pool where she had been fishing, the water mixed like soap suds and turned to slush.

Ellen shivered and while she shivered, watching, there was a streak across the pond. The water had turned to ice.

The aurora played that night, green and gold, orange and red, up and down, across, luminous. Ellen's cells played too, remembering other times. She could not sleep but lay still, disappearing from herself, returning, like the lights, like that old tern she had known for so long.

Suddenly the pilot leaped on her, reached for her throat. Pressed against the side of the cockpit, Ellen jammed her knee up to his groin. He clutched himself and rolled sideways, curled into a fetal position. "I'll get you for that," he grunted.

There was no Sigori to watch over her. Ellen pressed her back against the side of the plane, increasing the distance between them by another few inches.

The next morning, when he disappeared behind the tail, Ellen searched her medical bag. Quickly, her hands trembling, she filled a syringe from an ampule of morphine, not taking time to check for bubbles, filling it in the bag while she watched for him, afraid. She capped the needle and hid it in her pocket. That day she stayed close to the plane.

"Aren't you going for berries?" he said, his voice unused to speech.

"They're all gone," she said.

A mallard quacked. Ellen peered out the plane window to see its webbed feet frozen in the pond, its green head glossy against the white background.

The pilot stalked toward the duck, snapped its legs and wrung its neck. "He's mine," he said, holding him over the pot, daring Ellen to come closer.

His eyes darted back and forth so that Ellen did not know which one to pay attention to and found herself paying attention, instead, to the terror that crunched at her insides. What would he do next? Her jaws clenched and she felt as if her breath was prickling her vertebrae instead of expanding and nourishing her lungs. The pilot was crazy, like a madman abandoning his spirit so any malevolent being in search of a body might enter.

She thought of Ted, of his steadiness, his deep inner patience that contrasted with her own restlessness. Is that what makes him so unique? she wondered, remembering how she had been intrigued by him when they first met. *Does he have the patience to find me?*

All during that short day and long night, Ellen felt splintered. Part of her, wary, watched the pilot. Part of her suppressed cold and hunger, suppressed the wish to have the coat for herself. And part of her thought of Ted, of what he had said. *If only I had known that I love him . . .* Ellen sat up in shocked surprise at what she had just realized.

She didn't know how much later it was. She knew she had dozed a little when something woke her. Her eyelids cracked. Her spine crawled. The pilot lay on his stomach, arms outstretched to her medical bag. In a streak of light from the aurora she saw her scalpel glint in his hand like a bayonet.

Ellen reached into her pocket for the hypodermic syringe and flicked off the cap. She sprang on him, plunging the needle into his buttock. He twisted beneath her, bumping his elbow against the side of the plane. She grabbed his wrists, surprised at her own strength. The scalpel fell from his hand. He did not move.

Only when he was unconscious did her pulse settle. She tumbled off him, into a heap. Huge wracking sobs burst from her. She cried until there was nothing left.

On and on through the night one fear tugged at another until none remained. From the core of her being Ellen felt as if all of her had come together, all the parts that had flung her in separate directions for so long. She thought of Jason and blessed him for leaving, thought of Ted Kleet and knew she loved him, as he had always loved her. It was a different love than the one with Jason. Her love for Ted made no demands on him to fulfill that which she wasn't herself. With Jason she had confused love with something else, some other need. Because she hadn't needed Ted, she had thought it wasn't love. She heard Ted. *Where are you, Ellen?* he was asking.

"I'm here," she called out loud. "I'm here."

A ribbon of green luminous light played ahead of her, through the sky, like a trail home.

In the morning, the pilot did not waken. Ellen pressed his throat. Nothing. Wondering if her starved senses were playing tricks on her, she took out her stethoscope and listened to his chest. There was no beat of the heart, no drag of air into the lungs.

Ellen stared at him. Part of her was relieved, part of her remembered Spit 'n' Polish Patty and knew what she could do. Who could say what anyone would do in any circumstance? Who could say that Jason would not have married her anyway, even without his mother's plans. If he thought he owed his mother his life, then he probably did. For myself, thought Ellen, I owe myself my own life.

The choice between living or dying, surviving or giving up, she suddenly knew—without any confirmation from her medical texts, or Mrs. Ardley, or the shaman—was made in the core of one's being, like a kernel choosing to grow or ferment. What she, as a doctor, had been doing was making the person well enough to find that kernel. What a shaman did was guide a person to that center where the kernel could be nourished or buried. It was the choice of a soul, just as her soul had chosen to leave the tern and rejoin her body on the mud flats so long ago in Unaganik.

Ellen dragged the pilot out of the plane onto the ice, where he started to freeze. She gathered the silver fox fur around her and searched the sky, right to left, starting at the farthest end, working closer. A pale, low-hanging sun eased into the world. Its rays flared like the mane of a lion.

Turning, facing the dead pilot, she watched her shadow lengthen over the frozen pond, reaching the opposite bank where the puckered ice looked like wrinkles on a grandmother's neck. "This woman wants to grow old." Ellen spoke in Cheok's tongue. "She wants to love and grow old with Ted Kleet."

The dark grey shape of herself crossed the frozen pond and she turned again to the winter sun, stretched her arms, welcoming it in the traditional way, a *V* of victory, absorbed by the feeling of warmth in her body and light on her face.

Susan Saxton D'Aoust traveled extensively in Alaska, including 1,800 miles down the Yukon River, during her research on this novel. She lives on Bainbridge Island, Washington.

Special Offer
Buy a Bantam Book
for only 50¢.

Now you can have Bantam's catalog filled with hundreds of titles plus take advantage of our unique and exciting bonus book offer. A special offer which gives you the opportunity to purchase a Bantam book for only 50¢. Here's how!

By ordering any five books at the regular price per order, you can also choose any other single book listed (up to a $5.95 value) for just 50¢. Some restrictions do apply, but for further details why not send for Bantam's catalog of titles today!

Just send us your name and address and we will send you a catalog!

DON'T MISS
THESE CURRENT
Bantam Bestsellers

RELAX!
SIT DOWN
and Catch Up On Your Reading!

☐ 26264	**NATHANIEL** by John Saul	$4.50
☐ 27148	**LINES AND SHADOWS** by Joseph Wambaugh	$4.95
☐ 27386	**THE DELTA STAR** by Joseph Wambaugh	$4.95
☐ 27259	**GLITTER DOME** by Joseph Wambaugh	$4.95
☐ 26757	**THE LITTLE DRUMMER GIRL** by John le Carré	$4.95
☐ 26705	**SUSPECTS** by William J. Caunitz	$4.95
☐ 26657	**THE UNWANTED** by John Saul	$4.50
☐ 26499	**LAST OF THE BREED** by Louis L'Amour	$4.50
☐ 27430	**THE SECRETS OF HARRY BRIGHT** by Joseph Wambaugh	$4.95

Prices and availability subject to change without notice.

Buy them at your local bookstore or use this page to order:

- -

Bantam Books, Dept. FBB, 414 East Golf Road, Des Plaines, IL 60016

Please send me the books I have checked above. I am enclosing $_____
(please add $2.00 to cover postage and handling). Send check or money
order—no cash or C.O.D.s please.

Mr/Ms _____

Address _____

City/State _____ Zip _____

FBB—7/89

Please allow four to six weeks for delivery. This offer expires 1/90.